THE IVORY CROCODILE

Who knows him not, this web-footed saurian wearing rock-tough scales, this gigantic lizard as suited to underwater as to land, ngando, in short, the crocodile, evil creature forever pledging itself to the exclusive service of man against man, submarine-oriented servant of those who resort to its homicidal skills?

The fetishers and the ndoki especially are the well-known employers of ngando. They enter its body and have themselves transported underwater to remote locales, abduct their victims, and have themselves brought back with their human booty to their points of departure.

Occasionally, submitting to initiated groups, the ngando fulfill their dangerous missions independently, abducting human beings to be brought to those who have commissioned the crime.

Neither hunger alone nor a fondness for human flesh drives the small-jawed crocodiles to engage in this fluvial plague; rather, it is the wizardry of these mysterious men which inspires the animals' obsession with their grisly tasks. The chosen victim is first of all entranced—from a distance, of course—by a form of voodoo known only to select fetishers and ndoki. The spell is felt by the victim as an irresistible urge to immerse himself to bathe at some chosen spot in the waterways. As the victim enters the water, the commissioned crocodile approaches underwater from its hiding place in the aquatic brush and, with a vigorous, showy slap of its tail, stuns and knocks over the victim, snaps him up, and carries him off at full speed toward the distant banks where the perpetrators of the crime await.

Such is the part played by the ngando in our rivers and streams.

To render the ngando completely accountable, the evildoers bind themselves to the animals by blood. Validated in mysterious ceremonies, the vows are powerful enough to instantaneously kill the human partner if the crocodile should die.

– Lomami Tchibamba
from *Ngando and Other Tales*

The Ivory Crocodile

A NOVEL BY
EILEEN DREW

 COFFEE HOUSE PRESS :: MINNEAPOLIS

Excerpts from *Revolutionary Path,* by Kwame Nkrumah, copyright © 1973 by Panaf Books Ltd., published by Zed Books, used with permission of the publisher.

Excerpts from *The Wretched of the Earth* by Frantz Fanon, copyright © 1963 by Presence Africaine, published by Grove/Atlantic, used by permission of the publisher.

Exerpt from *Ngando and Other Tales* by Lmaami Tchibamba, copyright © 1982 by Presence Africaine, published by Presence Africaine, used with permission of the publisher.

Coffee House Press is supported in part by a grant provided by the Minnesota State Arts Board, through an appropriation by the Minnesota State Legislature, and by a grant from the National Endowment for the Arts, a federal agency. Additional support has been provided by the Lila Wallace-Reader's Digest Fund; The McKnight Foundation; Lannan Foundation; Jerome Foundation; Target Stores, Dayton's, and Mervyn's by the Dayton Hudson Foundation; General Mills Foundation; St. Paul Companies; Honeywell Foundation; Star Tribune/Cowles Media Company; Beverly J. and John A. Rollwagen Fund of The Minneapolis Foundation; Prudential Foundation; and The Andrew W. Mellon Foundation.

Coffee House Press books are available to the trade through our primary distributor, Consortium Book Sales & Distribution, 1045 Westgate Drive, Saint Paul, MN 55114. For personal orders, catalogs, or other information, write to:

Coffee House Press
27 North Fourth Street, Suite 400
Minneapolis, MN 55401

Library of Congress CIP data

Drew, Eileen, 1957-
    The Ivory Crocodile: a novel / by Eileen Drew.
    p.   cm.
    ISBN 1-56689-042-X
    1. Africa–Fiction.   I. Title.
PS3554.R438I96   1996
813' .54–dc20
                               96-3143
                                 CIP

10   9   8   7   6   5   4   3   2   1

Special thanks to Miles Rosedale

PREFACE

This story is a work of fiction. Although the characters are imaginary figures, they refer at times to actual people and events in African history. Kwame Nkrumah led his nation, Ghana, to independence from England in 1957; Ghana was the first African colony to gain self-rule. Nkrumah promoted independence for all African nations as well as a policy of pan-Africanism; he was a key architect of the Organization of African Unity, formed in 1963. As president of Ghana he grew dictatorial, and was ousted from office in 1966, when he fled to Guinea. He died in Romania in 1972.

In the wake of Ghana's independence, other African nations quickly demanded and received autonomy. Guinea received independence from France in 1958; Sekou Touré, the new president, allied himself with the communist nations. A dictator who suppressed dissent, he remained in office until 1984, when he died.

Patrice Lumumba was a hero and martyr in the Republic of Congo (now Zaire) in its volatile early years as an independent state. In 1960 Congo received independence from Belgium and Lumumba became the first prime minister. A series of internal uprisings set the stage for governmental instability; a grapple for power involving the Soviets as well as the United Nations and the U.S. ensued. Lumumba was detained by the forces of his rivals, Joseph Désiré Mobutu and Joseph Kasavubu, the president, and died in 1961 under suspicious circumstances. In 1965 Mobutu seized the presidency from Kasavubu; Mobutu, now Sese Seko Mobutu, remains in office today.

Angola did not receive independence from Portugal until 1975; since then, a struggle for power has engaged the country in civil war. The first president, Agostinho Neto, as well as his successor, José Eduardo dos Santos, and their party, the MPLA, have received support from the Soviet Union and Cuba; the government's primary rival, Jonas Savimbi and his party, UNITA, have received aid from the U.S. and other Western nations, and South Africa.

Frantz Fanon (1925-1961) was an eloquent author and spokesperson for violent black revolution in Africa. Born in Martinique, educated in France as a psychiatrist, he worked in Algeria during that nation's war against French control from 1954 to 1962.

Tambala is a fictional country.

The Ivory Crocodile

Part I: The Surface

I

MOVING

Not long ago, striding past a subway car, I locked eyes with a young African man seated by the window. I had just stepped off, I was dodging the clicking heels and swinging hems, when from the string of dazed expressions inside the train, one face surfaced. It leapt to the foreground like the key shape in a depth perception test.

It's hard to say why I guessed he was African. Skin that black, hair that snug, even the wide planes of his brow and jaw could belong to an American, but not his bearing. In the slim patience of his shoulders I recalled, I think, Africa's cramped spaces, people waiting ten to a bench, people crammed standing in trucks so loaded that others balanced like acrobats on the running boards.

His eyes were foreign, heavy-lidded, too serene for his fluid features—he had the eyes of an old person who has seen enough. The moment he saw me, his chin dipped in greeting. Did he know me? I slackened my pace, and his forehead knotted in confusion.

4

Perhaps he'd been one of my students in Mampungu, a decade earlier. It was a secondary school; he would be about the right age. I didn't recognize his face, but there had been so many. Possibly he'd sat always in the back of class, or had been absent a lot.

As I came abreast, he stared hard. Was it me, or someone else he thought he knew? Maybe he'd met a woman like me in his homeland, a pale volunteer in her mud hut—we must have numbered in the thousands. Or perhaps he took me for a double—perhaps, even, for Sadie, a little girl I'd resembled as a child. What if her life had paralleled mine, if she, also, had made her way back to Africa?

A step beyond, I glanced back; he was watching me over his shoulder. If I were his "Miss Nicoli," I must look different now, my hair styled, shoes tapered at the toe—I was dressed for the opening of an exhibit of my photographs. He could guess that I had settled down, married, that I had adopted America; he could probably guess that I'd left Africa out of the pictures in my show. Suddenly I regretted the celebration ahead. I felt light years from Mampungu, light years from this man whose train I had been sharing. Any second he would shoot through the tunnel in the opposite direction. Disappointment surged, the same hopeless ache that had driven me from Mampungu; he was out of reach.

Everything went too fast, we were always moving. As an infant, an embryo even, I moved. Conceived aboard an oceanliner, born in a boondock country. It went so fast I can barely remember. I had a habit, I've been told, of taking off my clothes in the street. All around were African kids without shirts—did I think that I was black? A few years later—and this I do remember—in Washington, my mother said something to my father about colored people. We were in front of a building, climbing steps, and I looked around for skin like rainbows, asked with excitement where they were. Yet my mother shushed me, nodding at some blacks, and I felt tricked.

In Conakry, Guinea, I was eight. My brother, Benjamin, two years older, climbed the palms and let the dead fronds drop. "Heads up!" he'd call. Odd notes fluttered across the lagoon. At night came the raw sound of drums. During rainy season's high tides, the ocean dumped fish into the swimming pool; in the morning they'd float crooked, scales glinting.

I drew the house before we moved there. In Washington my father described our future home and I ran for a pencil and paper so that I could fix the image of our pool shaped like a woman's body, most narrow at the waist. In the foreground I put the ocean; in the background, the imitation *paillotte,* or hut, that was our house, with its patio doors folded back like accordions, its thatch roof like a dunce cap. I had to draw it to see it, he said it was just right.

Juju, the black cat, sat at the tip of our roof in Conakry. Below this conical roof of thatch, three bedrooms and a kitchen wrapped around the central room, an irregular oblong with a dining table at one end, armchairs at the other. Behind the table, lining the concave wall, was a vast map of Africa, a tinged replica of an ancient one made for slavers, scattered with curlicued names for territories of the past. Meticulous ships were affixed to the seas like insects. The ceiling rose dramatically in a spiralling network of wood beams that sprinkled dust over the floor and the table tops. My mother cursed the termites, snapping rags at bookshelves.

In Conakry Benjamin learned French the best. I thought that French was learned through lessons, and I took our classes seriously, our first summer there. It was rainy season, and I spent the hours indoors reading, drawing, and filling a *cahier* with grammar exercises, impressed by the patterns on the page, the columns of words underlined in red, the lists in boxes.

Meanwhile, Benjamin trailed Ali, the cook, and although Madame got angry when his homework wasn't done, he could answer her in French. My mother used emphatic phrases with Ali, who would repeat them ceremoniously. *"Encore,"* he would intone, fingers spread like roots against his bleached slacks. But with Benjamin, Ali chattered. Benjamin listened until he got the gist, then translated.

"He says Juju's pregnant," he announced one day.

"How do you know, what's French for pregnant?" I tested him.

Smirking, he shaped with his arms a hoop in front of his belly. *"Beaucoup petits."*

Ali, watching from the kitchen door, laughed, whistling through his teeth, and wiggled a pinkie in his ear as if he'd been swimming. He was all bone and muscle under dull skin that brightened around his nose and cheeks. He made me shy. He didn't know his age; at times he acted old and wizardly, at times like a kid. His two personas were distinct: when cooking, he was the reverent chef and nothing could displace his deadpan, not even a skillet on fire. Otherwise he was my brother's ally, easily distracted from the mop or garden hose by my dolls held hostage in Benjamin's forts of sagging sheets. Sometimes Ali would crouch, knees jutting, to admire our miniature cities of Corgi Toy cars, the seed pods for pedestrians, or he shimmied to our Beatles records. We entertained him, I think, like a choreographed troupe—my parents, too, posing in our imitation *paillotte,* a world removed from Africa's lush ache.

The pool glittered. Tiny white and blue tiles lined the sides and bottom; a few drifted loose, unglued. Diving to collect them, I ran my fingertips along the gaps, prying at the intact edges. Nobody noticed the missing tiles; from above the surface the gaps were imperceptible. But seen through a mask underwater, the tile fabric stretched into focus, pitted. We swam and swam, mermaids, submarines. Lorraine was my special friend, then Linda, then Cass. With their fathers, they came to Conakry and left.

Benjamin played with the African boys drawn from the beach like magnets to stare through the pool fence, their eyes framed by chain links, their thumbs hooked around the wire. If my mother saw them there, she flailed her arms and shouted and they dropped away, grinning. A mere look from Ali, however, could make them vanish like magic.

I caught that look once, and recognized in it a hint of whatever he was outside our fence. Occupied with some errand, he was heading from the house to the pool, where I was treading water, but he did not acknowledge me. Instead, I saw his features freeze as he focused on something above and behind me, and rather than the swollen concentration of his kitchen face, I recognized anger. A frantic scuffle sounded then, and by the time I'd turned, the boys were gone. Ali, too, was gone when I turned again.

That anger, I think, was more than a show of authority. I had caught Ali stumbling upon the ambiguity of his role: how, allied to whites in their oasis, he must condemn the African kids whose fascination he shared. At the time, though, suspended in the pool, I perceived only his power; outside the fence, I thought, he must be an important man.

The gate was locked from inside, and Benjamin and I were allowed out to search for tidepools and shells. He made me promise not to tell my mother when he slipped off fishing with the boys, and, lingering behind on the lagoon's narrow beach, shaping blunt castles in the mudlike sand, I thought of the battered cans with wire handles dangling from their long, long arms.

In Conakry I was a double. I never saw the girl I resembled; she'd returned to the States weeks before I arrived. "Sadie!" I kept hearing. "Doesn't she remind you of Sadie?" Girls my age would slump, sighing, "I wish she hadn't left." People in the distance stopped, pale brows knitted, thinking she'd reappeared. The white community was small, each face memorized, intrinsic. Mine seemed to have preceded my presence.

One man, however, Mr. Baker, treated me from the first as more than Sadie's look-alike, convinced that I could be only Nickie. He knew. He was Sadie's father.

Left behind by his family, he was tying up loose ends at the embassy before his next post. One Saturday we drove down the dirt road to his house for lunch, passing the red dunes of an iron mine, and then the dingy concrete block that was a village school. Black girls in white blouses and green skirts danced in the yard.

"But it's Saturday!" I pointed at them. "And summer!"

My mother twisted in the front seat, her sleeveless dress baring a stark bra strap. "Vacation begins for them in late June, and for as long as school's in session, they go half-days on Saturday. It's the French system."

Benjamin scrambled to crane at my window. "I'm glad there's an American school, we get a better deal."

"Look at them jump," my mother applauded. We hesitated before a pothole as my father glanced from the wheel.

They were playing a clapping game in pairs, hopping up and down in tandem, chanting, slapping palms. Delighted, I projected myself among their coordinated steps, among their laughter and rhythm. But they were out of reach, fixed in my car window, an image, then an echo. Lurching forward, we left them behind, submerged by the green froth of bush.

Mr. Baker lived on a cliff. We found him standing on his patio as if marooned, tilting slightly, staring at the ocean. The horizon sloped like an upended bowl. When Benjamin whistled at the view, Mr. Baker swivelled neatly in his loafers and approached us eagerly.

"Ah, you're here, children and all! This is wonderful! I want you kids to make a lot of noise, it's been unearthly since my family left."

I braced myself for the comparison to Sadie, but as we were introduced he simply shook my hand gently and, rather than scanning my features, he focused on my eyes. His blue irises floating in pink looked sadly affectionate. He was older than my father, gray at the temples with creases that held the imprint of his smile, yet he was tan and agile. I thought he was the most handsome man I'd met.

Urged to explore the garden, Benjamin and I scouted out its limits by picking our way along the inevitable fence. The gate wasn't locked, and just as we began to bicker—Benjamin intent on the path down to the beach—I heard my mother calling.

"See? We haven't got time."

"She only wants you. Answer her!"

It was true, the summons was for me alone, just for a minute. The adults sat arrayed around a table facing the water, holding their drinks in soggy orange napkins. I dawdled at my mother's side.

"Go sit down," she encouraged, without explaining why, but the reason was clear. After setting his tumbler on the table, Mr. Baker leaned back.

"Yes, come and have a drink. The commissary's out of Coke, I'm afraid, but I can offer you a ginger ale."

I'd never had ginger ale before, but it sounded grown-up. The empty chair beside Mr. Baker faced the house—a regular western two-story—and with the other chairs angled toward me and the sea at my back, I felt as if on stage.

A houseboy emerged with a tray, and I wondered how he would react. Oddly enough, this man who had spent two years among Sadie's family reacted not at all to our likeness, serving my soda indifferently with stiff, careful gestures.

My mother, lipstick and black curls gleaming, sat holding the arms of her chair, pretty and vivacious, like a passenger on some exotic excursion. No doubt it was the debonair presence of Mr. Baker that sparked her femininity. Suddenly she was not the type to let her bra straps show. My father looked good, too, laughing confidently at her jokes, his long legs firmly anchored.

"So." Mr. Baker turned to me after a pause. "You do look very much like my daughter." He said it as if returning to an old subject, although this was the first—and only—time he mentioned her to me.

To my horror, I heard myself repeat the phrase I hated. "I wish she hadn't left."

"So do I." As if hard of hearing, he leaned in my direction, and I smelled alcohol, astringent and fruity, on his breath.

"Do you have a picture?"

"I do." He pulled a wallet from his pants and held it out to me, open.

Sadie hugged a fluffy dog and bared her teeth. A front one was missing, yet the mock grimace was framed by dimples, and her eyes squinted with pleasure. Her hands were hidden in fur. I recognized my blond bangs, my minute nose. She was, however, an exaggerated version of me, her features more defined, neater. A perfect me.

"She has a ski jump nose!" I approved.

"From her mother, yes she does." Mr. Baker licked his lips, and the lids below his eyes sagged slightly. "It isn't just your looks. There's something else. Something else that reminds me of Sadie." His staring face loomed, and he clenched his fist before his chest. "Something in your heart."

I nodded.

My mother gazed sympathetically, inquisitively, as she did when I was sick, and I felt warm. "What happened to the dog?" I asked.

Mr. Baker leaned back suddenly, chin to the sky, and laughed. "That too," he wheezed, "that too, is just like her." We were all laughing. "The dog," he answered, "is in quarantine. After six weeks, they'll take her home from the airport."

Shading her eyes against the sun, my mother stood. "Is that Benjamin? He's up a tree again. Benjamin! Come down here."

"You can see the fortress!" Halfway up the trunk of a palm, he obediently edged himself down.

"Now, that boy," said Mr. Baker, again the gracious host, "is one of a kind. He's spied our fortress, which you see only from my roof—unless you climb a tree. Would you like," he called to Benjamin, "some ginger ale?"

Benjamin hovered at the edge of the patio, claiming his own space.

"The commissary's out of Coke," I yelled.

Mr. Baker had sprung to pull up an extra chair, his old-world courtesy restoring his dignity. The wallet photo had disappeared. I understood that he was ashamed of his interest in me. Throughout lunch he spoke to Benjamin and me as a unit, when he wasn't chatting with my parents. Later, however, he led us all up an exterior staircase to the roof, and took my hand.

A ways down the coast, crowning a cliff, was an intricate blossom of turrets and towers poking above matted forest. "That's our Portuguese fortress," he announced, but my brother was already out of hearing, headed for a better vantage point, my parents trailing. Mr. Baker and I stood our ground, preferring the curving horizon.

"It looks like a haunted castle," I observed.

"Could be. They kept the slaves there, before they sent them away in ships."

"And they died?"

"Some did."

"Where did they go, in ships?"

"To be sold in America, mostly. You've heard of the plantations in the south?"

"Like George Washington's."

He chuckled. I persevered, "Does anybody live there now?"

"In the fortress, you mean? It's just a ruin, now. Just history."

I wasn't sure exactly what he meant, but I felt reassured by his thoughtful tone. He spoke as if we'd been friends for a long while, as if he already knew my favorite subject and what I wanted to be when I grew up. For a moment we didn't talk, and I was conscious of his dry fingers loose around mine. Benjamin's voice reached us as staccato inflections.

"But what am I doing?" Mr. Baker flinched. "I must be boring you. Wouldn't you like to go play with your brother?"

I shook my head, no. He'd been wishing I was Sadie, I knew, but I couldn't picture Mr. Baker as my father. My father never held my hand. Always folded up in himself, wrapped in papers and books, his method of reassurance was subtle. I felt closest to him when curled nearby with my own book, moored within his camaraderie. His faith in me was automatic. Once, scheming to surprise him when he was out of town, my mother taught me to dive. When he returned she led him to the pool and I performed. He stood smiling, arms folded, immensely pleased but not surprised, as if I had always known how.

No, Mr. Baker was not my father; he was special in another way. For months I drank ginger ale instead of Coke, and whenever I heard his name mentioned, I blushed. In the car on the way home from our visit, my mother had explained that he and his wife were getting divorced, and that he would not be living with his daughter. I thought that his wife must be very cruel. I could not imagine living without my father and Benjamin. For some reason I assumed that Benjamin would go with him.

In another West African town my father and I lived in a hotel. For a month we waited for housing, sharing a suite at the end of a hall. I was twelve, my mother had died, and Benjamin was in boarding school in New York. Every day my father took me to the nearly empty dining room for breakfasts and suppers, and the kitchen gave me sandwiches for school. In the afternoons I watched Josephine clean our rooms. She was plump and careful, she repeated her pidgin English patiently when I didn't understand. She had a boyfriend and took typing lessons and sometimes she stopped to smoke and do my nails. We both liked Precious Pink. Her brown hands darkened at the knuckles, and when she mopped she swayed and her white hem grazed her dense calves. I pictured her dressed like the African women in the streets, cinched in frilly blouses and platform shoes instead of her hotel uniform. Sitting beside me on my bed, wiggling her flip-flops, she smelled of cooking oil and ammonia and, later on, after I gave her a bottle of French perfume, of how I remembered church.

Some evenings, after taking me to supper, my father had to leave for dinner parties. Instead of TV I had the methodical glimmer of the fan's reflection in Josephine's glassy floor. The fan chirped and twirled, the windows closed against the bugs attracted by the lights. One night, my hands anchored to the doorknob, I watched my father slip away, his jacket swinging down the hall, room past room, his footsteps fading, and I wanted to call him back. I was filled with a crazy dread. What if he were gone for good? What if he got hurt, and I were left alone? I knew, though, that my fear was childish and I kept my lips pressed tight. I could not keep him safe, I could not keep him to myself: I could not count on him. He continued to recede, quick and frail as a moth, then darted around the corner without looking back. The empty corridor dilated, and I ached. I loved him more at that moment, I think, than I've loved anyone before or since.

I was sixteen when my father left his last job in Africa, and I made a pact with myself that I'd be back. Something was unfinished there for me; I knew I would return the first chance I got. It was as if I'd been snatched from the promise of passion—from a first kiss. I was old enough to plot the sort of life I wanted, and I had for models the Peace Corps. I'd seen volunteers bargaining in dialect for cassava and palm oil; they lived upcountry in huts. I could be like that, I thought—almost African, at home with the hot reds of hibiscus and chili peppers, flushed with laughter and the sun. When it came time at college to apply for jobs, I scouted out employers who could put me on a plane, and signed a two-year contract with AfricEd. The work was incidental; I would have been just as happy hired to weigh babies for a public health organization or to distribute food to famine victims as I was to teach for AfricEd, and I had no preference as to country. I simply wanted to live among Africans in the endless bush across the fence.

AfricEd assigned me to the nation of Tambala, a central African republic where I hadn't once set foot, yet when I arrived it felt like coming home. If the rickety lorries were known here as *camions,* if the women wore their hair sticking out like antennae in a style all their own, still the land seemed to pulse with the language of drums. There was no cellophane, no mistrust. Everything was raw and open and consumed right away. The United States might be rich, yet nothing there had ever felt like mine. Africa did.

Initially, I joined a crew of volunteers at a remote training camp for two months of acculturation and French immersion, a sort of decompression zone where we could get used to the country. Surrounded by Americans, I thrived, an experienced expatriate undaunted by the cockroaches and inoculations, eager to hear our Tambalan mentors speak the truth. We were still insulated, however, we trainees, and we studied the culture as if through a camera, frame by frame, fixing moments at our leisure, turning them over and inside out, putting down the camera when we got tired, and then relaxing as Americans, feet up on tables, heads on each others' shoulders, pining for M&Ms, a newspaper, a hot bath. I was good at this, living American in someone else's country; I'd been doing it for years.

The challenge began at Mampungu, my isolated bush post, where I was, indeed, among the villagers. None of them really had a chance to show me who they were. I was out of focus myself, and tended to generalize, looking for some idea I had of Africa in everyone I met, digging, defacing, as if for stolen treasure. I gave each potential ally the same part in my personal drama; it wasn't Mpovi I was trying to befriend, nor Bwadi, nor Diabelle. It was Africa.

I started defending Mampungu even before I got there. "It's exactly what I asked for. Remote, but with plumbing. I said I could live without electricity, but not without water. And I wanted a house to myself."

Paul eyed me skeptically from across the table. We were sitting out the rain in the annex bar, part of the American embassy complex. Having completed our months of training in the Interior, we were finally en route to our posts, stopping over downtown to stock up.

While he would be living in Nkisi, a residential satellite of Kimpiri, my journey south to Mampungu would take close to a day.

The room was dim and stale, a pocket of the States transplanted. Smoke recirculated through the cooling vents, and the rain against the sealed windows droned like a motor so that the place felt like a submarine. Baseball flickered silently on the TV console, the game taped weeks earlier and shipped from DC. There was no music, merely the lackadaisical thud of darts and the rise and fall of voices across the room, where three men hawed and chewed their ice. Other than the dart players and ourselves, there was only the bartender—an Asian occupied with drying glasses, squeezing his rag after each with a rugged twist.

"I can't see carrying water from some stream kilometers away," I went on, anticipating faucets. "In this heat I require at least a bath a day."

Paul leaned forward, glasses slipping down his nose. "You hire students to carry the water." His tone was thin and gritty, his long fingers graceful. He was older, a seasoned World Traveler who had explored the nether regions of being thirty years old. Brilliant and erratic, he always wore white and a piratical gold loop in one ear.

"Anyway, lucky for us, they saved the genuine *National Geographic* posts for the star volunteers." He pushed his glasses neatly against his face, using a thumb instead of a forefinger. "Neither of us will have to worry about water."

Nothing seemed to worry him about tomorrow's venture to our respective jobs. I did my best to follow suit. I rose to get us each another drink, another pack of cigarettes. I was hoarding Marlboros to get me started in the bush.

The Asian was mixing the drinks, milk splashing over ice, when a man settled on the next stool over.

"White Russians, huh?" His gray hair was scrubby, shorn close to the scalp, his flesh a weary hue of violet.

"Calcium."

He half nodded, his chin lodged in doughy folds. "Need all the vitamins you can get in this hole. What brings you to the heart of darkness, anyhow?"

His middle-aged drawl made me skittish, but I held my ground. I knew he was no diplomat, and guessed he was some sort of advisor, military or technical, perhaps an engineer. Kimpiri was full of shady goings-on. Everybody knew that the United States was funneling arms through Tambala to rebel factions in Angola. And that an American contractor had agreed to build a bridge to span the river down south. I wondered if this bridge would be near me. A drink in each hand, I stood as if for inspection, determined to be polite. "I work for AfricEd."

He drew back, as if insulted. "I thought Mankanzu sent you guys all home."

"That was Peace Corps."

"There's always someone." He wagged his head sadly. "What makes you want to ruin your health and pretty good looks in one of those dirty villages?"

"Oh," I said cheerfully, the bearer of good news, "we have a doctor here. AfricEd takes care of us."

"Takes care of you!" Suddenly he bellowed, and his anger was indeed legible, his face puffing, overripe. "Don't tell me they take care of you. You kids get sick and by the time someone brings you in, you're a mess. It's guys like Doc there who wind up saving your asses. Doc, come on over here a sec!" Waving a bearish arm, he spluttered toward the corner. A dart thumped.

"Cool your jets, Thompson, what is it now?" an amiable voice shot back. Sloping toward the target, a lean, bearded man plucked out a few darts, handed them to his partner. Then he swerved toward the bar.

"Tell this little do-good Miss what happens when she gets snakebite in the bush," Thompson urged. "She's one of those holy volunteers."

"Yeah?" Doc said with interest, ignoring Thompson. His dark hair lapped at his collar, and his eyes glinted alertly through wire rim glasses. He was not an old fart.

"Name's Mitch. I'm the medic down at Lufwidi. We're just setting up camp." He stabbed his hand toward my waist.

Heeling back, I took his hand, let go. "Nickie. I'll be at Mampungu, teaching English."

"AfricEd takes care of her, she says," Thompson swayed. "Tell her how many times you've had to truck out kids for medivacs."

"Once, actually, but I've only been here a few months. This guy out at Cheba got appendicitis. You know him?"

"Nope. What sort of camp is it you're setting up?"

"Getting ready to build a bridge."

"These monkeys sure ain't gonna do it on their own," Thompson snorted. He tried to focus on me. "You think you're going to bring them out of the dark ages," he accused, then looked confused, his train of thought lost. I started to turn, heading for Paul.

"Mampungu," Mitch stopped me. "That where that little mission is?"

I nodded.

"You got a radio out there?"

"I haven't been there yet."

"I'll drop by to make sure we're in radio contact in case you do get in trouble." His smile, overgrown with beard, was friendly, innocent, paternalistic. It pissed me off.

"Don't."

I made a beeline for Paul. "Hey," I heard behind me. "I only meant . . . I mean . . . Oh, well." In a moment the darts resumed.

"What was that about?" asked Paul as I slid back into the booth.

"He evacuated some Peace Corps guy. They're with the bridge project. They think we're all airheads."

Paul hunched forward conspiratorially, earring aglow. "Don't knock it. These engineers could come in handy for transportation. You're going to be out there relying on the random *camion;* it could take days to find a ride out. Hell, I wouldn't be so sensitive if I were you."

I told him about the monkeys in the dark ages.

"So he's drunk, he's a jerk. They're not all that bad."

I admired Paul's flexibility. After all, these were uncharted lands, where different rules applied. Alcoholic engineers came with the terrain. They were about as alien as missionaries to my imagined Africa, yet already I'd agreed to teach in a church school—church schools were the only schools in Tambala. Would I have to make peace with these bridge builders as well?

No. That night, anyway, I could not bring myself to look at Mitch or Thompson or their friend again. I bristled at the thought of my village overrun by drunken racists in trucks. Sipping silently with Paul, I clung instead to the prospect of my secret Africa, the childhood vista where clapping games were played in pairs and dinners fished from rocks. I wanted that life across the fence all to myself.

2

BLACK AND WHITE

Mampungu was a bush village abandoned by American missionaries, blessed with the remnants of their school and dispensary and
dead power lines. I was the only white there, yet a white like any
other: same damp skin, same pink squint against the sun, same soft
hair and face.

I might have been an ecclesiastic; I might have been a *colonne;* I
might have been a Portuguese explorer, five centuries before.
Ultimately we were each of us the same: *mundele,* white.
Mampungu and its environs had seen more of us than the rest of
Tambala, which extended far inward across Africa's equatorial belt.
Mampungu's corner of the country was near the coast. Upriver
from the Atlantic, heavily settled savannah, this region claimed the
port city of Kilu, and Kimpiri, the capital, as well as the asphalt
road that linked them, and the train. Seeping east and north, the
country spanned the mammoth rain forest that was a country unto
itself, home of Pygmies and elephants, home of the great river and

its crocodiles. Uganda lay across the Ruwenzoris, mountains of the moon. Spilling south, Tambala edged Lake Tanganyika, and spread back across the strategic mining region boasting copper, diamonds, and cobalt—not to mention a feisty tribe ever eager to secede.

Closer to Mampungu, directly south along the coast, Angola suffered its war. They still spoke Portuguese there. Tambala had become a French colony in 1885, when Europe divvied up Africa, cutting through old kingdoms, ensnaring rival tribes. At Tambala's independence, the Interior erupted into bloody troubles, landing the CIA-trained president, Mankanzu, his job. The U.S. had interests to protect, what with socialist Angola a domino away. The troubles stabilized; Tambala became a police state. While the mines made Mankanzu one of the world's richest men, most of Tambala subsistence farmed. People were poorer than I'd seen in West Africa. It was hotter, wetter, bigger, more overgrown—and still the people smiled. When I arrived at Mampungu, they smiled and whistled as if I'd been missed.

I was their gift from the benevolent West, from whence came schools and doctors and hydroelectric dams. I was their Nicole. All my life, when I'd heard myself called "Nicole" I'd cringed; I'd always gone by "Nickie." But I didn't have the heart to correct the village officials when they greeted me by my full legal name, memorized perfectly as it appeared on my documents. "Miss Nicole Spark," they articulated, grasping my hand enthusiastically as I stood dazed and polite before the yellow brick house where I would live. I decided then and there to let "Nickie" go. Soon enough, however, I was hearing "Nicoli," a Kikongo adaptation; Bantu tongues hate to end words on consonants. I thought "Nicoli" sounded lovely, the syllables clipped as if sung to drums.

I was equally delighted by the eerie beauty of the place. It was late in the dry season, the time when fields were burned to keep the brush from sprouting underfoot, and the temperature was compounded by the ash in the air, but I didn't mind the sweat trickling between my breasts and from behind my bent knees: I was in Africa. Crackling and charred, Mampungu was my private moonscape, its fires erupting, then dying into smoke as far as you could see across the brown savannah; after dusk, the red dots would keep on burning holes through the night.

This far *en brousse,* the language of choice was Kikongo; French was relegated to school and to other mission business, or to speaking to me. I taught English at the secondary levels corresponding with our grades nine through twelve. The students called me "Miss." They had no books, stole the chalk, and sold their dittoed texts to the market ladies as wrapping paper. Other than the material run off in the school office, no printed matter was available at Mampungu—no magazines, no news—and I was thankful for the miniature shortwave radio I had lugged from the States, coddled in a towel beside my camera in my backpack. Mitch, incidentally, would have been glad to know that the mission did operate a two-way radio, but I had no intention to call him.

I used my own shortwave to include in my classes facts and figures culled from BBC's World News, and the students seemed to thrive on the stories about wars—any wars—in Gaza, Afghanistan, Angola. The kids were bright and raucous, embittered by the slim prospects of their lives in poor Tambala. At the school year's end, the old principal had apparently waited to distribute grades until the students had been trucked to the train station, in case the ones who failed might try to break windows and smash desks.

"When you get married," said Mpovi, my next-door neighbor, "then you won't have to teach."

I didn't understand at first why she pitied me. What could possibly be enviable about her lot as a wife? I saw the students as a challenge; moreover, I was on their side. Mpovi, however, assumed me to be desperate, and took me under wing. She had moved to Mampungu that summer with her husband, the new *préfet,* or principal, and their infant son, as well as a veritable bevy of child relatives meant to board with them in order to attend the elementary school. Mpovi was beautiful, with soft impala eyes and skin like molten gold, and very young, I thought, when we met at the dinner party in my honor at her house.

It was my first evening in Mampungu, and the *Préfet* had assembled select mission functionaries to welcome me among their ranks. Suave and correct, he made introductions and small talk, aiming us at seats, his palms stiff as rudders. Although he, too, was new to the place, sent to set the school back on its feet, and although junior in age to several teachers, he oozed superiority.

A jovial pastor and a visiting doctor with a dense cap of white curls rounded out the group; we sat admiring the house, chatting in French, drinks placed carefully among the photos and doilies crowding the surfaces. To my pleasant surprise, the *Préfet* served us cold Empereur beer. If the bygone American Baptists had preached against alcohol, these Africans were now in charge.

The doctor impressed me with his worldly credentials as well as his concern; he'd been to school in Switzerland and to Philadelphia for a conference and he spoke of how badly he wanted to restore electric current to Mampungu. The men smoked up a storm on their raspy Gazelles, and I wanted to smoke, too, but I'd left my cigarettes at home, determined to ration my small supply of Marlboros, to cut down and quit, to drop the part of my identity that smoked. I was always this way when I moved to a new place, intending to leave behind all the things I didn't like about myself, to finally personify the perfect me.

I was forced to refrain; nobody invited me to smoke. At my elbow was a portrait of the *Préfet* flanked by two old people—his parents, I assumed—brittle and gauzy as wings. I peered, but the light from the gas lamp across the room fell short, obscuring their expressions. Pictures and dishes lined shelves on each wall, and photos hung everywhere, some framed, some cut from magazines, all portraits—human forms shaped like dark eggs mounted on bottles. Someone here, I thought, loved photographs as much as I.

Narrow cushions padded a sofa framed with wooden armrests, and austere desk chairs had been offered to the less venerated teachers. Murky floral curtains puckered in the breeze; beyond the screen, insects sawed. The home was sophisticated, decorated with purpose, tropical and cozy. Mpovi flitted in the periphery, now busy at the dining table, now disappearing through a door. The child boarders were not in view.

Yet finally she approached us slowly, regally, her own baby in her arms.

"*Ah, voilà,*" the *Préfet* announced. "*Madame le Préfet,* and our son, Malewa.*"

I was the only female guest; for protocol I took the men's example, rising, leaning forward to shake hands with the mother and to admire the child.

"He's tired," I approved, confronted with a hazel face embedded in crochet. His druggy gaze was fixed somewhere above his mother's shoulder.

"He was sleeping," she agreed, magenta lips fully arched in a smile. She retreated in a curtsy, and delivered Malewa to the *Préfet* at my right on the couch, then perched at my other side. Together, we watched the boy bounce and chortle, and for a moment the scent of flowers and acrid milk blocked the steamy smell of chicken and palm oil. She posed demurely, wrapped in the elaborately patterned fabric called the *pagne,* the weight of her matching headdress pulling her chin high and her back straight. Meanwhile, the men cheered the *Préfet* and his namesake, invoking vitality and cleverness, and the baby rallied, fanning out his fingers.

"OK," the *Préfet* turned to me. "I think he's had enough of Papa now." Before I could protest, the child came gliding toward my lap.

"He doesn't mind strangers?" I asked hopefully, but the mother vouched proudly for his good humor, and my hands formed awkward braces as he touched down on my thighs. Oblivious, the *Préfet* let go and the baby strained in the direction of the receding arms. Then his baffled gaze swerved and zeroed in on mine and we were stuck, equally helpless.

"*Chance, Chance,*" his mother cooed. I didn't know what to do, he was warm and unpredictable in my frozen hands. I saw his facial muscles catch, slowly crumple, I could see the screech coming as he sucked air into his wet, pink mouth.

"Oh?" I said.

He was safe in his mother's clasp before the long note hit, shrill as a siren. That was all; once absorbed in his mother's folds, he calmed. The party rocked with laughter, and I smiled sheepishly.

"I'm sorry, I'm not good with babies."

Laughter flared.

"No, no, no," wailed the Pastor, "it's not that!"

"It's not you," said one of the teachers, remarkable for his exaggerated afro, "it's your skin!"

"My skin."

"You must be the first white he's seen!" Rocking forward, the teacher clutched his knees in glee, rocked back. Then, refocusing on me, he suddenly frowned. It was the first of Bwadi's long, curious stares. Avoiding his eyes, I pretended to smile at the baby, although I was battling dismay, a rush of shame and resentment hitting like a blizzard inside. While the others at the party chuckled and poked fun at the child, Bwadi seemed to understand that they were also laughing at me.

Mpovi hadn't caught on. Preening, the child snug and innocuous against her shoulder, she reassured me cheerfully. "He'll get used to you. You call him Chance, that's our special name for him. You call him Chance, and he'll be like your son."

Chance. Luck. She spoke with conviction, as if she meant to make it happen. I wondered if keen, bushy-headed Bwadi thought she could.

After school the next day, as I crunched along the blackened path to my front door, I heard Mpovi call out an invitation. She was waving, swinging her whole arm. "I'm coming," I yelled back. I was sticky and tired and a little traumatized, my hands snowy with chalk, my heart loaded with all those round eyes staring, confusing America with me. "You are rich," the kids had insisted, "everyone there is rich." I had allowed discussion in French, this first day; I wanted to break the ice. "You are powerful." "You like little wars."

After that, Mpovi's guileless company appealed, and I quickly got ready to visit her and Chance. When I emerged on my porch, she was still outside, crouched low on a stool. A mango tree sheltered her from the aluminum sky, ominously hot despite a high sheet of clouds. I had yet to see Mampungu blue. The slash-and-burn fervor had not spared the mission lawns, which had been burned for snakes and scorpions, leaving a bleak plot of charred roots between my house and hers.

Activity had scuffed a clearing in the shady area that stretched from Mpovi's mango to the kitchen door. Opposite the rubble of a cook fire sat a concrete washing block beside a tap. The baby slanted naked along a straw mat, aiming at his mother, whose hands were busy in a basin at her feet.

"You came right away." Rocking back, she wiped her hands on the faded *pagne* covering her knees. Bare-shouldered, purposeful, she was in her element, her stool a throne. Yet the hugeness of her smile, drawing her chin up and her eyes half shut, was sweetly naive.

"It's too hot to plan my lessons now. The papers all stick together and then I can't think."

"But you shouldn't be inside in the afternoon. It's like an oven, there's no air."

A child came outside, struggling behind a chair, letting the screen door slam. With her lips, Mpovi pointed me to where the little girl was planting the chair, testing for wobble on the uneven earth. I would have preferred a stool, but accepted the seat of honor—the same stiff-backed chair that had served as extra inside the cushioned *salon*. The child flitted away. I was to be continually mystified by this network of halting, silent elves that seemed to hover in the wings to wait on adults.

"Would you like anything?"

I assumed Mpovi meant, to drink. "No, thanks. I just finished eating."

"*Oui,*" she dipped forward with encouragement. "You have a lot of food!"

Perhaps word had gone around about the provisions loaded off the *camion* when I'd arrived. "Yes, I have food."

"Sugar?"

"Yes, I have sugar. And beans, like those." I pointed at the ones she was sorting through for stones.

She laughed. Then, a pause. "We need sugar."

"For what?"

"Coffee. Do you have coffee, too?"

"Yes."

"Coffee we can get. But there's a *crise de sucre.*"

"A sugar crisis?"

"The *commerçants* are all out. I'm almost out. Tea and coffee, I have."

"I only drink coffee."

"With milk and sugar?"

"Black."

"Then why do you have sugar?"

"I don't know. To make bread and cakes, I guess. I don't really need it. You can have some."

"I have milk. Do you have milk?"

"Yes, but I don't use that either."

Again, the odd, direct look.

"You take some of my sugar."

Her smile returned. "You're very nice." Now she was bashful. "So where are all your things? Did you leave them in America?"

"Yes, with my father."

"In your village."

"Well, in his village. I come from a different town, now."

"But your maternal village. You left your things there?"

This time, it was I who laughed. "I was born in Africa, you know. My father moved every few years, for his job. I don't have a maternal village, I never lived where he lives now."

Dismissively, she tossed a handful of stones collected from the beans. "Then where are your grandparents?"

"They died."

"But where they lived, you never lived there?"

"No, my parents never took me there." I shrugged. "It's very different in America."

"And now you've come far away by yourself. You miss your family very much."

Feebly, I agreed. I missed my father and brother the way you miss the past.

Mpovi stared at the immobile baby asleep. *"Kiadi.* I was so sad when I got married and left my family. We moved to Kimpiri and I was sad for a long time. Now it's better. My village isn't far."

"When did you get married?"

"Almost two years ago. I was twenty. I finished school here and went back to my village and then I left again."

"You came to school at Mampungu?" I tried to fit her among the classroom of anarchic eyes. In leaving it behind, she seemed to have eclipsed its aura of struggle, of spirited retort.

"There were five missionaries then, all old, though, with no children."

"We must be the same age," I realized.

"You're twenty-two?" She was impressed, and repeated the discovery.

"How old did you think I was?"

She looked genuinely puzzled, as if the question hadn't occurred

to her. I knew how she felt. Absorbed in our differences, we tended to neglect what we might have in common. Being the same age
both narrowed and deepened the gap. Equivalent, our worlds
touched at one point like fingertips to a mirror.

For a moment we didn't talk, and there was just the hiss of
Mpovi's beans shifting against the tin. Kids playing soccer in the
distance chorused; someone made a goal. The baby stirred, and
Mpovi scooped him to her shoulder.

"Chance," I said.

"Chance, Chance." Her mood lifted. "Do you have pictures?"

"From the States?"

"Your family, friends, where you lived."

"Would you like to see?" I stood, happy for a reason to get up;
the chair hurt my back. Mpovi nodded eagerly.

She was right: the heat tightened inside my house. The photos
lay tucked in a drawer; before handling them, I wiped my skin dry.
They were not snapshots, although they were of my friends; they
were my portfolio, the only one I'd brought. They were my document of leaving, a photo-essay about saying good-bye, to people,
and to craft, too—there would be no darkroom in Africa.
Determined to take myself seriously, I was a bit melodramatic then
about what I thought of as "my art." The prints were black-and-
white five-by-sevens, mounted on heavy bond, each adrift within
broad white borders, bound together as a spiral book.

They didn't work. Flipping through the pages, my throat tickling
with ash from the burning fields, I realized that I should have taken
snapshots. I'd tried to imprison familiar souls inside a format, and
each face defied my frame, evolving poses I'd forgotten. Figures
jogged ahead, tossed shoes into a corner, voices skated, refusing to
flow along this line of tension, to blend into that shadow. My photos
reduced my friends to flat abstractions. I missed them very much.

Back below the mango, Mpovi was still alone with Chance. In
retrospect, I believe our privacy that day was staged, Mpovi's other
neighbors deferring to the perceived officiality of my first visit.

She turned the pages slowly. "You don't have color?"

"Please be careful, don't touch the picture." I tapped the border,
where her fingers should go. "They're very special to me."

"That's snow?"

I nodded. My friend Anna floated in a mist of flakes.

"It's cold. Like the afterworld."

"That's up in the mountains, not where I lived."

"Ehi!" Pete and Susan were two masks suspended, eyes closed, surrounded by ripples in gray pond water.

"I took that picture from a boat."

"It's like the ancestors!"

"No, they're not dead," I laughed.

"Are they married?"

"No."

"And this!"

It was Davis; I winced. He'd known all along I meant to move to Africa; he hadn't tried to change my mind. Yet, if he'd asked, would I have stayed?

He loomed, surprised beside a cow, eyes global as the cow's, his mouth matching the cynical scroll of its lip. Suffused with bovine indifference, this shot was better than the others.

"That's mean! You don't like him, do you?"

She was right, the image was insulting. He seemed, however, to be the only one I hadn't killed off.

"Is this your sister?"

"No, I don't have any sisters."

"How many brothers?"

"Just one."

"Only two children in your family? Show me your brother."

"He's not here." I hadn't seen Benjamin for years. Of course he wasn't in this portfolio, this little showcase of the stand-in family I'd most recently left behind. I hadn't realized until a week after arriving in Tambala that I had brought no photo of Benjamin at all. Startled by my oversight, I'd written to my father requesting one—not to Benjamin, because he never wrote back.

She turned the last page. "And this is what?"

I'd ended with a still life, an abstract close-up of an ivory knick-knack I'd held onto from West Africa. It was a crocodile, jaws cocked, and the ferocious shadow it cast. What you couldn't see in the picture was that the long body was hollow, carved as a napkin ring for foreigners. This silly crocodile, violently sensationalized in black and white, represented for me something that belonged there, in California, something that I'd meant to leave behind.

"It's just a figurine," I said quickly, "of a crocodile. It's not a good picture."

"But where are your parents?"

"Ah! My father's picture is in my wallet."

"And your mother?"

"She died."

"*Kiadi.*"

As if to make up for not having her photo, I splayed my fingers to show off her gold school signet intricate with Latin. "This was her ring."

Mpovi drew my hand close, her breath warm against my fingernails. "It's pretty." Then she turned my palm up, examining, as if to tell my future. Softly, I recoiled.

"Do you have pictures of American children?"

I thought of negatives I'd left at my father's; I enjoyed photographing kids. "Not here."

"And everybody is white." Blinking with curiosity, she passed me the portfolio.

"There weren't many blacks where I lived."

"But there are many in the United States."

"That's true. But I didn't know any well." I squirmed, pressed my back against the chair. "*You* have a lot of pictures."

On the subject of herself, Mpovi was cheerful. "I have pictures of all my family, relatives, my village."

"Everybody."

"Except," she turned, pouting, and reached for Chance. "Except for my son."

"Why not?"

"Nobody at Mampungu has a camera. In my village the photographer came sometimes market day, or my uncle would bring his camera from Kimpiri. When Chance was born nobody had a camera, and now I have to wait."

"I have a camera."

"That's right!" She opened her mouth, excited.

"How did you know?"

"Of course you brought your camera. White people always have cameras."

I had been afraid of this, of my camera branding me as the probing outsider, perhaps as whites before me had been identified with guns. I had planned to keep my Pentax unobtrusive; here, however, was the golden opportunity.

"Let me take his picture."

"Like those?" She looked dubiously at my lap.

"No, I'll make him look nice. No ancestors."

"Color?"

"Sure, I have color film."

"No cows."

"No cows, no goats, no chickens. Just Chance and you."

She clutched her baby to her chest. "You're very nice."

"Today?" I scanned the sky and the burned earth grainy with stubble, a dusky, monochromatic landscape full of possibilities. Once again, I was thinking in black and white.

"Not today." Dreamily, she rocked, bare shoulders twisting slowly. "I'll have him ready in good clothes. When the sun is shining."

"For color, yes, the sky should be blue and the lawn green. You know, I can't imagine Mampungu like that."

"But it's always green. The weeds grow too quickly, you'll see, they grow taller than the *petits*. The dry season is ending now, we have only to wait for the rain."

Gradually, she stopped rocking and straightened, Chance firm against her breast, her eyes slim as if fixed on the distant first drop.

I had no photograph but I had this: Benjamin on his motorcycle in a tropical town, spurting down the broken road, dodging Africans. From behind, his short hair is a shock, the nape of his neck white as a scar. It's a Technicolor outtake from my life: the motorcycle balloon red, the street orange as rust, his elbows kola nuts, tanned hard. I was fourteen, and although he was simply scooting around the corner to see his buddies at the Marine House, I knew that in some way he was not coming back.

I hadn't yet realized that I was already gone, myself. I'd returned from my first term at boarding school to find a family that no longer fit—that had been strained at the seams for years. But, like an adolescent who, puzzled by her sprouting hips, prefers zippers that pinch,

I'd been telling myself that this was a temporary transformation and that eventually the lumps and bulges would deflate, that harmony and balance would prevail.

29

That year my brother and I had switched places: I lived in America; he lived in western Africa. Too many schools had thrown him out, and so he was living with my father, taking high school courses through correspondence. With his hair long and jaguar black, he'd been notorious for wily refusal, random recompense. Away at school, he stole cars and wrecked them, broke windows, crushed a roommate's typewriter with a trunk. He ran away and ran away. Any minute, I thought, he'll be gone for good.

My father had signed his consent since Benjamin was underage. Benjamin was joining the Marines. And, although his registration at boot camp was still months off, he had cut his hair to resemble the embassy guards'. He belonged now to this tiny clan of soldiers posted to protect the American mission, the five Embassy Marines. They were a likable lot, hosting happy hours and films at their place, willing to crew for my father in his boat. On duty, sharply starched, they carried guns.

So I flew in from Virginia to find my brother freshly shorn, the black patch on top tapering to skin smooth as ivory around the ears and neck, long untouched by the sun. It's too hot, he laughed, hugging me at the airport; soon enough anyway he'd have to shave his head. It's not just that he was ugly, it's that he was someone else. My father looked afraid. After he'd returned to work, I stood outside our house and watched Benjamin splutter off on his Honda, snagging, swerving free, his new head brave and sorry as a thumb, and I felt exposed.

The summer before Benjamin's enlistment, he'd thought that Volkswagens could float. "Let's see, in the lagoon," I heard him urge Rik. While I caught only snippets of his whispered campaign, I could see from the busy glint of my brother's head that he was talking a mile a minute. Idling across the pool on inflated rafts, he and Rik had left me anchored to the novel I was reading as they plotted for real. Stalling midsentence, wandering, my eyes kept settling on Rik's back.

Benjamin was still wearing his hair like a hippie then and could not keep still. His friend, Rik, was Norwegian, blond, bemused, adrift. His parents were always off on some project upcountry, and he seemed half absent, himself. His eyes were blue with privacy and intuition, and it was a sort of scientific curiosity, I think, that committed him to Benjamin's tricks. But then neither of them trusted the world.

That day, he agreed to sneak his mother's Volkswagen Bug for a spin.

"Coming?" Benjamin teased me, assuming that I would not. Eclipsing the sun, his face was hard to see. I'd ridden on his motorbike to the pool at Rik's apartment complex, but I could easily catch a taxi home. They were dry and dressed and ready to go. The keys mewed in Rik's pocket, soft as reindeer bells, and I glanced from his crotch to his quizzical smile.

Of course, I didn't really think we'd drive into the lagoon.

Cupped in the back seat, pinned within a whirlwind as Rik drove the harbor road, I squinted out the open window. The water looked smooth and solid as linoleum. Unlike the raw lagoon in Conakry, this prosperous waterfront was cluttered with piers and markets, the fallout of commerce and transportation. Out where the sea went deep and royal blue, you could always see international freighters inching past. Nobody chased crabs down here or fished from rocks, and expatriates in need of beaches migrated in speedboats to islands off the coast.

All except for the Russians, that is, the burly fellows dotting the outermost corner of the shore, up where it tapered into a breakwater. From our side of the bay, from where the vw was tracing a course along the rim, the four or five figures looked swollen and spent, aimless as seals. They were navy guys or something, notorious and pitied for their attachment to this brittle, dirty inlet. Likely, they were restricted from all the leisure spots where they might mingle with westerners and spill state secrets; likely they had no choice. Whenever we spotted them, my friends from school and I would point and wonder, anxious to reconcile this image of the enemy with Hollywood's communist spies. Rik and Benjamin, however, not intimidated in the least, had targeted that very section of the beach for the launch. We could follow the track that led to the breakwater, cutting across where the ocean was closest to the road.

It occurred to me that they were serious.

Benjamin was chattering about some movie or TV ad he'd seen in the States: a Volkswagen bobbing like a buoy, watertight. Loosely, Rik laughed. Women balancing basins of fish on their heads were struggling past, long skirts billowing psychedelically. Suddenly popular in Europe and the U.S., these African prints evoked a sensual, elemental way of life; vividly ingenious, the patterns appealed to people on drugs.

I wouldn't have known about that yet. Our American school, where I'd just completed eighth grade, was out of range of the sixties. It took kids like Benjamin and Rik, emissaries from boarding schools abroad, to stir things up. At parties, they would disappear and then emerge from gardens draped in sweetly dissipating smoke, and to this day I associate the smell of marijuana with the tropics, with the palm fronds and heat of my brother's last summer at home. This despite his efforts to keep it out of my sight—not because he didn't trust me, and not because he thought of me as a drag tagging along, but because, I see now, he wanted me to stay good.

It was Rik who thought I might be happier corrupt. "What's wrong?" he'd asked me a few nights earlier in the Apollo, where we kids hung out to dance.

I'd jumped as if accused, his elongated vowels modulating in my mind. "Nothing," I focused on my Coke. Was there?

"You always look so sad," he'd peered angularly, tilting his Viking chin. *You always look so hideous,* he might as well have said. Signalling to the bar, he'd concluded, "You need a beer. You'll have a better time."

I did not want taking care of; "I don't like beer," I said. Shrugging, he had let me be, asked another girl to dance. I was gloomy, I decided then, because I was not beautiful, not likely to inspire romance. Three years after my mother's death, I hardly imagined that I could still be sad from that.

Steering the Volkswagen with one hand that day we stole the car, Rik held the dashboard lighter to something between his lips.

"Now?" Benjamin protested, glancing back at me.

"She's cool," Rik squeaked through his teeth. When he blew the smoke through his window, some made it back to me.

Benjamin waved the joint away. "Nah, one of us better be on top of things. Just put it out when you're done."

But the blunt little cigarette was suspended now between the two front seats, and in the rearview mirror I caught Rik's blue gaze. "Try?" he asked.

I took the thing from his fingers, puffed once, twice, the way he told me to until, throat burning, I handed it back. Benjamin was shaking his head at me through the haze. I didn't feel a thing.

And then we were turning into the fish market that blocked the bypass to the beach. The joint extinguished, Rik leaned on the horn, and we bleated flimsily. The mom of one of my girlfriends often stopped here while we were in the car, and as we sat captive to the rollicking proclamations of "Good price!" "I give you better price!" bombarding the driver's window where the traderwomen swarmed, the accumulating ocean stench would make us swoon and gag. I hoped now that it would be strong enough to blunt the smell of smoke. Gleefully, Rik braked and honked and nosed ahead through the women gesticulating with their fish. Children skipped behind us as we broke free toward the breakwater, and Rik shifted up.

"Right down by the pirogues, there, see?" Benjamin scooted forward. A few local boys loitered by the slender boats, black oversized canoes curving gently at each end, and when Rik aimed us off the track toward the water, the kids shouted us away, arms flung up and out, eyes white, as if defending their vessels from attack. Benignly, Rik waved back, and we dropped onto the slope. Pebbly and steep, this was a poor excuse indeed for a beach; the solid surface, however, made for good traction. I saw that Benjamin had thought ahead.

To our left, the African boys were bordering on frantic, their horror out of proportion to any humanitarian fear they might have felt for our safety. Close to us in age, they seemed to know something we did not. What they knew, of course, was that any car in their possession would not be headed toward the sea. Not far beyond them, the Russians were rising up on elbows, shading their eyes, bulbously stirring in the sun.

Rik waved at them, too—a star acknowledging his fans—as we inched ahead.

"Stop," said Benjamin, twisting and turning in his seat. Accommodatingly, Rik braked.

"Cut the engine, we'll roll her down in neutral."

Emptied of the engine's growl, the air expanded with the hollow slosh of water, the sigh of gulls, a fishmonger's wheedling call from the main road. The waves unfurled like silk.

"Three's too many," Rik suggested.

"I'll get out," I volunteered, suddenly eager for the open, anonymous sky.

Benjamin hopped out and snapped the seat forward. I was walking away, I realized, walking backward up the incline, watching Rik and Benjamin position themselves to shove the car forward. The doors were open like wings, and Benjamin was grinning over his shoulder, motioning to the boys to come help push. Whenever I'd seen a car stuck or broken down anywhere in Africa before, a crowd of good samaritans had providentially descended en masse. These boys, however, having fallen silent, stood rooted by their boats, long hands limp in disbelief.

Then the car was sliding toward the water, and I felt ill, a kind of twisting in my abdomen mingled with disgust, one of puberty's tugs. All in a moment, the mayhem of Benjamin's voice erupted as the car lurched forth, he and Rik ducked inside, and the doors boomed shut. Yellow and diabolical, a kind of giant snail, the car advanced with a splash. Water swirled around the revolving tires, rising; the front end dropped forward, the bumper disappeared. Waves ruffled against the doors. And Benjamin was climbing out the window, leaping free, charging around in the water as if buoyancy could be invoked.

I sank down onto the ground, the stones comfortingly hard and warm against my butt. Rik, stoic and blond, loyal to his ship, remained at the wheel as the vehicle balked, stubborn as a rock. Benjamin waved at the fisher boys, at me. An eerie sibilance sounded in response, murmurings and whispers that seemed confined inside my head, wary, imprecise. But then I looked around. A flank of little kids had gathered at my back, the dozen or so children I'd noticed running in our wake. I recognized an open mouth missing its front teeth, a boy's T-shirt missing a sleeve. I exchanged a look with awestruck, jaundiced eyes. I'm sorry, I wanted to say. Children like these often laughed at us, at how we cut oranges rather than peeled them with our teeth, at our Band-Aids, our swimsuits. They were not laughing now.

Staring into the dingy amazement of one girl balanced on calloused toes, I thought I detected query and hope—her faith, perhaps, that I could intervene against these crazy conjurers with the
car, against this apparition, this mechanical critter blindly homing
to port as if toward the herd of tankers hesitating offshore.
Actually, I doubt now that those children felt any real alliance with
me; more likely, I projected this bond because I wanted so badly to
be on their side.

When I turned to face the water again, I saw the Russians
uncoiling, brushing grit from their legs and backs, lumbering
toward the shipwrecked car, and they appeared less ferocious close
up, their bulging muscles sunburned pink, their cleanshaven faces
soft with youth. Although hardly men, they certainly were not kids
like Benjamin and Rik. Water to their knees, they listened gravely
to my brother's scrawny appeal.

With an enormous shrug, one of them prompted what looked
like the beginning of a slow ballet, and, hardly splashing, they
encircled the car. Even Benjamin shut up. Rik got out, bending
with the others for a handhold. Grunting all at once, they strained.
The car didn't budge. Again. Flushed effort, eyes scrunched shut.
Again. The Russians refused to give up, and I could not imagine
why. Why should they help my brother and his friend, and me, for
that matter, out of this stupid mess? What did they think we were
doing here with Rik's mother's car? Evidently, they were in it for
the sport. Finally, the bumper emerged above the surface with a
loud, wet lurch. And then, easily, as if to mock the fuss, the vw
began rolling backward as they pushed, retreating from the water,
up the incline toward me. The rescue team turned rowdy now,
choppy Russian phrases cascading against Benjamin's whoops. I
sensed the children closing in behind me, poised in nosy suspense.
Coming up abreast, the car rolled past like a toy as the Russian
crew cuts bobbed, victorious, and Benjamin and Rik toiled shaggily
along. Glancing valiantly at me, one of the Russians called out,
"Olympics!" His swimming trunks tautly veiled the knob between
his legs.

They shoved the car onto the road, let go. It gleamed and
dripped and did not move. The African boys waited, frozen beside
their boats. I left my cluster of children, joining Rik beside the driver's

door; his shirt and shorts were sopping, the cotton blistering like skin. Stepping into the puddle that was forming, I leaned through the window, half expecting to see fish. On the floor, water winked.

Benjamin was busy shaking hands, the Russians holding sly fingers to their lips. And then they were off, their illicit mission complete, swaggering past the Africans, wading into the lagoon. Graceful as otters, they dove in and swam.

"What's wrong?" Rik startled me.

Looking at him sharply, I saw his soft, lost eyes rimmed in red, and I wanted to put my arms around his neck. "I didn't get high," I said.

He nodded solemnly.

Something Benjamin did, or nothing, perhaps, brought the engine back to life. Sliding across the vinyl, we all got in, and my brother's dripping head looked jagged as an inkblot from the back. He was singing, I remember, as we soggily drove off, but there were no children dancing in our wake.

"Ko ko ko? Miss?" Anybody home? A girl's voice pitched through the house to where I sat planning lessons. I did this every day right after school, before the torpidity of afternoon could short out my brain, while still charged with the images of class after classroom of smooth black faces, twenty or thirty to a room, girls interspersed among the boys, each wearing a white uniform blouse or shirt. I wondered, now, which student had followed me home.

She banged, the screen door rattled. "Miss Nicoli!"

"Just a minute!" I abandoned the table littered with books and papers, notes fluttering in my wake. The climate made everything stick, paper to my skin, feet to plaster, I was slow.

Diabelle stood shyly smiling behind the door. She was alarmingly pretty, a svelte upper-form girl with long arms and legs and long bones in her face. In class she sat in back surrounded by boys; when called on she sprang hopefully to her feet and caught me off guard with a dazzling smile as the boys whispered her the answers. Yet she seemed to revel in my attention and ignored the cues, making me lead her through a sentence. I knew she wasn't as dull witted as she put on. After lessons she came forward to dangle, watching, as I gathered my books and chalk, and sometimes blurted questions about my family and my country, or about whether I liked to dance. I wasn't surprised, now, to see her at my house because I'd told my students to come for extra help.

"You've come for help with English?" I ushered her in, pleased.

"No, Miss. I mean, not today." Flustered, she hid her mouth behind her hand. "I have one question, but it's not about your lesson." She paused politely, suspensefully.

"No?"

"I've come to invite you to attend a wedding in my village." Her message delivered, she straightened proudly.

I was flattered. "How nice! Whose wedding?"

"My sister's. The village is very near. You can go there and come back the next day—because the celebration goes all night. We dance all night! The third Saturday in November."

This was over a month away. "The Saturday before the school break?"

"Yes, Miss."

"I'd love to come. Thank you very much. How do we travel there? Do we walk?"

"Oh, no, Miss." She thought this was hilarious. "It's twenty kilometers. There will be transportation."

I quickly figured—about twelve miles. "I can walk, you know."

"But none of us will walk. It's not necessary."

I thanked her again, and offered her a chair, then a glass of water, half of which she swallowed immediately. She studied what was left. "Miss?"

"Yes?"

"Can I see your house?"

I laughed and led the way. Everyone wanted to see; I'd barely had time to settle what with all the visitors. Some had pretexts, students delivering communiques from school, or villagers asking for work, some came simply to talk, and already I'd been asked for things. "I wanted to know," said one eager adolescent, "if you didn't need your backpack now. The one you wore arriving." A man in glasses wanted advice on getting an American scholarship. It was like Halloween, answering the door to stranger after expectant stranger. Diabelle's invitation was a welcome switch.

There wasn't much inside to see, although the house itself was a dream come true. Built solid of brick and timber, it rambled beyond my scope, luxuriously vacant compared to the cramped quarters I'd always shared in the States. Instead of a mud hut, I'd landed in a missionary's labor of love, complete with wood panelling and glass set into cabinet doors and, of all things, a fireplace, a wacky tribute to another place and time. Mysteriously, black streaks revealed that it had actually been used, and I pictured my predecessors bundled here in comforters and slippers, roasting chestnuts as they might have in New England, as if via witchery, one wintry evening, their house had been extracted and dumped intact in the jungle and they had gone on living, eternally chilly, as if nothing had changed.

There were lightswitches on the walls, and empty sockets in the ceilings; now and then I flicked a lever and nothing happened. Around each, however, a blossom of hand marks proved that the electricity had once been real. Now the hydroelectric generator lay dormant, the turbine broken down in its little brick shed by the stream, deemed by the missionaries impossible to fix.

A few pieces of heavy, homespun furniture had been left behind, as well as a sofa like the *Préfet*'s with matching chairs whose vinyl cushions tended to adhere to my damp legs. I had taken down the frayed curtains and pulled cloths from the tables because empty space seemed cooler. A few dresses hung meekly in my bedroom, and a gas lamp claimed a surface here and there. In the living room I'd left the bookshelves full of missionary literature: a 1959 encyclopedia set, *National Geographic*s from the early seventies, hardcover titles like *Getting Things from God*. I'd found my kitchen equipped with a stove and pots and pans, and I'd stocked a cupboard with the tins and sacks I'd brought from Kimpiri.

Sipping as if at a cocktail, Diabelle posed in room after room, scanning even the empty ones.

"That's all, I think."

"The bathroom."

"Ah, the bathroom!"

Deductively, she marched toward the very door. Inside, she turned a full circle. "Ehi!"

"It's not what you expected?"

She said no. It was the gleaming tile she couldn't believe. My first day, it was true, I'd scrubbed away a layer of grime.

She opened the medicine chest and looked dismayed at its paltry contents, toiletries and a few pill bottles: chloraquine, salt tablets, aspirin, prenatal vitamins—prescribed by AfricEd for men and women alike. I encouraged her nosiness, thinking that it was good for her to see these things. There was nothing particularly private here.

"What's this?" she pointed at my first aid kit, and I opened it so she could see the scissors and rolls of gauze.

"What are you looking for?"

"But Miss," she turned the faucet in the sink, watched the water flow. Gently, I turned the water off.

She faced me, long lashes shifting with her gaze. "Don't you have any of those pills for birth control?"

It was time to draw the line. "That's none of your business," I said, attempting to be stern.

Her face fell, she glanced down at the water draining in the bone white sink. *"Pardon,* Miss," she murmured.

"Ça va," I said quickly, wanting her back. "You're curious, of course. You should all know more about birth control. This is something I can maybe teach you at school. In English," I added, teasing.

"In English! Then nobody will understand!" She was beaming again, flexing her knees in mock despair, her faux pas forgotten. At the front door, handing back the glass, she was full of promises of drums and palm wine and how I would dance. She made the wedding sound barefoot and wanton and surreal. Sashaying across my porch, she called good-bye, and then glided across the blackened lawn, uniform skirt swinging.

The thing is, I wouldn't have minded indulging her in girlish secrets, or listening to her own.

The ash settled and the air thickened, urgent with moisture, but the clouds stretched high and tight as a lid. I wanted rain. Everyone else reveled in the lazy time before planting could begin, passing the hottest hours in the shade, taking shallow breaths. My skin was damp at 7:00 A.M. when I arrived at school, blinking in the early glare.

Every morning, the teachers gathered in the lounge, reaching across the table again and again to shake hands with each arrival as we waited for the bell. *"Bonjour, comment ça va?"*

"Not bad."

"No better than you."

Once I answered, "I'll be better when it rains."

"Kiadi. It won't rain today."

"Are you sure?"

There was a rumble of concurrence. That day we were about ten, a healthy show. You never knew who would opt out, on strike, tired of teaching for free. My colleagues had received no money from the government since I'd arrived, and some had gone unpaid all year. Yet their delinquency, timid and sporadic, was more playful than irate, a sort of teacher's prerogative for an impromptu day off. Never had the whole school struck at once, and the *Préfet,* while preaching professionalism at staff meetings, ignored the isolated absences, angling to avoid, I think, the kind of trouble that would attract the *militaires.*

Reporting for duty today, we were sitting and standing, patting our pockets for chalk or cigarettes—I had begun bringing mine to school.

"So when will it rain?" I puffed as someone held a match.

"October fifteenth." Bwadi leaned against a faded map, arms crossed, hands tucked in his armpits, thumbs pointing up.

"Exactly the fifteenth?"

"Yes, the fifteenth." His face was sharp with assurance. He looked a little hectic, overblown in the mouth and shoulders, hair on end.

"How can you know the exact day?"

"But, we know."

"Yes, it's true, the fifteenth. It's always the fifteenth."

"How can it be the same every year?"

"But, it is." Everyone was grinning.

I looked at Bwadi. Already a scant history of mistrust had sprouted between us. Attentive, critical, he was always in the background, playing out this tether, apt to pull me up short, to keep me within bounds. "Zero, that's severe," he'd said last week about the cavernous red zeros I'd been stabbing onto student papers during break.

"Well, they've all cheated," I had said. "Look at this." I'd shoved two papers over to where he stood beside the table. Hands behind his back, he bent over them, and read.

"It's supposed to be an original composition on what they would do with one thousand francs, and everyone wants to 'buy one airplane in America.'" I translated the error into French.

He made the Bantu sucking sound of regret. "The United States would eat them up."

"That's not the point. They've all made identical grammatical mistakes, not just there, but all over. They've copied each other's papers. I can't give credit for cheating."

He had glanced up tensely, his curiosity replaced by harsh emotion. "You see, you want them to eat each other up. You Americans have ideas about competition, that everybody must succeed alone, but this is Africa. Here, what you call cheating, we call cooperation. Everybody helps each other here."

I had shut up, stung. Of course, he had a point. Wasn't this communalism part of what I'd glimpsed as a child, part of the reason I'd returned? Yet I stuck to my guns, distributing the zeros. The class had rebelled, staging a spontaneous protest by dropping their heads onto their desks. Even the kids who had received good marks spent the hour with their heads down, refusing to learn. I was impressed. You would never find such solidarity in the United States. Bwadi was right.

Today, however, I sensed frivolity, license. "I'll bet you a beer," I challenged him. I'd heard the teachers making bets on soccer matches or on when they would get paid. "If it doesn't rain the fifteenth, you buy me a beer."

"Ehi, Miss!" They all squealed like sirens, cracking up.

"But Miss, you don't drink beer!"

I flicked an ash out the window. "I don't smoke, either."

"But you can't drink beer at Mampungu!" Shamavu, the math teacher, swerved in a circle, wrists fluttering, ashiver with glee.

"What do you mean?" I was smiling, enjoying the scandal.

"Where are you going to buy beer? It's the Protestants, remember, there's no beer here."

"The *Préfet* has beer," I pointed out. "There was plenty the night I arrived."

"But he's the *Préfet!*"

"Unless, palm wine," a new voice chimed.

"She said beer!"

"Which beer?" Bwadi wanted to know, face loose with amusement. For all his worried nosiness, he, too, could fall apart, appealingly inane. It would be fun to get him drunk.

I dragged on my cigarette, exhaled. "Empereur."

"But there's nobody selling Empereur!"

"He'll have to steal it from the *Préfet*, then."

"Or you will."

Bwadi and I dusted fingers, shaking on it. The bell clanged and he was gone, the others jostling behind. I stubbed out my cigarette, and stashed the half left over in my pencil box. I was happy to have caused a fuss, to have prodded the layer of respect that shut me off, white and female, foreign. I thought that this time I had made the rules.

Increasingly, I sagged. If Mampungu was gearing up for rain, it apparently had to turn first into hell. I was suffocating in the heat, singed, spent. Perspiration blotted whatever I touched, my dresses bunched and clung; even when I sat motionless the drops trickled down my neck and back. The humidity was lurid. After school and a few lesson plans, I usually collapsed in a nap, then rose creased and groggy to tutor students, or, if none came, to plod over to Mpovi's to join the simmering business of gossip and food.

The mission had been landscaped half a century before so that now great trees mushroomed over every roof, but people would abandon their own trees to meet in Mpovi's shade. Often two or three neighbors sat visiting, sometimes more, the men dropping to rest a moment before being ushered inside to see the *Préfet*. The women came armed with chopping boards or threaded needles, loyal to their chores. Their children banded off apart, swooping, then receding. Chance yearned across his mat and Mpovi rocked and laughed, blurting commands to the idle army of youngsters. *"Petit!"* she would shout, using the special form of address for any kid who is not yours but who must obey you anyway because you are grown up. *"Petit!* Go and fetch some wood," she'd sing out, or *"Petit!* Call Mama Zola."

I could understand those words. I would arrive at Mpovi's armed with a notebook and pencil, jot down a few Kikongo phrases, and then abandon the task to sit empty-handed, counting on osmosis. I hated interrupting the flow and gabble, backing it up for a translation. Mostly I let the conversation wash past, shook hands as people came and left, and waited for Mpovi to lapse into French. Everything was slow motion, viscous, hot. They chopped and peeled, chopped and peeled, their babies patting the earth.

Often enough Mpovi turned to concentrate on me, ignoring the others just as they ignored me when they got to talking. She was pleased that I was there, she wanted to keep me coming back. At times I felt like a roadside attraction, obligated to appear. They watched me like a cherished wild thing, smiling encouragement when they met my eyes, willing me not to run away. I had the sense, too, that they were hoping for some show, some plan, that they wanted something to do. I had no plan. I sat there sweating, and so they entertained themselves.

Once I brought along with my notebook a musty *National Geographic* to leaf through when I got bored, but everyone wanted to see, and the four or five women crowded my chair, their children peeking around their hips. They laughed at the naked Aborigines and were startled by the Eskimos in fur.

We were always looking at pictures, Mpovi and I. She never did invite me inside her parlor; that was her husband's territory, where I imagined she must shrink into her pinched, hushed role as wife. But when I asked about her photos, she supplied me with an album, which I spread open on my knees. The pages were crammed with black-and-white snapshots, mostly unprofessional Polaroids of people outside doorways. Most were full-length portraits, showcasing outfits down to high heels and pointed oxfords. I admired a shot of Mpovi flash-lit, glamorous in a fancy *pagne* and gold earrings, simpering above a table murky with bottles and half full glasses. "That's at Club Viva," she proudly announced.

There were village pictures, thatch in the background, pictures of children and of cars. A monstrous black Cadillac, circa 1955, sat rusting before a small urban home, wheels embedded axle deep in the ground amidst scattered flecks of trash. A man in mirrored sunglasses grinned from the driver's seat. "Ehi, no," Mpovi giggled when I asked where he was going. "It's always broken-down. But it's beautiful."

"They're all gray," I said, closing the book.

"Ehi?"

"Gray. The people are all gray. Nobody is white."

She got the joke, blinked happily. "That's why I want color. Your pictures will be best, in color, and I'll put a picture of you, so not everybody is gray." She twisted her mouth into a noisy kiss of disgust. "Gray is no good. As soon as it rains, you come with your camera."

I looked forward to the fifteenth as if toward a holiday. The date was official, worthy of a calendar, and I couldn't help wondering if black magic and fetishers were not involved.

"Why the fifteenth?" I asked Mpovi a few days in advance. "Why not today, or the sixteenth?"

"No, the fifteenth."

The others nodded, distracted from their tasks.

"But what if it *doesn't* rain the fifteenth?"

"Then we have a drought."

"So it doesn't, sometimes?"

She was applying bloodred polish to her toenails, leaning down from her stool so her wrists lapped her ankles. Her bones were subtle, not knobby and prominent like mine, her joints simple dark mounds along the slope of her skin. She was smooth and solid, not at all fat. She had a dramatic way of standing to tighten her *pagne,* feet apart, snapping and tucking the corner across her flat belly. Her cloths were always slipping loose, and she was always rearranging, binding her baby to her back or peeling off a strip to lay below him on the dirt. Refastening the folds, she seemed to glory in her earthiness. It was hard now to think of her strutting at that dinner party, or at Club Viva, prim and snug in bold batik.

As she focused on her foot, I studied the top of her head, the gleaming crisscross of her scalp, the patchwork of tufted braids. She looked up and I followed her gaze to the lattice above of mango leaves and the metallic slivers of sky.

"This year it will rain," she said.

"But how do you know?"

"The old people say. My mother says. Myself, I can't say, but the elders know." Twisting shut the lid of her polish, she surveyed her toes, the garish dabs vivid against brown callouses. Then she glanced at my neutral feet. "You don't paint your nails?"

"No."

Her friend, Mama Zola, accepted the bottle placidly. Orbited by varying combinations of her seven kids, she was older than Mpovi, yet she seemed to be her closest friend. Women as young and newly wed as Mpovi came to visit, but Mama Zola's chair was always closest. As the Pastor's wife she was perhaps a peg above Mpovi in the local hierarchy; beyond that, she was loyal and reliable, accepting Mpovi's moods and schemes with a maternal sort of patience. Clearly she'd never been pretty like Mpovi. The way her features slid toward her jutting jaw reminded me of a duck's bill, and she waddled, too, when she walked, her long breasts sagging below her shirt toward her bulging stomach. I never knew her well, but I could see that she was gentle and kind.

Suddenly Mpovi was pointing, half rising, lacquered fingernails launched in a mobile display. "Miss!"

Diabelle was making her way toward my front door. It was after the window of time I'd set for student visits, but these kids had no way of telling time; all the watches I ever saw on them were broken, worn as decoration, evocative as charms. She had changed from her uniform into a mud-colored *pagne* and her hair was tressed into the generic antennae, but I recognized her willowy approach.

"Diabelle," I called, standing myself, my arm swung up high in a salute, dropping to bob at my side. I was getting much better at these elastic gestures.

She detoured cheerfully and strained across the yard, saddled with some tome she carried pressed against her chest. This was curious; the only study materials available to students were the dittoed texts typed up by teachers or the class notes copied into slim *cahiers*. She looked as if she'd won a prize.

Mpovi settled back onto her stool, skeptically kissing the air. She had a florid aversion to students.

"Miss," Diabelle said happily, headed for me. She hesitated, though, once inside the clearing, as if testing the water. Remembering her manners, she turned to Mpovi. *"Madame le Préfet,"* she said, dipping forward to shake hands. I saw her eyeing Mpovi's nails.

Next in line, Mama Zola offered her wrist, her nails still wet, and Diabelle lingered again on the splendorous red. The other two women were blandly polite, mumbling in Kikongo as they shook. At me, Diabelle's natural smile returned.

"I came to show you, Miss. We found this in the refectory attic."

"What were you doing there?" Mpovi interposed.

"For *salongo*, Madame. There's no planting yet, so Pistache told us to clean it out up there."

"Salongo" was the Tambalan institution of fieldwork after school, roughly equivalent to our phys ed. Theoretically, this kept the students busy and fit, as well as the kitchen stocked. Pistache was in charge. Dark as charcoal, burly and curt, he was the *Préfet de Discipline,* the resident thug. To us teachers, of course, he was diffident, promising punishment to any misbehaving classroom. He always disciplined en masse, not because he was tyrannical, but because it was difficult to pinpoint the true culprits of any offense; nobody ratted, nobody confessed. He'd put the kids to work at dopey tasks like carrying stones across the courtyard or digging pointless holes.

So far I'd avoided his services; I was not eager to resort to outside authority. It would be like saying to my students, "I'm telling," as I had threatened my brother when badgered as a child. They would invoke the name themselves, sometimes, when they saw me getting mad, whispering derisively, "Pistache, Pistache." Everybody called him Pistache; this was his given name, and no one I talked to thought it odd. Pistachio. I kept running into these zany names: *Jetaime,* the man who washed my clothes; *Sonata,* the fat lady who sold fried bread. It was as if the meanings of these words were irrelevant; some fanciful parents had simply liked the sound of the syllables enough to attach them to children. In any case, although *salongo* was a routine activity rather than a form of discipline, Pistache was in charge, and his name lended validity to Diabelle's visit now. Mpovi held her tongue.

Stepping around Chance, whose head wobbled attentively, Diabelle lay the book on my lap.

It was a Sears catalog. I hadn't seen one since living with my father, but all the flavor of picking and guessing and anticipating boxes from the States came right back.

Delighted, I let the pages cascade open, scanning. "What year?" I wondered aloud, and turned back to the front. Diabelle crouched at my side, and Mpovi posted herself upright at my other flank, conscious of keeping a space clear around her toenails as a little crowd formed. I showed what to look for on the cover. "Nineteen seventy-three. This is what they sold that year."

"It's different now?"

"Actually, not much. Nobody wears skirts that short anymore, or pants that wide." I pointed to the miniskirts and bellbottoms. "Each season there's a new copy, with clothes to fit the weather, and current prices. You write to this company for these things. If you like this blouse, for instance, you send your size and the price, and then the package comes in the mail."

Everyone looked at me, considering.

"Dollars?"

"Yes, see, it says here sixteen dollars."

Diabelle fingered one of her braids. "But don't they steal the money in the mail?"

"You send a check."

Mpovi explained the concept to the audience at large.

"But then don't they steal the box at the post office?"

I laughed. "You're right, it wouldn't work here. But in the States nobody steals at the post office."

Mpovi nodded sagely. "They're well paid there."

"Or well patrolled," I shrugged. "When I lived with my family in West Africa, our mail came straight from the airport to my father's office, so we didn't lose mail there, either."

"And you can't do that here?"

"I can. My mail goes to my office in Kimpiri. Next month I'll get it during the holiday."

"You're going to Kimpiri for the holiday?" Mpovi sounded surprised.

"If the rains don't wash away the roads." That could happen, I'd been told.

I turned the pages carefully while everyone looked on. Kids planted themselves in front, staring at the pictures upside down.

In the catalog white women perched and pointed, stiff and smiling, dressed for work, dressed for play like those Barbie dolls with bendable limbs that lock into athletic poses. I tensed with nostalgia. I saw my mother in Conakry, in front of the mariner's map on our *paillotte* wall, I saw her leaning close to read her tape measure at my waist; I heard her soothing voice as she pointed in the catalog, "Do you like this dress? How about this?" I felt again the swooning promise of new things, and her soft insistence that I be pleased.

Later on, I got to order by myself, and my girlfriends and I would flip forward to study the lingerie. How sad for a girl that age to be without a mother, I thought, sitting beside Mpovi and picturing my past as if it belonged to someone else. Yet at the time, planning my wardrobe with my friends, I hadn't known that I was sad.

Diabelle broke the silence. "That," she tapped the page. "I like that."

"Pants?"

"Ehi, pants."

"But pants are not for us!" protested Mpovi.

"Non, pas pour nous les Tambalaines," agreed Mama Zola. We the Tambalans, is what she'd said.

"You don't like them?" I asked. Tambalan women wore them in the city, I was sure.

"I like them," Diabelle declared.

"Some of us like them," Mama Zola explained patiently. "But they're not allowed. The president says that we must wear traditional dress."

"And the men don't wear ties."

"But my husband, he doesn't like pants on women," Mpovi insisted. "He says you can see the shape of everything."

A couple of the little girls choked, giggling, and I wondered how they would react to the lingerie.

"It's too hot to wear pants, anyway," I said. "I feel sorry for the men. I haven't worn mine since I arrived."

"You have pants?" Diabelle was impressed.

"But I won't wear them unless it cools down."

"Ehi!" Something in the catalog had caught Mpovi's eye. *"These women are pretty!"* She spoke with relief, as if the models so far hadn't made sense. We had hit the large sizes. Everyone admired the full-figure fashions, pointing to a rare black model whose inclusion in that section struck me as racist. Yet none of these models were obese, they merely had roundish features, and large bones and large breasts—really, they looked normal.

"You think it's better to be fatter?" I quizzed.

"Otherwise you are sick."

"Like you."

Not sure whether they meant that I was sick or fat, I stared at my dense thighs until a woman I barely knew patted my stomach and said, "You're good and strong."

I couldn't argue with their logic; the only times I'd felt triumphantly light were after illnesses, or after exhausting myself climbing mountains.

"Not too fat," Mpovi specified. "But not skinny, either. Not like Diabelle." She pointed with her lips, then said something in Kikongo, something cruel. There was a chorus of cheering laughter, the kids hopped and dipped in place; I winced. Only Mama Zola remained subdued, her soupy face closed.

Still sitting on her heels, Diabelle gazed stiffly at the ground, the nape of her neck murky, vulnerable. At that moment I saw her as precarious, solo.

"In the United States," I announced, "she would be gorgeous! *Magnifique!*"

Diabelle glanced up, wide-eyed.

"Skinny like that?" Mpovi would have none of it. "Like the women in that book?"

Exactly, I thought, but I did not describe my vision of Diabelle embellished with beads and ivory in the pages of *Vogue.* That sort of hollow, exoticized beauty would not impress Mpovi.

She barrelled on, full of steam. I'd seen her bossy with *petits,* but never before venomous, like this.

"Women like that have no use. They fall down in the fields, they can't give birth." She nodded at Diabelle, whose crouch now resembled that of something cornered. "She wants to be a modern girl in pants. She'll never have children."

The sudden silence seemed deafening. It seemed nobody wanted to breathe. Diabelle's brow was creased, her nostrils pink. Something taboo had occurred, magic words uttered, a spell set loose. Chance began to cry.

"Of course she will." I stood; I had had enough. This dramatic malice hinged on me, I was sure, although I was not sure why. Nor did I understand why the attack on Diabelle's fertility caused such dismay. I, myself, was happily childless. I closed the catalog, passed it back to Diabelle. I shook hands briefly all around, failing to make eye contact with Mpovi, who was suddenly preoccuppied with calming down her wailing son.

Diabelle's hand was limp. At a loss, I gave it an apologetic squeeze and left her there to make her own exit. But at my porch I turned to find her slowly halting several strides behind. Caught in the middle of my blackened lawn, she looked guilty and hopeful, needy as a puppy sure to be sent back.

3

PROTÉGÉE

Not long after arriving in Mampungu, I went one evening to join the women's choir. I'd heard them practice every week, their molten voices mournful as oboes, the pebbled swish of calabashes keeping time. My house would swell with the melodies, tidal and lavish as they spilled across my windowsill, and I would stop what I was doing, look up from my book, turn VOA off the radio, hesitate to sip my tea. Floating across the mission, the voices somehow gained amplitude. There was no white noise. No traffic, no electric hum. Only the gigantic saw of insects like violins, the hollow clang of a cook pot, a child's looping wail.

The students had a chorale as well; they sang in the afternoons, boys and girls together percolating rhythms charged with testosterone and innocence. Theirs was a different sound than the women's eerie lament, but both were hypnotic, equally expressive of something buried at the core of what I was. The kids' concert was punctuated by daytime sounds, interrogative roosters and disgusted goats and passersby chiming in from the street. Everyone knew all the songs. Except for me, that is, so when Mama Zola invited me to join the women's choir, I could not resist although I cannot carry a tune.

Mama Zola came to escort me to my first practice, which met in an anteroom of the refectory, a corner of the mission I did not yet know. It was after dark and we all carried storm lamps, most of which were perched, flames turned down, on an empty table as we sang. I kept mine lit on a bench, though, to help me read the lyrics—which I could not understand, as they were in Kikongo, but which I dutifully sounded out as I tried to learn the tunes. There were about a dozen women in the group, some of whom I recognized from Mpovi's, several with infants strapped to their backs. They were all polite and titterish, evidently due to me. Mpovi was not there; I understood she did not sing, and then realized I should have stayed home as well. But it was lovely listening, feeling the floor vibrate as I tentatively mouthed the strange syllables, keeping my own wayward voice breathy and discreet. By the time we were turning up our flames, standing to leave, I'd decided I must not hamper the abandon of these artistes, that I would not return. I was happy enough to have been asked; I felt that doors were opening up.

Shaking hands methodically, we each said good night, and then Mama Zola pointed me in the correct direction home. I charged off cheerfully, veered across a lawn, hot on the track of some short-cut; I was always walking too fast, they could not keep up with me. But a chorus of laughter snaked out, the plush slap of palms against skin. "Miss," I heard from the road. "Miss! It's not that way!"

I stopped, surprised. Houses telescoped around me, alien, identical. The cluster of storm lamps winked like fireflies as soft shapes swerved and bisected, hooting, choked. Lost, wrong, I had no idea where I was. I turned in a circle, storm lamp outstretched, its stingy light disclosing only the dead grass underfoot. They laughed and laughed. A long moment later, someone called, "Over there! Your house is over there!" I made out an arm pointing, and saw then what they meant, changed tack, lit out.

"I see," I yelled over my shoulder, falsely jovial. "Thank you!" My camaraderie was draining fast, but I wanted to give them the benefit of the doubt, did not want to take offense. I pretended not to mind.

What had tickled those women so enormously, I think, was not just that I was lost, but that I was so cocksure. It is a good image of me at that time, during my early months at Mampungu. Striding with inspired delusion in the wrong direction, then suddenly adrift in someone's yard, a mere few hundred meters off the mark. A sole bright angel with clipped wings stuck in a slow, listing circle. It was absurd that I could be so abruptly lost in such a tiny place; the Tambalans all knew the mission the way I have known only interiors, and the sight of me teetering on a lawn must have seemed as silly to them as I would find someone groping in a bungalow. I am sure now that this does not happen with Tambalans, at least, not with Tambalans in Tambala. They always, always, know where they are.

The day after Diabelle and her Sears catalog had caused such a fuss, I went to see Mpovi. It had not yet rained. Mampungu was a steaming blur, its edges meshing, a world compressed by the gray weight of static clouds. I hurried straight over after school, eager to beat the rest of the clique, and we were alone with Chance. The *Préfet* was due home any minute wanting his lunch, but Mpovi greeted me as always, pointing out my chair with her noisy lips, depositing Chance on my lap. She was all nodding smiles, unencumbered by yesterday's skirmish. It seemed not to occur to her that I might be upset. She may have been thick, or she may have been communicating in some African way I didn't under-stand. In any case, before I could broach the subject of Diabelle, Mpovi intervened.

"I had a dream last night," she teased, impishly poised on her stool.

Busy bouncing Chance on my slippery knees, I raised my eye-brows.

"I dreamed that you were brown, like us. Your skin was brown, and your hair tressed tight against your head."

"Was my hair black?"

"Ehi, black, just like ours, and your skin brown." She blinked generously.

"What was I wearing?"

"You were wearing a *pagne,* like ours, an old one for working."

It was, indeed, an image to nurture. "What was I doing?"

"You were just there."

I was flattered, yes. "Was it a good dream?"

"Ehi, it was good, we were happy."

Chance was beaming toothlessly. Worn out, I held him still. "I'm glad," I said to Mpovi. It felt something like a gift, this perception of me as black. We were quiet for a moment, but then the silence felt forced.

"Mpovi," I risked. "You know, yesterday, when Diabelle was here. I don't understand."

Her happiness collapsed. She shrugged, irked. "Girls like that always bring trouble. It's not good for you, she wants to be your friend."

"She's nice. Don't you think?"

"She's a student. She should be afraid of you."

"Is that really true? We aren't like that in the States. Teachers and students can be friends there."

"It's not good." She shook her head, her erect braids tracing slow arcs. "The students will make trouble if they're not afraid of you."

"I don't know." Maybe nobody had ever tried treating the students with respect. I didn't want to intimidate and, besides, I wasn't sure I could. Mpovi certainly had the knack. I flashed on Diabelle, sweet, keen Diabelle, cowering like a dog. "What made you say she wouldn't have children?" I asked. "Everybody was surprised."

"She's a skeleton!" Impatiently, Mpovi lunged for Chance, swept him from my lap. My knees felt cool, buoyant. "This is why you don't have enough children in America, if all the wives look like the women in that book."

In spite of myself, I smiled. Yet I was still confused. "Even if it's true, why did you tell her like that? It sounded so mean." I said this gently, helplessly, not trying to accuse.

"It's already been predicted. It's not a secret."

"Predicted by whom?"

"Her father told her that if she gets pregnant before she is married, she will lose that child and all the next."

"Why?"

"Already her sister is quitting school to get married."

I was getting nowhere. "What does her sister have to do with Diabelle?"

"Because Diabelle's father is afraid now that she will become pregnant and leave school, and he will lose her price, too."

It was the business of the bride-price, I realized, whereby the groom compensates the girl's family for her hand. I nodded, and Mpovi went on, "An educated girl is worth a lot; with a diploma Diabelle will be a very valuable wife. But if she leaves school to have a baby, she'll be worth nothing. So he has made this curse to keep her good. Already she's too wild, though, too modern in her ways. She'll be without children."

"Would that be so bad? I have no children."

Mpovi gave me a sorrowful look, then smiled, chin tilted up. "But you will, of course. Diabelle is different."

"How do you know this about the father's curse?"

Cradling Chance, she straightened on her stool, privileged, smug. "He shouted it out loud and the whole village heard. Mama Zola got it from her family there, and she told me."

"Poor Diabelle." I felt sympathetic not because she would never have children, which I did not believe, but because her father seemed so rigid and Africa so hard. "Does everyone at school know this?"

"Maybe."

"And does he really have the power to make her barren, if she gets pregnant?" I wanted to hear what Mpovi thought.

"Everyone must listen to his father. An angry father can take away your luck, can even make you die."

In the States angry fathers disinherited, took away money. I supposed it amounted to the same thing. Either way what was really missing was the love. I thought of Diabelle in my bathroom, snooping for pills, and felt a flurry of urgency, of stalled hope.

"Then what about the wedding? Do you think I shouldn't go?"

"No, you can go! That's good, it's good for you to visit villages, but you shouldn't be so friendly to Diabelle. To her parents and the other adults there, it's fine, but not to your students. They don't expect you to be."

I was silent, rebellious. Mpovi, however, giggled optimistically. "What will you wear?"

"Wear?" It was too hot to think of clothes; I was sweating rivulets. "One of my dresses for school, they're all I have. Which do you like?"

"Wait!" Mpovi caught my wrist, her own hand dry. "You can have a *pagne!* One like mine that you saw at my house. Fancy with the braided straps. Next week we'll find fabric at the *grand marché,* and then Madame Bulewa will sew it on her machine." Prancing with initiative, she unloaded Chance onto his straw mat. But no, it was the *Préfet* arriving home that made her prance; she was needed inside. We could hear him scuffing evenly up the front steps, the thwack of the closing screen door. Tightening her *pagne,* she promised me beauty, she promised me bliss. As if she alone knew how to succeed. Posing at her kitchen door, Chance on her hip, she was African and correct, as I could only be in dreams. But I would let her dress me up anyway, I knew, just as I had tried to sing.

The afternoon of the fifteenth, the sky purpled and softened and a dense, feisty breeze whipped the palms into tatters. Old fronds fell, doors slammed, and I was cavorting with the children, mouth open to the sky, arms spread, summoning thunder and floods. Angry mothers called in their kids, and soon I was alone on the concrete block behind my kitchen where Jetaime did my wash, alone as the rain came down hard, deliciously alone.

My Africa was coming to life. Things would grow in green, there would be corn, tomatoes, peanuts, plenty of food for months. Trees would swell with papayas, avocados. The mangos fell in February, I'd been told, bursting orange on the ground. Mampungu promised to be lush and idyllic, busy with brown, muscular people in motion against a cobalt sky, their *pagnes* vibrant as bouquets.

What I'd seen so far had been false, the charred horizon a mistake, the bloated air a temporary blight. I'd arrived at a barren, sulky time, when the real Mampungu wore a shroud. Perhaps my points of reference were all wrong; perhaps I'd chosen the wrong landmarks, learned the wrong words, misinterpreted signs.

If so, I was going to get my bearings now. Something about this watery tumult filled me with hope and relief, with a shiny conviction that the real Mampungu would twinkle forth, that what had seemed fuzzy and flabby before would take on clean, sharp edges, like an emerging photograph jostled in its bath. Suddenly I saw myself upright and heroic, wielding the drawing of a uterus, Diabelle rapt. I saw myself emulsified, inspired.

Pummeled, soggy, shivering, running my fingers along the goosebumps on my arm, I wanted to be cold, really cold, I wanted my teeth to chatter. The rain fell and fell but I was merely wet. After a while I went inside to fill my lamps before night came, and the metal roof sounded like an endless drumroll. I felt fluid, flushed as if in love. I released my hair from its customary bun to comb it down my back, I wrapped my towel at my chest to hang like a *pagne* to my calves, I poured Pastis from the bottle I'd been hoarding—for a rainy day, I heard myself thinking—and smoked and thought of men I'd known.

My wood panelled kitchen seemed placid and roomy, and I liked the prospect of someone sharing my bush home. Someone smart and tenuous who would tread carefully. Davis had been too careful, aloof, borderline; he would never set foot here. I felt proud at how little I'd thought of him lately. During the hot, charred weeks so far I'd been too gritty with sweat and lethargy to think of romance, too scrutinized, too preoccupied to feel the full brunt of being alone.

Finally comfortable, though, I felt surprisingly peaceful and dreamy, ready to preen my way back to my old self. I was waiting—but for whom? Not spotless Paul, serene in his starched whites. Solicitous Mitch from the embassy bar? He was not bad looking, I recalled, in a furry sort of way, studiously blinking through his mane of facial hair. Yet I could not separate him from his buddy, that sneering engineer who scoffed at blacks. No, these bridge builders had no business in my life. As far as I could tell, they'd left the local folk alone; my neighbors could report only vague sightings of the red Ford trucks, so I assumed that we were out of range.

The men at Mampungu, for their part, hadn't made any moves. They saw me as a fellow teacher, not as a *femme*. They didn't know how to reconcile respect with lust. And then there was Bwadi's contempt.

Perhaps my abstinence was having a missionary sort of effect; the next day, when the sun broke out, I felt galvanized to do good.

Armed with only my knowledge of biology, I invited Diabelle for an afternoon chat.

"Now, Diabelle," I began in my *salon*, "it's because I'm concerned about your welfare that I've decided to talk to you about birth control. You're too special to throw away your education for some unwanted pregnancy. But I'm not a doctor, so there's nothing I can give you except some information. And what you decide to do with that is entirely up to you."

She sat forward in her seat, hands clasped reverentially atop her knees, eyes soft. She might have been at prayer. I played the priest, balancing caution and benevolence, sticking to the facts. I did not want to discuss Mpovi's rumor about Diabelle's angry father; I meant to steer clear of family rifts. Impersonal, discreet, I meant to be a teacher first and last.

I marked out a calendar, drew the diagrams of female organs, the egg and sperm, the fetus curved inside the womb.

"It's like a snail!" giggled Diabelle.

"I'm not an artist, of course. But we're ahead of ourselves—the point is, not to get pregnant in the first place. You need to have a plan even before intercourse."

"But there is abortion."

"Women have abortions here?"

"We can see an herbalist for medicine."

"What sort of medicine?"

"We boil it, like tea, to drink."

"It's safe?"

She shrugged.

It sounded like a bad idea. "Well, all that can be avoided if you're careful beforehand. Look here." I counted out the days of a hypothetical cycle. "This is when you ovulate, when the sperm can find your egg. If you make sure not to have intercourse during this week, the chances of pregnancy are low."

"The same day every month?"

What a fool I was, encouraging calculations that were iffy at best. "You have to learn your own cycle," I sighed, "find the average length, say twenty-nine days, and then figure from that. If your periods are irregular, it's not a good method."

"Miss, I don't like math. Citizen Shamavu says I hurry too

much, and make mistakes." She looked suspiciously from picture to picture. "Isn't there any other way?"

"The best way is abstinence."

She gave me an angelic smile, endearingly false. I moved on to withdrawal. "However, with this method," I concluded, "you have to trust the boy."

"Anyway, it's better for me to get fat."

"What?"

"You know," she covered her mouth, her embarrassment, "to fill up with the man's juice."

"Where did you get that idea?"

"We always know when a girl begins to have sex because she grows, you know, more like a woman. Rounder."

I mopped at my brow, my neck, incredulous. "That's coincidence." I deduced that she was still a virgin, susceptible to such girlish myths. "It's the hormones that change a girl's shape, at puberty, with or without sex."

"Medicine says that?" She waited, patient, calm. Evidently, my word was gospel. I told her the truth.

I told her about the prescriptions you could get from doctors for pills and IUDs and diaphragms, the experiments in India with an injection, the condoms tucked in the billfolds of American boys. Her expression oscillated between wonder at these miracles and dismay.

"But Miss, isn't there anything you can find for me?"

I thought of our AfricEd doctor in Kimpiri, his prudish lecture on VD, his crate of condoms by the water cooler, jolly as lollipops. "Yes," I caved.

"Condoms are for men," she said when I explained.

"You'll have to ask them to cooperate. I'm sorry, it's the best I can do. After the holiday, I'll bring back a supply."

"Ehi."

She was reaching for my notes and sketches, tidying a pile in her lap, intending to take something, at least, home with her. Gently, I lifted them away.

"Diabelle, I can't let you take these. I wouldn't want the wrong person guessing what we talked about today. If anyone asks, you've just had a lesson here. No one has to know it wasn't in English."

Solemnly, she nodded, hands knotted against her gut as if

against a cramp. She was as practiced as any, I knew, in keeping a secret, and her African solidarity now lay with me.

The humidity slowly accumulated force until even the shade was oppressive and the clouds ballooned and sank and rained again and then the cycle was on track. A few days passed and the ground softened to a crazy sort of paste that attached itself to shoes step by step, building layers inches thick so that you had to stop every few hundred meters to pry it off. Edging the concrete walkway at school was a column of globs where everybody scraped their soles.

Between the fitful showers, Mpovi was busy planting, trooping off with Mama Zola and their crew of children toting hoes on their shoulders and basins on their heads, stopping to wave in tandem as they passed. When I saw them from where I sat grading papers or reading below my own mango tree, my heart swelled and I never quite knew why. Was it guilt or pity or gratitude? I thought I recognized a thread of triumph and an inkling, too, of loss.

We missed a market day, the road too muddy for trucks, and two weeks passed before Mpovi could take me shopping for the fabric for my *pagne.* By this time, the hills looked as if covered with green lint, and when the sun shone the mission lawns were vivid as neon.

Market days were like holidays. Every other Thursday, barring too much rain, the trucks rumbled through Mampungu to park at the obsolete runway, where missionaries in archaic biplanes must have landed and taken off, once upon a time. The runway crested a knoll at Mampungu's outskirts; I liked to walk there at sunset for the gorgeous view across the rolling savannah. Now the flat expanse of red, weedless earth served merely as the occasional marketplace, where *camions* parked in a circle like pioneer wagons and *commerçants* spread their wares on tarps or mats, arranging pyramids of onions and red peppers, rows of *cahiers,* cylinders of pencils, of fabric, sacks of beans or rice—some still packaged in woven polyethylene stamped in English with, "Property of the United States of America Not for Resale." AID rice disappeared at the docks and then resurfaced in the hands of local *commerçants* who sold it as superior quality American grain at luxury prices. I bought it.

This week I needed cigarettes. Mpovi wanted fabric, the teachers wanted beer, and now nobody wanted rain. We did have a respite from the showers for a couple of days, long enough for the roads to harden, and Mpovi and I made plans. After school, we would go together to the market and then, afterward, I would photograph Chance. Nobody was going to farm that afternoon, and the teachers, afraid of missing merchandise, were going to let the kids out early. All morning my students craned their necks as the trucks rolled past.

When I had finally let my students go, and had washed the chalk dust from my hands, I met Mpovi outside her house. She was all dolled up in an organic swirl of brown, red, and orange, Chance blending nicely against her back in his yellow wool cap. My fingers itched for my camera, but I'd decided not to bring it to the marketplace, where it would cause a stir. I had not forgotten how, as a teenager, I'd brandished my first camera in that harbor town, where people had darted forward to collect and pose by the dozens, used to Polaroids that spit out images on the spot. Other people tried to grab my camera and to break it, afraid that I had trapped their souls. Cameras could kick up trouble in Kimpiri, too, where citizens were more sophisticated but the government edgy about bad PR, worried lest someone record the sorry, crumbling condition of the city—or worse, some clandestine cache of arms, perhaps, or a ragtag convoy of troops headed for Angola. In any case, stories abounded of cameras confiscated by soldiers at roadblocks, of photographers dragged into police stations for exorbitant fines.

Cameraless, I fell into step beside Mpovi as we joined the parade along the village drive. Women balanced baskets on their heads, men carried straw pouches. As we walked, we kept stopping to shake hands and exchange greetings with Mpovi's acquaintances; she knew everyone. People had walked from nearby villages to shop and sell their own quaint wares, sandals made from old car tires, short-handled brooms with long skirts of thistles, batons of *chiquangue*—the manioc paste wrapped to ferment inside banana leaves, a bush version of fast food. I listened for familiar words as Mpovi rattled on, and I guessed that she was explaining to each new face our project to make me a *pagne*. "Like mine," she would model, touching her shoulders, smoothing the skirt as they stood admiring her.

She did not know, of course, how I'd connived with Diabelle. I felt duplicitous, yet stuck. I felt like a rat. Mpovi took my loyalty for granted as I heeled tamely to her small, slow steps. She looked so natural, so in sync, her fluid caution full of grace. Women here learned to see with their feet; balancing headloads, carrying babies on their backs, they navigated the potholes and rocks by touch.

Today the runway was relatively dry; no mud, at least, gummed up our shoes, but we had to straddle deep ruts where the road had caved under wheels and it was clear that all of the ten or so vehicles risked bogging down. Managing to slip off while Mpovi socialized, I made my own rounds quickly, stocking up on cigarettes, soap, rice. I checked for Empereur, as well, remembering my debt to Bwadi, but the teachers had been correct; there was no beer. I did see a grizzly old *tata* fumbling with a great *bidon* of palm wine, splashing up a storm as he funnelled it into bottles for sale. He seemed to revel in his arthritic ineptitude; arms and legs glistening, sandals sloshing, he continued to grin, bacchanal, darling. Impulsively, I decided to buy this for Bwadi instead, and accepted a sample glass as the old man corked my bottle with leaves. It wasn't bad; milky, fizzy, tart. Gingerly, I was packing the bottle into my sack when Mpovi loomed up.

"But Miss," she protested, "you don't drink palm wine!"

"It's not for me."

"Who's it for?"

"Bwadi. I bet him a beer that it wouldn't rain October fifteenth. I lost."

"But I told you it would!" She gloated, as if she, herself, had won. Then she flinched. "Why did you bet beer?"

I shrugged.

"But Miss, *c'est risqué!*"

"Why?"

"He'll be coming to your house!" She giggled, though, too festive to lecture, tugging me away.

Under her guidance, I bought the fabric for my *pagne,* and then we headed back for our photo session of Chance. I stopped off for my camera; Mpovi went to tidy up. The palm wine and the heat had made me feel woozy and diffuse, but the cool, metallic camera was lovely to hold.

I found two chairs waiting at Mpovi's mango tree, as well as a crate placed like a table. From inside the house came the gregarious sound of men's voices, drunkenly chummy. Alone, Chance was sitting up on his mat, ogling the door from below his yellow cap.

I set my camera down on the crate. "Ehi, Chance."

He gave me a wobbly look and, automatically, I stooped and picked him up. I was getting the hang of babies, or babies in Africa, where friends are expected to lay claim. I still couldn't bring myself to coo, so we studied each other carefully, and I genuinely thought that he was sweet.

"Ah, *bon!*" Mpovi was at the door, a bottle of Empereur and two glasses in her hands. Lipstick the color of red peppers exaggerated her smile; she looked happy enough to cry, speechless at my initiative, at Chance in my arms. She lifted the bottle; I saw that it was only partly full. "We'll have a glass?"

Surprised, I nodded. She set the glasses down beside my camera and poured with the finesse of a bar girl, tilting each glass, twisting the bottle's last drop, then tucking the empty behind the crate. Serving beer must be another of the wifely skills she'd perfected for the *Préfet*.

She took Chance from me and set him up at her breast to nurse, and then we toasted, *chin chin.* The open bottle was still fresh enough, the beer prickly and cold. It went down easily.

"Mpovi," I kidded, "did you steal this from the men?"

Head tossed back, collarbones gleaming like gold, she laughed. "It's for us," she protested. "You are invited by the *Préfet*."

I wondered if she always referred to her husband as "the *Préfet*," or when speaking just to me. Certainly Chance would know him as "Papa." I wondered what she called him to his face. *Chéri? Citoyen?*

"And chilled, too. Whose *frigo?*"

"The dispensary's. He keeps bottles there."

So the *Préfet* had been hoarding beer all along. I raised my glass. "What's the occasion?"

"Market day. The rain." She smiled garishly.

"To the rain." We clinked, drank again. Mpovi wiped her mouth on the back of her hand, brightening her cheek with lipstick, and I vowed to snatch at least one shot of the candid smear.

"So it's all right for you to drink?" I asked. I did not remember her with a glass at my welcome party, when I'd been served Empereur.

"Why not? Here with you, or when my husband is there, it's fine, a glass now and then. But I wouldn't buy a bottle for myself. Of course," she blinked indulgently, "you are American."

That gave me moral leeway, I assumed. I lifted my camera.

"No, not yet!"

I put it down. All the good shots were going to be taboo: the beer foaming away at her elbow while the baby nursed, the slack look of bliss in her narrowed eyes, the splotched mouth.

Soon she righted her top and fiddled with Chance, getting ready to pose. "I wanted to make him peaceful, but not to fall asleep." She hummed like a motor into his face and he tensed happily.

"Good." She pointed with her bleary lips to my camera. I did not like her telling me how to shoot, but went ahead. Forthright as a model, she confronted the lens, then stared primly at her kid, her round face posed, soulless as a statue. Before long I'd had enough. I left my seat, snapping quickly, circling, crouching, and still I didn't like the effect. With her misshapen mouth, she should have been laughing.

"You have something on your cheek," I owned up. "Do you mind?" Leaning, I rubbed with my thumb, and she submitted, trusting as a debutante. Her skin was dense and moist; the lipstick disappeared. Her glass now wore more of it than her mouth.

"*Merci.*"

I wiped my hand on my skirt, and resumed shooting, this time for her. She would like this series, her unblemished absorption in her child. "How about Chance by himself?"

Enthusiastically, she perched him on all fours in the center of his mat. He didn't go anywhere, but sat back on his heels, leaning on his stubby forearms into the camera as I stooped to his level. Then I rose slowly, aiming down, and he followed with his eyes, lifting his head. His mouth was wet, his expression blank with concentration, and suddenly I loved him, I loved his surprised, blurry expression ballooning above his dwarfed immobility. I identified with him. This shot, I knew, could be worth the whole roll.

I had that rush of feeling something work, that numb invincibility, and grinned over at Mpovi leaning contentedly against the brick. I caught her off guard. Click. She smiled sheepishly.

"Stay there, just like that." But already she'd clasped her hands together and stiffened her mouth.

"Try over here," I waved at the tree, "with Chance."

I snapped her lifting him, swinging him to her hip, glancing over her shoulder in dismay.

"Miss, you're too fast!"

"Mpovi, you look best when you forget about the camera, you'll see."

She stood reluctantly before the mango trunk, composed herself, and flashed a fine smile. I took it, gratified by the effect of her looping braids against the roughly textured bark.

"Just be yourself," I said, realizing, then, how strange those words would sound. I tried another approach. "You're gorgeous, just like the wife of a cabinet minister."

She jounced Chance, her eyes sparkling. With her, compliments always seemed to work.

"Put the bottle beside Chance on his mat."

"No."

Before today, I'd never attempted to order her around; normally she instructed me and I submitted, an apprentice on her turf.

"I thought the sun on the bottle would be pretty," I insisted.

"I don't want a picture of a beer bottle."

Luckily something behind me caught her attention, and she began to simper, genuinely Mpovi. I got it.

A motor had interrupted the languid rhythm of the afternoon. Assuming it to be one of the market *camions,* I turned to see Mpovi's view. It was not a galumphing truck at all, but bush-headed Bwadi, his long frame hunched over a valiant little motorbike, a creamy blue scooter with mud-encrusted tires.

"He has a moped?" I marvelled. This set him apart from those of us at Mampungu—as far as I knew, everyone except the *Préfet* and the Doctor—without transportation. Of course, bicycles were common, but engines, requiring expensive petrol, were beyond the means of teachers who were irregularly paid. I wondered how he managed his supply.

He veered into the yard. Uh oh, I thought, was he coming to see me, and would his visit put Mpovi in a huff? I did not know what to expect since Diabelle's trespass.

"You found petrol at the market!" Mpovi waved as if she'd been expecting him, and I relaxed.

"*Un peu.*" Standing his bike beside the tree, Bwadi grinned. "I've been waiting a long time."

"Lucky you," I admired. "I didn't know you had a motorbike."

"I didn't know you had a camera." He looked equally impressed; we all shook hands. "It works?"

"I hope so. Where have you been hiding that?"

"I hardly ever use it at Mampungu; it's too easy to walk. Today, though, since I got petrol, I couldn't resist." He quit staring at my camera to address Mpovi. "I've come to see the *Préfet.*"

"Miss wants pictures of beer!" Mpovi blurted laughingly.

"Ah," he turned to me, "you've found some after all!"

"No, the *Préfet* got there first. The market was dry except for palm wine. However, I will offer you a bottle of palm wine," I formally declared, "until I can buy beer."

"Ehi, Miss!" Mpovi was deliciously appalled.

Bwadi looked around nervously, as if about to flee.

"Sit down," Mpovi offered. "She'll take your picture."

"No, stand by the house," I said.

Unsure of what to do, he looked trapped. First I threatened him with palm wine, then told him where to stand for a photograph. But I was on the rampage with my camera, pacing, pointing. At a loss, he complied, and Mpovi giggled. I wanted her picture like that, too, but gave it up.

"Smile," I told Bwadi.

He did, tightly. Hair ballooning against yellow brick, he looked tough.

"Now try the tree. Yes, with your moped, right there."

"They're color," Mpovi encouraged. She was tickled to see Bwadi like this, under my spell.

"It's an ambush here," he grumbled good-naturedly, and then he was staring directly at me through the lens in a way I hadn't seen him do before, as if the contraption in front of my face dissolved some barrier. I was conscious of something warm and nice beneath his gruff rebelliousness. I clicked twice.

"I'll go in, now," he said, up against the tree. I lowered the camera and he moved toward the kitchen door, his gait light and airy, as if his broad shoulders had been inflated and he might float upward into the sky. "Thank you," he remembered to call through the screen door as it slammed.

"He likes you."

I looked at Mpovi. "Him?"

"Yes, him. He likes you." She gave me a friendly shove.

"He's so serious."

"He laughs when you're not there."

I imagined him loosened up at the *Préfet's* clubby party, laughing among bawdy men at lord knew what. I had not been included; I belonged with Mpovi, eking out our meager drops of beer. Yet this was her idea of a day off, this chance to pose for photographs, to engineer my evolution as an African *femme*. Ebullience was in the air, and I was tipsy, too, poised to sprout knotted braids, to flower in my *pagne*, to resuscitate the inklings of a childhood dream.

"Who is dancing here?" a boisterous voice, faceless in the dusk, boomed through my screen.

I left off typing, yanked open the door.

It was ironic Bwadi policing my porch, moped propped before my stoop. He must have wheeled it straight from the *Préfet's*; I hadn't heard him ride up. My music was loud, it was true, but not loud enough to drown out an engine. The crescent of his smile slacked across the shadows like a lazy moon.

I poked my head outside. "You have no lamp?"

"I've only come from next door."

"A long party."

"Yes, but without music." He nodded toward my radio inside. "That's Mama Lokata, with *Orchestre Ça Va.*"

"I know. Come in. It's Radio Cameroon."

"It sounds as if you're dancing, but I find you working instead." He strolled across the threshold, abandoning his moped without a thought. This did not surprise me. Thieves avoided villages like Mampungu where strangers were fingered from afar, where everybody knew who belonged to what. Slinking off on Bwadi's bike would not be smart. Despite this lack of crime, I'd been advised to lock my door when leaving, against the minor pilferings of school delinquents, and I always did.

"So where do you take your moped, if not to school?"

"Oh, around. I take small trips," he said vaguely.

"I wish I had one. It's expensive, isn't it? The petrol?"

He shrugged vastly, his shoulders distorted by the gaslight, and resorted to Tambala's wily refrain. *"On se débrouille."*

On se débrouille: you manage, you do what you can, legal or not—you buy and sell at a profit, you ferry people in the company truck for a sum, you sell grades to students, you set up roadblocks for bribes. Despite the fact that salaries went unpaid, cash flowed. A moped in Mampungu, I imagined, could traffic packages, letters, bits of urgent news. A gossip could make a living as town crier here. But Bwadi was too classy for that.

"Sit down," I let him off the hook. "While you're here, I have something for you." Heading for the kitchen, I left him to the throbbing strings and drums, the inquisitive scuff of static. I was eager to present him with his trophy of palm wine.

But when I returned, bottle in hand, Bwadi was still on his feet, perched at the doorway to the hall.

I put the bottle down. "Would you like a tour?"

He rolled forward onto his tiptoes with assent. He seemed to keep getting taller.

I picked up a storm lamp and began the standard tour, stepping into each room, panning with the light so that shadows lurched. We did not enter the bathroom, Diabelle's sanctum, and at my bedroom door I stopped. As always, it was open and, from where we stood, the bed was limply lit, the sheet pulled haphazardly up over the pillow—my version of tidy—but by lamplight it looked unmade, vivid with my sleep. I moved us on.

Bwadi eyed everything, humming interest, clucking at closets, windows, wood. As we neared the living room again, however, he dallied, like Diabelle.

"What have I forgotten?" I asked.

He was not shy. "Your camera. May I look at it again?"

"Normally it's not included in the tour, but for you . . ." I back-tracked to a bureau stranded in an empty room, Bwadi on my heels, and extracted the camera from beside my photographs.

"Know how this works?" I put it in his hands.

"Teach me."

"Let's go sit."

The living room greeted us with the Aladdin lamp's glare; I repositioned it from beside the typewriter to the coffee table, and we sat together on the couch to inspect the camera. I explained the aperture, shutter, light meter, and lens, basking in Bwadi's deference. In his large hands, the camera looked fragile. He put it to his forehead, scanned the room as if with binoculars, and settled on the bottle of palm wine.

"Ah!" he bristled happily. "You drink palm wine, too!"

"No. I mean, yes, but that one's for you. Until I can find Empereur."

"Then we must have a glass."

Bwadi was so different this evening from his peremptory school self. I recalled how he'd looked when my white face had frightened the *Préfet*'s son, how Bwadi had laughed so raucously and grabbed his knees before sizing up my dismay. He was limber and agreeable now, softened up once again, I guessed, by the *Préfet*'s beer. He was almost childlike, his friendliness personal, overt.

"The *Préfet* sent you away thirsty?"

"But he had no palm wine." Suddenly the village brew sounded like a special treat.

When I returned with the glasses he had drifted over to the typewriter on the table. Trumpets bleated from the radio.

"Nkrumah," he looked up triumphantly from what I'd typed.

"You know it?"

"I know Nkrumah in French," he said. "What does this say?"

"It's from his autobiography. I'm using it in fifth," I specified, citing the equivalent of our eleventh grade. I went around to the sofa, set down the glasses, tugged at the cork of leaves. Secretly I was pleased that my work had caught his eye. I'd taken to borrowing the school typewriter to type texts onto stencils for the office to run off, and this one contained an excerpt from Kwame Nkrumah's work. "It talks about a racist incident in the States, when Nkrumah was refused a drink of water because he was black. I was going to title the lesson, 'America will eat you up,'" I smiled, pouring, "but then I decided to let Nkrumah stand on his own."

"You're making the effort!" Bwadi congratulated me, but then he turned, and my satisfaction was spoiled by the smug slant of his mouth.

Frowning, I offered him a glass.

"To the memory of Nkrumah!" he toasted, and we clinked.

After a thirsty swallow, he exhaled, revived, swung into a chair.

"Kwame Nkrumah. The great architect of African independence. Like your George Washington."

"Or Lincoln, who freed the slaves."

"No," he cocked his puffy head, "no." History was, of course, Bwadi's subject. "Washington. Washington repelled British rule, then became the first modern democratic president. The first to step down from office, to trust the people to choose. An enormous gesture, one we have yet to accomplish in Africa."

I swallowed some palm wine, puckering. "Nkrumah never stepped down."

"No, he held on tight until he was overthrown." Bwadi looked suddenly forlorn. "Yet he led his people to independence, and then Ghana paved the way for Africa. Self-rule was an amazing achievement in itself. Don't forget, we are at a disadvantage here. Washington's Americans were colonists, but we are the colonized. Next you must give your class something from *Vers la Liberté Coloniale,*" he decided. "'Imperialism is the policy which aims at creating, organizing, and maintaining an empire,'" he quoted in French. A splash of static burst like applause from the radio.

"It's a class in English, not in African Nationalism."

"No, but Nkrumah wrote in English. It's a vehicle."

"Like your moped."

Surprised, he hesitated, militant hair haywire. He did not get the joke. There was no joke; it was childish nonsense, sabotage.

"Should I teach them as well," I carried on, "about how Nkrumah squandered all the cocoa credit reserves Ghana inherited from the U.K. at independence? How he passed over the cocoa farmers for white elephants—all those monuments to himself, skyscrapers, expressways to nowhere?"

His footing restored, Bwadi scoffed, waving his glass. "That was the fault of the English from the start, for withholding the world price just to honor their own arbitrary price controls. Why did they not pay Ghana the fair price to begin with?"

"Everything was rationed then, during the war, and later they were reconstructing, trying to control inflation when cocoa became scarce. At least they kept the credit building in banks and handed it over at Ghana's independence."

I stopped, amazed to hear myself defending imperialism of any sort. We were sparring, of course, niggling over an obscure point, testing for acuity, finesse. To be talking politics at all was a coup; women did not engage in such discussions here, and nobody did at school; students might spread the word, advertently or not, toward the perked ears of Mankanzu's government police—the *Force Intérieure de Tambala,* or FIT. While delighting in my small entrée into Bwadi's world, however, I wondered if this intellectual foray would muddy my femininity. For the moment I decided not to smoke.

"Anyway," Bwadi dismissed the argument, returning to what was, for him, the point. "Nkrumah was bestowing a myth. He was an inspiration! Africans need to see leaders as extravagant, invincible. That is how they saw the English and the French; that is how the ancestors saw their tribal chiefs."

He spoke of Africans as if he were not one himself. I, myself, tended to think this way about Americans. "Where are you from?" I had to ask.

He glanced at me. "Angola."

"Angola! I thought you were Tambalan. You speak French without a Portuguese accent, and Kikongo, too. What are you doing here?"

He shrank away, offended, or angry. It startled me to think that the question had been rude; if so, I'd been insulted many times.

"There is a war in Angola," he reminded me. "And this is what I mean about Nkrumah. If Mankanzu had gone the way of Nkrumah, Tambala would not now be fueling a war next door. Nkrumah understood that the greatest obstacle to African strength is tribalism, which the superpowers have learned to exploit.

"'The imperialists of today endeavor to achieve their ends not merely by military means,'" he launched anew into a quote, "'but by economic penetration, cultural assimilation, ideological domination, psychological infiltration, and subversive activities even to the point of inspiring and promoting assassination and civil strife.' It's the CIA, isn't it, sending arms to the rebel forces in Angola? They don't like socialists in charge of oil, don't want them threatening Tambala's copper and cobalt. You see how it goes? They make our countries into playing fields." Slumping, his empty glass skewed in his lap, he looked all done in, and I regretted his disadvantage.

I motioned with the bottle for his glass, which he obediently set down. Picking up the camera, he weighed it, turning it toward him, staring morosely into the lens. Accusingly, he looked up. "It's the CIA, isn't it?"

"It's no secret. It's been in the news for years."

"They say volunteer teachers like you work for the CIA," he said evenly. The *soukous* had been suspended; a hearty announcer chortled on in French.

"AfricEd is not a government agency, like Peace Corps," I said. "But I don't know, maybe some of us are CIA. I'm not."

I am always this way when falsely accused—I state the facts, wash my hands. I refuse to feel responsible for someone else's poor judgment. Besides, the idea that I, or any volunteer I knew, could be a spy was a joke; we had laughed, back in training, when we'd heard that Tambalans might think so. But Bwadi was serious. He squinted at the camera's solid eye, the vast, black pupil gleaming in his grip. That moment was perhaps a turning point with us. After a moment of creased deliberation, the gaslight glinting off his tightened brow, he widened his eyes and smiled. He sat back and smiled.

"*C'est bien,*" he said.

Diabelle had promised we'd dance all night, and I envisioned the wedding as some kind of crazy bush circus complete with grass skirts and masks and streaks of war paint. Although I'd lived for years in those African cities, I still managed to reproduce the cliché images of travel brochures when I tried to picture the bush life I'd missed.

The Saturday of the event, I taught my morning classes as usual, and then went to Mpovi's so that she could tress my hair and fit me up properly in my new outfit. She'd been absorbed for days in my preparation, negotiating with the village seamstress on how to sew my *pagne,* painting my nails purple like bruises, resigned, herself, to staying behind. "Yes, I know Lufwidi," she had said about Diabelle's village, "but Chance is too young. A new mother doesn't travel."

That day in her clearing she was like a fairy godmother, and I her Cinderella. Amenable, I sat as tall and still as possible below the mango tree, trying not to wobble in the chair. Revelling in the attention, I couldn't help but hope that I'd be prettier now, that I'd begin to fit in. At least I would have Mpovi's respect. Behind my back, she minced skillfully, dipping and sidestepping, lunging for a handhold, tugging back to twist and knot clump by slippery clump, darting and dodging as if my hair were evil and alive.

"*C'est sauvage,*" said a loitering *petit.* About ten kids had gathered, whispering and elbowing, their mouths open slightly, like pink dents. Their school uniforms had been replaced by faded scraps of dresses loose at the shoulders, or, if they were boys, shorts tied by string to their waists and dangling to their knees—hand-me-downs worn by brothers and sisters and perhaps, originally, by children in Europe or the States.

"How can my hair be wild?" I responded, combing with my fingers through what still hung loose, airing my shoulders.

"Sit still," Mpovi grumbled, mouth full of thread.

Stepping forward, the ringleader, swaybacked with audacity, reached out to touch. "Only people sick in the head let their hair fall long like that, because they don't take care of themselves. You see them in the street in Kimpiri with hair like that."

"You'd have to be sick in the head to wear long hair, in this heat," I laughed.

Thick and wavy, flaring at the neck, my hair was not unlike blond dreadlocks. Until now, however, few people at Mampungu had witnessed the drama of my hair down; oppressed by its dank weight against my neck, I wore it up always in a slipshod knot. The heat had continued to mushroom. Because the rainshowers had stopped, all the recent moisture monopolized the air, clogging the oxygen, thickening space. At times, moving felt like swimming, and objects in the distance wavered as if undersea.

I zeroed in on the little girl. "Do you think it's ugly long?"

"It's better up. But anyway, with so much hair, don't you get bugs?"

Mpovi laughed above my head, grasping a clump. "There are no bugs here," she announced, then stooped to pry the comb from her baby who, sitting up naked, had put it in his mouth.

Next she dove for my hair as if trapping something wild, and I heard the comb ripping through tangles. "Ehi," I protested, blinking. Perhaps this business was wrong for the fine, feeble hair provided by my northern European genes.

Mpovi relented. She was doing her best, I knew. Her skill was noted among the community, and by habit she attacked her task with the rough twists meant for the resilience of a black woman's hair. I persevered, bracing my back, imagining metamorphosis. I tried to picture my double, Sadie, in African braids.

As the hour droned on, the kids grew in number, heads tick-tocking as they licked their lips, and Chance dribbled and smiled as he pushed around the bright pink comb discarded by Mpovi on his mat. I drowsed, lulled by the swish of pedestrians, the hollow pop of barefoot soccer, the sloping vowels of dialect, the throb of birds. There was a beat to everything in Tambala, it seemed, as if every atom obeyed the logic of some soggy orchestral score.

"Ehi, Miss!" someone broke my reverie. I squinted at the undulating road. Hands were up, waving; a few of the teachers, grins floating like gulls, had spotted me in Mpovi's yard.

"You've changed your mind?" I called, scanning for absent Bwadi. The teachers had all pledged to attend the wedding that night, but the tools they carried now revealed their plan to farm.

"Ah, no," Shamavu, the math teacher, yelled happily. "First the fields, then the celebration. Even bachelors have to eat."

"But Miss, you're wearing your hair *à la Tambalaine?*"

"We'll see," I resisted lavishly, waving them away. But they had no desire to stop. Nodding, chirping noises of accord, the group bobbed on down the road, for all the world like teenagers on holiday in their ratty T-shirts and sandals, hoes perched at jaunty angles, virility implied. I'd never seen these guys so relaxed; at school they wore their button-down shirts and slacks meticulously pressed, their lace-up shoes shined. I'd never seen such exuberance in the teachers' lounge, such spring to the step at classroom doors. Supposedly farming was women's work; wives tended fields, men had jobs—or, once upon a time, fished and hunted and built huts.

Supposedly the educated elite of Africa scorned manual labor, but these teachers seemed to find farming a relief. They were like Americans, I guess—gardening on weekends, emerging from their days of work indoors to delight in dirt and activity and tiny new sprouts.

Tying off another tress, Mpovi clucked. I felt the tension loosen as the thread unravelled. "These flagpoles don't want to stand up," she complained, referring to the Tambalan antennae that stuck straight out from the skull.

Exploring, my fingers found a braid completely encased in thread, sagging over my ear and pointing toward my shoulder. "That's fine," I approved. "I won't look exactly like you, but it will be my own variation. Not flagpoles, but palm branches."

She giggled, snipping thread with her teeth. "Yes, it's like a palm branch."

Mechanically abrupt, a metallic purr disturbed Mampungu's lazy symphony of footsteps and goats. I smiled, the sodden mass of my anatomy perking up. It was Bwadi, of course, putting past on his moped, a short-handled hoe and machete strapped to the back. Since our soiree he'd been bumming cigarettes, insinuating collusion at school. Evidently I was an accomplice of sorts, in cahoots. I'd begun to notice how he set himself apart, and this solo expedition to his field was a case in point; rather than chumming along with the other teachers, here he was scooting off alone. I didn't mind. After all his hot air about African cooperation, his independence seemed very Western to me. Initiative and efficiency would have him at the party on time.

Drawing abreast, he turned his head, ferreting me out. Suddenly self-conscious, I waved timidly, half expecting him to detour toward the mango tree, park his bike, and join my audience of kids. But no, hairstyling was a feminine domain, albeit public, performed outdoors rather than clandestinely as in American salons where women dyed their hair. Men were free to join these women as they gossiped and plaited on their shaded straw mats, free to see the transformations take place; apparently they preferred to steer clear. After lifting his fingers from the handlebars in greeting, Bwadi fled on down the road.

"How much is left?" I asked Mpovi, who had shifted around to tackle the hair above my left ear. My temples felt tight, my eyelids too small.

"I'm almost done." She giggled. "He'll be asking you to dance."

"Let me see a mirror."

Self-appointed, a *petit* ran inside to find one, and I continued to finger tress after flaccid tress. For some reason, I had not told Mpovi about Bwadi's visit to my house, and I did not care to discuss him with her now.

"Your face is beautiful," she sighed, circling to the front.

Whatever the coiffure, I knew, I could not expect to match Mpovi's poise. Her masterpiece complete, she stood tightening her *pagne,* snug in her universe. I, on the other hand, braids drooping, felt like a jumble of loose ends.

Banging through the screen door, the little girl delivered my mirror. Automatically, I held it up; what it revealed could only make me laugh. My audience exploded, too. Instead of flagpoles, a crown of floppy tails emanated from my head. "It's not flagpoles, and it's not palm branches, either," I gasped. "It's snakes!"

The children darted and twirled, chanting the Kikongo word for snakes. I joined in, and then stopped, mouth full of air. For a moment I saw myself as they must, slimy and fetal as a snail without its shell. With or without tresses, I was perverse. The night I'd terrified Chance, I'd had this same numb rush of something intimate exposed. Now, Medusaesque in plaits like snakes, spooking the kids in fun, I felt freakish again, a sorry monster fated to turn people to stone.

"Let's see how it looks with the *pagne,*" Mpovi encouraged stubbornly. Although she grinned indulgently at the din, she was not prepared to trash her own artwork.

Heading for my house to change, hilarity echoing in my wake, I noticed that the lawn was plush enough to hold the impressions of my feet. Already the savannah had matured from citrus green to the glossy hue of malachite, and I now believed the local wisdom that if the vegetation were not annually burned, the forest would creep back to reclaim the buildings and the roads. Man could clear and construct and fortify, but the jungle would always prevail. It was primordial; it would reduce the twentieth century to rusty debris. Hard surfaces and straight lines crumbled in this heat and rain, this humus and oxygen, this relentless abundance of life. Everything grew quickly in the tropics, even my hair. My mother had kept it cropped short, and as a kid I'd wanted long hair so badly I would fasten towels to my head to feel the weight against my back. My real hair never reached my shoulders until after she died.

In Kimpiri I'd bought one of the fringe hemp bags generic to the region, as popular with old women lugging tobacco pipes and kola nuts as with men on business trips, their roadside baguettes poking through the drawstring tops. Into mine I dropped a toothbrush, a bandana, a Swiss army knife, cigarettes, matches, cash—Mpovi had suggested a wedding contribution of twenty kulunas—and my camera padded by a change of clothes. The camera made sense; I would offer my services as the sort of roving photographer who had shot many of Mpovi's village portraits, and between poses snap frames for myself.

Next, I fumbled with the African outfit, hoping to secure a knot that would keep the skirt from dropping onto the lawn on my way back to Mpovi's for her final adjustments. Satisfied, I locked up.

By now it was midafternoon, and everything shimmered in the heat. Mpovi and the kids were like dark fish hovering in liquid grass, as if all the weeds and trees beyond her clearing had imploded to envelop them. I approached in what felt like slow motion, listening to the buzz of heat—of the insects wheezing and the hint of leaves and bark expanding, of the aluminum roofs arching. Mpovi's teeth gleamed jarringly as she waited, hands on hips.

"You're beautiful!"

The children covered their mouths, and I detected a ripple of respect. Nobody dared swat at my tresses now, nobody dared a word. Of course I'd never get inside black skin, but it seemed that, inside a *pagne,* I could begin to imagine how African women felt.

Mpovi dove right in, eager to perfect the angle of my folds, drawing the cloth tight across my belly and rump. "Where is your nice stomach?" she jabbed me in the back. "You must show your curves." After tightening the knot at my waist, she brandished a safety pin.

"Isn't that cheating?"

"No, everybody does it, especially to travel."

"I'm only going twenty kilometers."

"To dance, then. The knot will loosen and you won't know how to fix it," she insisted, fastening the pin. Then she tugged at the ruffle at my waist, part of the top that overlapped the skirt. "Now try to walk."

My ankles met resistance within the confines of the narrow hemline she'd created.

"Take little steps, little steps." Still the children didn't laugh.

As I strutted along, it occurred to me that my natural gait involved steps much larger than what Tambalan women considered normal, and that everyone must see my walking as clumsy, alien. Nobody clambering forth as I liked to do could ever balance a headload.

"You don't have other shoes?" Mpovi was frowning at my flat sandals.

"No."

"I'll lend you mine," she announced with finality. "The white ones with the heels."

The brave *petit* detached herself from her friends, but hesitated at my protest.

"You're very kind," I said to Mpovi, "but I can't wear shoes like that. What if the truck breaks down and I need to walk?"

"You carry sandals in case. Heels are much better with a pagne. And you others always wear nice shoes."

By "others" she meant white people.

"No, really, I never learned. I don't like them. They keep you from walking very far."

I'd invoked a familiar theme. Mpovi tended to insist that I could never make it on foot to the train station, seventeen kilometers northwest. Convinced that white people were weak, she refused to believe that I'd often hiked that distance in the States.

She didn't want to argue now, however, and dropped the issue, distracted by my shoulder straps. The top, stitched to zipper up the spine, was tight as a bodice and had ruffles for straps that matched the ruffle at the waist. Her fingers probed at my shoulders, tucking my bra straps into place.

She whispered confidentially, "You have many good brassieres."

I looked at her, puzzled. "I have a few."

Pretty hollows formed in her smooth brown cheeks as she tried to pull a sour face. "I don't have many."

Since she was always braless when she breast-fed her son, I'd assumed she never wore bras. "Can't you find them in Kimpiri?"

"Not good ones like yours, like in that book from the store. And if you do find any, they're too expensive."

I doubted she'd ever seen my bras, all broad-strapped, sturdy things good for long bumpy truck rides across the savannah. She could only have seen them by peeking through my bathroom window, where I hung my underthings to dry—the only part of my wardrobe that I didn't give Jetaime to wash and hang outside.

Clearly, whatever the style, she wanted one of mine. I only had a few; I wanted to keep them all. Besides, giving away bras was absurd, even more absurd than borrowing shoes—chest sizes were personal, specific; how could one of mine fit her? Studying her bust, I tried to gauge how similar in size we were. I had no idea. My image of my own breasts was created by the mirror, a straight-on view with my shoulders held level. I had no concept of myself in three dimensions—or in four—of how I moved through space, leaning, sagging, bouncing. Who did? Wasn't self-image, anyway, just the echo of what others saw, of what their faces revealed when you walked into a room? I felt oddly shipwrecked. The Americans who'd shaped my idea of what I was were out of the picture now. Had I changed? Was I bigger, smaller, looser, askew?

Following my gaze, Mpovi studied herself. Her chest was full, full enough to need a bra. "Don't you have one you could give me?"

She'd never before asked me for anything outright, preferring instead to hint around until I offered things from my pantry, and to send a *petit* for them later on. Of course, a bra was highly private, something no one was likely to hand out. Or maybe only an American would feel that way. Or maybe only me. Perhaps I was overly possessive, or shy. What would my childhood double, Sadie, do now? As I deliberated, Mpovi strained, her chin tucked against her neck, eyelashes fluttering, and she struck me as deprived.

"Sure, I'll give you one to try. If it fits, you keep it."

Re-animated, she demonstrated how to drape the extra piece of fabric around my shoulders if I got chilly at night—something hard to imagine in the wet heat—and then how to fold it properly inside my sack. She caught sight of my camera.

"But Miss! We must have your picture taken!"

Mysteriously, I felt reluctant to immortalize my African transformation. "Do I have time?"

"But it's you who can decide when to go."

I waffled, debating. The school *camionnette* had already trundled off the *Préfet*'s lawn toward the *petit marché,* the place where vehicles loaded up. The teachers, however, had yet to return from their fields.

"Plenty of time," Mpovi lobbied. "I'll call the *Préfet,* he can use a camera."

"Why the *Préfet?* You can use a camera, too."

"Me! I wouldn't know how." *Je ne saurais pas.* The phrase I kept hearing that drove me up the wall, that people used whenever afraid to try something new. I wondered if the French used the phrase, as well, or if it translated literally from some mother tongue expression, a local choice of words.

"You'll know when I teach you. Watch."

I left the lens filter screwed on, and adjusted the settings for the strong light. "All you have to do is hold the camera like this." I placed her fingers on the metal and she gripped.

"Be careful not to let your finger go in front of the lens. You don't want a picture of your finger." I showed her where to squint, pointed her at the cook fire, where yesterday's charred wood was encircled by hefty stones, and told her to keep looking as I adjusted the focus. Her muscular grace froze and she barely breathed; a sweet, fruity scent hovered on her skin.

"Tell me when the rocks are clear."

"They're clear," she mumbled, and I double-checked.

"So, first you make sure that I look very clear, by turning this knob. Then, when you're ready, press this button." The shutter clicked and she winced. "Let's practice on the kids."

From behind, I pointed her toward the brazen child, who, elated, arched. "Focus on her nose."

The girl laughed. "Now," I said, and the shutter snapped.

"You've got it, you see? It's easy. Now, me."

Against the mango's great trunk, straddled by two vast roots, I felt my cheeks ball up as I tried to smile. I had to admit, there was nothing natural about facing a lens.

She snapped, then lowered the camera, fascinated. She turned it over, upside down. She loved it, I could tell, and I couldn't help thinking of her in the States, the product of a different background. As a college student, chic in jeans and tank tops, a day pack instead of a baby on her back. As a heartbreaker, driving a red convertible to work. As a photographer. She recognized the magic in the little black and chrome box, the power to stop time.

My own love of photography was, I think, connected to my aimlessness; my pictures recorded where I'd been and who I'd been, establishing chronology. Like Hansel and Gretel's bread crumbs, my photos showed me the way back. I'd followed my brother out the door, left my widowed father behind; I'd lit out for that sweet gingerbread house in the woods. Yet my woods seemed limitless, diffuse. My photos were my map.

Mpovi, however, was as fixed as a person can be. She knew where she was from and where she was going: they were the same place. She meant to live her mother's life, to stay put in the past. Perhaps she collected photos as a way of drawing others around the axle of herself.

"Go on, take some more," I encouraged. "Come close, focus again."

She took one of her small steps, moved the dial, shot again. Then, impulsively, she swung around to snap Chance's bobbing rear end, and I admired her instinct—how well I knew the urge to capture candid moments! She had the photographer's opportunistic confidence, she had the knack. Yet rather than victorious I felt a strange hint of resentment. I wanted my camera back.

Mpovi, however, had no desire to compete. One more shot of her son, and she brought me the camera extended carefully in both hands.

Once I had the camera back, I relaxed. "You are a real photographer," I said, as if bestowing an award.

She walked me to the *camionnette*, and I was glad for her company amidst the ruckus aroused by my dress. Kids lined the road, their bright palms swinging above their heads, and adults called from beneath trees. Matching Mpovi's gait, her rhythmic, miniature steps, I felt as if on parade, and indeed, glancing behind us, I saw a skipping retinue of children. I wanted to hurry but was shackled by the narrow skirt. While Mpovi beamed like a queen, my own grin hurt my cheeks. The houses, faces, and trees blended together, magnified in the heat.

For the first time that day I felt embarrassed. What if the old friends in my photo album, the ones who'd helped to shape my California self, were to see me now? I focussed straight ahead through the humid blur, through my own sweaty remorse. Mpovi minced along, oblivious, humming greetings, proud as Pygmalion. Her wifely garments drooped, a tribute to her domesticity. She primped only for selected events—parties, market days—otherwise she seemed to take a certain pride in disarray.

The avenue's wispy palm trees converged upon the *petit marché,* a gay froth of brown gestures and flamboyant prints. Voices came bantering as if from above, seeming to filter down from heaven rather than from the crowd ahead. In the center of the commotion I spotted the *camionnette,* a blue hump gawking emptily, cab doors wide open, ready for boarding. They were waiting for me.

Swaths of cloth unfurled and flapped as women began to layer their hair and outfits against the dirty breeze they'd be battling, riding in the truck's open bed. Then Diabelle glided forward, splendid in a gold-and-black print, laughing wetly as she reached for my hands. Like a dark, tropical fish, she swerved off to dip briefly in a curtsy for Mpovi.

Mpovi's shield, however, was up, her smile restrained; she even recoiled, stepping aside. Her so-called disciplinary behavior struck me as downright rude, and I sensed something more at stake. Telling me good-bye, she blinked obliquely as we shook, me pumping her arm as if to replenish her good will. She pulled back and my heart sank. Was it me? She'd seen me suddenly, perhaps, in another light, and regretted my makeover. I stood unhappily, ignoring Diabelle, reluctant to leave Mpovi in this dingy state, the carefree charm of her work clothes reduced by her scowl to nothing more than rags. Pointing with her mouth toward the truck, she smacked her lips disapprovingly. "They're waiting for you."

I bristled. It was she, after all, who had insisted I hold everybody up while we took pictures. She who'd put me in this *pagne.* What was the big deal, anyway; why was she so bent on seeing me as an African *femme?* It was more than curiosity, more than a lark. She liked the power, perhaps, of her role as mentor, guide, of converting me to her camp. Or perhaps she was afraid. Afraid I was going to change her territory, make Mampungu modern and the life she loved obsolete. Yet Mpovi, herself, was modern to an extent—she was, after all, an educated wife, one of the valuable ones with a high school degree. Could the difference between old and new really be so black and white? It wasn't, for me; I wanted to learn. More than Mpovi's friendship, I wanted to learn. I actually believed there might be wisdom in tradition, bits of which might come in handy in my wobbly world. Mpovi's petty reprisals, however, I did not need.

I set off with Diabelle, who didn't seem the slightest miffed by the snub. A second later, though, I stopped cold, assailed by Mpovi's voice—piercingly plaintive, straining as if for something lost. The sound reached beneath my skin, suffusing my soul—I hear it still, plain and pathetic, making me sorry, sorry for Mpovi and for myself, for the world's borders we're born into, for her country and for mine. I still hear the final note of plea, twisting the last syllable incongruously—*"Vous êtes belle!"* You're beautiful, she begged, as if for something back.

By the time I swivelled she had started home, a patient, regal figure receding, hailing no one. What she'd seen between Diabelle and me, I think, was the defeat of something African. Mpovi was not simply jealous, reluctant to share the magnanimous white Miss; she resented Diabelle's girlish need to rebel. Mpovi understood her as a type; she knew what to expect. All of Mpovi's efforts to make me African wouldn't stand a chance against this girl's desire to lead a modern life. I was Diabelle's idol. The two of us would fight what Mpovi was: traditional, obedient, fixed. If Mpovi saw herself in defeat, though, she also saw Diabelle's demise. As a role model, Mpovi thought, I could only hurt Diabelle. And so she left us to play our parts: Diabelle to reaffirm the westerner in me while I chiselled away at her African core. Her family would not want what was left. They'd let her go, all her African potential reduced to broken pieces, the chips of a gem glinting among shards.

I'm generalizing, of course. I can't be sure what, exactly, Mpovi saw falling apart; some things about the West she loved—things, really, as opposed to manners and behavior—photographs; nice, lacy lingerie. I did wind up giving her one of my athletic bras, and not long thereafter, I spied, instead, black satin straps inside her blouse; she'd gotten the bra she wanted somewhere else. Even so, she never offered to give mine up.

83

4

DANCING

We were going to Lufwidi, a river village twenty kilometers south-west, maternal village of Diabelle and Mama Zola, home of Diabelle's sister, the bride. Already at Mampungu, marriage was in the air. The crowd at the *camionnette* surged, laughing, jostling for places in the back. Tembo, the school chauffeur, hulked beside the cab door as Diabelle ushered me into the passenger's seat. An old, deflated woman with crooked hands flattened against her thighs sat opposite the gear shift. She ignored my greeting, not even turning her eyes from the windshield ahead. Perhaps she was deaf. A child was lifted onto my lap, and in response to Tembo's gentle Kikongo crawled to wedge herself between the lady and me. Then another little girl landed on my lap, and the door banged shut.

The small face was round and tentative, full of downy obedience. "How are you?" I said, low on Kikongo, and made myself go limp. Those few words, however, from my thin mouth delighted both girls and they fell into conversation, exchanging shrill, impulsive phrases as my charge swung her legs. The old woman stared rigidly forward.

Twisting in my seat of honor among the helpless, I watched the able-bodied fill the back, Diabelle among the ranks of a dozen or so familiar faces, people I'd seen around Mampungu. She was the only student, I was surprised to note, and the only fellow passenger I really knew. The other teachers, I assumed, were on their own, broke, bereft of whatever fare the *Préfet* was charging for the school truck; they would straggle in later on foot, perhaps, all except for progressive Bwadi on his motorbike. As far as I knew, I, the fragile emissary from afar, was riding for free.

The truck rocked as Tembo boarded and the woman beside me moaned as the cab shrank with his pungent presence. He gripped the gear shift and she mumbled, her gaze still stuck on the horizon. Perhaps she was blind. As we rolled into first, the cheering of the crowd seemed to push us along, and the excitement was contagious. I loved it—the African fanfare, the hullabaloo erupting out of sodden routine, how the flabbiest pretext united strangers in some common purpose—passersby converging upon a stalled car, or these neighbors gathered as if to send us off on some intrepid pilgrimage.

We picked up speed down Mampungu's hill, lurching through a pothole which caused the old woman to wail. Tembo chuckled; the girls shrieked happily.

"Are you all right?" I tapped the woman's papery hand.

"It's her first time in a vehicle," Tembo said.

She paid me no attention. She was petrified, mumbling what must have been prayers, calling out pitifully at each dip and crunch of the shock absorbers, sending the girls and Tembo into gales of laughter.

"*Mama na ngai! Mama na ngai!*" My mother, my mother, she was shouting, and I admired her cosmology. Who better to call upon, who in heaven would ever help, if not your dead mother?

I was in high spirits, exhilarated by Tembo's mad driving, steeped in the thrill of precarious speed. For over two months, I hadn't moved faster than my flurried walk. For over two months I'd been with neither car nor electricity, not a light bulb, not a wheel turning. I'd probably slowed down, possibly taken on the rhythms of the sun and moon. Conceivably, my contours had changed, eroding here, hardening there, but how was I to know? Unable to interpret what I saw, I'd been avoiding the cracked and corroded mirror above my sink, avoiding my surprising foreign face, so bleak and permanently white.

Tembo charged the puddles, gauging at the last second whether or not to bank away, tipping us on two wheels, maniacally making time. The crew in back were grinning as they strained to brace themselves low, apparently impervious to fear. This was their amusement ride, the local roller coaster—the only note of protest was the old woman's prayer. I thought she had a point.

Unexpectedly, then, another truck careered into view, as hell-bent as we, squealing up against a bank to let us pass. Veering, we plowed straight through a pothole, the *camionnette* bucking with dissent, and I caught a glimpse of the white man at the wheel, vivid as a Viking, his red crown of hair a shock.

"Who was that?" I asked Tembo as he yanked us back on course. Yodels of approval sounded from the back. Evidently, no one had been lost.

"Those men are for the bridge," he yelled above the mama's groans. "They're always driving this way now. They're always driving too much."

"From where?" Hadn't Mitch told me the name of their camp, ages ago, in the embassy annex? But as nobody at Mampungu had been able to fix the existence of these guys, I'd sort of purged them from my mind.

"The river."

"Yes, but where? How far?"

Tembo raised his eyebrows at my niggling, sly. "Eleven kilometers downriver from Lufwidi. They are American, too."

Already, I was guilty by association. I shut up, hoping the redheaded road hog had seen my tresses flapping as I jounced; I hoped he would consider me bushstruck and tell all the others at his camp to write me off. I hoped he'd tell Mitch.

The girls clung gleefully to me and I wrapped them in my arms. Each time that Tembo reached for the shift stick the woman hollered and we laughed. The road was a red, splotchy ribbon drawing us across lumpy savannah; we crashed through groves of dank forest to emerge climbing plush and sunny hills. My hair was tautly tressed and my legs curtained in wild cotton; the kids were molded against my sides as if I were their mom. I didn't feel white. Mpovi's son, I recalled, had screamed at my first touch; I wondered what it was I'd learned to do right since then. Something more than how to dress, something about my smile, or my tone of voice, or the pace and pressure of my gestures. Mpovi had trained and suited me up like an astronaut, and I felt strangely self-sufficient, inspired and confident as if a part of me had woken up. I was as African now as I could get; I had finally arrived. Long ago, from inside that fence in Conakry, I'd yearned for this moment, and there was no place now I'd rather be.

Every time my family moved, I thought I didn't mind. When we moved from Washington to Conakry my best friend up the street vowed to write and wait for me; I expected to return in two years to find everything the same. Instead of fearing what I'd lose, I focused on what I would acquire: a swimming pool shaped like a woman's body, a house with a roof like a hat. Mostly, though, I anticipated my own wonderful metamorphosis.

Lying in bed, my eyes clenched with the excitement of our pending flight, I envisioned myself wise and gentle and surrounded by friends. I wanted to be one of the child saints we'd heard about in catechism. Our move would be my miracle, my lucky chance to begin again where no one would connect me with the mortifying things I had done. Never again would I snitch dimes from my Lent collection, cheat in class, or laugh at the fat kid. Never again would I get bonked on the head by a softball, or fall into a well.

Even the time I'd played doctor with the boy across the street would be wiped clean from my slate; I'd arrive in Africa with a fresh, glossy soul. I pictured my soul as a flat, two-dimensional sort of organ outlined by my skin and made up of a smooth white substance as vulnerable as the glaze on hot cross buns. Each sin made a dent; too many could deform the spirit's shape. I meant to keep my new soul shiny white.

At that time I was a Pollyanna, faithful that good friendships last and small sins fade, American enough to think anything new is good. As it turned out, the correspondence with my best friend fizzled, and by the time we returned to Washington she had moved away.

I didn't pine much over lost friends; I suppose I never believed they were out of reach until so much time had passed that I no longer cared. I had learned to assume that until we met again, they'd go on sighing, "I wish Nickie hadn't left."

In Conakry I played Barbies with Linda, sewing minute outfits from blazing market fabric, a whole pineapple for a dress. When her parents were out, we followed our brothers into her father's den to spread *Playboys* across the zebra rug. I blushed furiously, as if I'd never seen a woman's breasts.

I had, of course, but the women I had seen were black, my Guinean neighbors who did their chores topless. Passing their compounds, I would notice, over the low walls, their breasts swinging as they pounded yams. Somehow they didn't count. They didn't make me curious about my mother, or myself, as these *Playboy* models did.

And then one day, the mother of one of my American classmates came to show us how she nursed her newborn. The teacher presented the event as a lesson in biology, clearing a place on her desk where the woman could sit in full view. The dark nipple was a shock. When the baby's mouth closed over it I was scandalized, yet thrilled. Had my mother, too, unbuttoned her blouse in public? After the demonstration, I began regarding with awe all the black neighbors cradling infants at their breasts. Suddenly all nursing women were personally significant to me, whereas before, I'm ashamed to say, I'd observed the Guineans' maternal behavior with the same amusement inspired by our cat nursing her young.

Nobody had warned me about Lufwidi's great cross. As we crested the hill, it towered, two gaunt wood beams soaring above the usual orange mud homes.

"What's that?" I called to Tembo, unnerved, but he didn't hear me above the crescendo in back; everyone had broken into song, a Kikongo hymn I recognized from the women's choir. I still did not know the words, but the tune echoed regularly at Mampungu during practices, during their performances at church. I never went to the mission church, much to the Pastor's surprise. Sundays I took my weekly dose of chloraquine, the malaria suppressant, and puttered and dozed, tapping time to the nasal pulse of bass and the raw emotion drumming. Sometimes I'd nod off to dreams of ice cream cones and chandeliers—chloraquine can have exotic side effects.

Now I yelled again to Tembo, "What's that?" and pointed at the giant cross.

He waved gaily as faces turned to greet us, his own dark cheeks thickly dimpled. "That's our cross."

"What cross?"

"An old one, very, very old."

I could see that for myself as we chugged along in first gear, tracing a circle around the monument. Creviced with age, the beams stood about twenty meters high inside the remnants of a low stone wall, a ring of mounds crumbling like headstones. Through the gaps I saw a small cannon the color of moss.

"*How* old?"

Tembo shrugged, navigating through the children running to jump onto the fenders. At first I wondered if our grand entrance was not some ritualistic homage to the cross, but nobody paid it any notice except me. The two little girls scanned for relatives and strained toward the windows. The old woman's eyes were tightly creased shut.

Rectangular houses rimmed the plaza, their broad wood doors painted mint or milky red, their flat roofs sloping slightly whether made of corrugated iron or thatch. Continuing around the cross, we lapped our tire prints, and through the trees I noticed a coppery flash.

"That's the river?"

"The river!" Tembo agreed. "At the water the *bac* carries us across."

Disoriented, I thought for a second we'd keep right on going, roll down onto the ferry to ford the water and prolong our one-truck parade. I leaned forward hopefully; going felt good. As it was, we inched to such a subtle stop that I missed the impact of arrival, that definite sensation of momentum snapping back. In a way, I just kept on flying, although I felt myself handed down to the sweet airlessness of an excited crowd. Wails of admiration sounded among the hissing sibilance of "Miss"; my costume was a hit. I felt sick.

Diabelle took charge then, claiming me as her official guest, and I found myself shaking hand after hand across a moatlike barrier of toddlers, mumbling my greetings through a nervous smile. She introduced nearly everyone as her sister or brother, but I couldn't believe her family was that large.

Then, escorted by a few females trailing children, we moved off and she sat me down outside one of the green doors. Mine was the only chair there; I was to sit alone, as if on display. Diabelle disappeared and for the moment I welcomed solitude, too weary to talk. It was the heat, of course, nothing more. The malaise was familiar: the swollen ache of my skin wanting to burst, the sizzling sensation of my dizzy brain, my tender sweating stomach. I closed my eyes, regretting my poor skull clenched in braids.

"Miss, *ça va?*" Diabelle stood before me, pouring Coke into a glass. She looked competent and domineering, nothing like a student. The others kept their distance, as if conceding space to her authority. I was happy to be in her hands.

"Fine," I said, between sips. In the States I never drank Coke, but here the warm, syrupy soda worked like medicine.

She watched me, hands on hips, her lower lip protruding. "You want to lie down?"

"No, no. *Ça va.*"

"The truck made you sick."

"Not the truck." I was loyal to the truck. "The heat."

"Ah, the heat." She glared as if to scold the sky.

Coincidentally, the engine revved below the cross, and I felt instantly better, anchored by the motor's hum.

It rolled in our direction, picking up speed, and swept right past, empty but for Tembo squinting at the road ahead. On my feet, I yearned after the tailgate as if abandoned by a friend.

"Where's he going?"

"Back to Mampungu, for the others."

"The others?" I sat down, frustrated, not that there should be more guests, but that, once again, I'd got the picture wrong. This kept happening: I'd be breezing along confident that I was part of a plan, in the know, only to find that I was bustling in the wrong direction. If Tembo were running a shuttle, why, then, had everyone been waiting for me? And what about that stupendous send-off—

was that to flare up once again? True, I'd seen no money change hands; conceivably the truck had been rented for the day and everyone was riding for free. I wondered if the next load would be as boisterous as ours, if what had seemed to me extravaganza was merely par for the course.

Diabelle was standing, hands on her hips.

"You don't want to sit down?" I said hopefully.

"*Si!*" She twirled her hand skillfully, and a chair arrived, thanks to the halting bravado of a small boy. "My brother," Diabelle said with pride, settling in her seat. He remained in place as if awaiting another command.

"Everybody is your brother or sister."

"Ehi!" she laughed. "We call them brothers and sisters, we have only one word in Kikongo. But some are my nieces and nephews and cousins, like that, in French."

"And who's getting married, then?"

"That's my sister, from the same mother and father. You met her at the truck."

I didn't recall.

"Is the husband from Lufwidi?"

"From another village, not far. He was at school, too, last year. But they're going to have a baby, so now he'll have to stay and work the fields." She frowned, whether in disapproval or pity, I wasn't sure. I resisted asking about her father's curse.

"So what about all your school friends? Are they coming?"

"Ehi, no." Again she laughed. "The *Préfet* won't allow it."

I wondered if it was he who had kept Mpovi home. "But he let you come?"

"It's my family."

I nodded.

"Miss," she went on, "me, I'm going to finish my studies before I marry."

"Yes! You must," I agreed. Then I teased her, "Who? Who will you marry?"

She crumpled with mirth, burying her face in her knees. "A rich man, very rich!"

"And what will you do?" I felt better now, relaxed.

"Go to America!" She ended the phrase giggling uncontrollably, finding herself absurd. Yet I thought that I could see her in the States. She reminded me somehow of myself in twelfth grade, whereas Mpovi, my age, had veered long since into another realm.

I smiled sympathetically. "Why not? Maybe you will. You should go there to study. You and your rich husband."

"I'm going," she said. "I am. I'll go to America, and Emolo will come and live with me."

At the mention of his name, the boy sucked in his cheeks. I gave him the rest of my Coke.

"Non, c'est pas comme ça," a tough matron intervened as I settled in among the women shelling peanuts. Content with a corner of their straw mat, I'd arranged my legs Indian style, *pagne* tucked modestly. She wanted me to sit properly.

"I can't."

"Si, si." They thought I could.

"Mpasi," I pointed to my feet to show that they would hurt. Every time I tried the pose at Mpovi's, folding my legs together like theirs, rear end balanced on my heels, my feet fell asleep.

Commiserating, they nodded slowly, grinning, and gave up. Even in their clothes I was white, different, hopeless. Although I'd resisted that attitude for months, at the moment, still relatively queasy, I was inclined to see what they meant.

My wedding photo session was evidently not in the cards. It was too late, Diabelle had told me, the bride and groom were too busy now. Diabelle, herself, had been summoned to help her sister at the *source,* the village stream, and I was not invited, either out of ceremonial privacy or prudence for my weak white head in the sun. I was left to wedge myself among the women shelling peanuts and brood about my photos-not-to-be. I could not help picturing those anthropologists' stories of archaic rituals, the things a third world bride might undergo before a wedding—clitoridectomies, crude methods of devirginization—even though this was the twentieth century in a civilized village, even though the girl was already with child. Besides, a clitoridectomy—the ritualistic removal of the clitoris—would have been done long before the wedding day, if the bride were to be expected to walk. I hadn't actually heard of any such custom in Tambala, not in our briefings at training, nor from village chat. I'd heard of clitoridectomies in Kenya; doctors there had made a point of alerting the world when girls kept winding up infected in hospitals.

An aluminum vat seethed nearby over a cook fire, and a woman stood stirring it with a baton that reached to her waist. The only smell I caught was the thick, tinny flavor of afternoon sun on dirt. All the younger women schooled in French must have accompanied the bride to the *source,* for there was no French here, and it had taken a bit of pantomime, after I'd strolled up, to make the group understand that I wanted to help. Quickly, I got the gist of their job, to remove the peanuts from their shells. It was impossible, however, to duplicate the adroit knitting of fingers letting go a steady rain of empty shells. One hand manipulated each shell, breaking and extracting, while the other caught the kernels until a whole fistful could be tossed tinkling into the ceramic bowl. The sound was intermittent and lovely, an accent to their lolling conversation, most of which I didn't understand. "She can't, she can't," I kept hearing, cracking one shell at a time. "White . . . weak." A few narrowed their eyes and drew their chins close against their necks, mouths smacking with finality, condescending. But they liked my watch, my hair. "Camera," I heard; they'd seen me taking pictures of the cross.

I had not been able to resist the spooky monument. The little cannon at its foot looked ancient, from another era, evocative of Portuguese explorers wearing velvet, pointing muskets. Children had darted through the crumbling wall to pose and I'd let them into a few frames, retreating so as to include in the viewfinder the top of the cross. At its foot, the kids were dwarfed like dolls.

I pulled out my camera now, stepping off the women's mat. There was a flutter of timid alarm, giggling, the staccato bicker of advice.

"Don't come, don't go!" I blurted in baby Kikongo from behind the lens, wanting them not to move as I began to shoot. Confused by my oblique instructions, most of the women froze, some smiling as they made eye contact with the lens, some frowning as Mpovi had when caught off guard. Before they knew what had happened, I was sitting down again, Indian style, my camera tucked away.

Sighs of appreciation rippled; it seemed I'd done something good. Automatically, the women resumed their work, cracking nut after nut after nut, muttering to each other, glancing curiously at me. "Camera, camera," I heard, and someone leaned forward to touch one of my dangling braids. When I told who had styled my hair, they all nodded with such excitement that I was proud to be Mpovi's friend.

But was I, really, her friend? I wondered, crushing a shell slowly. The closer we got, the deeper the rift between us grew. Here I was, sitting in her clothes, in her place, going through the motions, bored stiff. How could you sit for hours shelling peanuts? Nobody behaved as if a wedding were to take place, there was no flurry of anticipation, no rush. Anchored in the moment, these women were happy with the task at hand. They didn't know what waiting meant—or what it meant to me: looking forward always to something better ahead.

"What is it you're cooking?" I asked eventually, interrupting the rhythm of their gossip.

One lithe woman motioned energetic pounding in a mortar and pestle, and gestured toward the cook pot; I understood peanut something, and answered that it sounded good, asking, "Is it special, for weddings?" Perhaps peanuts symbolized fertility, like our rice in the States.

To my disappointment they said no, that peanuts simply were in season now. They asked me what foods I ate; I told them anything except *fou fou*, the slimy manioc paste I had yet to learn to like.

"Is this how you prepare peanuts in your country?" I understood the lithe mimist to ask.

I laughed, unable to describe the combines and factories and jars of peanut butter on supermarket shelves. *"Ko."* At least I knew the word for "no." And "no" was enough for now, for later, too. Why did I want to learn Kikongo, anyway? The more I learned, the less I wanted to hear. I did not particularly care to understand their comments on my white self.

Peanuts rained handful by handful into the bowl; I was surrounded by shells like tiny capsized boats. Camouflaged, blending into this tableau of feminine purpose, I felt immaterial: nothing but an empty costume, paler than white. The real Nickie wasn't here shelling peanuts—she couldn't be. Who, then, was fastened in this African dress, and where had the real Nickie gone? I hadn't the foggiest idea who the real me was or had ever been.

Impulsively, I stood. Where was Diabelle? I wanted someone, anyone, to talk to in French. Better yet, English. English was what I'd missed most in Mampungu, more than electricity, more than vehicles—English, my own mother tongue.

The river was the color of rust and stretched smoothly across a green strip of savannah. The sky yawned above. The *bac* lay splayed on the surface like a monstrous water insect. A different thing entirely from the Staten Island ferry, it consisted essentially of three parallel pontoons supporting a platform large enough for one transport truck at best. Oddly, both ends of the platform curved upwards, pulled taut by wires connected to a sort of buttress rising from each side like wings. An example of appropriate technology, it was a mad scientist's delight.

Even stranger was the steel dinosaur embedded in the hillside. A tribute to days gone by, to the colonial machine, this ferry had literally bit the dust. The hull was sunken as if rooted in the earth, and the weeds around it had flourished, so that branches poked through eroded holes. Unlike the feeble *bac* in the water, this monstrosity had, in its time, been worthy of a hefty payload. A second platform was suspended above the bow, with ladders still intact where passengers must have climbed, and above that, a roof. I took pictures from all angles, close up and from the distance, completely carried away. I even debated about venturing inside, but resisted, daunted by the prospect of crawling and climbing in my *pagne*.

Still gawking, my camera warm in my hands, I was distracted by a splash. Children were diving from the little ferry in the water, putting on a show. I watched as a group ran naked from the bank onto a makeshift dock and jumped in the boat, not stopping until they'd leapt off into the river. The water looked fine. I wanted to get wet, to get my costume soaking wet, to peel it off and let it float down the river. The kids cheered as I drew near, aiming my lens.

The mythical bridge intervened. I could almost see the steely, skeletal structure superimposed in my viewfinder, children poised on girders and cables as if inside giant jaws, falling, arms akimbo, striking the water splash after spiky splash. Disturbed, I was glad that the bridge would not be built here.

Again, something made me turn my head. Diabelle, observing me from down the bank, but no. She only looked like Diabelle, with the same lanky limbs and slender jaw, the same almond eyes and wide brow, but with something different, too. I lifted my camera, clicked. A little girl came into view to lean in against her skirt.

Picking my way along the riverside, I was grateful for my sensible sandals. The woman, I saw, was barefoot. Her hair, though, was immaculately tressed in the style that Mpovi had tried on me; instead of drooping, her antennae stood out stiffly, radiating like a crown.

"*Bonjour.*" I used French instinctively.

"*Bonjour.*"

"I came to see the *bac,*" I explained, without bothering to introduce myself; everyone knew who I was. "Were you at the *source?*"

She shook her head, pointing behind her at a miniature settlement of a few mud houses, a sort of annex to Lufwidi, a tiny satellite. Then she pointed at her little girl, dressed charmingly in a yellow shift and anklets and black patent leather pumps. I didn't know what she meant. "Is that where you live?" I asked.

She straightened. "I'm from Kimpiri."

"Kimpiri!" Cheered by the mere mention of that city's name, I had, indeed, been in the bush too long.

"My husband works there."

"Did he come to the wedding, too?"

She scowled slightly, as Diabelle did when I asked her to be quiet in class. "No, he had to work."

For once I was asking the questions, partly because I identified with this woman from the city, partly because something about her didn't quite add up. "Do you know the bride?"

"She's my sister."

"And Diabelle, also? You look just like her."

She beamed proudly. Her teeth were straight and large, her lips violet.

"How do you like the village?" I pressed. "Compared to Kimpiri?"

"Kimpiri is better," she said promptly. "There's more to do, elec-

tricity, films. You can go around when you want. You can buy anything in the market." She spoke wistfully of her husband's car and
the hair salons, as if she'd been away for months.

"Was you hair tressed in a salon?"

She nodded vigorously; still the spikes didn't waver.

"Mine is crazy." We laughed, and she pinched one of my sagging
braids.

"Who did this?" she demanded abruptly, as if someone had
caused me harm.

"The *Préfet* Mpembe's wife, at Mampungu."

"Mpovi." She said the name neutrally. "She was one of my classmates."

I wondered if they'd been friends.

"You know," she said, "it might work in another style."
Absentmindedly, fingering her daughter's sleek braids, she was still
studying my hair.

"No." Having learned my lesson, I didn't fudge. "Next time I'll
do my hair myself."

The sun was getting low, and the bugs were bad here by the
water, causing me to smack and wave as we spoke of how to travel
to Kimpiri. The train, she said, was best: slow, but you sat comfortably instead of standing jammed like cattle in an overloaded
camion. I stored this information for the trip I was planning for the
school break next week.

Fed up with the mosquitos, we started back, the little girl skipping ahead. "So what happens at this wedding? When does it
begin?"

"After dark. The drums begin and we listen to the chief speak,
and then we dance." She spoke calmly, as if describing the most
mundane routine. Probably she found the village as boring as I.
She struck me as advanced, not the type to spend hours each day
preparing food. For some reason I pictured her not among women,
but men.

"Why didn't you go to the *source* with your sisters?"

She shrugged vaguely.

A flamboyant whistle sounded, and we looked up toward
Diabelle strutting in the middle of the road, a black-and-gold pea-
cock. "Miss!"

Rather than meet us at the bottom of the hill, she posted herself at the village edge, waving us on up, equal to the stares of everybody drinking palm wine at the village bar. She was a spectacle, born to turn heads, one of those people who can make a roomful of strangers revolve around them in ten seconds flat.

My companion balked, and I assumed she was ashamed. I hung back as well.

"She is ready with your food." She wanted me to go.

"Aren't you hungry?"

Sternly, she shook her head, no.

"Will you have a glass with me later?"

This was acceptable; happily, she nodded.

"What's your name, then?" I asked.

"Catherine."

"Not a Tambalan name?"

"Catherine."

The Western name made a difference. Tambalan names were pure rhythm, meaningless to my foreign ears despite the fact that most were common nouns: Strength, Intelligence, Beauty, Love—words I never understood when being introduced. "Catherine," however, was packed with associations, with people from my past, with characters from movies, books. It was a name that felt at home on my tongue.

I wasn't hungry but I supposed I ought to eat. I had no choice, really; refusing food was rude. Diabelle led me back to the two chairs planted vacantly outside the green door. Across the way, the peanut women waved and sent Emolo over with a covered dish. Earlier, I'd managed to extract myself from their tedious midst by pleading the need for a bathroom, and they'd sent me off to the latrine with a child guide. Now children with covered dishes were being dispatched to the palm wine bar. Emolo carried mine toward me carefully, hardly looking up, his long lashes dense against his cheeks as he set it on a chair. From his pocket he pulled a spoon, which he placed alongside the plate. Then he turned to me.

"Thank you." I expected him to bring another plate for Diabelle, but he held his ground. We all held our ground.

"Go ahead." Diabelle motioned to a basin of water I hadn't noticed below the chair. I dipped my hands and wiped them dry. She motioned to the other chair. "Sit and eat."

"Isn't there a chair for you?"

As before, she took this as an unexpected perk, and shrugged bashfully.

"Aren't you going to eat?" I insisted.

No, she would not, trained in the custom of serving dignitaries first, of giving them first crack at the food before it ran out. Aware that the cooks in the distance had gathered to watch, I felt like the lion in a zoo at feeding time.

Diabelle settled on the stool brought by Emolo, and we both traced his ramble back across the plaza.

"But Miss, why were you working with those women?"

"I was bored. I wanted something to do. And I want to learn about village life."

"Yes, but you can ask me. You don't have to work like that. You're a guest, you shouldn't be sitting on the ground."

"Why not?"

I removed the upside-down plate that functioned as a lid, and found the bowl full to the rim with a yellow-gray pudding floating nuggets of meat. Peanut stew with goat. Since I had told them that I didn't like *fou fou,* there was nothing on the side.

"It's their job to cook for you," Diabelle explained as I took a bite, "you shouldn't do their work." But she brightened, nodding at the stew. "This is the village specialty."

"It's spicy." My mouth was on fire.

"Too spicy?" Ready to cause trouble, she shot a dark look toward the anxious cooks.

"No, fine. Very good." I took another bite, and gestured thumbs up to my audience. I could hear their pleased laughter, and applied myself, determined to make a dent. All I could taste was *pili pili,* the red pepper, and the musty palm oil. I never would have guessed that the powerful flavor of peanuts could be disguised, but *pili pili* did the trick. I returned to the thread of our conversation. "But I always sit with the women at Mpovi's."

"Even with Mpovi, you don't have to act like that. Miss, *vous êtes professeur, célibataire. Très intelligente.*"

She said "single" as if it were a plus; this was the sort of compliment I liked. My African dress might be beautiful, but intelligence was the stuff I wanted to strut. My throat flared; the perspiration at my temples felt like blood. I took another bite.

Meanwhile, Diabelle focused on the low sky, on nothing, listening. I heard it, too: the *camionnette*.

"They're coming back," she said.

"Who's coming this time?"

"I don't know. The other teachers, I think, except for Citizen Bwadi. He came already on his *moto*. And the Doctor brought his car. This time Tembo may have stopped in different villages."

"Did the *Préfet* donate the school truck?"

"Him? But he can't encourage us. He's afraid we'll all get into trouble and quit school. No, not him. My father had to rent the truck."

"Did I meet your father, too, when I arrived?" I could not quite believe I'd be able to forget this do-it-yourself sorcerer who supposedly could curse his kin, but I'd felt so woozy right then. "I have a wedding contribution to give him. Mpovi said he gets the gifts?"

"Ehi. I'll introduce you at the *boîte.*" She inclined her head in the direction of the palm wine bar, which had begun to emit filaments of sound, bloated scratches, horns. "Listen!"

"It's the radio?"

"A record player."

"On batteries?"

She nodded, resigned. "There's no electricity."

After I took a few more bites, the truck roared into view, its bumper and front grill cresting the hill. Nobody was singing. Diabelle snatched the extra plate and clapped it atop my food. Lumbering past, the vehicle kicked up slight puffs of dust. I was happy to glimpse Lukau and Shamavu, my teacher pals, perched in the back. Bwadi had yet to show his face.

"Miss, in Paris I'm going to study fashion design," Diabelle declared, scanning my tailored top.

"Oh, do you sew?"

"I made this. I took it to sew on my neighbor's machine."

I pictured her pumping the pedal of an antique, the sort my own seamstress had used. Diabelle's *pagne* had panache: the top understated with classic, simple lines, the back cut low. I wasn't familiar enough with Tambalan trends, though, to tell the outmoded from the chic. Possibly my frilly straps and waist came off as frumpy. I made noises of approval, then asked her opinion of my style.

"It's good, very nice. But I'll make you one like mine." She moved to uncover my dinner.

"No," I stopped her, "I've finished. It's for the others"—for whoever wanted my leftovers.

"Next time you go to Kimpiri," she said, "buy the best cloth, the Dutch wax. Then I'll make you beautiful."

Evidently Mpovi had not succeeded.

"In Paris I'll learn to sew jeans, too. I'm not going to be like Mpovi when I marry."

"Who will you be like?" I thought of Catherine.

"Like you!"

"But I'm not married."

"No." She considered, her pursed mouth lengthening her brown cheeks. "You will marry a white man, won't you?"

"I don't know."

"I want to marry a white man, too."

I laughed. "Why?"

"Then he can take me to America."

"Maybe." I shouldn't encourage her, I knew. Bwadi's phrase unraveled in my brain: *America would eat them up.*

"I want to be like you, living in different places. Have you lived in Paris?"

"No. I've been there."

"I'm not going to live like Mpovi."

"No, you're going abroad."

"Or even if not, I'll live in Kimpiri and have a profession." She was serious. "Mpovi follows the old ways. I think her life must be very dull."

"You're going to be like Catherine."

"Catherine?" She looked puzzled.

"Your sister from Kimpiri. The one I was with at the *bac.* She looks just like you."

"Ehi, Bumfwidi!" Diabelle was amused, shaking her head. "She told you 'Catherine?' She tells many stories. But it's true that she lives in Kimpiri."

"Is she your sister?"

"Yes. But some people don't like her here. These villagers are so old fashioned! She stays with the Angolan refugees."

"There are Angolan refugees?"

She motioned angularly with her chin. "In that compound by the river. They build their own houses."

I recalled the lonely huts. "How many are there? Will they come to the wedding?"

"Just a few families. They're everywhere in Tambala, their own country is no good. Citizen Bwadi is Angolan," she filled me in.

"I know. Did he grow up here?"

"Not in Lufwidi." Slumping, she stared hard at our long shadows. "My sister, Bumfwidi, she has many problems in her life. She loved one man and went with him to Kimpiri. But then he left her alone, and she didn't want to return here, so she stayed in Kimpiri. Her only way to leave Lufwidi was to go with this man. Now she's been there a few years and she sees many men, and she can live that way. The old villagers here say she's been cursed."

This sister seemed more influential to Diabelle than today's bride, and I wondered if her escape to the city did not figure in the father's fears for Diabelle. Mpovi had not told me all. Clearly there was a history to this father's despair.

"Who would put a curse on her?" I allowed myself to probe.

Diabelle pursed her lips in noisy contempt. "They say anyone who talks to her will get bad luck, and they scream at her to go away."

"Mpovi told me a story about a curse. She told me that your father threatened to put a curse on you."

Diabelle's eyes narrowed. Silence flared. I didn't know what to say.

"I'm not like them," she blurted then, righteously taut. "I told you, I'm going to be like you."

"So it's true? What Mpovi said?"

"I don't know what she said. My father would rather have me barren than pregnant too soon. He says that if I'm bad, I'll never have children. He wants me frightened, he wants a good bride-price. He's getting almost nothing now for Allouette."

"The bride?"

"You met her at the truck when we arrived. You forgot already."

"And what about your mother?"

"You met her, too."

"I mean, what does she think?"

Diabelle softened, shoulders folding forward. "It's she who invited Bumfwidi back for the wedding. She loves us no matter what; she has confidence in me. But my father is in charge. Since I'm the last daughter in school, I'm his last hope. I must bring the price of an educated bride."

"You will."

"People worry that I'll have problems like Bumfwidi. But," she lowered her voice, "now I know about birth control, and I won't have to run away. I won't go to Kimpiri until I'm married, and then I'll go to the university."

"'Catherine,'" I mused. "Why do you think she told me 'Catherine'?"

"Bumfwidi is a village name. I would change, too. My name isn't a real village name," she said proudly.

"'Diabelle?' It sounds Kikongo, like Diakubama, or Ditumweni."

"No, my mother made it up. I was her jewel, so *'diamant.'* I was a beautiful baby, so 'belle.' Together, *'Diabelle.'*"

"Or *diable,*" I teased.

"No, no, not *'diable.'* Everyone tells me that. But I'm not a devil."

"And the ones who are superstitious don't worry about that name?"

"Because devils are only in the white church. The old people worry about ancestors, not devils. They don't use that word. They use *nkisi* and *ngando.*"

"*Ngando?*"

"*Ngando* is the crocodile that becomes human long enough to lure people into the water to drown. It steals children."

"What about the cross, then? Christianity must have been here a long time."

She glanced blankly at the monumental cross. The sun, disappearing, cast a spell of hesitation. A goat and her two kids, ambling through the plaza, gradually halted, blinking in the red melodrama. The tinny music had stopped.

"That's from a battle," Diabelle said thoughtfully, "the battle for this land. I'll ask my father to tell you the tale; he keeps all the stories from the past."

The cross seemed more a symbol of an epoch than of faith. "Poor Bumfwidi," I said, thinking of her banished, stuck between eras, the future and the past.

"Poor Allouette. I would rather have problems in the city than live in the village all my life."

"Allouette won't go to Kimpiri?"

"Not with this man. He's a farmer, a backward boy. But she wouldn't know what to do in Kimpiri."

"Then she'll be happy here."

"Because she's a stupid girl." Disgusted, Diabelle smacked her lips. "I'm going to be smart, Miss." Her voice was low, full of resolution. She looked up. "You're not lonely?"

"No." Was I?

"You must find a man, Miss."

This advice always made me smile, making loneliness seem trivial, a sordid cliché.

"Not to marry," she clarified, "but for company. You must be lonely at night."

Of course, she was right. Embarrassed, I said nothing.

"And don't you know a white man I can meet?" Illogical, sincere, she really was a teenager at heart. "Will you introduce me?"

I gave up. "So do we trade, a black man for a white?"

She thought it was a fine idea.

"Miss! You become Tambalan!"

I recognized Shamavu's excited voice within the buzz and murmur at the palm wine bar. Waving blindly toward the murky depths of the crowd, I trusted that the kind dusk softened the horror of my hair. A few older *petits* had begun lighting gas lamps, but for the moment even Diabelle was at a loss, flinching impatiently as she scanned the shadows for her papa.

"There!" Suddenly she plunged ahead, dragging me by the arm, dodging populated tables, protruding chairs, sprawled legs. I liked this place, this roofless commingling of sweet breath and sweat and camaraderie. I liked the license and promise of night.

Three men wedged into a corner watched us approach; I recognized Tembo from the truck. Flanking him were two delicate-looking elders, white-haired, spare. Tembo allied himself, it seemed, with the infirm: the old woman and the little tots with whom I'd shared his front seat, these wizened fellows on the bench. Yet as I neared I saw that the one on the left was not nearly so ancient as I'd thought; ruggedly taut, his face expressed shrewd concern; greeting me, his handshake was spry.

"Mon papa," Diabelle explained as he elegantly sank back into his seat. He was sporting a Mankanzu suit, a style made popular by the president. The African answer to the business suit, it consisted of slacks and a short-sleeved jacket whose nehru collar negated the need for ties. He looked like nobody's fool.

"Pour les mariés," I said, pressing my envelope of twenty kulunas into his leathery palm. With an efficient bow, he tucked the gift into a bulging jacket pocket, and I wondered if the bride and groom would see a cent.

The third of the trio turned out to be the village chief, and he was genuinely old, furrowed and askew with arthritis. I was hoping that Diabelle would squish with me onto the bench, but after mumbling a few phrases in Kikongo, she excused herself, slinking away, and I was on my own. Accepting a glass of palm wine, I gently edged in beside the Chief. Serenely, he steadied his glass on his knee. Hunched over his drink so that his bald head protruded from his neck, he brought to mind a dignified turtle.

"He's the one who can give you the story of the cross," Tembo said to me in French, inclining his head toward Diabelle's father, who leaned forward to address me around Tembo's girth.

He launched right into what sounded like a memorized spiel, although much of the language escaped me. He mixed a lot of Kikongo with his French, but I thought I grasped the general scenario. A tribal war had taken place in ancient times. The Portuguese—I'd been right about the cannon—had supplied the local people with weapons and a god, and when the invaders came over the hill the unearthly booming of the cannon and its plumes of smoke appeared to them as angry ancestors in the sky. Frightened at this omen from the afterworld, the enemies ran away. Understandably, then, in honor of their miraculous victory, the Lufwidians had erected this cross.

"How long has it been there?"

"A long, long time."

For an official historian, the man was short on facts and figures. But then, unlike Diabelle, he'd probably been deprived of school. He did possess the quiet confidence of an intelligent soul. Braininess in a provincial context, I supposed, might erupt into curses and decrees; after all, wasn't superstition simply a mind game?

"Are you the only person who can tell the story?" I asked, sure that I would have understood more of Tembo's French.

It seemed, however, so, and the performance was *fini*. Refusing me an encore, Diabelle's father sat back against the wall, receding behind Tembo's gut, and I was left to wonder: could those crossed wood beams really have survived since the sixteenth century, when the Portuguese were busy spreading religion and guns? Nothing, I believed, could weather the tropics that long.

"And the *bac,* buried there in the ground," I aimed toward my chronicler, "is there a story for that?"

"That one," he sighed forward, "is finished."

We sipped our palm wine thoughtfully, and I was savoring the acerbic fizz when a drum began a lazy beat.

Diabelle's father downed what remained in his glass. "It's time." Jarringly, he stood.

"The ceremony's going to begin?"

"Soon, soon," he frowned impatiently. He was apparently in charge. Tembo and the Chief rose as well, Tembo apologizing profusely, fussing at the thought of me abandoned alone.

"My friends from Mampungu are here," I reassured him, rising, myself. "I'll go and sit with them."

"Over here, Miss!" From across the room, Shamavu's voice came to my rescue. Extricating myself from the departing trio, I bumped and squeezed myself toward the vaguely undulating arm.

At his table, one chair was free, an empty glass waiting. I identified the wispy form of Lukau hooked at Shamavu's side, and the lacy froth of the Doctor's white hair anchored to wire rim spectacles. I started shaking hands.

"You are Tambalan, Miss!"

"You are beautiful!"

"And do you know Nurse Pinzi?" the Doctor asked.

"Ehi, I know his handwriting," I joked, as I rattled, rather than shook, the nurse's spidery hand. I knew him as an entity, the power invoked when kids were missing from class. "Nurse Pinzi," the others would cover, "she went to see Nurse Pinzi, she's sick." Sometimes I saw the proof of Pinzi's careful printing on an excuse slip, sometimes not. I didn't bother to keep track.

"*Bonsoir,*" he said feebly. He was the size of a twelve year old, and looked in the darkness as if he had no hair, although his voice and skin were young.

"May I sit?" I didn't see Bwadi.

Shamavu hurried to pull out the vacant chair, to offer me palm wine. He was happy-go-lucky; he'd graduated recently from the secondary school and had not yet got to university, but teachers were in short supply, so he'd been hired to teach math. He reminded me of a puppy with his large head and large, soft hands, and with the way he pounced.

"I've been hoping," the Doctor cleared his throat, "to share some news with you." He enunciated perfectly, his French careful and melodious, his tone businesslike. I regretted my kooky braids.

"It's about a project. Finally I have received funding for family planning."

I flinched, suspicious. "Really? From whom?"

"From my government. So I'm ready to begin. The first stage will be a survey here around Mampungu, and another in Kimpiri, to discover the attitudes toward birth control. We're going to see what traditional methods already are in use, and which modern ones might be acceptable. Nurse Pinzi's dispensary at Mampungu will be one of the headquarters."

If he'd heard anything about my own proselytising, he didn't let on. This project was official, his presentation polished, refined from months—years, perhaps—of drumming up funds. I recalled him at my arrival dinner at the *Préfet's,* how he'd spoken of his visits to the States for medical conventions, and of his years in Switzerland at school. He had impressed me then with his commitment to raise revenue for repairs on the hydroelectric generator, to restore light.

"Is this anything to do with fixing the electricity?"

"Ehi, no, but that, too, may come. There is so much we need to do."

"If I can help at all," I offered, "please let me know."

"Yes, thank you. But I'm sure you're very busy at the school."

"Not so busy." I thought of my idle hours at Mpovi's, of the other teachers' extracurricular fields.

"As I said, then," the Doctor launched forth, "since I'll be at the Kimpiri office, Pinzi's clinic will be the rural station; we'll collect questionnaires there. My interviewers must all be local women who speak Kikongo, you understand, but you might help to code the questionnaires. That's the first stage, which will continue until next year, when we will begin to make the birth control devices available."

"Wonderful," I gushed. I had no idea what it meant to code a questionnaire, but I was eager to give it a try. Instead of vegetating afternoons at Mpovi's, I would Code Questionnaires.

The Doctor went on a bit and then sat back, smiling abstractedly. He was happy, I was happy, we were all happy. A beam of light looped onto the wood table, and footsteps stopped behind me. Bwadi appeared, lifting a storm lamp to hang from a branch.

"How nice, a lamp. Oh," I realized, "I took your chair." I wanted, suddenly, to get out of reach of the lamplight, to hide my silly tresses. Bwadi's broad afro mushroomed in the shadows; I cringed. I could almost feel him trying to figure me out. My braids felt huge and awkward and alive. I began to escape.

"No, no, I'll get another," he said gallantly, and disappeared.

Damn, I thought, I've scared him off. Rays of light oscillated as the lamp rocked itself still. The dull thud of the single drum pulsed.

"Is this a special drum?" I addressed the table at large.

Shamavu jerked to attention. "The tam tam. The talking drum. It calls for people from all over to come to the wedding."

"From other villages?"

"Sure. There are several that can hear."

"It's late, isn't it, for people to start walking now?"

"Ehi, of course. Most people have already arrived by *camion-nette*. Earlier, this morning, he played the drum to tell everybody to get ready for the truck."

"What's he saying now?"

Everyone wrinkled their foreheads, listening. No one ventured a guess.

"So, you mean, he can play a sound that people understand as *camionnette?*"

They all attested to this fact.

"It's slow," I observed. The drums across the lagoon in Conakry had been frenetic, syncopated. These echoing thuds must be like Kikongo on the scale of the BBC news programs in Special English, excruciatingly clear. Patiently, I waited for someone to provide a translation, and something glinting on Pinzi's chest caught my eye: a stethoscope, draped from his neck as if forgotten, like an airplane passenger's plastic earphones. Absurdly, I pictured Pinzi tuned in to a movie screen.

"Soon," the Doctor sighed contentedly, "this will be a modern village. This bridge that's coming will bring electricity, commerce, perhaps telephones. From the road, at night, people far, far away will see the lights shining here, like stars in the night. It will be beautiful. Like the United States. But tell me," he roused himself, clearing his throat, "I would like to know about your country. Three things." Even his casual conversation had to be meticulously organized. "There are three things in the United States which I do not understand."

"There are many which I do not."

"Assassination." The drum thumped. "And the custom in nightclubs of women with no clothes. And suicide. These three things I do not understand."

"I don't understand those clubs, either," I laughed.

"Some people took me to a club in Washington and the women danced with their breasts bare. All the men were really enjoying this."

"Maybe because my people think sex is evil. Since they're always hiding, they never get to look at each other, and so the men think naked women are very exciting. But that's a question you must ask an American man." I heard Bwadi approaching with a chair.

"Where do you keep disappearing to?" Lukau nagged.

"I was talking to a friend."

I fingered a braid self-consciously, tugging at the string. Somebody tossed Bwadi a fresh glass.

"And suicide," the Doctor persisted. "Why don't people in your country want to live?"

"They're crazy, I guess. They get so lonely and depressed, they can't imagine happiness and can't stand the way they feel."

"But why?"

I stopped, figuring. Everyone waited.

"Has anyone you know committed suicide?" Shamavu wondered.

"No. It's a form of mental illness, I think, the depression that causes suicide. They say it's genetic. They say it's maybe not enough sun."

The Doctor blinked. This was evidently news to him.

"It's a theory. The lack of sun does something to the brain. But," I ventured, "I think it's also cultural. The u.s. is a hard country to be happy in. People worry so much about money, and being independent. We're all so individualistic that ultimately we don't care enough about each other. We're too competitive." I glanced at Bwadi, who had slouched into his chair, arms resting on the table. Raising his eyebrows, he half shrugged, turning the hand closest to me palm up. It was a sexy move.

"And assassination," the Doctor cut in, backtracking to point one.

"Assassination." I took my eyes off Bwadi. "You mean when somebody kills a president, like Kennedy?" Kennedy was a hero in Africa.

"Yes." The Doctor's forefinger pounced on the table as if to trap a bug. "I can't understand why. In Tambala, in Africa everywhere, presidents are murdered by men who want to take their place. We call that *coup d'état*. But in the United States that is not the reason. Why did that man shoot Kennedy?"

"He was crazy, too."

Pinzi giggled.

"It was a conspiracy," Bwadi contradicted languidly.

"No, no," the Doctor snapped. "Nobody believes that now. There was a congressional investigation."

"The Warren Commission was controlled by the cia, and so were the journalists, the White House, everyone involved. Kennedy, himself, would not cooperate. So you see, it was a sort of *coup d'état*."

"But did the government change afterward?" Lukau challenged.

"Johnson became president," I helped Bwadi out. I did not entirely disagree with him.

"The change was provided for in the American Constitution, of course," Bwadi said. "The vice president takes office in any emergency. So structurally, nothing changed. But then Johnson was conveniently persuaded to escalate the war in Vietnam. Ask Nicole."

It was a pleasure to be addressed, for once, without the title, "Miss." Just to keep the ball airborne, I amiably countered, "It was Kennedy who landed us in Vietnam in the first place."

"Kennedy saw his mistake, though, and the CIA interfered precisely when he threatened to let Vietnam go."

The Doctor snorted, but chose not to disagree. I sensed that he was scoping Bwadi out, listening for something else. He seemed to have abandoned any hope of psychological insight into assassination from me.

"And why," fretted Shamavu, "would the CIA want this war in Vietnam?"

"The CIA represents the military industry, the arms barons who manufacture the weapons the government buys. The Cold War has been very profitable for the United States."

Bwadi stopped short of declaiming the CIA arms pouring through our very watershed into Angola, and I wondered whom he didn't trust, who might possibly report him as subversive to the FIT. It was the first time I'd been acutely aware of a conversation's heart cut out, of eyes aimlessly downcast, of drinks held too eagerly to lips. Something spidered up my spine, and the spies and trouble in Tambala seemed suddenly real.

"If people are so rich in the United States," Shamavu recouped, "why are they so unhappy and insane?"

We were back to the Doctor's original question, one Bwadi did not care to field. I, however, was no good to them at all.

"I wish I knew. People want too much. With so many possibilities, they expect their lives to be perfect, and feel cheated or guilty when they're not. It's so easy to feel you should have done something else. Because of this independence, you see—if you're responsible for yourself, then when things go wrong you're also the one to blame. But I can't say. Our society is complicated, with many problems. Our families are weak. We've forgotten how to behave."

"Yes," observed the Doctor. "The old people live in buildings separate from everybody else, in institutions not unlike jails."

"And children live far from their parents," I admitted.

"You think this makes them crazy," Lukau pressed.

"And other things. I don't know." Suddenly, I was sad. They seemed to notice, and we fell into another silence, more gentle than before. Bwadi tipped the bottle toward my glass and leaned in close.

The bride was plump and sullen, the groom distracted as they sat side by side, surrounded by a circle of people seated in the plaza. The drum had stopped and so we'd assembled, about a hundred of us, chairs in tow, for the official ceremony. I scrutinized the sluggish couple. This was the first I'd seen them together, and now it was too dark to use my camera. The moon cast gauzy shadows, the lamps dangling from thatch awnings and from branches, glittering like stars within reach. The bride wore a Western knee-length shift of floral polyester stretched taut in front by her pregnant belly. Her fiancé sported neatly belted slacks and a shirt with creases still fresh across the pockets. Colors were hard to tell, the silverized edges of straw, leaves, faces, and arms pooling into fluid black. It was the sort of contrast I strove for in photographs.

Elfin and grizzled, the Chief snuck into the arena and began to mug and sermonize, full of stylized authority. In the background, the couple floated disconnected, stony and surreal.

"He says they will work hard and prosper," translated the Doctor, who had kept me by his side. It sounded like a sentence of hard labor.

A good guest, I held my tongue, storing up questions. Each time the audience erupted in a choral response I jumped as if I'd missed a cue. "Life," I caught; "strength," "happiness." I couldn't tell whether they were invoking ancestors or Christian saints. The cross towered uninvolved at the other end of the village.

"The wife must obey the husband," the Doctor thought I ought to hear. "The husband must protect the wife."

This was what I hated about marriage, these prescriptive

assumptions. Even in the States, even these days, marriage reduced you to something standard and arbitrary. Women scrubbed, men mowed lawns, women shopped, men watched the game. Wife. Husband. Your world was warped into a dull sitcom and then, likely as not, you wound up divorced. The idea of marriage terrified me, for its predictability, as well as for, paradoxically, its pure unreliability. I couldn't see myself as a wife at all. Nevertheless, I was lonely; Diabelle had been right.

Across the arena, she was sitting dreamily among her bland sisters. Scanning, I spotted Bumfwidi-Catherine standing at the outskirts, gazing stoically across the tops of heads. The Chief finished his performance, and that was all. When the drum began a sharp tattoo, people rose and milled about, hanging onto their chairs as if to dance partners. Eventually the drum drew everybody near the drinking tables, and I found myself again seated with the Doctor, disappointed, the feeble beat putting me to sleep. I remembered how in Conakry, falling asleep in our imitation *paillotte* as drums fluttered and thumped across the lagoon, I had pictured myself dancing among the African children, mastering their steps as they clapped.

"Is that all?" I turned to the Doctor, and his drowsy eyes blinked politely. "They're officially married now?"

"Ehi. They registered already with the state."

"Was any religion involved?" I hadn't seen Mama Zola's husband, the amicable Pastor at Mampungu who'd exempted me from church. "I mean, in my tradition we usually want a priest or clergyman."

"I know your tradition," he smiled. "I was married at Mampungu. Here in the village everybody prays together, after the Chief."

"To the ancestors?"

"And to God, also."

"Has the ceremony changed, since you were a child?"

He folded his hands atop the table, concentrating, seeking accuracy. "No."

"But they wear Western clothes now."

"Ehi, that's true. But," he lifted a finger, "you'll see that the dance is the same as ever. This is the real beginning of the celebration."

"And the bride and groom," I couldn't help asking. "Why did

they look so sad?"

"*C'est normale.* Their lives will be different now. They have many adjustments to make. The girl already has the boy's baby. And her father is not pleased with the bride-price. Pregnant girls are a liability."

"If that's true, then wouldn't the man always want the woman pregnant, so he could pay less?"

"Ehi!" The Doctor chuckled. "Such accusations do occur. But few would choose the disgrace."

"Poor things. You can see they're not in love."

"Your marriage for love, that is a modern concept. This is what the Chief was explaining, that they will learn to love. You don't begin to love until you begin to build a family."

Was that how it worked? Where I came from, first came love, then family, then divorce, if you believed the statistics, and, as none of my friends had married yet, statistics were my major source. But some of their parents had divorced, and Mr. Baker, from Conakry, had left a strong imprint. How had Sadie, his daughter, my double, felt about leaving her father behind? Had she grown up eager to get married, to have kids? Would she eventually abandon a husband, and, like her mother, pick up her children, and leave? Divorce was splashed all over American culture, our heroes and heroines all traumatized by failed love.

"The Chief also explained the bride-price. For this girl the father received two goats, some *pagnes* for his wife, and palm wine. An educated girl might bring hundreds of kulunas in cash, a radio, a bike."

"Do they ever try not to have the child?"

"You mean abortion."

"Yes."

"An old story. It's against the law now, and it's always been against custom, but yes, it happens. Girls will use a traditional bark remedy, or an overdose of chloraquine, anything, really, that will serve as poison. It's very dangerous. Sometimes the girl dies along with the unborn."

"Doctors don't perform abortions?" Too late, I realized I was putting him on the spot.

"Our purpose is to keep people alive. And I'm a product of superstition as well as of science; we say that the wronged dead return to do harm." Both reasons seemed to carry equal weight.

Shamavu trotted up. "Miss, you're not dancing?"

A knot of people undulated near the drum. Sticky and stiff with sitting, I was ready to give it a try.

The dancers circled the single drummer, each pair of hands riding the hips of the person in front, each pair of feet shuffling right then left, right, left. Shamavu and I broke in, his touch at my waist respectful, and I held onto a wide woman I recognized from the cooking group. "Move your foot right," he instructed; "left!"

The rhythm was impossible to miss, flowing from the hips to shift my legs right and left along with everybody else's, as organic as a long breath divided into beats; we almost didn't need the drum. Palms pounding, face clenched in black concentration, the drummer worked the tam tam until, hypnotized, we catalyzed each other. People dropped out and back in; the chain never thinning as couples shared the drummer's limelight, dancing inside the circle for a few steps, changing partners, everybody dancing with each other. Dropping out, I sipped palm wine until dragged in again, braids flapping at my brow. Diabelle dropped in, dropped out, danced together with me in the center. I didn't see Catherine. I pulled in the Doctor; he pulled in a woman with a headcloth. I saw Lukau, I saw Bwadi, I did not see the newlyweds. Bwadi shimmied good-naturedly with the old woman who had been so frightened in the truck; on her own two feet, she grinned and swayed toothlessly, all her senses restored.

I rallied, I dipped, I watched Bwadi leave. Dragging in Emolo, Diabelle's little brother, and then gargantuan Tembo, I anticipated all the while Bwadi's corrective touch, his tug shifting me to his side, his hands tilting my hips, his persuasive breath at my neck. What I wanted, I realized, was a slippery moment off with him alone.

Drunk and honest, I saw all my wanting channeled toward his long-boned aplomb. Mpovi's premise that he was after me appealed and I swooned, giddy with the guarantee of imminent love. Around and around the drum I went, dallying, available for Bwadi's grasp, weathering the bubbles in rhythm each time the flinty strains of pop music clanged out from the record player to interrupt the drum, each time a palaver ensued between the hipper guests who yearned for a bit of jazz and the old folk who thought the drum should beat all night. I noticed the circle had shrunk.

The mood was now bordering on wild, the old men especially licentious and getting on my nerves, half humping whoever was in front as they shuffled left then right, grinding, the mamas shrieking with glee. This was not my idea of a romantic *pas de deux*. Giving up, I stepped out and kept on walking, detouring for cigarettes, annoyed. Where had Bwadi been? Probably he was off whispering politics with comrades in some scratchy field.

I headed for the *bac,* gulping the fresh air, greedy for space after the orgiastic spree, feeling my way with my feet—although the moonlight defined the dips and stones, bright enough for me to walk right onto the dock and then onto the ferry itself. The boat rocked subtly and I balanced, enjoying the motion under my heels. Carefully, then, I stepped along the platform where I'd seen the kids playing, and walked on out to the end. The water shone darkly and the wedding was a distant, rumbling glow. Across the river, the ribbon of land was straddled by two moons.

The Bakongo afterworld was underwater, I'd learned in a book the missionaries had left behind. The land of the dead mirrored the land of the living, the two like mountains opposed at the bases and separated by water. When the sun rose and set, the living and the dead exchanged day and night.

I was the fish out of water. The negative among the living black. Sinking down to perch myself inside the pontoon, I leaned over the edge and caught my shadow; in the night river I was as dark as any African. But my tresses drooped like an impostor's and the frills at my shoulders looked like wings. Bwadi had not been duped. I unfastened the safety pin at my waist and let it drop overboard to puncture the surface. My silhouette wrinkled, my limp tresses trembling. Pulling at a braid, I found the thread bound tight, the knot neatly buried, wrapped to last this night of dancing—and what else? Mpovi had misjudged.

I yanked harder at my hair, but it only hurt. I needed my Swiss army knife. My Swiss army knife! Who did I think I was, a Girl Scout on solo? Chiding myself, I leaned back and lit a cigarette. The pontoon curved spaciously around me, a private crib rocking. The moon in the sky was all I saw. I puffed and let the smoke slink out of my mouth.

When had I last set foot on a boat? My father had sailed for recreation, equipping himself at our boondock posts with the latest, fastest racing boats, competing in expatriate sailing clubs, usually winning. In Conakry once he sailed past our imitation *paillotte,* and I waved at him from the rocks. He was a quietly reckless man. Once I'd seen him capsize and wrestle the boat back upright, tacking off nonchalantly with his drenched cigarette still dripping from his lips.

We were all cartoons, we whites in Africa. Yet I wanted badly to talk to one of my own, a fellow fool with the wrong skin. Could pristine Paul have ever felt as bushwrecked as I? Perhaps I was wrong for development work, too malleable, flawed. Yet weren't all of us wrong in Africa, all of us Americans and our little wars?

The boat shifted, spurred, although I hadn't moved. The current was changing, I thought as I flicked an ash overboard, not looking to see it drop. I tried to think of what I still had left, here in Tambala. My mother's signet ring. My camera. This hot night sky in the water, these two moons burning face to face.

The rocking began again and didn't stop. It wasn't me. I sat up, riding, grasping a rail. Then I heard voices. Of course: the breathy pleading of sex. I took a last drag and flung away the cigarette, cussing my luck; I had stumbled onto lovers' lane. Why did clandestine lovers always choose vehicles? I decided not to stay and listen, and cautiously stood up, my knees giving with the oscillation. Who was intruding upon whom, here; who had found the *bac* first? But it didn't matter, I'd had enough of my own brooding. I meant to be discreet, to tiptoe past without a glance, but the commotion was distracting as I straddled the last pontoon, and my curiosity won out. Gilded by the moon, the exaggerated afro was unmistakable, the woman's antennae resilient as ever, the tense, metallic planes of her face and his shockingly sharp. My gaze or my steps disturbed their timing and Catherine's eyes swung open onto mine. Bwadi half saw me, his lids half open. I slid on past.

Part II: Underwater

5

À L'AMÉRICAINE

The next week at Mampungu the students went on strike. Although school strikes were a kind of institution in the country, up until now I'd heard only of teachers walking out. As an AfricEd volunteer I was supposed to be apolitical, to stick to the classroom no matter what, but I couldn't see much point in lecturing empty desks.

I'd returned Sunday morning from Lufwidi feeling foul and tyrannical and had spent the day devising spiteful quizzes that would eat the students up. I felt masticated myself, spit out. *"Indisposé!"* I'd shouted at Mpovi when she came to my door. Not much later, a *petit* appeared with a steaming cup of something that smelled like mold. "For the head," he quoted Mpovi, who believed I'd drunk too much. Out of sight, I poured it down my sink. I was already on chloraquine, drugged enough in my antimalarial haze. The church choir wailed till noon and then the school truck made its second run from Lufwidi; I never did hear the tinny dribble of Bwadi's motorized bike. I hoped he had a flat.

Monday's exalted prank took me by surprise. Evidently others had been tipped off Sunday while I dozed and sulked; when I showed up for work I found the school deserted, the teachers' lounge a void. Poised at a classroom window, I stared in at the portrait above the blackboard of the president in his leopard cap, at the static herd of desks. Kikongo graffiti sprawled across the walls. A door slammed. Footsteps ticked.

Pistache, the *Préfet de Discipline,* was marching up the hall, bristling with emergency and intent. For a moment I assumed he'd expelled all the kids.

"Where is everybody?" I demanded, sticking out my hand.

Head down, he caught it in an avid grip, shook loose. "They ran away."

"The students?"

"They left early for the holiday. They ran away yesterday, and took the train." He seemed impressed.

"Over a hundred students ran away together in broad daylight? Come on," I scoffed, dropping my briefcase, folding my arms.

"They are on strike," Pistache grunted defensively. "The *fou fou* was green."

This threw me for a loop. "Green?"

Nodding thickly, Pistache pressed his advantage. "A note was left in the refectory. And the cook admitted that the students were angry about the food. That he'd been using old flour."

"You mean we've been poisoning these kids?"

"They all left Sunday morning while the *camionnette* was in Lufwidi."

"And why didn't anyone tell me? I could have been halfway to the train station myself by now, if I'd known we'd already started the holiday." Running away did not seem a bad idea.

Ducking his head still further, Pistache appeared neckless. Shifting his weight guiltily, he sidled back. "The *Préfet* said you were sick, and shouldn't be disturbed."

"Sick? The whole school runs away and I'm the one who's sick?" I stalled then, jarred. Never before had I inspired such trepidation, not even in a kid, and here I was lording it over the administration's tough. What was he afraid of? All at once I saw that I was playing the white—the snotty boss, the imperialist pig. It did not feel good.

"You're right," I capitulated, studying my toes. "I was feeling sick. Maybe I got some of that green *fou fou.*"

When I looked up I met a gappy smile as he swelled forward, reassured.

123

"A strike against green *fou fou*," I marvelled. "What will they come up with next?"

Pistache frowned philosophically, trying to think, as I picked up my school bag.

"Well, I'm going on strike, too. I'm getting out of this crazy place. *Bon congé.*" Wishing him a happy holiday, I headed off to pack.

I could not bear another minute in Mampungu. Mpovi had adorned me in the emperor's clothes, and Bwadi had got the joke. Now even the students had let me down, robbing me of my job, rendering my fine intentions to befriend them a farce. Diabelle, doubtlessly in on the trick, hadn't said a thing. Of course, I was a teacher, allied with the *Préfet* and Pistache; what could she have said? Nevertheless, I felt left out—betrayed, bereft, yet airily autonomous, as well. I was cutting loose.

Sun hat flopping, water sloshing in my pack, I slunk off down the avenue, crookedly dodging the potholes and fissures in the red clay that was collapsing so ironically between the colonial rows of palms. Cries of "Miss Nicoli!" cascaded down the road, and whenever someone called out "Where are you going?" my response inspired ribbons of Kikongo, minor eruptions of alarm. "Kimpiri," is what I sang out. I was going to the city and I was going now.

Not until the last rusty roofs had given way to the patchwork of fields did I slacken my pace. Alone, I could relax to scan the landscape, to absorb the velvet hillsides pooling into inky forests along the gully streams. Birds flitted and sighed; distant human figures stooped and swayed, weeding. It was precisely the scene I'd imagined for years, the melodious life across the fence from my expatriate childhood, and I was in the picture now—yet I was simply passing through, traversing at a snail's pace this Africa that was not mine.

Even so, I was not ready to quit Africa cold. America's neon and steel and suburbia did not appeal; a mere American or two would do. Anticipating Paul's spotless hospitality in Nkisi, the American English we would speak, I fell into my long-strided American gait. Like a trekker nearing a mountain resort, I beamed, envisioning the amenities ahead—hamburgers and Marlboros at the American club downtown, my letters waiting from the States. Unexpectedly, then, this idyll collapsed, for, up ahead, there was Mpovi in her field, the familiar print of her *pagne* flashing in the distance like a vivid bug.

Her back to me, she was tilling soil, and I could have snuck on past, but something made me turn off toward her plot. I did not understand the woman, and I blamed her foolish costume for my failure with Bwadi, but I believed that she'd be genuinely hurt if I left without a word.

Turning at the sound of my footsteps, she smiled, teeth blooming. "Miss, you're wearing jeans!" was her first response.

Anticipating rough truck rides, grimy stops, I had, indeed, donned my Levis. "For travelling," I agreed, and offered my hand. The last she'd seen me I'd been sporting her couture, poised to leave for the wedding, and the mournful twang of her voice calling *"Vous êtes belle"* echoed in my mind. I wondered if she thought so now.

"You're better, then?" she frowned maternally as we shook. My hand came away studded with grit.

"It was your medicinal tea, I think. Thank you so much."

"And where are you going?" she monitored. Indeed, a bit of malice lingered from her change of heart at the *camionnette.*

"To Kimpiri. Pistache says we have no school."

"But how will you get there?"

"I told you, Mpovi. I'm walking to the train station. Like the students. I'm running away." Grinning, I extracted a bandana from my pocket to wipe my face, and glanced at my watch. It was 8:10.

"No, Miss. Wait until Thursday. The *Préfet* is taking the *camionnette* to buy food for the refectory. He can drop you at the train station then."

I'd had enough of Mpovi's advice. My pack shifted as I shrugged. "I'm ready to go today. And if I don't get started, I'm going to miss that train. Thanks for the offer, though."

Abrasively, she caught my arm as I turned, and I froze, confused by the concept of combat. But she merely wanted to know about Lufwidi. "Did you dance?"

"Yes, I danced. And everybody asked about my *pagne*. I met some-one you might know," I risked, not eager to divulge my failure with Bwadi. "Diabelle's sister, Bumfwidi. She said she was in your class."

"She came down from Kimpiri?" Mpovi snorted, then pursed her lips in distaste. "She's the worst of the family. Diabelle will be the same."

Something primal and indelible flavored Mpovi's grudge, some-thing personal and secret, some man. She hadn't mentioned this renegade sister when warning me of the father's curse; the omission evoked a history of rivalry and defeat, a chapter Mpovi wanted closed. I could see it all, Mpovi jilted by a high school boyfriend for jazzy Catherine—perhaps even the *Préfet* had been lured. My own face must have revealed a few hints to Mpovi, as well, for she tilted her head gently and guessed, "She kept the men busy all night."

I understood jealousy then as I never had before—the propri-etary anger, the shock of ambushed love. I understood Mpovi's bile. Even so, I, myself, felt more hostile toward Bwadi than toward Bumfwidi-Catherine, and less pity for Mpovi than for the city prostitute. What choice had she had? More than ever, I felt com-pelled to help shape a different sort of future for clever Diabelle.

I got away from Mpovi. My way out of Mampungu was not clear, however, for a few kilometers down the road a restless buzz materi-alized as an approaching motorbike, a milky blue missile jockeyed by a pom-pom of frizzy hair. There was nowhere to go.

Clinging defensively to my pack's shoulder straps, I advanced.

Bwadi lifted his chin cheerfully as he neared, one hand flapping up from the handlebars. "Ehi, Nicole!" he putted to a stop, engine running.

I had to shake his hand.

"*À l'Américaine!*" he indicated my Levis, approval in his eyes. "I was wondering if you would ever wear jeans. Where to?"

"Kimpiri."

"No classes this week?"

"The students are on strike. They've all run away."

Bwadi received this with a great guffaw. "And I rushed back for my 8:50 class!" His night of frolic, his motorized sprint had rendered him sportive. Why could I not have that effect? Either he didn't know or didn't care that I'd seen him in the *bac*. Assumably, he was returning fresh from another night with Bumfwidi-Catherine.

"Well, I'm trying to catch a train," I started off.

"On foot? *Non, non, c'est pas comme ça.*" Tinged with amusement, his voice lacked its teacherly edge. "I'll give you a lift. But I have to return home first to refill the tank; I'm too low to make it to the train station now. Hop up."

"Thanks but no thanks," I called, lengthening my stride.

"OK, I'll be back," Bwadi laughed as if he hadn't heard. With a belch of acceleration he shot away, while I, underpowered, lurched toward Kimpiri at a sorry trot.

Sweating, my fingers puffing with circulating blood, I marched. Already I'd turned from Mampungu's access road onto the primary track between the river and the asphalt highway known as the *grande route*. There I could easily hitchhike, but it was twice as far as the train station, and I needed to be off the road before the noonday heat. I meant to spurn Bwadi's ride. In my haste to escape him I was pacing myself poorly, overheating; I stopped in a scrawny patch of shade for my water tasting of plastic. Would he really show? The thought launched me stupidly forward; zipping and shouldering my pack, I cursed my clinging jeans. Then I balked. Why was I the one scrambling when he was the jerk? I should take advantage of his moped, I mused, commandeer it for my flight, let him ferry me about. If he did reappear, yes, I would travel in style.

Exhaling, I stretched out, and the walking began to feel therapeutic. The savannah billowed infinitely, luminous with green yearning for the gray, moist sky. It seemed now that I could walk all day. My breathing stayed deep and even; I thanked my resilient feet. Bwadi or no Bwadi, I would enjoy my vacation. I passed a village of mud huts, children playing in a pile of abandoned thatch, and then I heard the whine. A motor swelling, shrinking. Bwadi in my wake?

No; the sound escalated, accrued, took on the stampeding proportions of a chassis and four wheels. Hurtling toward me from behind was one of those clattering red trucks, chariot of the engineers. Hah! Delivered out of Bwadi's reach! I didn't care who was at the wheel; even an hour of Thompson's bigotry would be worth leaving Bwadi in the dust. I raised my hand and grinned.

I could not believe my luck. It was furry Mitch, begoggled in sunshades, slowing to a graceful stop. His face expanding happily, he ducked to unlatch the passenger door.

"Well, hello," he called as I ran up. "I was hoping our paths would cross. Where you headed?"

"Kimpiri, but I'll just ride as far as you're going. I can get a train at Mwindi, or hitch another ride on the highway." The English felt like heaven in my mouth. I climbed up.

"Nickie, right? We met at the Yank Tank. Or maybe I shouldn't bring that up. Anyway, name's Mitch." After clasping my hand in a short, neat chop, he snapped the truck into gear. "Perfect timing. I'm going to Kimpiri for supplies. I insist on driving the vaccines myself, to make sure they keep refrigerated. Kind of hot for walking, huh?"

My damp bandana was not much good for sopping up my sweat. "Look," I floundered, "I'm sorry about that night at the embassy bar. Your friend—"

"Hey, don't worry about it. Don't blame you a bit; he's a real Neanderthal. Guess you don't hold it against me, though, that I never did drop by? I really have been planning to."

I was holding onto the dashboard, braced for bends and ruts. "You haven't missed much. It's pretty quiet up there. I've been counting the days till this break." Regretfully, I detected desperation in my voice.

"This isn't your first trip back to Kimpiri, is it?" He gave a little sixties whoop. "Wild. And walking! What's wrong with that little green pickup I see tooling around? Don't they let you drive that?"

"Officially, I'm just a teacher. No special privileges. Besides, I was looking forward to the hike as much as anything. I hiked all over in the States."

"Oh, yeah? Where at?"

"The Sierras. Yosemite. The Blue Ridge Mountains, when I was a kid." At some point, it seemed, I had ceased to be a kid.

"Californian, huh? I spent some time down there. Damn beautiful country. Too crowded, though. I'm from Hawaii, most recently."

We sat there grinning as if about to break. Mitch was pale as plaster, his arms delicately scribbled with hair. I understood the Africans' impulse to touch.

"So you're the doctor with the engineers?" I managed.

"With Eckhart, Incorporated. So far they've sent me to Indonesia and Yemen. First time in Africa, though. And it's different. Man, is it different."

"Where, exactly, is your camp?"

"We call it Lufwidi, but we're actually eleven clicks downriver from the village proper. We always take the name of the nearest settlement."

"I was in Lufwidi last weekend, for a wedding ceremony," I exoticized, falling right into character as the intrepid adventurer, the jungle bunny, Jane.

"A wedding ceremony!" Mitch approved. "And I was cooped up watching flicks, babysitting a bunch of drunks."

"Movies?"

"Clint Eastwood videos taped stateside. I don't know why they send the crap."

"You show movies at your Lufwidi camp?" I hated Clint Eastwood, but right then anybody on film sounded good to me.

"Open to the public," he said casually, braking for a pedestrian. "Check it out."

"Tambalans watch?"

"No, no, I take that back. Private screenings in our little air-conditioned lounge. I was trying," he grimaced in my direction, mock exasperation in his voice, "to extend an invitation to you."

"How genteel. I'd be delighted," I surprised him. We flew into third gear.

"How about Thursday, then? We're throwing a little shindig for Thanksgiving at camp."

"I'll be in Kimpiri," I laughed, not about to cut my vacation short.

"Crud. I'm driving back down to Lufwidi tomorrow A.M. Then, the end of next week I'm going to Madagascar for R and R."

I swallowed my envy. "Maybe when you get back. How long is your trip?"

"Two weeks. Two weeks off every six months. Keeps up morale.

Where you staying in Kimpiri? We could do something tonight."

Mitch was nice. Upbeat, open, an open book; Bwadi, on the other hand, was a fragile tablet of angry hieroglyphics. There was nothing wrong with Mitch. Tonight, however, was logistically awkward.

"I'm staying in Nkisi, with another volunteer. Kind of out in the sticks," I admitted. "AfricEd only puts us up downtown for business or medical visits."

Miffed, he charged a puddle.

"Who's the redhead who drives like a maniac?" I changed the subject, recalling the Viking type who might or might not have witnessed my tressed hair. "He nearly ran us off the road on our way to Lufwidi Saturday."

Mitch gave a sort of feline exhalation: "Hshee! Vince, for sure. A real bozo. You wouldn't believe the guys I deal with, like overgrown kids. Last week he got drunk and fell out of a tree. Stick these guys in the bush and before you know it they've lost all traces of civilization."

"I don't know, I never heard of a Tambalan falling out of a tree drunk. There's a lot we can learn from these people. They're not all fucked up in the head like we are." Was this really true?

"Hey, I'm with you all the way." Conciliatory, Mitch rattled a pack of Marlboros in my direction and, after skimping along on raspy Gazelles, I was in no mood for restraint. Mitch punched the lighter in the dash.

"I want to tell you, I'm impressed," he insisted, elbows lifting earnestly as he cranked the wheel. "You've got to have guts, and an awful lot of good karma coming your way. Believe me, when I got drafted, I wished I had joined the Peace Corps."

"You were in Vietnam? Talk about roughing it."

"Company medic. Got out of there and did some bush doctoring in Hawaii for a while, then signed up with good old Eckhart, Incorporated. And here I am."

He clunked into low; we were jouncing into Mwindi. The train station looked deserted. Adrift amid a slew of empty tables nearby, a woman raised a beer bottle in greeting. Empereur, so close to home? No longer committed to Bwadi's bet, however, I relegated the beer I owed him to the realm of mistakes to be erased.

Mitch stuck his head outside in answer to the woman's salute. "Hey, Mama!" She was very dark and wore her *pagne* wrapped loosely, as if she'd been interrupted on her way to bathe. "The boys spend time here," he explained, retreating inside the cab, "when they want a quick beer."

"Better than Lufwidi palm wine, I guess. The villagers there don't seem to know much about the bridge."

"Nah, we keep out of their hair. We cut a new access direct to this road, so we don't have to drag our equipment through the villages. For entertainment we head down to Kilu."

Kilu. The port city to the south. At Kilu the river swung directly west toward the Atlantic and the opposite riverbank became Angolan soil. Something I had yet to see. "That's a drive, isn't it?"

"Hour and a half. Couple hours after dark. When they're over the limit I make them spend the night. Cute little city, though, dancing, nice clubs. Open to the public," he laughed, "for real." Glasses glinting darkly, he accelerated out of town.

Of course, I was glad he hadn't dropped in on me at Mampungu with his consort of thirsty boys. I'd been right to scare him off. But look at what I'd missed! While I'd been orbiting Mpovi, the whole country had been passing me by.

"You smoke?" From his pocket, Mitch was pulling a hand-rolled cigarette.

Evaluatively, I frowned. "Local stuff?"

"Congo gold, from those mountains over there." He waved whitely to the north, joint clamped thinly between his lips, then fiddled with the tape deck balanced between us on the seat, preparing for take-off. James Brown grunted forth, and Mitch lit up. We were cruising now, Mwindi shrinking at our backs, Mampungu a speck of history. I exulted at the thought of Bwadi wasting gas, limping into Mwindi on his lousy bike, listening to the sultry bargirl report me in the Eckhart truck. Probably he fucked her, too.

Plucking the joint from Mitch's fingers, I puffed. The smoke was dense and sweet, overripe. Silently I calculated the power of the rush, puffing again when Mitch passed back the cigarette, waving away the third offer. I was fine, just fine, floating along on James Brown funk, the breeze divine against my cheeks. Beside Mitch, insulated in our steel cocoon, I felt invincible, in love with Africa again.

"So what do you think of Africa?" I asked.

"Too damn hot."

I could appreciate that. I accepted another Marlboro.

"Good money, though. Guess that sounds pretty shallow to you," he added, humbly. "You're doing something special. Getting down to basics. Food, shelter, people helping each other. Getting rid of hang-ups."

I listened with interest, the American tobacco like silk against my throat. He reminded me of when I'd first arrived, idealistic, making allowances, simplifying. Full of Kennedyesque generalities infused with nothing more specific than good intentions. Help the people help themselves. What, exactly, did that mean?

"But tell me," Mitch said, jabbing the roach out the window, letting go. "What brought you here? Way out in the wilderness?"

The Question. "I was born in Africa." My stock answer sounded foolish now. Shouting above the cacophony of music and the muscular engine, I continued with the edited synopsis of my life: my birth in Cairo, how I'd moved a lot and lived sometimes in the States, how I'd always pined for Africa—and I realized that I was skirting the real question: why?

Mitch didn't seem to notice. Smiling benignly, he was chasing some hazy train of thought. With his round wire rims, his flattish profile, his beatific mane, he reminded me of John Lennon.

Before long, our road bisected the highway, and when we turned onto the tarmac we accelerated like gods. I was happy to be back in the twentieth century, speaking English, doing drugs. We talked shop, Mitch describing how he oversaw the health of the Eckhart team.

"Saturdays I open the clinic to the local staff. I see anyone who works for us, and their families. Hasn't gotten out of hand, so far. I'm not that strict about papers, and we've got medication to go around. I like to think I'm doing something constructive here."

"What do you treat, mostly, in the Tambalans?"

"Worms. Worms and malaria. They all have worms."

"Distribute any birth control?"

Caught off guard, he glanced at me, trying to gauge my drift. "Condoms. Everybody gets condoms. And my routine little pep talk on vd."

Condoms I could get, myself. "But the women, I mean. I'm just curious because I'm going to be helping with a family planning project at Mampungu. The first stage will survey what forms of birth control are already in use."

"Nah, I don't have any of that kind of stuff. Maybe we could coordinate, though," he perked up. "You could come out and meet with the ladies, or something."

"Right now we don't have anything yet, either, to distribute. And the survey sites will be picked at random. But in a year or so most of the women around us should have access through the local dispensaries."

"Those places! They don't even have running water! I was appalled!"

I sighed, as if at blame. "They have a long way to go."

"You're going to be here, then, in a year?"

"Who knows? Maybe there'll be a coup, and we'll all get thrown out."

Mitch chuckled. "Not unless the u-s-c-i-a wants a coup, will there be a coup, and this Mankanzu dude looks pretty tight with Washington, at the moment."

"As in, 'Let's build a bridge to Angola?'"

"Hey, not one inch of it will be on Angolan soil. We made good and sure to choose a site upriver where Tambala owns both sides. Somewhere it's not likely to get blown up."

"Good to know I'm not in the war zone."

"It's closer than you think, no kidding. 'Course, with this shitty infrastructure it's a week's bushwack to the border and then a river crossing to boot, but put in a good road and a bridge and you'd be cruising from Mampungu to Angola overnight."

"So this *is* a military project."

"Eckhart is a private company. But who knows who's pulling the strings? Fact is, there's arms caches all over our neighborhood. Our surveyors just ran into one. We're supposed to look the other way. Probably got dumps around your place, too."

"Better watch out," I said mischievously. "I might be CIA, myself."

"Wouldn't be any news to you, then," he smiled, knowing I was not. "It's all American goods."

Oh, how pleasant to be among one's own, to be able to interpret haircuts, slang, politics! To know where you stood. Even bellicose

Thompson was more understandable to me than Bwadi or Mpovi. "I've already been accused of that at my post," I confided. "Of being CIA."

Mitch was amused. "Without a car? Hardly. Without electricity? How would you wire your bugs? How would you entertain your informers?"

"I think I'm supposed to be the informer. I'm going to Kimpiri to be wined and dined by my case officer," I improvised.

"Well, then, there's not much hope for me. All I can offer is Clint Eastwood videos and pot."

I looked at him, and a sly silence evolved. Clearly, we were going to be friends. We were friends, now. This was not love at first sight, or animal magnetism, or anything like that. It simply made sense. Our claim to each other was as natural as that of old marrieds grown alike. Banished to the same tight corner of the bush, two lonely souls dangling amid a crew of rednecks and a Bantu clan, we recognized each other automatically. There was no urgency, no risk.

Silence surged and ebbed as we zoomed along, flipping tapes, smoking Mitch's Marlboros. We stopped for peanuts and Cokes and each took leaks further up the road, slipping off matter-of-factly behind trees. We slowed for towns, for sagging *camions,* hummed along the straightaways. We made fine time until we reached the outskirts of Kimpiri, where a roadblock backed up traffic. *Gendarmes* in ragged fatigues hopped up among the passengers in the truck bed ahead, gun muzzles pointing at everyone's feet.

"Shit," I breathed. "What about your dope?"

"These guys are always here," Mitch yawned reassuringly. "They just want their *matabish.* Got it all ready here in the compartment."

Matabish, "dash" in West Africa, graft. A little gift, grease for the palms, payola—this was how things got done. And if you did not comply, some trouble was invented, you got carted off to the police station until someone could come up with an even bigger sum to bail you out. Reaching in front of me to pop open the glove box, Mitch gaily extracted an unmarked envelope from which he pulled, one at a time, five crisp pastel notes in ten-kuluna denominations. All the Tambalan cash I'd seen before was dingy and torn, including my salary issued straight from the bank. I imagined the *gendarme* would be tickled pink.

When we pulled up, the soldier nuzzled the space at Mitch's window, gun pointing up, over the roof. Did it have bullets? Tambala's military was pathetic, manned with soldiers culled from the streets by force, boys literally kidnapped for conscription and underpaid, if at all. They resorted to roadblocks for fodder. Rumor had it that the government could not afford to keep bullets in supply, but who would challenge the long barrel of an m-16?

Accepting the *matabish,* the *gendarme* vacated the window, leaned back on his heels, nodding, counting, pocketing the money, then swooped forward to study me in the passenger's seat, the pack at my feet. I remained glumly respectful. Dropping away, he took a few swaggering steps, spun, waved us on.

"I'm glad I didn't bring my camera. If we'd been searched I probably would have kissed it good-bye."

"You kidding?" Mitch scoffed cheerfully. "They wouldn't dare. We're American!"

His arrogance made me nostalgic. My childhood in Africa had felt so charmed, so immune to threat. There had been danger all along—anti-American riots, *coups d'etat*—but all of that had remained across the fence. Under house arrest in Conakry, Benjamin and I had giggled at the soldiers through the gate. Even my parents hadn't understood. "You Americans were not courageous," reprimanded the Guinean ambassador, after the u.s. had been kicked out. "You were stupid." Later, he was called back to Guinea from Washington and shot.

I'd heard this story only recently from my father, as a kind of cautionary tale before I'd left. Now I wondered, was this lurking violence partly what I felt compelled to explore, this pulse driving the laughter and the dance?

Mitch was gazing ahead, confidently barging past the ramshackle houses, the tin roofs sloping above bleak tracts. Equipped with *matabish,* the crisp, frivolous bills like toy money to burn, we cowboyed into town.

Mitch and I roamed the market, tracking Paul. The footing was a challenge, beset with flapping chickens, squashed papaya, slop. Eager for a stroll, Mitch had abandoned his truck beside the school when we'd been pointed there. He needed a break there before tackling the traffic downtown, he said; he'd never seen this part of Kimpiri. We were in Nkisi, the sprawling fringe of the city, the residential *cité* where manioc and corn proliferated in front yards, where damp *pagnes* flapped like flags between power poles. We were at Paul's post.

The marketplace was dense with merchandise, the tables layered, the inventory dangling from above and spread on blankets on the ground, the peopled aisles swirling and pulsing with loud colors clashing, with dark limbs waving, figures darting, teeth glinting, tilting grins, with tomatoes and pepper bulging neon red, with the pale gold crystals of sugar sparkling, with rows of aluminum pots smeared with my reflection as if my face, too, had been mass-assembled, and with strips of sunglasses mirroring my distorted self. There were pieces of me everywhere.

In a polyphonic drumming of syllables, voices called out in Kikongo, "Come and buy!" Or, "Best buy here!" Meandering through the buzz of flies and children murmuring, I was seduced. I had to shop. Not for provisions, not for rice or beans or the new wick I needed for my Aladdin lamp—all that could wait—but for an impulse trinket, a flamboyant lark. I ogled the sunglasses, contriving a squint against the sun. Mitch grabbed a pair from the display and slid them against my face. The market darkened, polarized, the cookware robbed of its glint.

"Not those," he said, pulling them off.

I detached a pair with green rims, put them back. The *commerçant,* babbling behind his table, waved alternatives like a juggler preparing an act. I tried on, took off.

"Hah!" Mitch decided. "That's it!"

Snugly straddling my nose, the wraparound black frames had dropped a curtain of sudden dusk. I wagged my head for the *commerçant.* "You know Ray Charles?"

Inspired, he mimed a piano boogie. *"Aveugle,"* he beamed glarelessly.

"What'd he say?" Mitch did not speak French.

"'Blind.' He knows Ray Charles. Tambala knows Ray Charles!" Impressed, I dug fuzzily for my wallet, unable to see inside my pack. *"Combien?"*

My dirty cash smelled of mildew, felt like wet muslin. Peeling off a limp bill, I draped it across the merchant's palm. He didn't bat an eye. It was legal tender to him; the change he returned was equally droopy.

Sauntering off with Mitch, I scanned the newly dim crowd, dodging children wielding *baguettes,* on the lam. Then I spotted Paul ahead, his tennis hat and T-shirt religiously white, his shoulders vulnerably sloped. Rooted, he looked mesmerized, absorbed in the sales pitch of an elderly *commerçant* pointing out pieces among the collection of wares spread at their feet. From the distance I thought I recognized *objets d'art;* I recalled how in West Africa the tradermen would come laden to our door, and how I would encourage them to spread the blanket on the porch and unwrap the items one by one— a statuette, a mask, silken strips of kente cloth, ivory napkin holders carved like crocodiles. I liked best the brass gold weights from Ghana, the exquisite figurines of birds or men or abstract ciphers used in ancient times to weigh gold, and with my allowance I began a collection. Once I took my newest purchases into the pantry to ask our cook if he believed that they were really old; he laughed and laughed, amazed that I could spend what to him was a great deal of money on such paltry bits of junk. Later, however, all of my gold weights disappeared during one of my father's moves. He had moved while I was away at school in the States, and I arrived the next holiday in the new house to find my possessions transplanted into a designated room, the inventory complete with shoe boxes full of pencil stubs, rusted hair pins, rubber bands, gum wrappers, my drawers having been emptied indiscriminately by the embassy packers, Africans who could not identify a white person's litter. Even so, my precious gold weights had been pilfered, and my only consolation was that they must, indeed, have been worth something.

Mitch in tow, I picked my way toward Paul, and saw that despite a few mangled statuettes, this display was not of art but of fetishes— piles of flaking bark, twigs tied together, small bundles wrapped in leaves and hemp, mounds of brilliant powder. In one corner were strings of pills mounted in foil, a veritable cache of unidentified pharmaceuticals, of black market medicine.

Mitch whistled discreetly.

"Paul," I pulled up, touching his immaculate sleeve.

As if shaking off a fly, he jerked, fixated on the old man. But when the *commerçant* flashed me a toothless welcome, Paul turned his head and shifted gears.

"Nickie!" he suddenly exulted, colliding for a rickety hug.

I introduced Mitch.

"You're a medic? Here, get a load of this. Traditional medicine extraordinaire." He turned back to the *commerçant,* whose mouth continued to work silently, as if unable to turn off his spiel.

Mitch and I angled up close.

"What's that?" Mitch addressed the man in English, pointing at a ribbon of white pills. "Ask him what it treats, and how it should be taken," he nudged me familiarly in the back.

"Pour le fièvre," the man answered me. He had no name for the pills. You took four at the onset of a fever, and four a day until the fever stopped.

"Chloraquine," Mitch surmised, fingering a string, studying the tablets through plastic bubbles on the cards. "Not American, though. Wonder where he got them."

"Don't ask," instructed Paul in his World Traveller voice, the voice with the jaded edge that put tourists in their place. To ask would be accusatory; such pills came from clinic administrators who sold them for profit on the side.

Freeing the string of pills, Mitch pounced next on a cone of ocher dust, squatting, dipping close to sniff. "Ask about this stuff."

The old man expounded in a fluent blend of French and Kikongo; I understood some phrases: "pains in the back," "getting a baby," "to win football." Indicating sticks and packets, his hands revolved one around the other to mean "mix."

"What have you got for sleeping?" Paul interrupted in Kikongo.

I translated for Mitch; we exchanged a glance.

For sleeping, the *commerçant* reiterated the cure for winning football. Same succession of powders, same twigs. Same dose of tea, three times a day. For each ailment, in fact, the remedy sounded exactly the same.

Paul, his Kikongo better than mine, banged the heel of his hand against his head—an African gesture—and said a phrase I didn't know.

"All right, pal, come on," Mitch interceded, squeezing Paul's elbow. "You don't need any of this. What you need is a cold beer."

No wonder Mitch's patients were all drunks, if this was his method of counsel. Strangely docile under Mitch's touch, Paul obediently stepped away, thanking the *commerçant* over his shoulder, pointing toward a row of kiosks. Before following, I thanked the old man as well, superstitiously apologizing for having bought none of his cures.

"But he might have something I can use," Paul was insisting as I caught up.

"No, no, no," Mitch cajoled, corralling us into peeling chairs. "That guy didn't even know how to use those things. He was just pointing at random, a little of this, a little of that; he gave the same exact routine for different ailments." Fishing out one of his candy-colored bills, he flagged down the *patron.* "I'm buying. Hope the *frigo* isn't on the blink."

Suddenly exhausted, I wiped my face with my bedraggled bandana, guzzled bottled water from my pack. Paul slumped, digging for cigarettes, his single earring metallic, adamant. I was sure I'd never seen anybody so white, so ceramic. His pallor could be blamed on chloraquine, which was known to kill one's ability to tan, but there was something dispassionate about him, too—something bloodless and aloof. Uniformed in white, prophetic, cool, he evoked renunciations and vows. I could not imagine him in love— not with a woman, not even with a man. Wryly, he struck a match, an unlit Gazelle wobbling in his lips, and returned to the subject of cures. "Haven't you ever heard of a panacea?" he addressed Mitch.

"Not of one that worked." Mitch's pack of Marlboros victoriously landed on the table, solid as a royal flush.

"Seriously," Paul exhaled, "you can't deny that some of it's effective. This student of mine, for example, just managed a home abortion with some bark." Smoke expanded seraphically around his head.

I removed my new glasses, looked through them backwards. "And she's OK?"

"Returned to class, good as new. She was pretty sick for a few days, and the doctor here was pissed, but look, it worked!"

"Lucky she didn't abort herself in the process," Mitch grunted as the beer arrived. "Probably took some natural poison. Lucky she's alive."

I told Paul then about my prospects for family planning work. "That bark should show up in the survey as a traditional method."

Paul nodded vaguely, distracted by Mitch's vivid cash in the *patron*'s dubious hands. The man was examining each bill, turning it over, holding it up to the light. Finally pocketing the sum, he sullenly scuffed off.

"What's that, fresh from the mint?" Paul's interest fit; the spanking bills would certainly complete the effect of his blemishless attire.

"Don't ask," Mitch responded, worldly as Paul. "Fresh from the church, actually, good old Saint Ignatio's of Kimpiri. The Catholic exchange."

"You're paid in dollars," Paul reached for the beer, "of course."

"You get the black market rate at the church?" I quizzed Mitch.

"They've got the perfect scam. Close as you can get to legal, in this place."

"We're fucked," Paul lamented, aiming his cigarette at me. "We're paid in kulunas. Even with a pay raise each quarter, we still can't keep up with inflation." Swirling the splash of beer in the bottom of his glass, he added reflexively, "For the ancestors," and emptied the few drops onto the ground. This Tambalan ritual served nicely, I thought, to rinse out questionable cups. Filling his glass to the brim, he wondered, "How's your salary holding up?"

"Mine? I've hardly spent a thing. There's nothing to buy in Mampungu. I can lend you a few hundred, if you want." Volunteers were unspokenly pledged to spreading the wealth, helping colleagues in need. My own needs were minute—a kuluna here, a kuluna there for handfuls of produce, a few cigarettes. Jetaime's cash on wash day. A splurge on market fabric and the seamstress. What else was there to buy? For this trip I'd taken two bundles from the stash in my desk drawer, expecting to spend more this weekend than I had in a month.

Paul shrugged gratefully. "Amazing to think I could live on a dollar a day in India."

"Cheap beer there, huh?" Mitch kidded, his moustache frosted with foam.

"No beer at all. Hindus don't drink; Muslims either. Good deals on hash, though."

"As good as here?" intimated Mitch.

"I couldn't say. I pretty much had my fill in India. Talk about dabbling in unknown substances."

"Stick to weed, you're usually OK," muttered Mitch. "Look, what do you think you're doing here, anyway?" he tacked. "I thought you volunteers were supposed to be setting an example, converting people to scientific progress and all that. You shouldn't be validating this voodoo crap."

Paul flicked an ash. "I'm not here to change the world. Anybody here to change the world might as well go home. Remember Quentin?" he looked at me.

I smirked. "That guy with the shitty guitar, always starting up hootenannies!"

"That's right, Mr. Hootenanny. He's gone." Paul thumbed his glasses against his head, an absentminded gesture blending expedience with a hint of condescension. "He wanted his villagers to mix corn into their *fou fou*. For nutritional value, you know, since manioc has none. He had this theory that if Tambalans would just start mixing corn flour into their *fou fou*, the nation would suddenly sprout MBAS and technology, join the ranks of the NICs. The night before he flew out I saw him at the Yank Tank, ranting and raving about his *fou fou*."

"Victim of the dreaded *fou fou*," Mitch grinned.

"The thing was, the villagers did not take kindly to corn in their *fou fou*, they wanted to keep it plain and simple, straight manioc, like it's been for centuries."

"Actually, they probably ran him out of town because they couldn't bear another awful hootenanny," I said. Everybody laughed. The beer, delightfully antiseptic against the throat, cheered us up. The late afternoon clouds were tinted gold. Kiosk doors banged and *commerçants* sang out as they closed down displays.

"And that guy, Glen," Paul languidly recalled, checking me for recognition. "Always spouting on about grass roots activism? He's gone."

"I liked Glen," I blinked.

"Too idealistic; he gave up. See, you can't just barge in and change the way people think."

"Or their taste buds," Mitch aimed his pack of Marlboros at me. "The question is, do you really want them to change you?"

I succumbed to another cigarette. "I don't know about fetishes, but there must be something to the African approach." I paused. "Last weekend I was asked to explain suicide. Think of it: there's no such thing as suicide here."

"And what did you say?"

"I don't know—I babbled on about our lousy families, how people feel so alone. We're too independent, too competitive. Every man for himself. Did you know there's no such thing as cheating here? It's called 'cooperation.' I actually got into trouble for giving the students zeros for cheating. This teacher told me that's what's wrong with the States—no one helps anyone there."

We were silent a minute, puffing. I waved away a fly.

Paul offered, "There's no suicide here because it's so easy to die. Life is short enough."

"So if all the people who attempted suicide were shipped here they'd be cured?"

Mitch pulled at his beard. "It's not that simple. You can't just drop a whole mindset. Maybe anyone raised here would never get to that point, but once you've lived in the u.s. you're going to be confused."

"Confused how?"

Mitch squinted. "Complicated. Stressed out."

"So," Paul countered, "an African living in the States could become suicidal."

This seemed plausible, we all agreed.

"See, everyone changes when they change cultural environments," I insisted. "It's impossible for us not to change. I don't mean we're going to 'go African,' or magically discard all our hang-ups and mental woes, but now and then I find myself acting out of character. Like the other day, all of a sudden I was calling this kid, 'Petit!'"

"Hooray," Paul approved. "You're learning the ropes."

"But I hate those ropes. I hate the way kids get ordered around by people they don't even know, I cringe every time I see it happen, and then here I am, doing it too! It's like I've been brainwashed!"

"When in Rome, do as the Romans. It's not a matter of choice, it's a matter of survival, of how to get things done. You won't get anyone's respect until you throw your weight around a little."

"I know," I said miserably. "But think about it. If we behave like power mongers, then we completely negate the whole theory behind development—help them help themselves."

"And whose theory is that? Pure Western interference. They didn't ask us to help them help themselves. What they want is money and technology, bridges, dams." Paul nodded toward Mitch. "They've got more use for engineers than for English teachers. How come you're not teaching, anyway?" he challenged me. *"Congé* doesn't start till Thursday here."

I laughed. "The students ran away."

"Ran away!" Mitch still could not get over this.

"They were protesting green *fou fou.* They all snuck off yesterday and caught a train. They don't have much use for school, I have to admit. You can't blame them. Most of them won't be able to bribe their way into university; most of them will be unemployed. What good would English do?"

"Bribe their way into university?" quizzed Mitch.

"It's part of Daddy-o's Tambalification plan," Paul leaned toward Mitch. "Keep the people stupid. Discourage higher education by limiting access to the universities. First of all, don't build any. There are only three in the whole country, remnants of the French, with space available for only a fraction of each year's high school graduates. Second, don't fund them, don't fund study abroad, don't pay the professors. Your populace remains undereducated, uninformed, uncritical. And Daddy-o stays in control."

"'Daddy-o?'" I smiled.

"There's always Mother Nature," Mitch offered. "Maybe he'll get hit with syphilis, or something, like Idi Amin."

"Watch what you say. His fetishes have ears and if they hear the slightest hint of dissent, they'll zap you dead." A student had actually told me this in earnest when I'd asked, confidentially, how a whole nation could put up with the antics of one man.

"Not me, I'm white. I'm indelible," Paul deadpanned.

"Exactly," Mitch emptied the last of the bottle into Paul's glass. "Exactly why only the CIA can make a revolution work."

"We're already dead, anyway. Did you know they thought the first explorers were from the afterworld, because of their white skin? Because spirits of the dead are white." I'd been storing up facts from the missionaries' books.

"I thought I was feeling peaked lately," said Paul.

"I'd prescribe a vacation, if I were your doc. Do you guys ever get out of here?"

"Christmas," Paul sat up, addressing me. "After we get paid next month, we should all head for the beach. There's supposed to be a little expat resort set up there. It's smack on the Atlantic, just up the coast from the river mouth. The trip out is rough—two days of trucks with a ride down the river from Kilu in between—but once we're there, we can rent rooms cheap at the Catholic mission, or all pile into a cabin at the hotel, right on the water. Split six or seven ways, it would be affordable. We'll take our sleeping bags."

"Six or seven?"

"We'll recruit when everyone comes into town to do their banking. I'll be putting some people up. We'll nab them and drag them out to the beach."

"You mean other volunteers," Mitch clarified.

"Yeah, but you're invited, too. Come one, come all."

"Sounds great. I've been hearing about this place, a real paradise. But my vacation's already planned for next week, and once I'm back I'll be stuck at work." He looked at me.

Paul drained his glass. "Where you going?"

"Madagascar. Supposed to be some nice beaches there. Going with a few of the guys, for R and R." He ducked his head sheepishly, as if embarrassed of his cushy perks, then checked his watch. "Speaking of which, I better be off. Gotta clock in at Eckhart before they send out a search party."

Amazing how easy it was for Mitch to get around. How easy it had been for me! Whisked away by this knight in shining armor, I'd transcended Mpovi's skepticism, Bwadi's defiance of my projected hike. If not for Mitch, I'd still be hostage on the crawling train, halfway here. If not for Mitch, returning to the bush would seem bleak indeed.

Traversing the market single file, the three of us instinctively quick-paced as we headed, teamlike, toward the truck, I felt as if I'd finally arrived—not just in the city, but in the country, itself. Mampungu seemed already light years away, a fusty, forgotten outpost, dramatically provincial, serenely self-absorbed. Nothing much of what I'd felt there mattered to me now; mysterious Bwadi seemed a joke, mulish Mpovi a mere pest, my school a fiasco. Instead, like Dorothy enchanted by her green glasses in Oz, I envisioned the place anew. I would return, I understood, to a village linked to the future, one complete with family planning and swift red trucks and films and escapes to the beach. Yet, even if Bwadi had no heart and Mpovi had no brain, Diabelle had courage and I could help her wish, at least, come true.

"So you coming to camp?" Mitch dissolved my reverie, jingling his keys beside his red door.

Paul was dallying a few strides off, flapping a sandal to loosen a stone.

"Sooner or later," I shrugged, suddenly shy. "Just let me know when you get back."

"You bet," Mitch agreed, triumphantly jabbing his key into the lock. Glancing back at Paul, he hollered, "Catch you at the Yank Tank," and then tugged open the door. We did not kiss good-bye.

Paul always danced alone. Even opposite glitzy bargirls strutting daintily in place, elbow to elbow with local pals in airless clubs, Paul danced alone. We went out every night, and I could see why he was broke. Yet if he'd drunk up his own funds, he was flush in friendly sponsors; everyone wanted to buy us beer. He drank until he danced.

Everybody did. Nkisi at night thrived, the neon hissing, music chugging, cold beer fizzing in glasses smeared with condensation, skin slipping against skin. A sort of African magic seemed to settle after dark, rekindling the fried spirits of afternoon, inviting abandon in the rare cool hours often wasted on sleep. The actual catalyst was, of course, electricity—that inspiration missing in the bush. Rather than humping like zombies in a circle 'round a drum, Tambalans in the city danced to bands, to scratchy records of African pop—electric guitars winding melodies across swelling drums and horns, amplified on patios or inside *boîtes*. No one could resist. Pulled to the crest of the crowd's pulse, organic, you rippled, breathed, pushed and followed, you didn't think. Hips collided, the scent of sweat and hair oil surged, you let go from the heart and the rest came undone. Polyrhythmic, haunted by the same Latin strains that inhabit the rumba—a style that had ricocheted to Cuba and back—with vocals chiming in a liquid chant, the music picked you up and moved your limbs. The room would be chugging, shuffle shuffle *whoosh whoosh,* heating up, when all of a sudden the volume would drop. *"Bis! Bis!"* Other side! Mock anger, a communal moan, motion suspended as the record got flipped, then the explosion of the needle touching down to drive on through the song, shuffle shuffle *whoosh whoosh,* dancers elaborating with single-note bird calls, equatorial yodels, the music tinny and heroic in the crackling speakers, the chairs skewed empty, the beer going flat. You could not stop drinking and sweating and I never felt drunk. Buoyed by the crowd, with a stranger for a partner, I'd glimpse the dank, pale face of my white cohort across the floor, immersed. He was always there, over there, my odd white friend, and although the point was to drift apart and integrate, ultimately we would come together and share a dance, dancing African like toys wound up, unable to stop.

You were never too tired to dance, you could never say no; when you forgot to even try to stop, you knew that Africa had taken hold. Back at AfricEd training, we'd haphazardly been coached: invited downtown by amicable instructors on Saturday nights, we'd learned to calm down our yanking limbs, to calm down and sway, side to side, a simple shift of weight, a shift to weightlessness. We'd learned that after an initial flurry of timidity everybody danced; if you couldn't—wouldn't—you might as well go home, home to America, like the Baptist ex-missionaries who'd given up Mampungu after half a century of fighting drink and dance. At training Paul had been one of those who had skulked sipping in the shadows, wispy, remote; he'd said he'd never danced in the States. Now, in Nkisi, he was dancing, his teeter an exaggerated replica of the African flutter. Yet Tambalans danced very much in pairs; attuned to each other's choreography, partners interpreted and adjusted as they went, mimicking steps and gestures, dipping in tandem, launching simultaneous twirls. I loved this intuitive yaw, the thrill of sync, the anonymous belonging for the length of a song. Paul, however, would wag his hands and gaze above his partner's strobed head, his mouth open as if asking something of himself, the planes of his face readjusting, Picassoesque. Coolly oblivious, Paul would improvise alone.

I was guilty of oblivion of another sort that week at Paul's. Seduced by expatriate amenities, I trundled downtown each morning when Paul set off to teach, wedging myself inside a *camionnette* jammed with grumpy citizens who'd been up too late. Like a country bumpkin, I found the looming edifices and the clamor of traffic a treat. Taxis bleeped urgently, radios blaring music and news; children in uniforms intrepidly jaywalked. Descending at Independence Avenue, fanning away the flies and dust, dodging briefcases, I made for the air conditioning.

My first stop had been AfricEd. Discovering a glorious crush of mail in my box, I ripped right in, amusing the secretary, Corrine, a cheerful blonde who set me up with coffee at an empty desk.

Officiously, I read the memo announcing the pay increase to match inflation. Then I rummaged for my father's letters, for the one marked, "Picture: do not bend." Out fell Benjamin in color, wallet-size, gussied up in military dress, a gleaming black patent visor slicing above his eyes. Dark eyes, like my mother's. Why had my father sent me this, of all pictures, when Benjamin had been out of the Marines for years? Yet Benjamin had been out of touch, too; the reason I hadn't written directly to Benjamin for the photo was that I knew he would never get around to writing back.

Disturbed, I slipped the photo back inside, put away the unread letter. A package had come from my friend, Anna; she'd moved, it appeared, to an address in the mountains. I knew that her box would be good for a few laughs, and, accepting scissors from helpful Corrine, I slit the tape, then tore at the cardboard, scattering crumpled newspaper on the office floor. Plenty of food: freeze-dried camping dinners—beef stew, macaroni and cheese—cake mixes, powdered eggs, packages of yeast for yogurt. Old magazines, *Atlantics, Rolling Stones*. I dumped them onto the desk. A ribboned box from a swanky department store, something serious? I'd told people not to send anything valuable; packages got lost. But no, this was a joke; a note inside read, "send a photo dressed in these digs. . . ."

I pulled out a floppy cloth sun hat dyed a lurid mess of pink and yellow, like camouflage for a Walt Disney ride. Sweatbands for my wrists and brow, and then sunglasses in hot pink frames with red hearts at the temples—now I'd gone from zero pair of sunglasses to two. Next I found orange flip-flops. Finally, what I thought at first was a silk scarf dotted ludicrously with leopard spots, black against gold, but which kept unfolding into a nightgown. Corrine erupted in a merry squeal. Polyester leopard sleepwear, the sort of thing you pulled off dime-store racks; in fact, all this stuff smacked of a beachside drugstore in August. I held the nightgown up so that it stirred, a sheer curtain in the air-conditioned breeze. A door sucked open, and Gus, my director, emerged from his office.

"Hah! Another deserter loose from her post," he nodded, squinting at my leopard lingerie before retreating behind his door.

"He'll want the full bush report." Corrine kissed the air, miming African disdain as she indicated Gus's door, and then snorted happily. She was married to a Tambalan, I recalled. Hurriedly, I repacked my toys, plucked the paper from the floor.

Gus responded laconically to my knock. "Come."

He was standing before the air cooling unit, hands in pockets, nodding thoughtfully as if in conversation with the humming machine. I told him of my students' strike.

"Well, you can always build latrines," he smiled cynically. Implicit was the policy that teachers had to make themselves useful; if the anticipated job fell apart, we were to scope out something else to do.

"Oh, they'll all be back Monday," I promised, and then filled him in on the family planning moonlighting I had up my sleeve.

"Not putting any time in on that bridge, are you?" he obliquely quizzed. Graying, stooping, professorial, he was shabbily dignified, as if to set an example for us frayed volunteers.

"I just met my first Eckhart neighbor," I saw no reason not to confess. "He gave me a ride out of Mampungu. I guess their camp is pretty close."

Gus grunted noncommittally. Doubtless he knew more than I about this bridge operation; he would probably hear when I visited Mitch. I didn't care. If Gus found my behavior irresponsible, he could send me home. What did I have to lose?

And yet it did not occur to me to quit and leave. Conspicuously, I lounged around Kimpiri for the next few days, lunching at the embassy club on leftover turkey from some Thanksgiving bash, buying Marlboros at the Yank Tank. Mostly I hung out at the air-conditioned USIS library, avidly flipping through *New Yorker* cartoons, devouring fiction when I wasn't culling facts and figures for the texts on aggression and world strife that the students so loved. Gus believed I was developing a methodology for teaching current events.

I took the train home and got robbed. It wasn't my giant backpack full of Anna's presents and my local market supplies—the batteries, toilet paper, and stencils for my student texts, the sugar for Mpovi and condoms for Diabelle. It was my day pack, the little one I carried like a purse; it was the things I could least afford to lose. My passport. My keys. My Ray Charles sunglasses, my letters from the States. Benjamin's picture. It wasn't money. After Paul's loan I had little money left.

After my week of carousing I had an angular headache and little money left. I was waiting at the station. The train was hours late, the afternoon a furnace; everybody sagged. I was leaning against my pack against a wall; I was asleep. My little pack at my side. I dozed for a minute; when I woke it was gone. Long gone: a long minute gone. Woozily, I glanced about—yes, it was gone. I yelled. People were propped everywhere—kids and teachers travelling back to schools, vendors with *paniers* of *chiquangue, commerçant* mamas with city supplies for bush resale. Fatigued men in suits. Everyone craned, groped, a cry went up. Almost as quickly, the excitement ebbed. Another *voleur,* another dumb white. A few boys grinned.

The stationmaster was contrite; it happened all the time. I told him my name and address and what, exactly, I'd lost. He wrote it down; he would file a report. I'd never see the stuff again. It was too hot to fuss.

Aboard, I missed my passport the most. I'd lost the tangible evidence of my immunity: my amulet, the eagle embossed in gold that I could raise like a crucifix to ward off the evil M-16s of the drunken *gendarmes*. I'd meant to distance myself from the U.S., but when push came to shove, I was an American first and last. My country was greedy and crude and cold, but it was safe. I was like a child who runs away from home and then turns around, tummy rumbling, at milk-and-cookie time. I owed my whole adventure in Africa, in fact, to my American advantage—to my college degree, to my right to leave the country and return.

The savannah straggled by like an overexposed film. From my remaining luggage I dug out Anna's pink sunglasses with the hearts at the temples and put them on. I slowly drank a liter bottle of Empereur and felt like someone else. Stripped of my documents, the keys to my house, a comb for my hair, I could have been anyone just then. A sham, an amputee, I lacked some crucial segment of myself. Without my magic passport I was just another random human slouching along behind a border; I was anybody white.

I thought about the letters in my stolen backpack. My father's descriptions of the weather and the dog echoed, promising me nothing. My brother's picture came from a moment I'd never seen; I barely knew him since he'd left high school for the service. I had left my father and brother both half a globe away, yet living near them couldn't bring us any more close. Rocking toward Mampungu, I saw myself through Mpovi's eyes, as an orphan of sorts.

I was distracted from my thoughts when a man entered the car. Tidy and heavyset, he was Western-dressed, the buttons of his white shirt straining over his stomach. He hesitated, swaying, his brown fingers flexing eagerly as he scanned the passengers. The seats were crowded with students headed back to their mission schools in the bush; I recognized a few of my own, but, intent on savoring their last moments of freedom, they had no desire to infringe upon my privacy.

This intruder, however, showed no such restraint. When his eyes met mine, he nodded with happy recognition and came my way.

Did I know this man? No, I decided, he was simply another colonophile fixed on picking my white brain. I glared out the window.

"*Bonjour,*" he said heartily, sticking his hand nearly into my lap. Distastefully, I accepted his handshake. Modest sideburns trimmed to perfect right angles overlapped gleaming dark jaws; he smelled of oily perfume. I did not invite him to sit.

He made himself at home, however, on the seat opposite my dwindling bottle of beer. Ancient, the train's interior was made entirely of wood polished soft with age, brocaded with graffiti carved out by knives. *"Biri, désormais,"* I read on the window frame. *"Nous souffrons."* Creaking, my worn bench yielded like a saddle as the train rolled ahead.

"Where are you travelling today?" the man asked brightly.

I told him.

"Ehi, chez les missionaires!"

"I'm not a missionary, I'm a teacher."

"You teach! And what do you teach?"

"English."

"Ehi, good, good. English is very good."

He praised English, he praised the train, the leisurely atmosphere, the comfort, the safety.

"It's slow," I said toward an acacia limping past.

"Ehi," he chuckled, dropping his hand to his knee. "Merely a delay. A delay is no danger at all to anyone. Anyway," he leaned forward jovially, "with Jesus Christ we don't have to worry, do we? You, I believe, are Catholic?" He indicated my beer.

"Pagan." I faced him through my shades.

"Oh!" He sat back abruptly, perplexed, impervious to sarcasm. But I had opened Pandora's box. Taking a breath, clutching his ample knees, he launched into a pitch for God. Clearly, *he* was the missionary, this train his turf, the passengers his captive victims. He'd assumed I was a colleague, but, thrown for a loop by my paganism, he rallied to the challenge, his voice melodious with inspiration, the voice of a pro.

Mampungu's Pastor never nagged me about church. With a dimpled grin, he'd hail me from afar, steering clear. This ecclesiastic, on the other hand, was a pest. Sweating, sipping, I let him prattle on and refused to answer when he begged me to explain how I'd fallen from the fold; I was in no mood. Actually, there was some truth in my declaration; I did favor the animist principle that recognizes a spirit, a sort of vital force, in each and every object—although experimenting with fetishes was not my style. In any case, I liked the idea that humans and rocks amounted to the same thing: bunches of atoms held together by an electric charge. Electricity, I thought, that's what I believe in, although I didn't tell my interrogator that.

He sighed. He'd done his best. I was mute, a lost cause. "Well," he said, ever cheerful, "if you'll excuse me."

I nodded curtly at the landscape as he rose and shuffled away, on down the car.

The school *camionnette* was waiting at Mwindi station, floating reliably in the twilight; as I stepped onto the platform, several students, already disembarked, jockied for my pack. "Miss, Miss," someone squealed, "your glasses are fine!"

I had forgotten I was wearing them, and the world brightened considerably when I swept them off. "I thought it was night already!" I blinked, slightly delirious from the beer. The chauffeur, Tembo, shook my hand hard as if amazed by my return, and cleared a path to the cab through the morass of students.

The kids were in high spirits, chanting as we inched into gear, "Three weeks! Three more weeks!" Jungle whistles trilled, and I thought that we had much in common, these boarders and I, and that we should be allies, rather than adversaries, in their devilish pranks.

But this Mickey Mouse school, I'd decided, was no longer my concern; I anticipated making a fresh start. While I would not neglect my classroom hours, my new purpose would be family planning, my new friend Diabelle, my diversion Mitch. Recharged, I would begin again as Nickie, leaving Mpovi and Bwadi to rehabilitate someone else.

"Everyone is happy about the long holiday," Tembo said.

"Ehi." Remembering that I was locked out of my house, I was suddenly tired. My whole body hurt, and I closed my eyes.

Passive Tembo let me rest, and night had solidified when we arrived at Mampungu twenty minutes later. Everyone descended at the *Préfet*'s house, the truck's official resting place. I went to knock on his door.

Mpovi answered right away, smiling in the feeble light of the storm lamp she carried.

"I'm sorry to bother the *Préfet*," I began, "but I lost the keys to my house. Do you think he has doubles?"

She straightened, concerned. "How did you lose them?"

"I don't know." I didn't want to explain. I wanted my keys, a bath, bed.

"Maybe they're in your bag. Did you look?"

"Yes. They're gone. But I brought something for you," I said, remembering her sugar.

She seemed to shrink a little, childlike with gratitude. "For me?"

"Yes, for you. A surprise. I guess they took my bag already to the house." I squinted toward the truck.

"Oh," she said, in a hurry now, "come inside."

For the first time since my arrival dinner, I was escorted into the gallery of photographs, the *Préfet*'s salon. Attired casually in a white T-shirt and slacks, his lawn mowing outfit, he rose from the desk where he'd been working by lamplight.

"Ah, *bonsoir.*" Bounding forward, he surprised me, as Mpovi had, with an aggressive welcome. I had the sensation that they had both feared I'd disappeared for good.

"You've arrived with the others, exactly right," the *Préfet* nodded, rocking on his heels. "You haven't missed a thing; the classes were all cancelled last week." He thought I'd come to apologize for my early escape.

"Miss has lost the keys to her house," Mpovi informed him, her lamp swinging gently, causing shadows to twist across all the photographs.

"Oh?" Neatly, he cocked his head. "How did that happen?"

"I don't know."

"You looked for them?"

"Yes." I bristled, defensively sullen, aware that I'd violated some tenet of his systematic domain. One was exempt of responsibility when factors were beyond one's control—when the students went on strike or salaries went unpaid—but, as if to compensate for the messy bigger picture of Tambala, one must orchestrate with precision the minute details of one's life. One must not lose one's keys. Dodging his disapproval, I scanned the portraits hung like masks, detecting only shapes and, in places, eyes. All of a sudden I wanted badly to feel the dense weight of my camera in my hands.

Instead, I accepted Mpovi's storm lamp as she went to light another, disappearing toward a chorus of children's yells. The *Préfet* turned curtly and left the room; I heard a drawer scrape open. In a moment he returned jingling a set of keys, his good spirits restored by his own efficiency.

"One of these should work," he beamed, and as Mpovi returned with her extra lamp he held them out to her as if I could not be trusted.

"The Doctor was here," he said then, conversationally. "He spoke to me about your offer to help him in his work at Mampungu."

"I need a project for the vacation months," I parried.

Yet he nodded mildly, eyebrows raised. "You're to be commended for your generosity."

Whatever, I thought, anxious to try the keys.

"As a matter of fact, he left a communication for you." Prancing over to his desk, he plucked a white envelope from the top of a pile.

"Thank you." I looked at my full name penned in elaborate script, aware of the *Préfet* poised in anticipation, and decided to read the letter later, alone. "Shall we see about the keys?"

After a polite good-night, I slipped outside with Mpovi and strode behind her to my house. Sure enough, my pack lay sagging on the porch. Mpovi fiddled with the keys, and I set down the lamp and began rooting around; identifying the lumpy sack by touch, I pulled out the sugar.

"For you," I said as she tried another key.

"Ehi, *c'est quoi?*" Hovering, she was unable to tell in the dark.

"Taste." Grabbing her calloused fingers, I dipped them into the granules; she lifted a pinch to her mouth.

"*Sucre!*"

"*C'est ça.*"

"All of that! For me!" Truly excited, she abandoned the keys for the sack.

I gripped the familiar handle, turned the lock. "It works! I don't believe it!" I'd been envisioning a break-in through the kitchen window, dreading the destruction of some door; the locks could not be freed even from inside without the skeleton keys. I crossed the threshold, threw the key ring onto a table, and with the Doctor's letter still clutched beside the lamp, I inhaled the opaque scent of my habits at Mampungu: coffee, must, the tang of kerosene. I stood grounded, breathing in like a fool as Mpovi dragged my luggage inside, as she called out warmly, "*à demain,*" as the screen door banged with a rumbling echo. Stuck in the cavernous dark of my living room, a sole immobile point hanging onto my flame, I almost felt at home.

Looking forward to reading the Doctor's letter, afraid of misplacing it in the flickering light, I tucked the envelope inside my belt. When I touched a match to the mesh of the Aladdin lamp, the room came up yellowish; as I moved away, my shadow careered around the walls. In the kitchen I checked the countertops for signs of rats and poured myself a glass of water. My bedroom looked undisturbed, my imprint in the sheets circled by wrinkles like ripples in a pond; I pitched my shoes beneath the bed just in case, but nothing scuffled. The bathroom gleamed reassuringly as I set Mpovi's lantern on the fill tank of my nice commode and started the bath-water running full blast.

I lay the envelope beside the lamp, and again I had the urge to hold my camera. Leaving the water thundering into the tub, I grabbed the lamp and headed for my chest of drawers.

I meant to examine the mechanism as I had sometimes taken inventory of my jewelry in the States, picking pieces one by one from the box, dangling an earring, trying on a ring, saying to myself, "Now why don't I wear this?" Most were costume gems from my mother, glamorous, intricate perhaps, endowed with sentimental associations, but not really to my taste. I loved them anyway, loved that they were mine.

Opening my camera drawer, I froze. Impossible. The camera wasn't there, its niche empty beside my stash of kuluna bills. Distinctly, I recalled how it had looked Monday, patient and magical as I'd extracted money for my trip. Cameras in Tambala wound up confiscated, smashed by the police; I hadn't figured mine could be stolen from my locked house, my haven in Tambala, my haven in the world.

Quickly, I counted the stacks of bills, the water pounding away in the tub. The money was all there, the hemp knots intact, the bundles wound tight as gifts—except for one corner roughly cropped, nibbled by rats. Whoever had taken the camera must have left the drawer ajar, and the rodents had gone to town.

I tore around the house, storm lamp swerving as I turned off the faucets and inspected the windows and the locks. Everything was fine, the thief's tracks covered. The attic? A secret trapdoor?

At a loss, I headed for my bath, peeled off my clothes, stomped into the tub and then stood, the water cool and disturbing at my ankles. Sinking, I slid beneath the surface, blew bubbles. There would be no pictures now, no document of me in my dime-store get-up for Anna, no way to gauge in the future who I had been here. Unless, of course, I got it back. I could inform the authorities, demand a missionwide search. Or I could snoop around, myself. Coming up for air, I reached for the Doctor's letter as if for a clue.

"To the Esteemed Miss Nicola Spark," I read in ornately penned French. "It is with extreme pleasure and pride that I regard your generous interest in my evolving project concerning family planning. Your valuable assistance will be all the more effective if you accept my commission to designate one assistant, for the purpose of enlisting help as well as in order to train that individual to carry out your anticipated duties which, I understand, you will be obliged to terminate in less than two years' time. My budget permits me to provide a salary of K200.00 for the aforementioned assistant, and K500.00 for you, per month. I proffer to you the utmost gratitude and anticipate with enthusiasm our months of combined endeavor."

He'd signed it, *"Le Docteur* Yela Vutudi."

I might have smiled at his pomp and circumstance, I might have noted his financial generosity, but his reference to my leaving made me mad. At that moment, two years in Africa felt like forever, yet in his view I was just passing through; in a drumbeat I'd be gone. They'd begun planning for my departure the minute I'd arrived, the kids staking claim to my shoes and watch. *I've come to ask, Miss, if you will give me your glasses when you go.* Of course, they'd seen us come and go for centuries; they'd learned how to hook the booty fast because we were only as good as what we left behind.

Of course, they were right. Objects were what lasted, permanent and raw. It occurred to me that, with my camera, someone had absconded with all I was worth.

6

NGANDO

If not stolen, lost. Gold weights from Ghana, the pool tiles in Conakry that fell off and drained into the sea. Searching for shells along the rim of the lagoon, I found the lovely blue squares and, less often, white ones glossy as scars against the sand. My father gave me a cigar box in which to collect them with shells.

One day Benjamin singled out a tiny mottled cowrie shaped like a cone.

"This is like a skeleton," he said.

"What?"

"This is what's left after it dies."

"After what dies?"

"The snail, dummy. This is where the snail lived, inside, like a house. When it died and fell out, the shell washed up on the beach."

"It's not a snail! It's from underwater, in the ocean!" I hated snails.

"Same difference. Snails can live underwater, too, like fish. Even in those shells that sound like the ocean, big, fat snails used to live in them. It's true, ask Dad."

For a day or so I was horrified, then I returned to the sand with new respect, as if to a cemetery. Eventually I got used to the idea of shells as bones and could concentrate once again on their beauty. I imagined a fantastic dragon dying to leave behind the pool tiles like scales.

The cigar box of treasures got tossed somewhere along the way, although I still have my drawing of the imitation *paillotte,* as well as a couple of ivory crocodiles, a few trading beads, tapestries, and masks. Now I guard these objects carefully, as if, like fetishes, they house some African spirit; these bits and pieces are all that I have left. Even my obsolete passports—all but the one, of course, stolen in Tambala—have a place in my files. And I still have an envelope of photos of Chance, as well as shots of me decked out in garish fabric, my hair snaking out from my strange skull. I've yet to print copies to send to Mpovi. By now that baby must be ten.

In Conakry, where I was nine, the blue and white tiles that lined the swimming pool slid down the drain and into the lagoon to be exposed at low tide among the shells of water snails. It was 1966, eight years after Guinea had won independence from France, the pool was crumbling from within, and Americans were going home. President Sekou Touré, militant, resentful, forced us out when we refused to let go.

My family left six months before completing our two-year contract. By that time, all Americans except for the embassy staff and missionaries had been officially kicked out. Because of Touré's socialist leanings, the United States had cut back on monetary aid and now he was irate, railing over the air against us imperialist capitalists.

During the past month, the American school had been shrinking as my classmates failed to appear, without warning, without good-byes. The little school bus fairly rattled with the few of us left, and my brother summed up the situation perfectly one day. As we were descending at our house, he stopped beside the driver and announced to our remaining friends, "Maybe see you tomorrow, maybe not, who knows? Tomorrow any of us could be getting on the plane."

That was how evacuation worked. Unexpectedly, your father came home with orders to leave and suddenly everyone was packing up a storm, filling crates as tall as I was with the personal effects that would follow by ship. The next day, you were on the plane. It was always "the plane" in those countries growing up, not just any plane but the proverbial plane waiting to take you back where you belonged.

I loved Conakry. I loved the glittering swimming pool and my cat Tang, one of Juju's offspring; I loved how she perched, orange and regal, on the tip of our giant *paillotte* roof, level with the palm fronds. I loved the tiny crabs scrabbling, hundreds in tandem, across the sand to vanish simultaneously into holes or under bits of debris or inside one of our sagging castles, and I loved the water fights we American kids would wage around the pool, shooting from syringes like guns that we saved from our periodic inoculations. My brother had grown darker and quicker than ever and my mother more pale. She smiled from her patch of shade on the patio, legs casually crossed, a sandal dangling from her toes, her eyes patient and dark, the hair at her temples hinting at gray. My father would crack his yellowing newspapers and would sail.

I must have assumed that my dwindling circle of friends was simply a part of the place. I had no sense of threat that I recall. I didn't understand the president's French broadcasts, and the Guineans I saw daily—our gardener, our *garde de nuit,* the kids at the fence, and Ali—were as amiable as ever. In the ivory circumference of our expatriate lives, things were just as they had always been.

People got robbed, people got sick, there was no TV, no telephone. There were tremendous thunderstorms that my father enjoyed. When the electricity failed at night, we'd gather around lanterns in the living room, and he'd stand at the window, his back repeatedly outlined by lightning. The sea would rise and waves crashed through the fence, and afterward, in the morning, Benjamin and I scooped fish from the pool and raced them in buckets to the lagoon's salt water. We found some, of course, too late; poisoned by the chlorine, they were already floating on their silver sides.

Even in clear weather, the pool took its toll. Once Benjamin called me to where he and Ali stood staring at the ground below a cactus tree, and I expected they'd extracted another drowned crab or bird. Instead, I saw the sleek wet fur of a dead rat the length of my arm, its tail curling even longer, the hideous color of flesh. Stopping cold, I looked away to where we'd carved our names between the spines in the soft paddles of cactus.

"It's a grasscutter!" Benjamin proclaimed, crouching near the narrow, toothy muzzle. "Look at its fangs!"

"Ugh," I whispered. "It's horrible."

Ali was grinning like a hunter, nudging the thing with his toes. Amused by my disgust, he told me it was good to eat.

I don't know why I was so surprised when, shortly before leaving, we were robbed. It remains a crisis I have yet to transcend, a disturbance in my child's garden of Africa, a poison dart that pierces, now and then, my longing for palm trees and heat. Though our evacuation was inevitable, a function of politics and my father's job, and what happened to my mother a few years later had nothing to do with Conakry, I can't help tracing the trajectory of my family's dissolution to this one particular night.

I woke to the sound of doors banging, then the drum of bare feet slapping past my room; tumbling from bed, I opened the door to see my mother streaking past, her nightgown billowing as she sped across the *salon* to the patio outside. Stunned, my first thought was that she was running away. My father lurched forward as he struggled with the waistband of his slacks, and my brother darted after, his pajama bottoms flapping at his ankles. Tentatively, I followed in their wake, my feet chilly on the floor tiles, my head throbbing with dismay as I passed the accordion doors neatly folded back. At that time of night, they should have been locked tight.

The darkness was thick and sweet. Up ahead, my mother's nightgown skimmed like a great moth along the garden steps, skirting the pool and shooting through the gate to the rocks beyond. Feeling numb as stone, I hovered by the pool, left behind by my father and brother, who had followed my mother out the gate. Then I saw the slim flutter of her lingerie disappear, as if she had simply closed her wings and slipped into another dimension.

"Get back!" I heard my father shout. "Do as I say!"

Benjamin protested in his familiar whine.

With my fingers hooked around the fence wire, I waited, the pool gaping black as ink; I spotted the white dab of my mother on her feet entangled with a figure I took to be an African, but it was my father darkened by the night, walking her forward. They advanced, her nightgown hanging meek as any nightgown, Benjamin jaggedly pulling up the rear, his arms poised at odd angles to his waist as he kept his token distance.

When my parents passed together through the gate, I stared at my mother's ceramic glare, at the small black hole of her mouth. Then I ventured forward to meet Benjamin.

"What happened?"

He latched the gate behind him and stood a minute panting, and I sensed his panic in a way I never have since. He looked trapped, frantic as a wild kitten faced with human hands.

"Thieves," he breathed in my direction, and his voice caught. After a raw silence he continued, "She fell on the rocks." Then he headed tautly toward the house.

Inside, my father was lowering my mother to a couch. He'd turned the lamp on and, as he leaned, the knobs of his bare spine looked swollen and hard.

"I'm all right," she was saying, but then she winced and put her hands to her head.

"You kids change your clothes," he turned to us. "We're going to the doctor's house."

I hurried into my shorts, and when I returned, the accordion doors were extended shut and latched and I heard the car whirring to a start. They were leaving me, I thought as I broke into a run, leaving me to the thieves; as I crossed the kitchen, however, I stopped at the sight of my sweet Tang staring with expectant trust. Protectively, I scooped her into my arms. She liked the car; often enough, my mother had allowed me to bring her along on errands.

"In the front," my father called as I approached, and then he jumped out of the driver's seat to lock up the house. I slid in beside Benjamin.

"You can't bring her!" he huffed at Tang in my arms.

"Shut up!"

I turned to see my mother stretched out in back, and Benjamin twisted, too, following my gaze. "Mom," I whispered loudly, "Mom!"

She opened her eyes and smiled and she looked peaceful there, merely tired. "I'm here," she said, and closed her eyes. The only blood I saw was a gash along her arm.

My father slipped back behind the wheel, and Benjamin began whining about Tang. "Dad!"

"I don't want to hear it!"

Silently, we sped the mile to the doctor's house, until our headlights illuminated the muddled form of his night watchman propped sleeping against the wall.

My father parked and leapt out to knock on the front door.

"I'll go shout at Billy's window," Benjamin offered. We knew the house well because Linda and her brothers lived here. But Mrs. Randall opened right away, dishevelled in a robe.

She ushered us inside the familiar study, giving me a look of mock reproach when she saw me holding Tang. She was a generous, delicate woman, always calling us from our games to cookies or juice; I'd never heard her raise her voice.

My father went away with her, and Benjamin and I were left alone in the room. Sitting on the Naugahyde couch, I fingered Tang's sweaty footpads. Since she wanted to investigate, I lifted my hands, and she dropped onto the floor to stalk and sniff the walls.

Benjamin went straight for the desk drawer where we knew the *Playboys* were, pulled it open. "Yup, they're here," he said, pushing it shut. He came to sit by me.

We stared together at Tang sniffing the edges of the zebra rug. Then he said softly, "It was Ali."

I felt my eyes widen. "Tonight? How do you know?"

"I saw him. I saw his face. I heard Mom shouting and when I went to my door he was running out of Mom and Dad's room, but he didn't see me. He had her purse in his hand."

I pictured my mother's beige leather bag. "It couldn't have been Ali. He likes us. He took all those kittens to his compound." My mother had allowed me to keep only Tang.

"He took them to eat."

I clenched my eyelids shut, and a swirl of orange and green neon streaked across the blackness. Gripping the cushion, zooming forward, hearing a roar, I wanted to stop.

Someone was at the door, and I opened my eyes to see Mrs. Randall's bright grin.

"There goes Tang!" Benjamin yelled, but I didn't move.

"He won't go far," Mrs. Randall reassured us, her voice sing-song. "We'll find him in the morning. Right now it's time for you to snuggle back to sleep; you're going to spend the night here. Your mother looks like she's going to be just fine, she only bumped her head. But she's going to stay here until the doctor can do tests in his office in the morning and your father's going to stay, too. I'll be back in a jiffy with sleeping bags and pillows."

"Oh, Tang," I whimpered when she left.

"Forget Tang. Don't you care about Mom?"

"Did you see her fall?"

"She slipped. Just like you do all the time." He jabbed me with his elbow, teasing. But I didn't respond giggling with my customary pinch.

Mrs. Randall set up our sleeping bags and pillows on the zebra rug, and when my dad came to pat Benjamin's shoulder and to kiss me good-night, I didn't tell him about Tang.

As it turned out, Tang was lost by the time we were shuttled off to school in the morning; in the afternoon we found my mother home, perched as usual in the shade. The patio yawned around her as she gazed up into the palms, serene, detached. "Nickie," she kept asking me, "have you seen my sunglasses?"

"Ali took them in your purse," I'd say, and she'd look worried and reply, "Oh, that's right."

My father explained that her concussion slowed her down, and the next day she did seem better, and the next. Ali and our night watchman never returned to work, and that week, alone at home, she busied herself battling the termites. I still recall her waving the dust rag as we left for school. Then it happened: Benjamin and I returned one afternoon to find my father surrounded by packing crates, my mother dashing from one to another.

"Here, Nickie," she called, dragging one into my room. "Start packing, we're going home." Her cheeks were flushed, her voice exuberant. "Put in the things you want most, first, because we might not fit everything."

Happy to see my mother happy, I started with my stuffed animals.

Toys, books, clothes; I must have sacrificed the cigar box of shells and tiles. When the crate was full, I hurried out amidst the chaos of boxes knee-deep in crumpled paper, and my father flashed me a harried smile, his arms full of shoes. I ran into the kitchen, then outside. My mother was there in her chair, absorbed in the horizon, in the ocean's blue edge.

"Nickie," she said conversationally, and turned to point beneath a bush. "Where did that come from?"

"Tang!" My orange cat was poised hopefully, waiting for my move. I swept her to my chest.

"Is that your kitty, sweetheart?" my mother asked, and I pressed my burning eyes into the fur.

Tang stayed behind with the imitation *paillotte;* she did not belong amid our scramble for housing in the States. After we got settled, though, and the kids in my new neighborhood asked me to speak French, I would think of her. *"Chat,"* I would say. *"Petit chat."*

The doctors insisted that my mother's head was fine, driven off balance those few last days by fear and shock perhaps, by too long in Africa. I never saw her confused in that way again, not once before her auto accident in Washington. A random wreck, a local intersection, alone with groceries at her side—it was such an American death. Yet whenever I begin to picture it, another memory intrudes. I always flash on her running through the night, a flimsy breath of white sailing toward the black water, out of reach, a ghost.

Scooting forward in his chair, the *Préfet* tucked himself neatly in against his desk. Seated opposite, I squirmed, working the three fresh sticks of chalk against my palm. Every Monday while the secretary across the hall stood ready with a box, each of us teachers filed in for the week's supply, which we then carried around from class to class as a precaution against the pilfering kids. Today I'd presented myself to the *Préfet,* as well.

"So, you've found your keys?" he smiled affably.

I shook my head. "I've come because of something else. My camera, actually. My camera's missing from my house."

His eyebrows contracted, fuzzy with distrust. "From your house?"

"Last night I noticed it wasn't where I'd left it, beside my money in a drawer. This morning I looked everyplace. I thought I'd better let you know."

"And the cash?"

"Nothing's missing but the camera."

"You didn't take it on your trip?"

"No."

He sat back, hands flat on his desk. "It's serious, then. Whoever has your keys is coming in your house."

"No, I don't think so. I mean, I'm positive I had my keys yesterday morning, so they must have been stolen with my backpack."

"Your backpack was stolen in Kimpiri? Ehi, *kiadi.* This I did not understand." He gave a little shiver of exasperation. "It's too dangerous in Kimpiri these days, thieves running up and pulling things from people in the streets. How did it happen?"

"It was in Nkisi, at the train station."

"At Nkisi, even way out there! Did you report this to the authorities?"

I shrugged. "I told the stationmaster. I was on my way here."

Sitting forward, the *Préfet* clasped his hands together with intent. "What, exactly, did you lose in this satchel?"

"My passport, my *carte d'identité.*" Documents, I knew, would carry the most weight.

"Your embassy must reissue them at the earliest possible convenience. Can you wait until the midyear break?"

I nodded. This was just three weeks away, toward the end of December—the national school vacation that spanned Christmas and New Year's, missionary style.

"For the interim, I will draft an official letter of introduction, to discourage confusion. One must not be caught without papers in Tambala." Already, he was reaching for a pen.

"But about my camera," I persisted, "it must have been taken by someone else. The thief with my keys could hardly have arrived yesterday, before me. How would he have known where I lived? Besides, a total stranger would have been conspicuous in broad daylight."

"Oh, oh, oh," the *Préfet* lamented, "to think this rogue could be a member of our own community! Yes, yes, it's possible. A student might have seen where I was keeping those spare keys, or someone clever could have picked your lock. *Oh, oh, oh!* Twice you have been robbed now, after all your generosity! They forget you are a volunteer!"

Patiently, I fingered my chalk.

"And to think this thief with your satchel could still arrive!" he concluded with a snort. Clearly, he preferred out-of-town suspects.

My favorites, however, were the giggling children always lurking at his house, the prying fingers privy to his desk. How many eyes had seen me taking pictures with Mpovi, had scoped out my possessions while I led my little tours?

As the *Préfet* began scribbling my makeshift commission, I considered claiming an arbitrary day of strike, bypassing my classroom to conduct my own inquest, to root through dormitories, desks. Yet it was his home, actually, that I wanted to search.

"Where were you?" the students were calling out in English, miming my response to tardiness as I crossed the courtyard toward their classroom door.

"On strike," I smiled ironically, going in. They didn't understand.

"Last week," I pointed behind me, my signal for the past tense, "you were not here. Monday, Tuesday, Wednesday, Thursday, you were not here. Where were you?"

"On a fait la grève!" someone yelled.

"Strike," I said, writing it on the board, "to be on strike." Turning, I pointed from one kid to another. "You were on strike. You were on strike. You, you, and you were on strike. So who was on strike?"

"We!" they chorused. "We were on strike!"

Seizing the opportunity, I led them through a drill. "I was on strike," they chanted, "he was on strike." We changed tenses, added qualifiers. "We go on strike. We will go on strike next month." I appointed a drummer who tattooed in time, palms against his desk; one guy in back spontaneously erupted to boogie a few strides.

"But," I stopped them, raising both hands, withholding cues. "But, but, but. Where was I last week?" I pointed at myself, shook my head: not.

"You were not on strike."

I made a gloomy face. "I was alone." Everybody laughed. "Next time, you must tell me before. I will go on strike, too."

"You, too, Miss?"

"Yes, me. Me, too. I will go on strike, too."

It had been one of my best lessons so far. Below the title, "Green *Fou Fou*," a collective essay bristled whitely on the chalkboard. Squinting, licking their lips, the kids copied with urgency into their *cahiers*. It was their story in their words, the English a key. Glowing, I stepped outside, headed for my next class, but my happiness froze at the sight of Bwadi poised in the walkway, ready to pounce.

"What are you doing?" he hissed.

"Teaching. Do you mind?" Haughtily, I minced past, only to be shackled by his blunt grip on my arm. I spun to confront him, the inflated halo of his anarchic hair, and he let me go.

"C'est suicide, ça!" he practically spat.

"I have no idea what you're talking about." This time, I veered off across the courtyard, but he was on my heels, my neck, his whisper humid with fury.

"Your ignorance will put us all in jail! Except for you, of course—you can always fly back to America. Meanwhile we will be interrogated, the school closed down because you've been organizing strikes!"

"I have not."

"No, but try explaining your lesson on green *fou fou* to the FIT!"

"Green *fou fou* is hardly a political issue. If your English were as good as you think, you'd know there is nothing sinister about that text."

"And how much English do you think the *gendarmes* know? They're sure, in any case, to know the word, 'strike.'"

It occurred to me that Bwadi had had the whole period free. "So you've been listening at my door since seven o'clock? The real spymaster here, it seems, is you." Dismissively, I took another stride, Bwadi in hot pursuit. Lurching across the bleak courtyard, we whispered, disengaged. I could not help thinking how easily this could be taken for a lovers' tiff.

"Who could miss your class chanting, 'strike, strike, strike'?" he nagged. "I was walking past, on my way for chalk, and I thought the revolution had begun. It's lucky that the *Préfet's* walls are so thick."

"But nevertheless you did inform him of this impending insurgency, I'm sure."

"I was there," he huffed, "at his request. He wanted me to give you this." The paper he shoved into my hand was the improvised commission, a baroque announcement of my engagement at *Institut Mampungu,* typed and signed and crowned with an authoritative stamp.

I looked up, at the perspiration glinting on Bwadi's knotted brow. Something flared, and suddenly I laughed. "And what about all your noble politics? Nkrumah's victory with Positive Action? Don't tell me righteous Bwadi is afraid of the word, 'strike'!"

A flood of emotion darkened his face; he seemed to rear, tall and wild-eyed, stepping back. "This is no place to talk," he checked himself, but then his fist snapped forward with a violent chop that released a spray of chalk. Breaking into vivid bits against the red dried mud at our feet, the shards nearly sparkled, precious as shells. I would have stooped, reaching, but Bwadi's brown leather shoes swivelled curtly away. "Of course," he was calling to me over his shoulder, "a woman who can vanish into air has no need to worry for herself."

Puzzling in place, I watched him duck through his classroom door. Solid, round faces bunched at each walkway window, room after room. I felt abandoned, exposed within my tiny island of scattered chalk, a witch at the stake. Immobile with guilt, I stood accused of magic access to airplanes—until, that is, I understood the real gist of Bwadi's taunt. Surely, by "vanishing," he had meant my disappearance from the road to Mwindi with Mitch.

I couldn't help smiling as I marched toward my next class. A few intrepid students darted out behind me onto center stage, diving for the fragments of chalk.

At midmorning recess, the scene of my skirmish with Bwadi reverted to student turf. Kids sauntered across the sunbaked plaza to cluster in margins of shade where, fanning their faces with graded papers, they rolled their eyes.

I sent for Diabelle. A rush of insight had brightened my last class while, laboriously, the students penned their answers to my palliated question, "How did you spend your holiday?" No strikes, no *fou fou*, no politics from me, just in case. Robbed, insulted, drenched in sweat, I was sulking at my desk, debating the wisdom of my commitment, when I remembered Diabelle. Everything fell into place. There was still the Doctor's project, there was still Diabelle. If she'd been in that class, I would have called her up to my desk then and there.

Now, outside, she waltzed cheerfully across the yard, skirting a group of girls, her brown face bright with trust as if, from me, only good could come.

Reaching for her hand, shaking, I blurted the news. "I would like to offer you the chance to work with me for the Doctor." In the tree branches above us, insects wheezed.

She dipped to scratch a calf.

"He's doing a public health survey on family planning. Our job would be mostly paperwork, several hours each week, and the Doctor would pay you two hundred kulunas each month." Worth about twenty dollars at that time, the sum was quite respectable by Tambalan standards. As a volunteer, I, myself, was pledged to forgo extra income, but Diabelle had no such restrictions.

Alert, eyes fixed, she was listening, taut as a gazelle. She wet her lips. "Family planning for whom?"

"Everybody. He hopes to make counselling available at local dispensaries, for women in the bush."

"For me?" She glanced around.

"By the time the dispensaries are equipped," I laughed, "you'll be off in Kimpiri. You see, I'll be training you to carry on the job when I leave, and you could eventually be offered a city position, or maybe a chance to study public health."

It was overload. Trying to figure all the angles, she narrowed her eyes at the ground, the neat furrows of her scalp gleaming between her many tight braids; she looked almost wily, prone to deceit. She had, after all, kept the kids' scheme for last week's strike secret from me. I had to respect, however, her uncertainty.

"Don't decide right now," I said gently. "Think seriously, first, and then accept only if you're really sure you want the extra work on top of your classes at school."

Biting her lip, she looked up. "Why must you plan to leave?"

She took me by surprise. Was this what was boggling her response? Rather than calling dibs on this rosy future up for grabs, she seemed stymied by the thought of me gone.

"My job here only lasts two years," I slowed down; for the first time, it sounded short. "Look, I'm not going to forget you in the States. We'll keep in touch; maybe I'll come back to visit, or you'll go study over there. But that's such a long way off, let's think about today. If you'd rather not be distracted from your studies, maybe you could wait until summer to start. In the meantime, though, I'd probably have to ask someone else."

"Ehi, no, Miss! Don't ask anybody else!" Her wail was shot with teenage challenge. "Tell me again what I would do?"

Describing as best I could how we would read questionnaires about village birth control, I felt, for the second time that morning, my words hit the mark. Like my chanting students heralding strikes, Diabelle rallied, electric interest in her eyes.

"And Miss," she sidled up when I was done. "About those things you promised, from Kimpiri?"

The bell was ringing, recess was up. "Come this afternoon for extra help," I nodded before slipping into class. Sweetly elusive, I felt for all the world like Glenda, the Good Witch.

Acknowledging Mpovi's ardent wave, I lifted my own arm in feeble greeting as I returned to my house. Moments later, my screen door rattled: a *petit* bearing a plate of glittering cookies, sugar sprinkled on top. "From Mpovi," the girl swooned, delirious, it appeared, from the aroma.

Accepting the gift, I offered one to her. "Sugar, sugar, sugar," she chewed dreamily. "And in our tea! We all had sugar in our tea this morning!"

"You drink tea, too, already?" Thinking, I tried to fix her age, her name. This was Nsasa, I decided, Mpovi's nine-year-old niece, brazen doyenne of the neighbor imps. I pictured her skulking through my house, camera clutched against her chest.

"Give Madame my thanks," I turned, abandoning the girl in my *salon* as I headed for the kitchen with the plate.

"But Miss Nicoli!" she called, too polite to follow, "you must come yourself; Madame invites you for a glass!"

"Today, you mean?" Beer was the last thing I wanted after my profligate week, but I'd avoided Mpovi long enough. "Tell her I'll be over in a while," I instructed, bustling little Nsasa out the door, watching her skip friskily across the lawn, buoyed, no doubt, by the knowledge of my camera's whereabouts. Likely, she'd left it to molder like a fetish underground.

I pictured it: blind, symbolic, encrusted with mud. It was better there, perhaps, better than in my high-tech hands so attuned to dials and levers and arpeggios of steely clicks. Wasn't it a part of what I'd wanted to let go? Only, I would have preferred to single someone out—Mpovi, probably—to accept it as a legacy when I moved on. What did I have left to offer now?

Listing in the kitchen, I chided myself for pretending to suspect the child; it was easier, however, than accusing adults I needed to trust. Mpovi? I dismissed the thought: sly, covetous, yes, but too transparent; besides, she wouldn't dare risk the *Préfet*'s wrath. And if it were the *Préfet,* himself? I'd prefer not to know.

After lunching on a couple of gritty cookies, I collapsed for a nap, then woke dull and sticky, pinched. Coffee rarely appealed in the afternoon, instead, I splashed water on my face, lit a cigarette. Odd: a few hot puffs worked magic against the sudden coolness of wet skin. The ritual complete, I waded through the billowing humidity to Mpovi's clearing.

The same old crate stood ready beneath the tree. Nsasa, swinging through the door, glasses in hand, swerved back inside at the sight of me as if nonplussed. Once again, I wanted to reach out, grab her hem, make her talk, but then I realized she was simply hurrying to let Mpovi know I'd arrived. Emerging in a bright *pagne,* Mpovi cradled her baby and a bottle of beer.

"It's true?" she blurted, concerned.

"What?" A lot was true these days.

"Your camera! Has it been robbed?" Scooping my news, she sat abruptly, vivacious with alarm. "The *Préfet* says someone took it from your house."

Upstaged, I felt helpless, limp. I felt thirsty, after all.

"It was while you were away?" Passing Chance to Nsasa, Mpovi began playing the hostess, filling tilted glasses, scolding the foam.

I claimed a stool, tapped a toast to health, drank. I described the gaping place in the drawer, all the intact locks.

"But doesn't Jetaime have his own key?"

"No, I let him in before I go to school." I hadn't thought of Jetaime, of his eager greeting early Monday each week, of his dignified *merci* when I paid him later in the day. Of how he'd come begging to work. A veteran houseboy, he'd learned from the missionaries how to clean the bathroom and kitchen, how to swab the floor. Diligent Jetaime. He would set up the ironing board outside in the shade, and I'd arrive home to find him using the iron stoked with glowing coals to press my clothes. I was absolutely sure it wasn't Jetaime.

"My husband thinks the same thief stole your satchel yesterday."

"He couldn't have," I scoffed, addled by how much she'd been told. "He would have needed a car to beat me here from Nkisi, and anyone rich enough to have a car wouldn't bother with a camera. Plus, how could a stranger have just opened up my door yesterday in broad daylight? Someone would have seen." Foam expanded in my mouth as I gulped, glancing at top-heavy Nsasa, Chance balanced on her hip.

Mpovi, starchily perched on her stool, looked miffed. "The *Préfet* is making inquiries right now," she defended him.

"He's very conscientious," I agreed quickly; "I do appreciate his help. But you don't really think he'll find it, do you?"

"We'll get your camera back."

Was this a fact? Was she privy to some strategy to wrest my camera from a local crook's lair? To return it unharmed, perhaps mysteriously, to its drawer in the dark? Her prophecy sagged, however, with the same false promise of her other auguries: I would be beautiful; Citizen Bwadi would be my beau.

"Oh, Mpovi," I sighed, low on oomph. "I'll survive without my camera. I'll be too busy for photography now, anyway. Afternoons I'll be working for the Doctor."

Changing gears, she scooted forward confidentially. "He came to the *Préfet* to explain while you were gone. He said you would be needing an assistant." Demurely, she sipped.

It came as an honest shock that she might have liked the job. I squirmed. "I asked Diabelle."

"Ehi?"

"He wanted me to hire a potential full-time employee. Someone who could travel later on. Diabelle has none of your family responsibilities; she's always wanted to live in town. I just assumed all your energy was taken up with Chance. Besides," I continued as she reached for her son, "you've never mentioned any interest in family plannning."

She looked at me. "Has Diabelle?"

Clumsily, I blushed. I'd actually forgotten that Diabelle was due at my door any minute now to collect her promised condoms. "She wants a career," I said.

Mouth screwed up disdainfully, Mpovi aimed a kiss nowhere. Impulsively, then, she pressed her baby's face against her own, and she appeared to soften as I watched, golden and rosy, both pushy and yielding at once. A hand winged minutely up.

My high-tech fingers itched. "We have the other pictures, anyway," I said, mainly to myself.

"The others?"

"The ones I took of Chance. I sent them off already to the States." I looked away, an odd nostalgia intruding on my efforts to appease. Mpovi in her festive *pagne,* the pliant brown of Chance's skin, the emerald of the bush, everything seemed harshly beautiful and out of reach.

"In Lufwidi," I tried backtracking, "we danced around the drum."

"Ehi," Mpovi laughed, on cue. "And who did you dance with?"

"Everyone."

"The dance around the drum. It's good, isn't it?"

"A little slow. I like the clubs in Nkisi better."

"In Nkisi, did you dance?"

"Every night."

"With all those people you don't know? Me, I like the village. I like the quiet, and dancing with my friends."

"I have friends in Nkisi."

She dipped forward, startling Chance. "I heard," she whispered, glancing at lurking Nsasa, "that Bwadi was angry at you."

"He's always angry at me."

"Today, I mean. In the schoolyard. The students saw you have an argument."

"He's always criticizing how I teach." Tipping my glass, I slowly drained the dregs. It was best, I decided, that word get around we'd had a private tiff. It was best to respect Bwadi's political willies, to play down my inadvertent incitement to strike. Probably, it would be best to assume that, rather than stupidly indifferent to matters of state, Mpovi was shrewd. After all, I had no idea whose side she was on.

"There's Diabelle," I tried to weasel out, pointing as I saw her wafting up the road. "I forgot, she's coming for a student conference."

"But why," Mpovi persisted, "does Bwadi criticize?"

"Probably, he thinks I should stay home and bake cookies, like you. They're delicious, by the way."

She exhaled, dimpled, pleased, completely ignoring Diabelle. Despite her recent ambition to join the Doctor's project, she resorted to her standard response. "When you're married," she recited, "you won't have to teach."

Over the next two weeks, there was a lot of rain, but that wasn't why I quit idling outside. Bereft of my camera, my passport, my hope of ever fitting into Africa, I was making my own way. Instead of calling on Mpovi afternoons, I met at the dispensary with Diabelle, drifting later among the evening shadows at home with a book lit yellow by my kerosene lamp. Soon enough, I was sure, I'd hear from Mitch; if neighbors wondered at my isolation in the meantime, too bad. Surprisingly, they did not. Only when I quit faking a future among the Tambalan wives, only when I matched the whites of Bantu folklore, bleak and weak and crazy with too much thinking, could Tambalans begin to approach. The fact was, my place was on the fringes, like the Angolan refugees whose huts stood removed from the local villages. Naturally, my allies must be renegades themselves.

Diabelle was on my side; together, we holed up. I'd never actually visited the dispensary before our first staff meeting with the Doctor there, but from the moment he greeted me in the road out front, I knew I'd come to the right place. Calmly professional in a white button-down shirt, sleeves rolled up, in belted slacks and oxford shoes, he seemed to symbolize the modern world.

"It will rain," he had dismissed the sky.

The building was as dilapidated as the rest at Mampungu: screens curled back from the window frames; rust stains laced the walls. Predictably, a froth of mango branches sheltered one corner from the sun. The clouds that day looked resilient, dry as the white fuzz on the Doctor's head, yet it was painfully humid, the air like stew, my brain glazed and stupid as an egg hardened in its shell. Straining for a hint of the wind that must precede itinerant storms, I felt only the heat pressing, penetrating like pins into my pores.

"I'm very pleased that you've hired a student," the Doctor mused as we waited for Diabelle. "If we succeed, I can perhaps recommend her for some scholarship to study abroad, such as I received from the Swiss. It's of the utmost importance now for Tambala to increase the availability of trained professionals."

Hearing him echo my hopes for Diabelle, I felt pardoned for having overlooked Mpovi. "It was good of you to let me decide whom to hire."

"Ehi, but you know the community here better than I," he flattered me; "this way I did not have to investigate a lot of applications. I spent too much time hiring the interviewing team. But we have a good group now, I believe. They're working already in Mwindi; I dropped them there on my way here. It will be better when the new Land Rover comes, so that we don't have to share transportation. Of course, then I'll have to hire a new chauffeur. Ehi!" He raised his whitened eyebrows, swinging his hands to his hips in a gesture of approval as Diabelle approached.

She wore a *pagne* of Sunday quality tucked around a cotton blouse. The Doctor knew her already from Lufwidi, and he watched her lanky gracefulness with evident appreciation—calling into question Mpovi's scorn for lanky girls. Although lean, Diabelle was perfectly proportioned, and an intelligent expression animated her delicate face. I bristled protectively when the Doctor dropped his voice to confide, "She's a promising young girl."

Eagerly, she hurried up the path, her sandals picking up mud. *"Bonjour, Monsieur le Docteur,"* she said with a brief curtsy as they shook hands. "I'm sorry I'm late."

"Not at all." He peered through his spectacles, not quite smiling, and minced past to pull open the screen door, aiming his forehead at the jamb above. "There will be a sign," he told us, *"Centre de Planification Familiale, Location de Luzawa, Département de Santé Public, République de Tambala,* with a government seal. I ordered it last week."

Diabelle trailed behind, scraping the mud from her shoes onto the edge of the concrete stoop, and the Doctor waded ahead into the dim room. He moved like an aging dancer, I thought, his carriage subtle, efficient. Waiting for my eyes to adjust, I detected another human figure shadowing the far wall.

Pinzi took shape, stethoscope curving down his chest. In Lufwidi the instrument had reminded me of airline earphones, but now I thought of snakes. I offered him my hand as the Doctor officiated.

"I've asked Nurse Pinzi to join us in today's meeting, so that we can all become acquainted. Shall we take a seat?" Herding us over to a table, he tilted his beaklike chin to indicate the chairs lining the wall. In the corner loomed a refrigerator, silent and gothically pale. In the other corner, beyond an empty bookshelf, were the two desks meant for Diabelle and me, and across the room sat Pinzi's, equally free of clutter. Perhaps his job involved no paperwork. No illumination, no air. The atmosphere was dense and hot, pitted with the aroma of ammonia, rubber, and mold.

Dragging chairs from where they'd been arranged for patients, we assembled around one end of the table, and the Doctor distributed copies of the questionnaire. Barely able to decipher the print in the darkness, I wondered how Pinzi managed to see his patients during their exams.

Oblivious to eyestrain, however, the Doctor presented the document and the art of coding. The questionnaire involved eleven pages of personal questions about sexual habits and reproductive experience. "How often do you have intercourse?" the women would be asked. "How many wives does your husband have?" "What methods have you tried to keep from getting pregnant?" It was the traditional methods that interested me, that later would unite Diabelle and me as we laughed at the responses penciled by the interviewers: "urinating," "taking quinine," "the belt worn around the waist."

Our job was to enter the numerical codes that corresponded with each of these answers into columns at the margins. We were also to check for inconsistencies in logic; for instance, if a woman had said she'd had five children, and she'd been pregnant only three times, we were to flag the questionnaire.

The work looked easy enough, and the Doctor's drawl made me sleepy; my eyelids wanted to close. Diabelle was all attention. With great effort, I lifted my gaze, and focusing on the door behind Pinzi's desk, I woke a little as I wondered where it led.

The Doctor didn't miss a beat. Concluding his presentation, he looked directly at me. "Allow me to show you around." He stood, and we all scraped our chairs, following his lead. I felt Diabelle at my side.

"First, we have your workstation." The Doctor posed, palm extended. "These two desks I brought just yesterday from the hospital."

I smiled at the desks, at Diabelle.

"They're good," she whispered.

Stepping neatly behind one, the Doctor motioned us to come and see as he opened each drawer, one by one, as if he, himself, had invented them. I admired the empty interiors.

"Over here, of course, is Pinzi's desk." The Doctor took a few long strides, then hesitated, contemplating the block of wood, and when I glanced back at Pinzi I thought I detected a trace of panic in his pursed mouth, as if he feared that the Doctor might discover something hidden in his desk. Cough syrup? A camera? Yet the Doctor stepped blithely away, and we trooped to the mysterious door.

"The examination room," he announced, leading us through. In the gloom I made out three beds along the far wall, curtains suspended between them like tall specters. Cardboard boxes were stacked beside cases made of glass, and a sink glowed beneath a shuttered window.

"But it's so dark," I marvelled, looking at Pinzi. He had yet to speak a word.

"Yes," drawled the Doctor, "we keep this room cool, as comfortable as possible for the patients."

Sweat was trickling down my belly, my back; I kept thinking I heard rain. As he positioned himself beside a case of gleaming scissors and tweezers and knives, I felt the insides of my elbows and knees pang with squeamishness. Instead of modern medicine, the dusty display evoked a surgical museum. Diabelle was lingering at a different case, trying to read the labels on containers the size of cookie jars, her nose almost against the glass.

Abandoning the instruments, the Doctor darted to her aid, his hand just missing her breast as he reached to turn the lock. Diabelle jumped back as the door slid open.

"After I've written a prescription, Pinzi dispenses from this supply. In emergencies, such as with cases of cholera or malaria, he dispenses on his own authority."

"What are these?" Diabelle pointed.

"That is ampicillin, an antibiotic for infection."

"And those?"

"Chloraquine, for malaria."

Methodically, she pointed a third time.

"The panacea, there, for pain."

"Aspirin?"

"Ehi, you'll make a nurse some day!"

Pleased, Diabelle lowered her gaze. But the Doctor, inspired by her interest, proceeded to present each supply jar, enunciating pharmaceutical terms, symptoms, cures. He might have been Paul's wizened charlatan showing off potions and herbs. There were drugs against infection, lozenges for cough, pills for sleeplessness and fluttering hearts. Powders for diarrhea, ointments for sores. Diabelle blinked and nodded, enthralled, just as she'd responded when I'd supplied her with her condoms a few days before. Pinzi seemed to be asleep standing up.

Finally, the Doctor locked up the case, removing the key to press it into Pinzi's palm, whether to validate his function as nurse, or because Diabelle and I were suspect, I wasn't sure. Back in the front room, we clustered around the refrigerator.

"Our *frigo* here runs on *pétrole,*" the Doctor explained. "You must take care that the pilot flame is always blue. When it's not, the mechanism isn't functioning properly, and if the temperature gets too warm then all our serum will go bad." Squatting, he yanked the grate from beneath the storage compartment, so that we could take a look.

"Pinzi will teach you how to refill the tank with *pétrole,* and to adjust the flame. Everybody must be responsible for the *frigo.*"

"I see," I said as he replaced the grate.

Straightening to his full height, he pulled the handle, and I inched forward for that blast of frosty air. Happily, the Doctor exclaimed, "Someone has foreseen our thirst!"

Luxuriating in the draft, I noted the beer bottles lying on their sides on the top shelf.

"Whose are these?" the Doctor asked Pinzi.

"Citizen *Préfet's,*" the flimsy voice replied.

Nodding, enjoying the chilly air, I watched the Doctor point out the precious boxes of vaccination serum on the lower shelves. Then he reached for a bottle of Empereur, and shut the refrigerator door.

Already Pinzi had got hold of glasses and was headed back to the conference table; clearly, in this situation, he knew what to do.

"I'm sorry," the Doctor was telling Diabelle, "we have no Coke, no Fanta to offer you instead. Could you take just a sip for our toast?"

Pinzi was pouring, tilting foam into a glass. Diabelle shook her head. "If the *Préfet* were to hear," she smiled.

Then the Doctor raised his sweating glass, and I wanted to lift mine straight to my cheek, to my aching forehead, but I suspended it aloft, savoring the coolness in my hand.

"To family planning," intoned the Doctor.

"*Skol,*" we replied in weak unison. Wielding an imaginary glass, Diabelle sipped at air.

Mostly it rained afternoons or nights, and in the morning people set out with sticks, stopping every few minutes to scrape the mud from their shoes. The kids who came daily from local villages wore thick black sandals made from old truck tires, and if it rained any time near dawn, they didn't come to school at all.

My aluminum roof was watertight and loud when the rain drummed down; each time it began I closed my eyes and listened, hearing again the congas in Conakry booming across the lagoon. Everything seemed waterlogged, as if the walls, books—even my own waist—had swollen with humidity; everything had blurred. Sudden as Jack's beanstalk, the leaves pushed at the screens, twisting up from what three months ago had been charred earth. The whole mission was soggy, saturated, lush; the oxygen laced with a mineral hue. Walking, you slid, stuck, and sank; you almost took root. In the bathwater my ankles looked knobby, tuberous, and my fingers floated splayed as if searching for light.

At the dispensary, I smoked, turning my head to exhale toward the clutch of mango branches outside the window I kept open. I'd ripped the shutters off my first day there, and Diabelle had stitched curtains from an old *pagne* to hide the nail holes and chipped paint. Atop the bookshelves, emptied in preparation for our anticipated stacks of questionnaires, she had placed a black ceramic water jug and I thought of flowers, but Africans never cut hibiscus or bougainvillea for display indoors. Rather, they kept the forest at bay.

I confiscated beer, once, twice, as the Doctor had, except that I hoarded my bounty to take home. Pressing the deliciously icy bottle against my chest as I left, I would invite Pinzi over for a glass, but he merely grinned as if in pain; he never showed up. He must have spread the word, however, because before the week was out, Lukau, my teacher friend, appeared smirking sheepishly at my door, rabbit teeth shining in the light of his storm lamp.

"Miss," he came right to the point, drawing back his skinny shoulders, "I've come to ask if we might spend the night together."

I laughed out loud. Was this how Cupid struck in Africa? Lukau laughed along, proud of his shot in the dark. Evidently he had nothing at stake, wasn't smitten in the least.

"I don't think so," I said. "Sorry."

Cheerfully, he cocked his head and aimed his brittle hand; we shook as if sealing a pact and then he disappeared, the arc of his lamplight fading as he squished off into the night. I shook my head. Drinking beer had, perhaps, rendered me a *femme libre,* a free woman, up for grabs; Pinzi must have thought my invitation loose.

The next day at the clinic, I told Diabelle; she saw the joke. "They will all be coming after you," she wrung her hands with delight.

"They will all be sorry, then."

"But why don't you like Lukau?" she teased. "He has two very nice goats always eating his front yard."

"Then he can sleep with them."

"And what about Pinzi? If he arrives, too?"

Pinzi was out of the office just then, fair game. He was out of the office more and more, repelled, perhaps, by all our talk of wombs and tubes and calendars, our giggles over data—over women walking backward after sex, sipping brews, reciting names, anointing abdomens. When methods were referred to in Kikongo, Diabelle translated, and I was beginning to learn: *"vuata nsinga,"* for wearing string around the waist; *"lomba,"* for traditional words. For the moment, however, Pinzi was the brunt of the joke. "He's married," I scolded Diabelle.

She nodded: so what else was new? Apparently, infidelity was not an issue here.

"I couldn't possibly make love to a stethoscope," I parried, flipping with finality to the next page of my questionnaire.

Diabelle clapped both hands gleefully over her mouth. "And the *Préfet?"* she recovered. "After all the beer of his you take?"

"If he bothers me, I'll threaten to quit. I can always work for the Doctor, instead."

"And the Doctor?" She squinted darkly, treading a reckless line. Indubitably, we owed him some respect, yet he was still a man, a man. "He would be," she whispered, "very exact."

She was talking about sex. She spoke like a pro, and it dawned on me that her box of condoms was not lying idle, waiting for the right guy. Sex came earlier here in Tambala—to all girls, not just to the flirts. Likely Mpovi had slept around as well. Even the conservatives here were sexually loose.

Western, prudish, out of step, I'd pictured Diabelle like the virgins on the pill in my high school dorm, the ones packed off with prescriptions by their worldly moms. Reverentially, my friends would reach into their bureaus each morning for the plastic dispensers while we, the unprepared, looked enviously on. Birth control to us then was an entitlement to womanhood rather than a need.

What Diabelle's manner now evoked was a more recent past, when, at college, we all accepted sex as sport, preaching easy attachments, slick rifts. I'd kept pretending like hell that breaking up didn't hurt.

"The Doctor," I answered her, "is too old."

Unchecked, she dipped forward eagerly. "Yes, your Bwadi is *dur."*

"Dur": difficult, tough, hard.

"My Bwadi?"

"Yes, Miss! You were so good arguing with him! You made him very mad!"

What, exactly, had she seen that day at school? Trying to picture the squabble from her eyes, I saw something like a mating ritual, vivid plumage, garish feints.

Resentfully, I flipped another unread page. "Bwadi's not my type."

Diabelle sat back, staring, a slow smile tightening her face. "I know, Miss. It's what I told you before. White men are best."

Then Bwadi showed up one night, literally out of a storm, dripping morosely onto my porch. Although he wasn't carrying a lamp, I glimpsed his profile strobe-lit in the flash before he knocked.

"It's you," I complained, opening the door. "Come in before you get killed."

"There's too much mud. I've been pushing my moped."

Leaning across the threshold into the damp slap of rain, I caught sight of handlebars. A wicked gust whipped my hair into loose mutiny, the frantic strands like stinging bees, and I snapped back inside, fingers combing. After my bath, I'd left my hair hanging long in the fresh rain air. Bwadi had never seen my hair down.

"Hurry up." I swung the door open wide. "I'm not standing in the rain."

He slopped inside, pooling where he stood. His pants were splattered knee-high, smeared across the thighs; his palms, suspended sheepishly, looked as if he'd been holding mud. The beads of rainwater in his kinky hair glistened, and his wet shirt clung as if absorbed in places by his skin. He didn't look hurt. He didn't look drunk. He looked as if he'd emerged from a bog.

"What happened?"

He let his hands drop. *"Je suis en panne." I am broken down.*

"You, or your bike?"

He shrugged. We were smiling now, in spite of ourselves. Or he was smiling; I was smiling back.

"Strange touring weather. Has the holiday begun early again?"

With the official Christmas break now a week away, I expected to hear at any moment that school had closed. My veiled reference to last month's student strike, however, put Bwadi out. He stiffened, lord of his puddle on the floor, and announced to the shadowy walls, "I've been wanting to see you." When he focused back on me he looked confused; I'd never seen his eyes so round.

"You're in trouble," I said.

He looked away.

"You'll have to wash." Irritated by his secrecy, I spun off toward the bathroom. The storm lamp I placed on a shelf illuminated the windowpane's watery blur; it looked as if we'd sunk. Supplying Bwadi with my one extra towel, I pointed to the soap; he stalled, afraid to take a step.

"It's American style: a sink, a tub, a commode," I condescended; likely the bathroom in his quarters was the same.

"It's too clean."

"First it's too muddy to come in, then it's too clean to wash." Closing the door, I shut him in alone.

The tile and ceramic amplified his laugh.

I groped for matches, lit the stove. The kitchen was dark, but I knew my way around by touch as I filled a pan with water, fit the lid. Lightning flashed and my hands looked blue; thunder cracked, rattling the silverware in the sink. Bwadi made me nervous, a stranger to myself. Why had I let him in? What was he doing in my bathroom? I'd put him there, I supposed, to give myself a chance to think—or maybe just because I couldn't stand to see him wet and desperate, stray. Come out and fight like a man, I felt like shouting, reaching for the tea. Come out clean, smart, superior, so I can say something cruel. Clearly he'd had some motive for showing up; he could have limped on home from wherever he was—with Catherine in Lufwidi, probably—without stopping here. He could be muddying up his own bathroom. He could have sought shelter from the storm at the *Préfet*'s, been offered cold beer. And if his motive was remorse, he could have come before.

Yet he had said he'd been wanting to talk.

Something boomed against the roof, at first I thought lightning but there was no illumination; a branch, maybe, a torn palm frond. In Conakry when the night storms raged we would gather at the center of our giant *paillotte,* all of us humble in pajamas, my father smoking nonchalantly beside my mother, brother, and me together on the couch. The storm lamps flickered on the end tables, but inevitably he would meander over to the window for the lightning's silver panorama, his calm shoulders haloed like a saint's, the smoke trickling upward from the cigarette in his hands clasped behind his back. Oddly, I ached for that childhood scene, recalling it as cozy, the coziest ever, my father in his element, quietly reckless, my mother's shoulder soft against my neck, my brother straining to keep his toes, insulated in their tennis shoes, pressed against the floor.

The water on the stove began its hollow boil; I spooned the tea leaves, poured. Timid noises carried from the bathroom: the blast of pounding bathwater instantly quelled, the toilet handle jiggled too gently to flush. A few thumps, silence: towelling dry? I tried to picture Bwadi careful and sleek, but all I could imagine was a murky creature turning in place, dark, warm, coarse. *Dur.* I could not imagine telling him about our Conakry *paillotte.*

Filling two mugs, I decided to serve the tea black, American style; nothing sweet or creamy to soften the bite. Padding out to the *salon,* wondering if my flip-flops would be enough to ground me now, I set a cup for Bwadi on the coffee table. Mine I carried to the desk where I'd been reading when he'd appeared. Finding my place, I stared at the page.

He emerged barefoot and shirtless as a sharecropper, slacks shortened to his knees, water trickling down his calves. He must have rinsed the cuffs and rolled them up wet.

I nodded at the coffee table. "There's tea."

"No Empereur?"

"Are you still waiting for that bottle you won?"

"I hear you've been giving it away."

"Actually, I've drunk it all myself." I turned back to my book.

After a moment, I heard, *"C'est gentil,"* and the sudden velvet in his voice caught me off guard. *It's nice.* Did he mean the tea, the bathroom, me? He was looming now, posted at my shoulder as if to monitor my paper grading in the teachers' lounge. Yet this was different. I heard him blow, slurp, gulp his tea, palpably close. Rather than severe, he felt to me forlorn, as if hulking for reassurance as a horse does beside a human it trusts.

"Thomas Mann. *The Magic Mountain,*" I said in English.

His arm, reaching around me for the book, was dry and scratchless, fragrant with my soap. "For your students?"

"For me. Not every moment of my life is spent on them."

"No, you've abandoned us for the dispensary." Coolly, he added, "I never find you home."

Disobediently, my heart skipped.

"This matter I want to discuss," he lapsed into formality, gingerly replacing the book, "is not for anybody else. So I've been waiting to find you alone."

This didn't sound like any apology. Rising, I carried my tea to the coffee table and flounced into a chair, fed up with his thick chest in my face.

He did not sit down. "I need your cooperation at school."

"Bwadi, I have the right to teach as I like."

"The right!" He stiffened. "Do you think you are still in America? This is Tambala, there are no rights here! This is where you are pulled from your bed at night and thrown in jail. This is where you disappear without a trial. Where boys are stolen on their way to school and sent to fight in Angola. Where the *gendarmes* are anarchic, stealing, raping, drunk. No, I don't believe you have the right to attract them here."

"I would translate the text, explain that the green *fou fou* was a joke," I bristled. "I'm not afraid."

"Then you are stupid. You do not explain here." His arms chopped sideways in disgust; tea slopped. Silent, he struggled a moment, his recessed body seeming to undulate as some private battle raged within. Back arched, chin torqued, legs flexing, he looked like someone in a dream whose feet refuse to run. What he was fighting was the urge to hurt, I understood, the urge to hurt me. Yet rather than frightened I felt a little thrilled, amazed to think that I could tame this beast.

The words he finally found were bleak. "You do not explain here," he repeated limply. "You watch your brother beat unconscious before any questions have been asked. You watch him taken away and never know if he's alive."

The sky churned. Shivering, I pulled my knees up against my chin, the hem of my skirt around my feet. He was in trouble, yes.

"Tell me."

Maneuvering clumsily, Bwadi swung toward the chair beside me so that it grated as he sat. Flopping forward, he leaned his elbows on his knees, letting his hands dangle loose and large. I could not see his face; he was studying the floor, ankle deep in shadow, his hair an exasperated tangle between his shoulders' silky slope. A gust jogged a windowpane.

"They thought he was helping the MPLA," he said. "Giving information about troops, supplies."

"*Caches d'armament,*" I put in, remembering what Mitch had told me about the CIA shipments en route to the UNITA rebels in Angola. My thoughts raced; my whisper hardly rose above the rain. "I didn't know you had a brother nearby."

"I don't anymore. This happened over two years ago."

"But—" I puzzled. "Tonight?"

He refused to talk about tonight. Was I supposed to guess? Whether or not this brother had been actively involved, I knew that Bwadi, for one, was socialist: loyal, I was sure, to the Angolan regime. For the first time I acknowledged that he was honestly on the other side. That I wanted to be there, too.

"I'm sorry."

The phrase was out before I reminded myself that the apology was supposed to come from him. Yet what had he really done to me? Belittled my professional efforts, made a fool of me at school? To hear Diabelle tell it, I'd come out on top in the courtyard. So he'd avoided me at the drum dance in Lufwidi, foiled my masquerade as a Tambalan *femme*—at least he'd joined our table at the palm wine bar. There had even been a moment of collusion, I recalled, against—against what? I thought back, trying to recall exactly what had caused the conversation to veer from the Doctor's topics to—to no talk at all, to that chilly hush of suspicion and guilt. Blaming the CIA for JFK's assassination was an old story in the States, yet something about the concept had struck a nerve that night. Studying the corner beyond the lamplight's scope, blood rushing, I noticed my hands radiating warmth, my eyes burning as things began to make sense. Bwadi on his moped, his mysterious errands. His tendency to spy.

"Was the moped his?" Bwadi's brother's, I meant.

He lifted his chin, up, over, showing me his eyes, the pale crescents like eclipsed moons. He nodded; it felt to me like release.

"For gathering information."

"Oui."

"What did you see tonight?"

He glanced away, not quite willing to admit that this was really about him. Whatever was true about this brother, Bwadi had the moped now. Had brought it broken-down to me.

"Let me help."

Leaning back against the chair, he unfolded, flexible yet dense. I sensed acquiescence although he didn't tell me anything, and I knew not to quiz, just as I had with my father whenever conversations had faltered as I stumbled onto some weekend meeting, whenever he asked me to stay away from the house.

Suspended in Bwadi's wooden silence, I pictured possibilities. Bwadi digging in the mud for buried M-16s under cover of the storm. The petrol for his moped financed by the MPLA. Perhaps it had been a meeting tonight that had forced him out, some crucial assignation too tricky to postpone. Tense, surreal, limbs jutting bent at the elbows and knees from the low armchair, he evoked a sort of black grasshopper, a refugee. No—I was the refugee, temporary as the plush spider that often spanned my reflection in the bathroom window. They come in from the rain, spiders and refugees, men, too, floating, flexing, eager to adhere.

Thunder exploded the sky, the lightning dangerously close. Clutching my armrests, feeling the shock wave vibrate my spine, I thought of the high tides of Conakry, the dead fish floating sideways in the pool. I put my hand around Bwadi's arm.

We sat there, listening, neither of us inclined to move, until the crash that seemed to split my skull. For an instant, the whole room was lit not blue but a harsh yellow, and sparks flew from the ceiling light socket; it was brighter inside than out, painfully bright, the smudges explicit on the walls. When the darkness returned, the room receding from the reach of the Aladdin lamp, I found myself on my feet, up against the wall, Bwadi at my side.

"Ngando," I thought he said, his breath against my temple. It felt
singed.

"What?"

"Ça va?"

"Were we hit?"

"The electric wires. The current carried through the circuit."

Full of awe, I considered the phenomenon. "All the buildings
were lit, do you think?"

He shrugged, watching me, thinking something else.

"Have you seen it before?"

"In Kimpiri."

"So for a second Mampungu got its current back." I imagined
the poles lining the mission drive, the wires still intact, attracting
electricity. Neither of us budged.

Then Bwadi said it again: *"Petit ngando."* He said it sadly, sort of
helplessly: "little crocodile." I was sure I'd heard him right. I didn't
ask what he'd meant, though; the lightning was flashing elsewhere
now, the thunder seconds late, and Bwadi was moving me across
the floor, toward somewhere safe, I thought, but then we were in
my room, my bed, touching flanks, legs and bellies scraping, and I
was pressing my fingers against him, one place at a time, not sure if
I was pushing away or not.

7

PAILLOTTE

The next morning I woke curled into a knot, bare and ivory as an egg. Bwadi was gone. Early light fell milky and silent through the window and I ached for his hot breath in my ear, for his evolving hold, for the whole harsh blur I'd had to abort, arching away. He'd let me go and I'd undressed, but I was also fishing for the box from which I'd supplied Diabelle, and when I banked back against him and pressed the cellophane envelope into his adamant hand, he winced. He knew what it was, knew what to do, but all the lush inevitability of giving in was gone, doused by fumbling suspense. He didn't stop and didn't stop but then it was over too fast, over for far too long, the bed taut with our mute insomnia until finally I woke alone.

There was no more rain. Classes would be small today, the village kids unlikely to ford the soupy road; I resolved to rely on review, to busy the students with crossword puzzles and role-plays while I pondered my next move. Thudding out of bed, I tried out shame and triumph, anticipation and disgust, but I really had no inkling how I felt.

The bathroom, however, inspired definite ill will. Bwadi had left his mark: the towel crumpled in a loamy pile, the toilet bowl sunny with piss, rings of debris in the sink and tub. I cursed out loud and then caught myself relishing the mess as male; they were, it seemed, all the same world round. I pictured myself yelling at Bwadi, but I couldn't see him kowtowing to my rules; rather, he'd twist my criticism into something selfish and Western, unjust.

The sink required a scrubbing; I wanted to wash my face. Biting my pride, I stooped for a sponge; I would leave everything else to Jetaime, leave the crudity of men to men. And then I was humming, fussing, flossing through my morning *toilette,* waltzing toward my paltry wardrobe, reaching for the dress least bleached, for the fabric whose stitching still matched. Spiffy, grinning like a twit, I was dressing up for Bwadi once again.

The bell for school assembly was clanging from the church by the time I stepped outside, arms juggling the paraphernalia of play: backgammon, maps, bingo, password, masks, posters, pens—a veritable Romper Room in English to replace my sober texts. Twisting to turn the *Préfet*'s spare key in my lock, I stiffened with a start, then welcomed what I saw.

Bwadi's broken-down moped threatened to take root on my porch. All the blue splendor of technology had succumbed to a muddy crust, the chrome gunky and fecund. It struck me, though, as charming, allegorical, an angel on the blink. I could see it in sepia, like the Cadillac jalopy in Mpovi's photograph, the one with foliage filling the windows, the axles sprouting weeds.

He didn't come back for it; he didn't come back. At school, he receded out of reach, dimly swooping into a distant room; I twirled off to class with my unwieldy props, clowned and orchestrated, made the students laugh. Did they know? Or did they ascribe my manic antics to the nearing holiday? Some must have noticed, on their way from the dorms, Bwadi's moped planted like a flag on territory gained. Yet no allusions reddened my ears; even Diabelle remained in character as a traderwoman pushing fish, bullying, bargaining her way through the anglophone marketplace simulated by the kids.

In the clinic, however, she ingenuously asked, "Can you drive that moped, too?"

"Not that one." I peered into the bowels of the *frigo,* at the hot blue flame. "It's broken-down. I used to drive my brother's, though."

"No!"

"Sure." I straightened, satisfied of the *frigo's* promise to run cold. "When we were kids." Instructing from behind, he'd told me when to crank the clutch and open the throttle, when to lean into the curves; we'd cruised the lagoon road at forty-five. His was a full-blown Honda, not a pedal moped like Bwadi's, and he'd wanted me to go too fast.

"Was it good?"

"Actually, I didn't like it much."

"Why not?"

"Too much noise."

Pen poised, secretarial, she cocked her head. "You like the quiet here."

"At Mampungu, yes. You'll see what I mean after you've lived in town a while. Cities have no stars. You look up at night and see empty black."

"Miss, *non!* Where can they go?"

"Well, they don't all disappear; a few, the brightest, stay visible. But nothing like here, in the bush. All the electric lights block them out." I hesitated, hearing myself make no sense. "It's like when you hold a lamp to your face, you can't see out into the dark. The city lights keep everyone from seeing very far into the sky."

"Yes, Miss!" she abruptly cheered, charmed by her own insight. "Because our pupils shrink! Citizen Limbewa explained how it worked last year!"

This was exactly what had endeared her to me from the start—the drama of her intelligence, the seeable ripple of bliss. With this knack for biology, I thought, she had to be destined for medicine, for a career in health. "You continue to amaze me, Diabelle. Soon you'll be teaching me."

Suddenly modest, she busied herself with a questionnaire; a moment later, she sighed. "Miss, there will be too many of these waiting for us after vacation!"

"Don't you worry about that. You just worry about school. I may get back a few days early and start catching up."

"Then you must send someone to tell me in Lufwidi! I'll come and help."

"Sure," I laughed, "you can stay in one of my spare rooms."

"Yes, Miss? I'll cook for you and Bwadi, and clean!"

She was utterly sincere. Bwadi and I had transcended the realm of innuendo, it seemed; we were now prosaic, a fact. Was this due simply to his moped on my porch? Or had she begun to sense sacred turf—that to me, Bwadi was no joke? She was canny, this girl; no fool at all.

I gave myself a mental shake, and focused on her image of our happy family. "We'll cook *together*," I revised, "you and I. Jetaime comes in to clean." Idolized, I felt flattered, yet eerily endangered, too. An impostor, I knew only how to play along.

I folded away into myself, my stack of interviews, the private secrets fresh for dissection into code, and for a while we worked in silence, the whispered friction of the pages loud. Then Diabelle's voice surfaced, reciting like a child's, "You take a *camion* to Kilu, spend the night, go downriver in a ferry the next day, take another *camion* all the way to the beach."

It was Paul's itinerary for his proposed trip, the plan I'd told Diabelle.

She looked my way. "It seems such a difficult journey just to see the Atlantic Ocean. Why do you want to go?"

"To cool off. To swim."

"Are you still hot?" A maternal frown blossomed as it had in Lufwidi that day, when I'd arrived so woozy at her house. She seemed to think I hadn't cooled down since.

"I don't think we others ever really adapt."

"But you were born in Africa."

"I've got European genes. Did Citizen Limbewa teach you genetics, by any chance, as well?"

"Yes, why we are all like our parents." She scowled. "But I'm not like my parents at all."

"Your grandparents, maybe?"

She shrugged, annoyed.

"You're like your sister, Catherine, no?"

"Like Bumfwidi, yes. So," she brightened, "I must have an American name, like her. Give me an American name, Miss."

I said what came to mind first. "Virginia."

"Ehi, Virginia!" She mimicked my anglicized vowels. "It's a place, isn't it?"

"Our first president's home state."

"George Washington."

Iffily paid or not, the teachers here had done a damn good job. "I'll have nothing left to teach you at this rate."

"Say it again?"

We practiced the pronunciation, Virginia's crude soft "g," and I wondered if ultimately language would be all I had to give.

"*C'est joli,*" she concluded. "Prettier than 'Catherine.'"

"But not as nice as 'Diabelle.'"

She patted at her tresses, pleased, and we fell back to work, interpreting, assigning, tapping each other's recall: "What's the code for menopause?" "Is it four for stillbirth?" The student choir kicked in, lament and exultation rising from the church like a tide. Later, locking up for itinerant Pinzi, I pinched another of the *Préfet*'s bottles of beer, for Bwadi this time, for us. With Diabelle as witness, I announced into the refrigerated air, "I'm keeping a log. I owe him for five now."

"Ehi, Miss," she dismissed my oral IOU. "It's for a good cause."

Something in her wording struck me: "a good cause." For me and Bwadi, did she mean, or for Bwadi's underground? For politics, or love? Snapping shut the *frigo,* I glanced for a clue at her optimistic face.

The church choir drummed; she was waiting to go. She looked like a teenage student, eager to get back to some powwow in the dorm, to the firm ground of friends. Probably she'd meant nothing at all. Empereur clutched against my chest, I did not ask.

Hypocritically, I cooked. I had never cooked for Davis in the States; I wouldn't cook for Mitch. Where was Mitch? Back from Madagascar, medivacked? Snatched from Africa by some high-tech emergency before we could—what? Probably he was busy at his Lufwidi camp with another willing white, perhaps a tantalizing black. I tried to imagine him sitting in my kitchen: stoned, soft rock chugging, smoking up a blue Marlboro storm. "We've got pizza at the cantina," he'd say. "Let's go."

Up until yesterday I'd have jumped into his truck. Now, however, my new Mampungu had eclipsed Mitch, had eclipsed my wistful vision of a trusty buddy who could share my Africa and laugh.

Bwadi would not laugh. I remembered him guffawing when we'd first met at the *Préfet's* house, when little Chance had screamed at my alien face. But then Bwadi had sobered at my flustered blush, and I'd hardly seen him laugh since. Mpovi said he laughed when I wasn't there. Still, his moped stranded at my door made me glad. At the sight of it that afternoon my spine had tightened, and the beer camouflaged within my armload of books had seemed hardly enough. Shoving crusty leftovers aside, I'd begun sorting fresh beans, soaking, stewing, measuring out rice, until here I stood, sweating alone, wood spoon poised above the stove.

He said I didn't listen. He said I didn't think. He said I was American: do, do, do. Sleek, smoky, jagged, he was a tourmaline crystal at the back of my throat. I never did gag.

I didn't let go. I helped him escape, but not from me, or maybe it was. Everything he said was true; he did not come back; he never told me a thing. My camera was for the cause: he never told me which. I didn't want it back. The night I tracked him down at his house he pulled it from a pile under the bed. I went to his house. Because finally I was leaving the next day for vacation and did he want his moped back? He said take me to the beach. He wanted me to take him to the beach. He lived alone. On an impulse at dusk I'd grabbed the bottle of beer and struck off toward the teachers' quarters. Kids scattered in the twilight, my flimsy pigment like death. Finally one who didn't run pointed to Bwadi's door.

I said let me help and he pulled me into bed and then later produced my camera as if from thin air. Is this your brother's, too, I asked and he looked away. He was skipping country with the film; he was skipping me. I imagined the prints: wood crates dug up, broken open, a fan of steely barrels spilling out. Black and white and gritty, molten mud, solid guns. Pictures for the press? For the MPLA commanders in Luanda? If I hadn't come here tonight, I asked instead, would you have simply disappeared? He said the moped for the camera was not a bad trade. I thought: you would have left it anyway; a pedal motorbike couldn't get you to the border, even if it weren't wrecked, even new. I thought: you tried to leave that night in the storm, but came sloshing back to me. Came back to disappear. And if I hadn't shown up tonight, I asked. He would have bushwacked to the river, bypassing the roadblocks. But *gendarmes* didn't bother whites. I don't know why I went. Like my camera, like enemy arms, my white immunity could be commandeered for the cause. Like the postal funds embezzled by the young clerk Lumumba, the crime for which he'd been imprisoned in the Congo until his fellow rebels could scrape up the sum. Like the whole white world we'd stolen from blacks: Fanon would say I owed it all back. Fanon, another of Bwadi's heroes—Frantz Fanon, the militant writer all for decolonization, for fighting foreigners with violence, Fanon, who had ultimately sought refuge from cancer in the satanic U.S. Bwadi would say that Fanon had been murdered by the CIA. But I said yes. I took him to the beach. It wasn't about sex, the sex was awful, brief, abrasive, parched. He couldn't wait, we couldn't go first to Kimpiri as I'd planned for my salary. Not even for my passport, my *carte d'identité*. My color was enough. It got a little crazy, illogical, me likely to hinder rather than to help, likely to confound *gendarmes* who could not read the document Bwadi had handed me that day in the school courtyard, the *Préfet's* baroque assertion that I was legally employed. Bwadi remembered with a flinch. And sent me home with a storm lamp to pack. He hadn't touched the cash beside my camera in that drawer; there was still enough. I was not afraid. I folded a ten-kuluna note into the paper and at the roadblock at the river the sleepy guy in fatigues did not ask me to explain, did not bother to rummage through my bag, to rout out the camera—Bwadi's camera—and film. Bwadi hovered like a lover. Were we not lovers, then? But he never said so, he never lied. I was a hostage, an accomplice, unable to say no. I paid the way. Beer after beer, I cleared my debt.

Instead of going to Kimpiri first, we took the train south to Kilu, the ferry the same day, the night truck to the coast. Diabelle had said good-bye at the clinic; she didn't see me leave. Mpovi didn't know. It wasn't a secret. We took the school *camionnette* to the station with the kids and spent the morning waiting with Pistache, their burly chaperone, and Tembo, the chauffeur, with the other teachers travelling that day in the opposite direction for the big city north. The students strutted in their pressed jeans, their tidy *pagnes* with headdresses that matched, and eyed us from afar. It was no secret, no. I was Bwadi's camouflage, I didn't mind. It was the most real dream I've ever had.

I went to him and he took me away. No, I took him. Neither of us belonged. He was Angolan, a refugee. I didn't listen, I didn't think. We'd been equally precarious, both perched to evacuate at a moment's notice, now he'd had his sign and I could not let go. I didn't ask a thing. He never told me why he'd appeared so abruptly that night at my house, what or who had told him to run to me, with me—or was I Bwadi's idea alone? He never told me how he'd broken in.

No. It wasn't about love. It was a grimy journey, sullen and bleary, the viscous forest floating past, sweating mud. We scraped our shoes on railroad ties, slept in seats, the night truck thick with breath, loud and liquid with snores. Bwadi's elbow kept digging at the curves. Arching over the rail, I was wide-awake, a witness to the stars: innumerable, discreet. I was tiny and unborn. In our *paillotte* at the beach I was huge. The French hotel rented us a *paillotte* with a bath. Thatch roof, tile floor, glass windows, a bed. Bwadi collapsed. I kept him one more day. Unfolding bill after bill, I had tendered the president's dingy image for fares, beer, food, a room. I could arrive in Kimpiri broke; I'd been robbed. In the *paillotte* I took up all the space. I brushed my hair down, found my swimsuit, changed. Bwadi's eyelids twitched at roadblocks, his eyelids twitched asleep. The sand was golden, hot and soft between my toes, each grain a speck of yellow bevelled glass. The beach sloped down from cliffs crowned green by bush and coconut palms teetering against the sky. After Bwadi left I sat and watched the sun emerge from there, a massive orb inching upward, dark and liquid as a yolk. That was the next day. First, the first day, I swam alone. The beach went on and on, sparsely peopled by Bantu fishermen sporadically gathered, tugging single file on ropes, hand over hand, dragging pirogues ashore. Or they set up nets, lines stretching from posts in the sand to the fizzing surf. The waves broke close in and gently; out beyond the white water you could float and roll with the swell, the waterline cool at your brow, your hair suspended like tentacles, pulsing when you flipped to dive, sucking sleekly against your neck when you popped through to the surface.

No Africans swam or sunned. At the resort, boys lingered in the distance, covering their mouths as they studied us sprawled pinkly on our towels. Multicolored umbrellas skewed, we were a few couples, a few families, teens, tan toddlers racing to the surf, a few women reddening on lawn chairs, tennis hats bobbing as they shared sunscreen. Single me. I stationed myself apart, a sort of sentry between the fringe of kids and my inevitable tribe; from behind my bubblegum sunglasses with the hearts at the temples, I watched them both. It was like watching a home movie, the echo of recognition tingeing scenes you were in before you can remember, the expectation that, any second now, your own face will inflate the screen. And then I did see someone, yes, someone from my past; skittishly, I froze. The name came easily, had always lain in wait, Mr. Baker, the sad, handsome man who'd held my hand in Conakry. Stomach down, he was propped on his elbows beside a younger woman, and his face turned speaking in her ear revealed the same twinkling gaze, the aristocratic chin, the feline tilt. He would be about that old, that fit, arms all bronze, hair white. Up there on his roof in Conakry, gazing at the turrets of the Portuguese fortress, he'd held my hand and wished I was his daughter, the one who looked like me, and I'd fallen in love.

Probably it was someone else. I shifted away, aware of my lily belly, round. Too much beer? Perhaps parasites. *The geography of hunger:* the phrase came back to me from somewhere, the image it always evoked: edemic bellies round as globes.

The African kids were gone.

I removed my shades, and inside my closed lids I saw the sunshine tender red. A few days here would turn me pink gold. Pink gold—the jewelers' term for the color of gold mined in Ghana, the old Gold Coast. Eighteen carat, tinted rose. Ghanaian gold had been so inexpensive and abundant that I had used to ferry rings to my friends at boarding school after visits to my father at Christmas. They paid me from their book money, each ring costing about the price of one text, whether designed in the shape of a "v" or worked from filigree or made up of the seven delicate bands. At one time I'd had one of each; I couldn't remember how they'd all got lost. Along with the pool tiles and gold weights, they'd drifted out of my circumference, and I'd hung on to other things instead: strings of trading beads, an ivory crocodile carved hollow inside. My mother's signet ring.

Bwadi hibernated, that first day, and I lolled alone, avoiding Mr. Baker's eyes. Would I still remind him of his daughter, Sadie, sacrificed in his divorce? What was she like now? Had she, too, wandered back to Africa, combing for clues? Scrubbed by salt and sand, purged of the journey's dirt, I'd never felt more clean. My skin tingled in the breeze, my hair dried long. I dozed, woke, dozed. I imagined Bwadi's fingers searching at my neck, separating strands. I'd never told him of my childhood *paillotte,* of our thiefman, Ali, of my mother evanescent on the rocks. He might not know she'd died. He didn't know Touré had kicked us out. There was too much to say. There was nothing to say. He would not come near this beach. This was independent Tambala, Africans could go where they liked, but they didn't like the beach. They didn't like colonial *paillottes.* Except for those kids, there, mobilized now at the water's edge, over where the curving cliff cut off the sand. Some hunched down and dug, some trotted back and forth, carting brush. Voices carried, piercingly sweet. I was up, strolling over, towel tucked around my torso, *pagne* style. At the fuzzy heads swivelling, the perfect round eyes all fixed on me, the slow, soft note of wonder in the words wafting out— "Ehi—" "Ehi—" "Ehi—" I laughed. *"Mbote!"* I called hello, a few more phrases in dialect, and, laughing, they agreed on glee. Showered with chatter, I couldn't understand a thing. Their sand castle replicated the resort. A long, lumpy bungalow, a cluster of knobs for *paillottes,* miniscule roofs of twisted leaves. There were no servants' quarters. Pebbles for cars dotted a parking lot, for the company Land Rovers driven by guests. Shells for umbrellas, bits of weed for towels. *"Ça, c'est vous,"* a boy tugged me to look, dropping a cowrie onto a towel apart. Startled with delight, I remembered the patterned shells from Conakry, the same soft ice-cream swirls calcified, *petite.* We had never used them for people; had never erected a castle as exact as this.

Back at the *paillotte* Bwadi was taut. "I lived in this style hut when I was small," he said, "but the floor was dirt. There was no toilet, no water, no paint. I lived there with my mother and aunt and six other kids. It was about this size."

It was the size of a toy house. I felt huge. I showered, sidestepping Bwadi's piles and puddles, opening fresh soap. "I'm hungry," he said when I came out. He'd put on a clean shirt. In the patio restaurant he was the only black sitting down. I was proud of his impolite afro. I was on vacation, he was off to war. There were no mosquitos. Plastic holly draped the rails, red Christmas bows. Conversation from adjacent tables swelled: ". . . devaluation but . . ." "Swiss bank . . ." ". . . Air Tambala," ". . . infrastructure. . . for strikes." Mankanzu this, Mankanzu that, in English, in French. Bwadi, listening, scowled. He wanted Tambalan food. I had to order fish and chips instead; in Mampungu the beans and rice I'd cooked for him had gone to neighbor kids. He didn't want me cooking African, hair tressed; he wanted me white. I saw Mr. Baker enter in effeminate shoes. He and his scented companion rustled by, scanning, too fast. "That man there," I said to Bwadi, "I think I know."

His eyes did not leave mine. "From Kimpiri?"

"From Conakry, when I was a kid."

"You were not in Conakry."

I blinked, surprised. "Yes. In Guinea. We were there a year and a half."

"I know where Conakry is. It was closed to the u.s."

"Not until we were thrown out. We were evacuated in 1967, I think. Maybe '66. I don't remember. I wonder if it's him."

Bwadi didn't bother to look. "He hated Americans."

"Touré, you mean. Yes, he did."

"And yet you came back."

The beer arrived; Bwadi lowered his eyes and I studied his lashes, a dense, trembling fringe. Linen sleeves ministrated, disappeared.

"Why did you come back?" He lit a cigarette, reached for his foaming glass.

"We are not in Conakry. Americans are welcome here." Granted, Peace Corps had been asked to leave, but obviously only because the volunteers were too indiscreet, too likely to poke around supply routes and squawk. AfricEd kept a lower profile. But I didn't want to talk politics; I didn't want to lose. "I wonder if it's the same man."

"Did you have waiters, too, in Conakry? Candles, artificial leaves?"

It occurred to me that Bwadi could not recognize Christmas. He wouldn't know that the dinner music, drowned out at intervals by the ocean's white roar, was Christmas carols jazzed up.

When I didn't answer, he pressed, "An ambassador's house must be very fine."

"My father was not ambassador." Many people at Mampungu, fueled by scanty facts, made the same mistake.

"A diplomat, I thought."

"I was a child."

"So why did you come back?"

Sliding a Gazelle from the pack between us, I nursed a flame, and watched the smoke unfurl. "Bwadi, all this time I've been living in your world, now you can try mine."

"You've never been in my world."

I looked away, around. Teenagers in jeans and skimpy tops, gold exposed, monopolized a corner table crowded with Cokes. Later—how well I knew—while the parents shared hardship-post anecdotes, toasting close calls, the kids would saunter off to the beach, smoking dope, making out.

Why had I come back?

As if mustering patience for a slow student, Bwadi sighed. "In the sixties, we left our village in Angola behind. My father said we were too young to fight. He wanted us to understand; in Tambala he knew we could go to school. He gave me books about the big men—Nkrumah, Lumumba. But he knew it was too late."

"Too late for what?"

"Nkrumah's dream. Peace. The foreign intervention was too strong. Already Lumumba was dead."

I remembered Bwadi's caution at the wedding in Lufwidi, how the conversation had stalled. Nobody had wanted to evoke Mankanzu running the CIA's arms. In my world, however, it seemed Bwadi could talk. With the electric lights dimmed, the pot roast and coffee wafting past, the ladies aglitter with diamonds and lipstick, the aura of insulation prevailed. Who could touch us here?

Afro bowed, Bwadi spoke of Lumumba, the Congo's only populist, eliminated by the CIA in 1961 for having leaned left. Pained, he seemed to have nothing at stake. I liked the idea of us overheard, of my fellow expatriates catching snatches of what a brooding African and diplomatic brat had to say. Perhaps I'd come back for this. In 1966, while Bwadi's father was preaching Nkrumah in their refugee *paillotte,* I was throwing water balloons at the man, himself. In Conakry, my friends and I could see him through the cracks in the compound wall dividing their yard from his. Exiled from Ghana after a *coup d'etat,* he'd holed up in Conakry, in league with Touré. He sat in his garden and wrote. Filling our water balloons, we knew only that he was an ex-president. He threw himself flat on the ground. Dogs had barked, servants came running. Water had splattered the path.

"Some Tambalan children made a fantastic sand castle," I told Bwadi instead above our crispy fish. "I wanted to show you."

He stopped chewing. "A sand castle?"

He knew as little of sand castles, of course, as he did of Christmas trees. I smiled. "They built a small replica of the resort out of sand. With all the buildings, and little shells for people on the beach. There was even one specifically for me."

He grunted, swallowing. "Did you think they'd copy their own pitiful huts? 'The look that the native turns on the settler's town,'" he began quoting someone, "'is a look of lust, a look of envy; it expresses his dreams of possession—all manner of possession: to sit at the settler's table, to sleep in the settler's bed, with his wife if possible.'"

I was not amused. "And I'm the wife, you mean." He'd gone combative, as if the first few bites of food had catalyzed attack. My own fish tasted like fuzz. He'd been quoting Frantz Fanon, I knew, the pro-violence Algerian; evidently he'd augmented his father's lessons, done his own research. Was it at university that he'd read Fanon, studied Kennedy's assassination, Nkrumah's decline? Yet at some point his education came up short. Blinded by an era's rhetoric, he made me think of the residual hippies in the States. I was blind, of course, too, confined to a parallel vision insipid as the Disney exhibit I'd seen at the New York World's Fair—the mechanical, multinational toy dolls joining hands, chanting, "It's a small world after all."

I didn't want to fight. Had we ever done anything else? When he'd come drunk from the *Préfet's*, that first time, wheeling his moped onto my porch, he'd behaved like an ally, full of respect. Heart sinking, I replaced a wedge of potato on my plate. It hadn't been respect. He'd coveted my camera from that very afternoon—from the moment I'd photographed him beside Mpovi's tree. He'd conned me into teaching him how it worked: trigger the shutter, advance the film. What a fool I'd been. Yet what else could he have done?

"'The national bourgeoisie organizes centers of rest and relaxation and pleasure resorts to meet the wishes of the Western bourgeoisie,'" Bwadi was reciting. "'Such activity is given the name of tourism, and for the occasion will be built up as a national industry. The national middle class will have nothing better to do than to take on the role of manager for Western enterprise, and it will in practice set up its country as the brothel of Europe.'" Gazing serenely toward the inky sea, he looked pleased with himself, pleased to have remembered so appropriate a quote.

"Wait till Eckhart sees this spot."

Swiftly, his eyes fixed on mine: warning? mistrust? Retracting, he hunched over his plate, shovelling forkfuls.

"They'll develop this whole stretch," I taunted, "high-rise hotels, disco clubs, motorboats à la Hawaii." Hawaii meant nothing to him. "You're like the students, you know? Trained to learn rote. Do you ever think for yourself, or do you just regurgitate?"

He studied a tablecloth stain. "After my father went to prison, I learned all his books by heart. He never got to hear. After a while we got his death certificate from the Tambalan police. It didn't say how he'd died."

I relented. I realized that we'd each lost a parent at about the same time. "He would have been proud."

"I have had no choice." Was it apology or regret—regret for his own lack of freedom—hollowing out his words? "He was my father."

"If that were true, wouldn't I be just like mine?"

Abandoning his fork and knife, his food, he braced his fists, arms flat, against the tabletop. "Who do you think you are working for here? The friends you make will learn to support u.s. interests. You are an evangelist, promoting your country, your bridge, your beach. Making our children want to be American, like you. 'The impressionability and sensibility of the young African are at the mercy of the various assaults made upon them by the very nature of Western culture.'"

"You make me sound like a snake."

Leaning back, he mouthed something sly; I lip-read: *"Petit ngando."* To think I'd ever heard it as a term of endearment. I straightened. "I'm here for personal reasons. I spent ten years in Africa growing up. I want children to like me, Nickie, not the U.S., not the CIA. The two are not, by the way, one and the same."

"You may elect your presidents, but it's the CIA who decides when to shoot them, even there."

Nobody was paying attention. Our strained voices had failed to distract our fellow diners from their own comments and retorts, their appetites, the ebb and flow of drinks.

"Do you really believe that a father can manipulate his child's fate?"

Still leaning back, arms extended on the table, he slowly opened a fist, palm up, shrugged.

"You really believe that if Diabelle defies her father, for instance, she can be made infertile by his curse?"

Perhaps he'd heard the rumor, perhaps it was a common hex; he did not seem surprised. He did not answer me. He seemed tired.

"I'm glad your father was not a violent man." I motioned for the bill.

Silently smoking, we put up with the wait. When I finally stood, Mr. Baker's table swung into view. Bwadi was already strolling out; I detoured.

"Excuse me," I smiled politely as the sophisticated man and his partner looked up. "Mr. Baker?"

Perplexed, he opened his blue, filmy eyes wide.

"Mr. Baker from Conakry?" I tried French. "I thought I recognized you from Conakry, Guinea."

A gracious shaking of the head, forgiving, debonair; narrow fingers spread in protest: no. Backing off, I was blushing, nodding my excuses to the curious blonde. She was much his junior, in her late thirties, perhaps, but I could see how she'd find this man attractive. An idealistic blue, his eyes promised paradise; his sleek amusement promised skill. He looked kind, in control, he looked like someone I could trust. But it was someone else. It was nothing but a double—Mr. Baker's double taking form in Africa after all this time. Unsettled, I caught up with sour Bwadi; he was right. Sadie, Mr. Baker, the mistaken man, me, we were all the same. My father, too. We were all doubles here.

In the *paillotte* Bwadi pushed against me as if I were getting away. "You will not let me be a man." I didn't listen, I didn't think; I rummaged at the wrong time. "If you had a child," he said into the salty dark, "it would be all right." Eschewing sweet nothings, he preached: the product of our dialectic, bridging our opposing natures, this child would embody black and white. For the first time I felt used. He held my hands still. He was a zealot, desperate, hanging on for life. For the first time I felt he was in love.

It was too late, though; I fended him off. Switching the lamp on, he got up, started tucking things away into his hemp sack as if all he were leaving was me, as if, had I made my womb available, he would have stayed. "Is everything you do political?" I asked when he stood looking at me from the door. "No," he said simply. And he was gone. I didn't listen, I didn't think. My throat felt ravaged, stabbed. Everything he said was true.

Smoking, I remembered sobbing in the shower when my brother had joined the Marines. At boarding school, I'd retreated from my inquisitive roommate to the mildewy stall to harbor my enormous disappointment—not that he'd get killed; we were losing the war in Vietnam then, de-escalating, and he did not expect to go there—but because I saw us spiralling into separate worlds. In those days my friends and I, Saturday hippies, would sneak away from the shopping district where we were bussed, change into the tattered jeans that we had carried in paper bags past bus monitors, and march in the leftover demonstrations. The idea of my brother's head shaved scandalized me, but when, months later, he visited me at school, I sat blissfully beside him in the car he'd bought with his own money, bursting with happiness—and with sadness, too. He was barely my brother anymore; he had grown up and left me scavenging for shells.

I went back to the beach. It was later, almost dawn. There were no electric lights. The ocean foam glowed. Smoking, I followed the waterline, the cool sand sinking below my bare soles; I passed where I'd lain on my towel in the sun. Remnants of the sand castle sagged. One high wave, perhaps, was all it had taken to sweep the settlement away. I could make out the slick dots of shells scattered as if frozen in flight. Tossing my cigarette, I gulped the sea air, confused by the beauty of the sky, how it yawned, luminous as slate, veined with stars linked into glittering strands. I took slow, deep breaths, wondering how long I'd have to wait to see the sun come up, considering, considering how many millions of those distant suns had already dissolved to dust.

I left the beach. That night, I saw Paul. Waiting for the ferry back upriver, I saw Paul, and my heart sank. The ferry was approaching like a phantom, thinly taking shape out of pinpoints of light. It was late, almost 3 A.M., the ferry was *en retard,* and I had slipped away from the dock to find a place to pee, had lingered alone beside the black yawn of night water meeting sky. Lapping at pilings, the river seemed to breathe; invisible boats creaked and knocked. I remembered floating at Lufwidi village in my pontoon, the scuff of Bwadi and Catherine making love, and I wondered if one day he'd come back to her. If one day he'd come back. I tried to picture huts on fire, bodies, blood, all the emergency of war, but I'd only ever seen Africa benign. Even under house arrest in Conakry, I'd found the *gendarmes* kind. In my Africa, choir songs wafted through windows; fruit grew. I could not imagine Pistache waving a machete, Mpovi running screaming with Chance. Yet the cross towering above Lufwidi attested to local battles, however long ago, and the country's recent history was splattered with vivid insurrections, with the army's gory retorts. This was my happy poor. Help them help themselves, we'd pledged, as if to offer them chocolate. I'd meant to scorn the thought of doing good, the myth of Western benevolence, but I'd fallen prey to the noble savage icon instead.

The pale ferry loomed. It might have been the one beached on Lufwidi's very bank, the old colonial dinosaur come back to life. I liked the idea of it ghosting downriver toward the coast, alive as local ancestors. But I could not deny the reality of a familiar bleached blot among the dark shadows at the rail, a crude illumination: Paul. My heart sank. He had nothing to do with where I'd been with Bwadi. He was American; what I wished I was not. Dimly, two—no, three—other volunteers jockeyed backpacks in line to disembark, wispy and translucent among the murky blacks. I understood perfectly how Africans had first seen whites as dead. Peering, I recognized Sherry, a witty biologist, despite a drastic haircut; Ross minus twenty or so pounds; meticulous Phil—all fellow trainees at last summer's *stage*. I had nothing to say. Paralyzed by a vague sensation of disgust, I hung back, but then I snapped into action. Paul owed me cash.

I had spent my last bundle of kulunas that morning checking out, planning to resort to stories of robberies for my travel fares. How Bwadi had taken my money and run. Actually, he'd taken nothing, not even the camera. By the light of day I'd found it in my bag; he'd given it back: sneakily, symbolically, just as he'd left his moped on my porch. Nevertheless, I felt pillaged, deflated, as if something were missing under my skin, something intrinsic as tissue, a soul. The camera was dead weight. I thought of hawking it among the pink-gold Europeans on the beach, but I'd had enough of them. Thumbing through my money, the man at the hotel desk raised a kinky eyebrow and asked if I were returning to Kilu alone; I shrugged yes. "And you have a ride?" For "ride," he used the word, *occasion,* the local slang that evoked so perfectly the iffy waits, the random fanfare of success. He brushed aside my plan to catch a market *camion.* "*Mais, non,*" he protested, "my partner is driving this afternoon to join his family in Kilu for Christmas!" How I had smiled. And Simon, the Lebanese partner, had sadly made leg room for me among coolers filled with fish.

He was a slow, craggy, sad man, tired of Africa, perhaps, certainly tired. Too sad to talk, he'd fed me raspy cigarettes during our sweaty, bumpy drive; solicitous, he'd followed me with droopy eyes during our vigil at the dock. The only *bac* in service was for some reason stuck at Kilu. I was up and down, dozing, pacing, hands on hips. Passengers from a *camion* had propped themselves against peeling walls; babies howled, goats brayed. Simon offered me bread that tasted of diesel and fish; he paid my way to Kilu on the *bac.* I asked Simon how much, but with a dejected sniff he'd dismissed my debt, avowing my fare had been included in the car's. Apparently, I could get along fine broke. But, just in case, I abandoned my hiding place as the ferry docked, and muscled myself back into the fray. Dodging a goat, a quarry of flour sacks, I hailed suave Paul.

He veered, flashing me a lubricated grin, gusting toward me from the shuffling throng, admonishing, "Where have you been?"

"At the beach," I skulked, suddenly shy. "I've been bad. I ran off with someone from my post."

"Ah," Paul nodded knowingly as Simon sidled up.

"Not him," I hissed. "He's my *occasion.*"

"Ah," said Paul again, shaking hands. Sherry, Ross, and Phil lunged forward, shedding backpacks, happy as crooks. They looked drunk.

"You'll love the beach," I said.

"Where do you think you're going?" Paul demanded, his bandit earring emitting a gleam. "You're coming back with us."

"Look, I'm sorry I screwed up and missed you guys, but my time at the beach is up. I've got business in Kimpiri; my pack was stolen on my way back to Mampungu last month, and now I've no passport, no *carte d'identité,* plus, after this excursion, I'm flat broke. In fact, I was wondering, Paul, about that little loan last month?"

He seemed to sober up. "No problem. What happened? How much do you need?"

"Enough to see me up the road to my paycheck. I was dozing, waiting for the train, and someone walked off with my pack." I shrugged. "Simon's only going as far as Kilu; I'll probably have to catch a truck." I glanced at Simon; his slim grasp of our English evidently filled him with despair.

Phil looked alarmed. "You travelled out here without a passport? What would you have done for money if we hadn't shown up?"

"I'd say I'd been robbed."

"Head for the post office when you get into Kilu," jolly Ross enthused; "there's a big party there, everybody's calling home."

"Right, you gotta call now," Sherry advised. "They're putting calls through all night, but then they're closing tomorrow at noon for Christmas Eve."

"Christmas Eve?" I stuffed Paul's soggy bills into the pocket of my jeans.

"Tomorrow's Christmas Eve," Phil confirmed, as Paul shoved me another bill.

"Here, for calling home. I'm still a hundred in the red, but you should have enough for a *camion* and a phone call. They'll let you sleep at the Catholic mission for free."

Sherry was wrestling me aside. "So where's your boyfriend?" She, at least, knew it couldn't be Simon. "What happened at the beach?"

"Oh, he left. On to his village, to more important things, you know. It was fun while it lasted. Listen, keep an eye on Paul, OK? He's a tad bush crazy, if you ask me."

"Oh, Nickie," she shooed away the thought. "Aren't we all?"

"I caught him shopping for fetishes in Nkisi. He appears to believe."

"He drinks, is what he does."

"Don't we all?"

"Hah! Seriously, from what I've seen, he's eating and sleeping well. But I know what you mean. He's kind of overboard."

"He's kind of a cartoon." I squinted; her new coiffure held the momentary spotlight of a passing truck's headlights as it lumbered down the ramp. "By the way, I like your hair."

"Yes, it is rather Mickey Mouse, isn't it?"

"It's AfricEd. What inspired you?"

"What's the point of long hair in Tambala?" She threw up her hands theatrically. "What's the point of anything here?"

Suddenly I felt cured. What was the point, indeed? Nothing mattered here at all, everything was hopeless, Bwadi, bridges, beaches, me; nothing could be done, I was sliding, sliding, back into the luxury of laughing out loud. Sherry was the first female volunteer I'd spoken to since summer, and she made me feel sane.

"I've got to go." Reproachful Simon was nudging my elbow; the *bac* sounded a mournful toot. "Catch you guys in Kimpiri," I called over my shoulder, trotting after Simon to his car. From behind the window, I fixed on the foursome; they looked whimsical, dissolute. Paul glowed and swayed; the others milled loosely around their little mountain of backpacks. I locked the car door. They looked like easy targets for thieves.

"Hey, there, partner! It's Dad!"

It was Mitch, cowboy voice booming unmistakably from a post office phone booth. Propped against my backpack for a nap, I lurched awake. I hadn't noticed him in there; I wondered if he'd seen me negotiating at the counter for my call. Expecting a long wait, I'd set up camp across the room from the people ahead of me in line, a motley dozen or so foreigners sticking to the single bench as if to high ground. Most were men sporting five o'clock shadows, dinged up briefcases, some gnawing on *chiquangue;* listing, pining, they were lonely entrepreneurs from all corners of the globe. One raggedly distinguished nun slept upright. I didn't have the heart to bother her about a room—a bath and bed were number one on my agenda, but I could go directly to the mission after dawn. For the moment, calling home had seemed a good idea; even if I'd missed the party, at least I would stay dry. I did expect rain. Midpassage on the ferry, I'd spotted clouds fuzzing up the Southern Cross, and the town air reminded me of Mampungu those nights I woke up chilly just before a storm.

The room was Kafkaesque, tall and dark, the light from one bulb in the ceiling falling short of the phone cubicles; focusing, I failed to locate Mitch. Long ago the booth doors had been carted off by vandals, I imagined, to be inserted into huts, laid flat as tables or beds, or broken down for cook fires and burned. The thwarted privacy struck me as perverse, the booths like confessionals deviously wired to amplify one's sins. A few pairs of eyes stared desultorily toward Mitch's commotion; the nun seemed to snore. I could smell the sour, smoky patience of the bench from afar; I could hear Mitch.

"No, no tigers here, chum, tigers only live in Asia. We've got monkeys, though. Elephants up-country. Gee, it's good to hear your voice!"

He sounded like a good dad. A dad with nothing to hide, probably divorced. I didn't recall a ring on his finger, but I was not surprised he had a kid. I wondered if, once inside their cubicle, each of the bedraggled men across the room would perk up like Mitch. Only those most determined to reach the home front would dawdle here at this hour.

Christmas was not my *fête.* I'd grown to resent all the holly and candy canes, the snowmen marching across cards. For me,

Christmas evoked crumpily wrapped gifts strewn like wreckage beneath the artificial tree my family shipped from post to post. More recently, my stateside Christmases felt inevitably stale, the echo of tradition fading fast, my father and I floundering like actors who've forgotten their lines. My brother and his family stayed away.

Mitch was talking up the odd ecosystem of Madagascar to his son. As the child got older, would Mitch find less to say? Would the terrible male love swelling his nasal twang diminish, disengage, withdraw? I remembered calling my father from college last spring, the familiar hesitation after he'd heard my name, the "Oh, yes!" as if he'd forgotten for a moment who I was.

"I've applied for a job in Tambala," I'd told him, after asking about the weather and the dog. "A two-year teaching contract. It would begin in June."

"Of course," he'd approved, as if he'd been expecting me to haul off to Africa for some time now. I pictured him nodding, absent-mindedly proud, just as he'd looked in Conakry when I'd first learned to dive. He'd always assumed that I was fine away at school, as long as his gentle letters came supplemented with checks. He never had phoned. What would we talk about now? Mr. Baker's look-alike at the beach? My angry African spy? My father would know more than Bwadi about what was going on. Who was help-ing whom in Angola, whose business interests were at stake. All I knew was that the u.s. and South Africa—and Tambala, too—were supporting Jonas Savimbi's insurgents, UNITA, while Cuban troops were fighting to keep the socialist government in place. Bwadi's heroes, the socialists. I wanted to hear my father's side. Instead, our expensive silences would reverberate, our hems and haws stall, and I would dwell once again on what he had become: polite, damaged, remote. Suddenly, I missed him too much.

Fleeing to the empty counter, I saw no clerks. *"Ko ko!"* I shouted, not sure if the greeting used when knocking on neighbors' doors was appropriate here. *"Ko ko ko!"*

Wiping her mouth, the mama clerk waddled out of an inner office, antennae tresses bent.

"Is it possible to cancel my call?"

"Vingt kulunas."

"No, I want to cancel. Stop."

"Why?" Massively, she crossed her arms.

"I just remembered it's a bad time to call."

"*Vingt kulunas,*" she insisted. "I've already processed the order." Noisily, she kissed the air, indicating a man asleep on a desk in back.

Rather than intimidated, I felt sorry for her pathetic thug, and pushed across the *matabish,* watched her tuck it into the fold of cloth at her waist. From the bottom of a pile, she took my order and ripped it up.

I marched toward the voice of Mitch. He was saying good-bye, exuberant with longing for his little tyke, and he appealed to me enormously right then. He was up-front, easy to read; he had access to trucks. He'd saved me once before from Bwadi; the thought of that blue moped left in the dust while Mitch winged me toward Kimpiri cheered me up. Bwadi had made me want to renounce my nationality, my childhood, my skin—and then he'd wanted me pregnant. Had he been that cynical in his pursuit of my imperialist heart? Or perhaps his rebellion against birth control was more about lording it over the white man's wife. I should have gone back to the beach. Should have danced and gallivanted with my fellow charlatans all over his shitty beach. I should take off with Mitch.

Furry grin bristling with delight, Mitch exited his booth. "So it *is* you!" He looked chipper and American, his beard tidy, under control.

Smiling, I felt itchy, grimy, in great need of a bath. "Fancy meeting you here." I smoothed my hair.

"Everybody who's anybody has been here tonight. I've been trying for hours, kept not getting through and then having to wait in line all over again. With only this one phone working, it's taken forever. I saw Paul and his gang, by the way, headed for the beach. You might still catch them if the ferry hasn't left."

"It has. I just got in on the return trip; I'm on my way back. We crossed paths already on the other side."

"That right?" We moved away from the booth so that the sleepy nun could take her place. "So you took off by yourself? Paul said you were supposed to travel with him."

"I went with another teacher from my post."

"There's another volunteer at Mampungu now?"

"Just me and the Tambalans."

"Oh, right." Flustered, he grappled with the same faux pas I'd have made in the Caucasian oasis of my past. There was nothing wrong with mixing, it's just that no one did. "Nice out there?" he recovered.

The sister's sudden deluge of French blanketed our words.

"Fine," I said. "Nice resort. All done up right for the holidays."

"What are you doing for Christmas?"

"Going to Kimpiri, I guess."

"You guess? You haven't got plans? Stick around here. The hotel's throwing a bash tonight."

I took heart; maybe it wasn't too late for me and Mitch. "The problem is, I've got sort of urgent business. I'm in dire need of my paycheck. Plus, my passport's been robbed."

"Really? But look, you're in no shape to travel today. You're bushed."

"Thanks."

"You've been up all night. My professional opinion is, you need a rest. Anyway, the banks and embassy will be closed by the time you're in Kimpiri. What's the rush?"

"Actually, I was going to hit up the sisters for a mission room. They rent free to volunteers."

"Don't bother. The mission's too far out of town. Come on over to the hotel, you can take a shower, relax. Tonight we'll party there, and then tomorrow we're celebrating at camp with steak flown in from Joburg. Next day, you blast off to the city compliments of Eckhart, Incorporated."

I shrugged. "When in Africa, never pass up a shower. Not to mention a ride."

He ducked off to pay his charges at the counter, darted back. "Hey, what about your call?" he protested when I began to gather my things.

"Cancelled. I realized it'll be too late."

Blinking deferentially behind his wire rims, he hoisted my pack onto his woodsy, gentlemanly shoulders. He didn't ask whom I would have called. I didn't ask about his son. It didn't really matter. At that moment, I didn't mind that he might have other commitments, that he might be married in the States. What I wanted was his company; I didn't want to care.

In the street, the darkness had thickened, blocking any hint of dawn. A black storm loitered above; a phlegmatic wind made my gritty skin crawl. The first silver drops fell.

Part III: Crocodile

8

THE BRIDGE

We slept through till afternoon. I woke first, gingerly avoiding Mitch on the floor; he'd given me the bed. Sun had preempted the morning's storm so that a trapezoid of light bisected his bare elbow. From the window I could see the river, ships. The water was brown, the sky blue, the air spic-and-span. Leaning over the sill, I saw tradermen unfolding tables beside the patio, straddling puddles, unrolling brass and ivory knickknacks out of tapestries, stacking baskets, straw hats. I saw the clean highlights of my own dangling hair. It might have been that West African harbor city where I'd lived a few weeks in a hotel when I was twelve: the tradermen tall and old and fluid in their long muslin robes, the wet treetops glistening green.

Kilu was a lovely town, carved out of hilly gold rock, its cobblestone alleys cluttered with huts overlooking the port. The ninth story of the hotel felt like the nineteenth. The smoke from my cigarette floated flat, a momentary stratus drifting left. I was wearing one of Mitch's shirts, but my skirt looked hopeless, streaked road red.

"Want coffee?" Mitch abruptly sat up. I had the impression he'd been awake a while.

"Sure. At the patio?"

"No need," he reached for his glasses. "There's room service." Shirtless, he hung over the sill beside me, finger-whistled, and waved at the waiter craning his neck beside the pink-and-white striped awning.

"*Café deux! Café deux!*" Mitch called down, *"Neuf six. Ici neuf six. Merci merci!"*

Nodding gravely, the young man in drill headed back inside.

"Phone's out of order," Mitch turned to me.

"And this works?"

"Always has. The milk and sugar comes with. How'd you sleep?"

"I missed the whole storm. You've learned some French."

"Pidgin. Just picked up where I left off in 'Nam." He was settling into a shirt, a chair. Back arched, arms stretching toward the ceiling fan, he yawned noisily. The table was strewn with his stuff: portable tape deck and Marlboros, wallet, glasses case, keys, playing cards, a rancid ashtray filled with butts. Everything faceup.

"So how's the bridge?"

He grunted gently, sucking a cigarette lit, exhaled. "It's all logistics, staff still arriving, local hiring on-site, calculations, blueprints. So far so good. It's a gig."

"Why not put it through here at the port?"

"Traffic will come through same as always, but get routed north to cross at Lufwidi. Once we put in asphalt, the detour will take less than an hour, and who's counting minutes in Tambala, anyway? See, the mouth's too wide here, upriver will be cheaper. Fact is, though, it's a matter of strategy. Not enough buffer between us and Angola at this point—cross over just a few kilometers down and you're on Angolan soil. Mankanzu wants to be sure he can keep the riffraff patrolled."

"Not to mention his own military convoys after dark."

"Not to mention sabotage."

"You think dos Santos will blow it up?"

"Nah, that would be an act of war."

I thought of Bwadi, Bwadi's photographs. Yet there was nothing clandestine about the bridge site; anyone who wanted could find Lufwidi. He'd been up to something else, I was sure, documenting arms caches, mug shots of fellow spies. Crouching at my pack, I dug below the incriminating camera for clothes. "Mind if I wash out a few things?"

"Make yourself at home."

Splashing around, I heard the coffee come; I saw the glum waiter smile at his colorful tip.

"Any ideas on how to kill the afternoon?" Mitch bellowed, pouring. From the bathroom he looked phantasmagoric, a wild scientist concocting a cure, his hair unkempt and overgrown, the steam entwined with smoke encircling his head with milky swirls that, backlit by the sun, resembled a halo. I flicked on the fan.

"All I know is that Kilu has a Catholic mission, a ferry, and a port." After hanging my skirt, top, and underthings above the tub to drip, I took my place in the dispersing mist. With the coffee, my brain seemed to tighten, comfortably snug. "A post office, too."

"Guess it's too late now for you to call."

I shrugged. The fan was turning in a slow, rusty circle. "I lived in a hotel like this, my father and I, while we were waiting for housing at one of his posts. There was a fan, a window with the same view of the *petit marché.*"

"He was in the foreign service, right?"

"We moved and moved."

"Nice houses, though, huh?"

"Colonial leftovers. Exotic gardens, swimming pools, brocade upholstery all wrong for the climate. Air conditioning." I smiled, wiping beads of sweat from my brow. "It was ugly and plush."

"It was home." Sensing my nostalgia, he let it swell, recede. He saw nothing wrong with longing for colonial props.

Suddenly fidgety, I put down my chipped cup. "Let's walk, then."

"I know where we can smoke a joint," he agreed, and I felt deliciously cunning and young, a kid in Africa again. Something about the blue collusion behind Mitch's spectacles reminded me of Rik, the boy who'd first offered me dope, who'd helped my brother push a car into the bay. The boy I'd wanted to kiss.

Downstairs, Mitch switched to sunglasses, scanned the patio. A few idle waiters shared a table near the bar. "I guess the rest of the boys are still sleeping off last night."

"Eckhart boys, you mean?"

"Yeah, there were a few of us trying to make calls. The rest will probably drive in after dinner tonight. Hey—" he indicated my Disneyland glasses, "what happened to Ray Charles?"

"Stolen." I gave him the details.

"Bummer. So," he brightened, "let's find another pair." He strode off, but when I caught up he'd been sidetracked by the tables of tourist art. Sleepy *commerçants* twanged out invitations, waved statues, beads.

"Look," I came up behind Mitch. Reaching, I singled out an ivory crocodile about six inches long. "I got one exactly like this from Ghana. I've even got a picture of it at Mampungu." Removing my shades, I squinted at Mitch through the hollow jaws as if through a telescope, sighting a wire temple, a dark lens.

"Pourquoi?" he asked the traderman.

"For napkins," I told Mitch, replacing my sunglasses. "For place settings, you know? Curry lunches and all that."

"How appetizing. Impaled crocodiles. Gutted, stuffed."

"Bon prix!" the *commerçant* blurted, as if cued. He wanted us to take six, eight, a set. Replacing the one, I thanked him, started slinking off.

Mitch, however, was digging for his state-of-the-art cash. "For one only," he managed in French, extending a candy-colored bill. No fool, the *tata* snatched it away.

"You should have bargained," I whispered as we retreated. "Seen how low he would go."

"Nah, it's Christmas. Merry Christmas!" he called over his shoulder. "Merry Christmas," he said to me, closing the trinket in my hand.

"I already have one, I told you."

"Now you have two. A set."

"Does that mean I have to invite you for curry?"

"Yes."

I examined the ivory scales. "I suppose you've heard about the crocodiles here." I didn't want the thing, didn't want any more to be the sort of person who collected tribal knickknacks, for whom Africa was an imitation *paillotte* on the beach.

"They eat people."

"But there's a special crocodile they call *ngando,* a magic crocodile that changes form. As a human, it lures other people, usually children, into the river for swimming or a bath. Then it changes back into a crocodile and strikes."

"They believe that?"

"They have great respect for crocodiles." I dropped it into my hemp bag, mumbling thanks. I didn't want it, but I didn't want to insult Mitch.

Lingering at a table of fruit, we picked bananas, a papaya, a paper cone filled with *nguba:* peanuts. We were too hungry, we decided; it was too hot to walk. Mitch headed back upstairs for his tape deck; I munched in the shade. Then he led me to a corner of the parking lot where three red Eckhart trucks gleamed like tomatoes about to burst. He opened the doors of one, let in air. Sharing nuts, we watched from the shade.

"There's no breeze," I observed. "You really think it's going to cool down?"

"No." Handing me the nuts, he dove for the driver's seat. I lurched in opposite. The interior reeked of vinyl and peanuts, of us. From the tape deck The Doors gurgled forth.

Downtown was deserted; we headed up into the *cité,* living quarters for the poor. Mitch drove fast, cultivating wind. But the streets narrowed, flanked by low mud walls crammed in front of huts. Chickens darted, goats stared. The aluminum roofs appeared to radiate. Children swarmed, lining our progress in waves, each compound alerting the next, each tiny tribe mobilizing to greet us with yodels, skinny arms upright. Ten year olds balanced two year olds sloppily, hips canted. We inched to a halt.

"Allez, allez, allez, allez!" Mitch suddenly sounded the *camion* driver's call, leaning out the window, arm rowing. Small dark bodies launched themselves over the tailgate, climbed the tires, filling the back.

"Where did you learn that?" I laughed.

"Longo, my assistant, always has me stop for passengers. That's how he gets them to board." Rolling ahead, he gave the stragglers a gentle moment to tumble in. About thirty kids jostled and shrieked with glee. We picked up speed.

"Fifty percent of this country's population is under five," I said.

"This isn't a country, it's an orphanage."

"Doesn't it ever bother you?"

"What? They're having the time of their lives." He glanced in the rearview mirror.

"A joy ride with the rich Americans. Doesn't it ever bother you that this truck is worth about twenty of their homes?"

"I'm just trying to keep a few people in good health," he replied, matter-of-fact. "A doctor without transportation would be pretty lame. We're doing good here compared to Vietnam. Nobody's getting bombed." Slowing, we turned back toward the kids' home turf. "I've met a few of your students, you know. They think you're the good fairy."

"Who'd you meet?"

"I don't remember names. I gave a bunch a ride near Lufwidi last month."

"My dispensary assistant is from Lufwidi. She's on the lookout for an American man."

He cocked his head, braked. Obediently, kids started jumping out. "Your students all cheered when I mentioned your name."

"Wait till I wave my wand and disappear."

He looked at me through his black sunglasses. "Shouldn't let it get you down. Think of yourself as entertainment. Just brightening up their lives for a while is worth something. Make them laugh in class."

I smiled. I liked Mitch, I did. I liked The Doors. We left the town behind, climbing a dirt track that traversed the hill. It was extremely green. Pedestrians were returning from fields, harvest balanced on their heads. Mitch tried not to splash mud. Higher, people grew scarce, the slope steep.

"This is it," he said, rounding a bend.

"What?"

"That. That's where we're going." He pointed at an orange ruin, a jumble of brick walls rising unevenly from a floor of weeds. Beyond, the site gave way to a panorama, down, down, down. Hills fell toward the valley, encrusted with jungle. The river was a glossy brown gap.

"Some view."

Watching for snakes, we walked. A flight of stone stairs led up, nowhere. The air was almost cool. We sat in the shade on the bottom step.

"Do you think we're trespassing?" I asked.

"This is just an ex-*colonne*'s half-built estate."

"I mean on someone's *champ*." I gestured at a few banana trees thriving in what should have been a room.

"We won't take any." He fussed, lighting his joint.

"Looks like a Portuguese fortress to me."

"Nah, it's not that old. Probably a French tycoon planned to live here until the troubles chased him out."

"The troubles." I savored the florid smoke in my throat. "I've never heard Tambalans call it that."

"What do they say?"

"La révolution."

"It worked, I guess. Whoever this belonged to must be gone for good. Nobody else has laid claim."

"We have."

We climbed higher, to where there should have been a balcony, a roof, and settled on the precarious landing. With one finger I traced the graffiti carved into the stone. Names, hearts. "Do you think it could collapse?"

"Kids come up here playing all the time."

We were level with treetops, redundant birds. The leaves looked plastic, too green. The birds sounded like toys.

"I saw slave camps in West Africa. Portuguese. They looked kind of like this." I indicated the crumbling partitions between rooms. "You could see the pits where the people were kept."

"This is just what's left after some guy had to evacuate."

"I had to evacuate once. I wonder what happened to that house." I tried to picture the *paillotte* without its cylindrical roof. My voice sounded far away, in the past. Mitch and the sky felt close. "My family had to leave Conakry. The president canned all the Americans. For a while we were under house arrest."

"No kidding," Mitch purred.

"My brother and I got to stay home from school. But we had to cancel Halloween. We snuck candy through the fence to the guards."

"Wild."

"I was going to be Mary Poppins. I had my father's black umbrella, my mother made me a black hat, I painted flowers on an old purse of hers for a carpetbag. I practiced standing up prim and proper, toes out, so I could lift off into the clouds. Then we really did go. We had a day to pack."

"Wild." Mitch's big voice drained away. He looked sympathetic, stoned.

"My brother broke house arrest. They hadn't posted guards in the back, and he just walked out to fish the tidepools. My mother went calling him to come in for cookies while they were still hot. She never baked. She didn't want the guards to hear anything wrong. When she finally got him inside, she hugged him on her knees. When my father found out, my brother said, 'What are you going to do, ground me?'"

It was just Mitch and me, two stories up, nowhere. The sun was almost within reach. Without his dark glasses, Mitch's eyes were tiny skies. He was riding an updraft, swooping into a dive. His mouth touched down on mine.

"Mary Poppins, huh?" Mitch was chewing, chopsticks flexed. The restaurant could have been anywhere exotic: Asian waiters, hybrid customers savoring the air conditioning, the sweet-and-sour pork. We were still in Kilu, though, back downtown. Christmas tinsel clung vinelike to an immobile fan. Red ribbons looped the walls. Mitch beamed. "Was that your favorite flick?"

"Until I saw *2001*."

"*2001!* First rate. I just saw that again at camp. The psychedelic part's a rush, where he gets sucked into Jupiter. But what was that fetal stuff at the end?"

"Rebirth." I hesitated, calling up the terrible beauty of that scene, the deafening heartbeat, the monastic pastels. "Rebirth into a new space and time. Nonlinear time, where the future and past happens all at once. Don't you ever feel that way?"

Mitch laughed, full mouth closed. Wagging his head, he swallowed hard. "Can't say I have. I exist for the future, I guess, can't stand for things to stay the same. Always looking forward to the next country, next job."

"You're entirely Western, then. Everything's progressive in the West. Do it better, faster, different, throw out the baby with the bath. Here it's the opposite extreme, equally perverse. These people thrive on tradition; they refuse to change."

"That's exactly it! They won't even boil water! Do they boil water out your way?"

I had to say no. "But the kids are trying," I amended. "I know a few ripe for conversion. Girls dying to be chic and cosmopolitan, to get real jobs. Boys fascinated with atoms, astronauts."

"Now that would be the ultimate trip—to be an astronaut."

"That's what I wanted to be when I grew up, for a while. After Mary Poppins, it seemed like the closest thing to magic."

"So what happened?" With his chopsticks, he indicated the earthbound restaurant, us.

"I guess I fell into the past."

"But," he hunkered forward, "maybe this country really is where the future's at. Not a bad place to sit out a nuclear war. Nobody would bother with us here."

"Like nobody bothered with Vietnam."

"Oh, hey," he adroitly segued, "talk about films, did you see *Apocalypse Now?*"

Vaguely, I recalled the flurry of controversy, acclaim. "I didn't catch it before I left."

"Phenomenal. Just phenomenal. Unfortunately, it's too new to get through Eckhart; I've tried. Anyway, they followed this CIA guy up the Mekong to take out Marlon Brando as this whacked-out general."

"That would be Kurtz."

"That was his name. How'd you know?"

"I read the book. The movie was based on *Heart of Darkness:* recommended reading for anyone headed to Central Africa. It's about colonial exploitation."

"Well, the movie is recommended *seeing* for anyone interested in Vietnam." Maneuvering a bamboo shoot, he looked tickled pink. Truly, he seemed to have left the war behind.

"I'd even enjoy Clint Eastwood at this point," I managed to keep pace. "Jerry Lewis, Doris Day. I miss movies more than anything, I think. More than food."

Nevertheless, I did accept seconds; I cleaned my plate. Food had never tasted so good; I'd never felt so earthy, so acute. It was Mitch's drug, of course; we'd driven straight from our private ruin on the hill to eat, and the stylized edge of euphoria had not worn off. Or perhaps it was Mitch. Perhaps it was my AfricEd buddies at the dock who had sparked this sudden zest for decadence, for living it up. At first, from across the water, I'd seen my clique through Bwadi's eyes, but then the vision had blurred, and now his hold on me felt like an illness in the past—like a sharp pain whose parameters you can't quite recall. He'd pushed and pushed until he'd pushed me back into my sandbox with my shells. Plucking at the water chestnuts flown in canned, I ad-libbed with Mitch. He smiled like a star; our athletic conversation felt rehearsed. We were speaking American, the language of Hollywood and television, of sports and rock and roll. We forgot it was Christmas.

Mitch lit up again on the way to the hotel and the river night felt like silk. Idyllic Conakry was just around the next bend; Mampungu receded like a fling. In the parking lot the Eckhart trucks had multiplied. Upstairs, I put my clean outfit on unironed and thought I looked artistic in the mirror, weathered and ethereal, rare. Experimentally, I revolved; the faded skirt flounced, my fluffy hair rose, my mouth winged up, amused. This was not a bad person to be, I decided; this was a person within reach. Mitch reeled me in, and all night people tugged.

On the patio, disco tinkled, the damp air clung. Rotating lamps stained the empty dance floor red, green, white: the colors of Christmas, the colors of Tambala's flag. Scattered African couples had already appeared: men buttoned up in equatorial suits, women in fauvist *pagnes*. Perfume wafted from an extravagant table of dark ladies alone, a ruffle of suspense. Farther off, a dozen or so white men slumped over drinks.

"Hey, Doc!" someone hailed.

"Doc, you made it!"

Following Mitch toward his friends, I grinned back at their incredulous teeth, their chummy grunts. Round-shouldered, long-legged, they were a rangy breed, closely shorn. Some had gone gray.

They were all happy to see Doc. He might have been their keeper, the wiry trainer with the whip, the benevolent *chef*. His sinewy limbs, his intricate beard made me proud. I relished my seat of honor at his side.

Timidly, the big Americans riddled me with gentle questions. Over the rattling disco, I gave the same old spiel; they looked confused. They were not so bad, really: simple, lonely souls. I didn't see the lush who'd insulted me at the Yank Tank, who'd called the Africans monkeys, me a holy volunteer. I didn't see redheaded Vince. Some were missing, Mitch leaned in close to explain, off on safari in Kenya, on leave. Singing the praises of our Chinese restaurant, he tapped his sneakered foot, poured Empereur. The talk fizzled when someone cranked the music up; smiling blithely at each other, we all sipped passively until eventually we'd drunk enough to dance. From across the way the perfumed women batted their eyes; one by one, the engineers puffed out their hefty chests and advanced.

Then Mitch and I joined the Eckhart troupe, the compliant hookers shuffling lazily in place beside the bobbing men. Uninspired by the loud French pop, most of the Tambalan crowd stuck to their chairs, their foaming glasses of beer. But as I did my little thing, swaying and dipping, the dancing hookers, at least, seemed to wake up. Flamboyant lips arched with approval, tressed heads listed, heeled, here and there from a distance a woman matched my step. Laughing, applauding, they egged each other on, in sync. I was out of my league, of course, among these impish vamps; their taut satin dresses and heels put my wrinkled skirt and practical sandals to shame. And yet they wanted to adopt me, it seemed; I had measured up. Flattered, I played along, loose-limbed, feet sliding, initiating swerves. Jigging Mitch didn't seem to mind. Bwadi's disapproval clung like a ghost. It didn't dance. Bwadi, of course, had bypassed the drums in Lufwidi for sex with Catherine in the *bac*. Wheeling, I shook him off.

Absorbed in their own worlds, the Eckhart men jerked and strained, against gravity, against time. Mitch kicked and pumped, all oomph and angles, all over the place. Buoyed by the girls, I grinned in friendly pity, twirled. He was alien, innocent, a gem. Song after song, we persevered together while the hookers changed partners, getting on with their business, working the floor. The mood began to shift as a healthy dose of respectable Tambalan couples began to dance; even Mitch succumbed to the infectious lilt of African steps. Things slowed down, the dazzle of lights merged; finally, the first tinny guitar chords of a local recording wheezed forth, and a chorus of appreciation rose. Mitch shimmied, adorable, motorized, tired. Impulsively, I took his hands in mine.

Back at our table, a few of my dance partners adhered cheerfully to men. Dabbing at perspiration, I reached for my beer, a cigarette, a light. The woman sitting closest to me detached herself from her catch to press my arm.

"Ehi, you smoke, too," I approved in French, offering her a Gazelle.

"But you speak French!" she giggled, delighted. Thick-waisted, very dark, she wore a slinky flowered dress of a nylon fabric that brought to mind my leopard nightgown. She appropriated a match. "Where are you from?"

Shouting above the music, I told her Mampungu, then America, explaining once again the whole deal, my teaching, my contract. She puffed hungrily, and I realized that she was the first Tambalan woman with whom I'd smoked. The men leered foolishly, sprawled all over their seats, basking as the prostitutes ran fingers through their short, sparse hair; Mitch serenely watched my conversation with the woman in the gown. She told me how she'd lived in Nairobi and Kimpiri, how she wanted to go to the States.

"And I wanted to come to Africa!" I laughed, touching glasses with Mitch.

I wanted to dance Tambalan, he wanted to rest. Rocking my shoulders, I was dancing anyway, I was back on the dance floor. The cigarette I'd given my dark friend burned between her fingers as she swayed, red, green, white. And then the working girls had circled us, dancing, clapping time. The men abandoned at our table looked perplexed. Red, green, white. Happy Mitch looked high. This was my initiation, my joke. The hookers rolled their hips, go-go dancers for a moment in our corner, on stage. We were not topless. There was no need for topless dancers here, for seedy hideaways, voyeuristic lust. There was nothing to expose. Dancing, we clapped in time, we were the schoolgirls in Conakry at their clapping game. Nobody minded, nobody came to take me away. It was where I'd always wanted to be.

At Mitch's metal settlement, Christmas Day felt like July Fourth. Men sweating in shorts lounged on lawn chairs, cans of beer balanced on paunches or wedged between legs. A sports game taped stateside erupted forth from a boom box. There were no plastic wreaths, no lank bows; the rectangular buildings simply reflected the sun. Mitch, driving, had pointed out the bridge site, the razed bank, the mighty wire fence that rimmed the whole bald lot.

There were no chickens, no goats, no children chasing tires. No choir songs lilted across windowsills; all the windows were closed. You could hardly hear the insects for the generator's roar. Mitch's camp was an eerie Africa, one I'd never before seen. No babies cried.

He ushered me inside his quarters for a tour. Stale and prefabricated, the place rattled with air conditioners, quarrelsome twangs, a television's blue hum. Sprawling, drawling, brawling, these guys were industrial cowboys, spurring their trucks around corners, transfixed by videos rather than campfires. They looked hot and soft, liable to melt. I didn't want to watch, didn't want to install myself in the lounge for what was left of Gene Hackman's role. Mitch invited me to choose the next film from a shelf, but I just shrugged. All my enthusiasm for movies fizzled to distaste. I saw the TV console as alien, an artifact, something I wouldn't know how to use. Mitch and I played backgammon and reggae in his cubicle of a room instead.

Dinner was a sunset barbecue; we all piled outside to find the drowsy sports fans revived, as if everyone's team had won. The boom box now blared Santana; the local cooks manning the coals were tapping fingers, feet, in time. Underlings laden with tubs of ice, potato salad, and sundry condiments charged to and from the kitchen, audibly encouraged by a strident American voice. In a moment the loudmouth emerged from the kitchen, and I tensed. It was the same rugged drunk who'd yelled at me in Kimpiri when I'd first met Mitch. Apparently this was Thompson's bash.

"You didn't tell me he'd be here," I nudged Mitch.

"Who, Thompson? Our miracle man?" Grinning, Mitch watched Thompson deposit a platter of raw steaks beside the grill.

"He's a wizard with supplies," a gap-toothed man agreed, having overheard. "Got connections from here to Timbuktu. Said he scored this steak in South Africa."

Sipping my Coke, I slunk back against a wall, wishing the sun down fast. It was that time of day when Africa sped up, oh so briefly, in the scramble for that last moment of light. Children and animals were called home, lamps refilled and lit. There was no such activity here at Eckhart, of course, yet even these cumbersome Americans looked recharged. Tinted red, eager for the feast, they craned. The African employees sprinted, under the gun. I lingered out of range.

I was just around the corner of the barrack, arms folded, my breathing slow. The jungle swam upward behind the fence, a tall tangle of shadowy trunks and brush. Still I heard no birds. Underneath the clatter of the barbecue ran the same electrical hiss. I smelled marinade; sweet, smoking meat. And then, as if invoked, two eyes met mine, the vivid, human whites suddenly lurid in the new dark. There had been no movement, they'd been there behind the fence all along, this single pair of eyes disconnected in the dusk. Shocked, I stared back, and gradually the contours of her face came up, the fragile brown arms, the faded shift. I might have been in a darkroom, watching a blank sheet of paper evolving the details of a print. It was a girl, younger than Diabelle, not as pretty, her hair tressed into severe corn rows.

Approaching footsteps made me turn.

"There you are." Mitch handed me a crowded paper plate.

"Who's that?" I swung to point.

"What?"

"There was a girl standing there, over in the trees."

He squinted. "They do that."

"Who?"

"The women come looking for Johns. They sneak around the main gate, find a place to climb the fence."

"But she's just a kid."

"Probably Eladia, one of our sadder stories. I don't know who she's with these days."

"God." I looked down at the murky steak on my plate. It looked rare. It didn't look like anything I could eat.

Licking ice-cream cones, we trooped down to the riverfront for Thompson's fireworks, belching gently, feet crunching on the pebbled landfill. The lack of electrical appliances was a relief; up by the buildings spotlights glared, bug zappers buzzed. Mitch and I stopped at the water's edge.

"Coast looks clear," he quipped, flashlight scanning the water.

"Do people come from Lufwidi by boat?"

"Nah, it's easier to walk than to drag the pirogues back upstream. Supposed to be crocodiles, though. Our head cook won't come near the place, says it's a perfect landing site."

"Seen any?"

"Not yet. I think our boogie-woogie generator keeps them all cowed."

There were no mosquitos, no waves. The water curled at the rim, transparent, then flattened away. Crouching, I dipped my fingers. You could not see the opposite bank.

At the first hint of a whistle, cheers sounded, and we looked up. With a tiny pop, a blossom of light veined the sky, fell apart.

"Yeah!"

"All right!"

Mitch and I ambled back toward where the guys had settled to watch. Transfixed, they looked dim and harmless, full of hope. I thought of the deadly Indians in the Amazon who, hearing the celestial strains of Bach, put down their poisoned darts. We sat, too.

"Where'd he come up with these?" a baritone asked, awed.

"These fireworks, you mean? Mystery to me."

"That's the guy you ought to get to know," someone breathed ironically in my direction. "The king of Service Supplies. Keep you in shampoo."

Others chuckled.

"Genie Thompson, that's right! Rub his belly, get your wish."

"Oh, no," I recovered. "I'd rather have Witch Doctor Mitch."

"Hah!"

"That's ripe! Witch Doctor Mitch!"

They cracked up. Delighted, they fixed on the elegant explosions, the fists of light opening like hands against the stars. Nobody had anything against sugar daddies here, against Santa Claus. Mitch's arm snaked around my waist. Perhaps I'd overreacted when I'd first met Thompson drunk. Paul may have been right. Yet the words still stung. *Monkeys. Dark ages. Holy volunteer.* They irked like slurs against my own family. I must have mellowed somewhat, though, because even if I could not worship Thompson, I could no longer resist Mitch.

We'd been there a while when, rustling, scuffling, a jolly troupe approached from camp. Loathe to venture too close, the band corked the path, a dozen sets of eyes and glowing teeth dangling there as the kitchen staff jostled; voices surged, the Kikongo vowels shrill, the laughs singsong. At each firework, they hushed.

They made me glad. At least Thompson had left them with a fresh platter of steaks. At least he'd piled a plate high and ducked inside the barrack, solicitous of the someone waiting, I assumed, in his room. Perhaps he was benevolent, as with prized dogs. Staring up, I imagined the aggregation of eyes aimed at my back.

When the show was over, Mitch and I stayed. His buddies rose with middle-aged groans, knees cracking, to lurch on up the vacated path. We lay back like friends, Mitch's head on his crossed arms, mine on his chest. We lay there a long time. We didn't have to talk.

"It's almost better without fireworks," he finally said, and I could feel his voice fill his ribs.

"You'll love the sky at Mampungu. No electricity, you know, to muddy up the depths."

"Must be quiet."

"It's loud. Bugs like violins all night long. Like a giant lullaby."

"And at the beach?"

I tensed. I hadn't thought about the beach for hours. "You hear the ocean there, breaking on the sand."

"Good waves?"

"I don't surf."

Rising on his elbows, he disrupted my headrest. "Who'd you go with, again?"

I sat up. "The history teacher. He went on to his village. He's not coming back."

"What did you do, scare him off?"

I smiled, not at Mitch, away. I stopped smiling. "I don't know."

As before, he let the silence ride, pulled me back, hung on. I was safe. He smelled of soap, smoky, a little of astringent and the plastic of Band-Aids.

I closed my eyes. "You're nice."

And then the generator sounded its slow moan, winding down, cranking off. I saw that the whole camp had receded, every light cut. Mitch wrapped himself around me, his fingers like a breeze. The insects could now be heard, pulsing tightly, left behind; chugging, they sounded engineered, nothing like Mampungu's organic throng. The river seemed empty of fish—of water, as well; Mitch and I might have been astronauts, afloat in air. I tried to imagine a bridge, a silver trellis arching like a tunnel through the night, bringing cars, taking them away. "This is what I wanted you to see," he whispered, and I saw that the stars, at least, had bred. Like the eyes at my back, they'd multiplied, like the eyes watching as my brother pushed a car into the sea. They were not going away. They were going to follow me back to the States.

"Where is Citizen Bwadi?" Somber, neat as a pin in his short-sleeved African jacket, the *Préfet* looked around my living room as if for clues. His creased forehead wore the same worry my students did as they needled me in English; our second week into the term, Bwadi's absence was concrete. Teachers were allowed a certain lag time from vacations, allowances were made—not only for teachers, but for travellers at large—for the unavoidable delays of bogged transportation, of cancelled appointments or banks out of cash. But Bwadi was, at this point, flamboyantly late. I, myself, had managed to return on time, even after lolling around the Yank Tank and the USIS library among fellow volunteers, comparing notes. Some, like me, were after salary infusions, some were submitting stools for parasite counts. Some were stuck between posts—old failures, new assignments. Some were going home.

My business fixed, I'd returned to find everything the same at Mampungu, until, that is, Mitch had whisked me off the first Saturday. Bouncing beside him in his truck, I'd waved jubilantly from the window and felt a surge of pride in the students we passed. Solitary, *cahiers* open, they strolled at the mission outskirts, preferring to study, they'd told me, *"dans la nature."* One was up a tree, mouthing words. Each had waved back, and by Monday all my classes were curious about my red truck. Not about the man at the wheel, but about the truck, as if he were simply my chauffeur. They'd never asked about the blue moped on my porch. "Where is Citizen Bwadi?" they were asking now instead.

"I don't know," I told the *Préfet* in my house. Hungry, drowsy, I was spoiling for my post-teaching nap.

"But you took the train with him from Mwindi," he puzzled, and I took pity then. Round-eyed, he seemed quizzical and help-less, not at all the debonair official who'd ushered me onto his staff, not at all the marital autocrat I'd pictured with Mpovi.

"Have a seat," I conceded, dropping onto a sticky vinyl chair. "We went together to the beach. For me it was an adventure. But then he left me alone." I posed, lovelorn. Wasn't that how it was supposed to look?

Slowly, the *Préfet* sat, hands on his knees. Evidently he was at a loss here in my home—or simply at a loss. Yet calling on me had been his choice; he could have summoned me to his office for a for-mal interview. He was after secrets, I assumed; he didn't want us overheard. Or perhaps he meant to appeal to me as a friend, as a neighbor in need. He looked afraid. Licking his lips, he frowned. "You had an argument?"

I smiled evasively. "He was going to his maternal village, he said."

"In Angola, then. He didn't say when he'd be back?"

I shook my head, no.

"You see," he mustered his professional voice, "I'm concerned about his classes. About if I'll need to rehire."

I knew this wasn't true. Yes, he'd have to cover the history syl-labus somehow, but what really upset him was the trouble that could mushroom from Bwadi's scam. He was afraid of Mankanzu's security forces, the FIT. With them or against, he was afraid. I didn't know which of us knew more about Bwadi's operation; tacitly we conspired to play dumb. If the authorities did come looking, it would be best if we could all plead ignorance. Bitterly, I realized that it was Bwadi, not I, who threatened Mampungu's peace; he'd objected to my silly repetition drills and green *fou fou* essay because he didn't want his own escape thwarted by nosy *militaires*.

In composed agitation, the *Préfet* stared tensely at the floor. It was a stupid time of day, too hot to think. The room was dark and ripe, the curtains closed against the green heat. The *Préfet's* knuckles looked vulnerable as they hugged his knees, and all his petty pomposity struck me as an honest way to survive. Proper, correct to a "T" in this police state, he remained above suspicion, above threat. As for his real politics, I didn't have a clue. Perhaps his ultimate goal was to keep his wife and son and children-to-be safe.

Abruptly, he clasped his hands together. "You've made contact with the bridge engineers," he observed.

"Yes," I perked up. "I've been to visit their camp."

"They are hiring more and more villagers for work. This bridge could bring much prosperity to our locality, but it could bring problems, too."

"Problems?" I flashed on the feral girl at the fence.

He could not, however, manage to voice any real complaints. Possibly he was loath to broach the subject of child prostitution— of sex of any sort, for that matter; he dropped the subject of Mitch and me as well. Hemming, he explained away his concern. "I don't want the boys quitting school for the work."

"I'll make sure my friend there knows," I pledged. Of course, there was really nothing I could do. Wrist skidding, I wiped my brow free of sweat. "You'd better find a new history teacher, I guess."

He got up, nodding, short neck taut. The hand I shook was amazingly dry. Ushering him out the door, I felt both that something had finished and nothing had transpired; suddenly, then, he balked on the porch. Gasping, he exploded, arms out. "What is this here, then?" he repressed a squeal. "What is this?"

He was fuming at the moped, not at me. It sagged exactly where Bwadi had left it nearly a month before; weeds had grown up through the spokes from the cracks in my cement porch. Queerly anachronistic, it was like a remnant from a modern kingdom gone bust. I watched a moment as the *Préfet* steamed, his neat back swelling and contracting with quick, bilious breaths, and I thought that he might, justly, cry. I thought of the Guinean ambassador who'd criticized American bravery as dense, of how, executed by his own government on some trumped-up charge, he'd been proved right.

I glanced away, scanning for snakes. My lawn had grown in too long, Pistache had informed me that day; he'd be sending a *salongo* team with machetes to cut it back.

"What is this?" the *Préfet* was whispering at the bike.

"I don't know." I turned to go inside.

Mpovi came over next. I'd had a chance to eat and doze, to splash water on my face, to make a few cryptic notes for school. Buckling up my sandals for my afternoon foray to the dispensary, I heard a knock.

"*Salut,*" I flung open the screen door, surprised. A barbaric insect, loudly armored, flapped through. "Come inside."

Mpovi entered eagerly, accepting the same chair I'd offered the *Préfet*. "I was just leaving," I let her know, "but I'll be late. Pinzi can open the dispensary for Diabelle." Fetching two glasses of water from my boiled supply, I fixed on the fitful insect in the sink. Awkwardly, it clanked against the stained porcelain. This specimen was new to me, its frantic wingspan wide as a crayfish. With a dirty spoon, I scooped it out of the sink; blindly, it collided with a windowpane.

"There's a restless soul in my kitchen," I joked, handing Mpovi her drink. We could hear it battering a wall.

"I'm sorry. It flew inside with me."

"Someone you knew?"

"Miss!" she protested, amused. "It's an insect!"

"Huge. Like a bird."

"They come this time of year. We chased one this morning with a broom." Leaning back with an expectant sniff, she began studying my living room much as her husband had, although I doubted she was after clues. She'd come at his request, I was sure, but I was glad even so; I'd avoided her for too long.

Watching her head as she panned, I saw her—finally and all at once—as an African would. Braids knitted flat alternated with gleaming rows of dusky skin, the scalp exposed in a pattern as if etched. I saw that beauty depended on absence here, on allowing the eye to move in a pure line unbroken from the crown of the skull to the long Bantu neck. It was a different ideal entirely from mine, from curls fluffed up to embellish, and thus bury, flesh and bone. I could see now what Mpovi had wanted for me.

Minimalism was not, however, Mpovi's taste in home decor. She'd never paid a formal visit like this; somehow it seemed too late to offer the house tour. She was appalled, I guessed, by my ascetic response to the heat. Where she had displayed all her family photographs, I kept surfaces empty, walls free. I'd gone back to curtains to block the sun; Diabelle had sewn me some from old dispensary sheets. Behind the dining table where I worked, I'd hung only an airline calendar depicting a sapphire sea. My own photos still lay bound in a drawer.

I listened to the bug. "They're not dangerous?"

"Only when they dive," she giggled. "You have to watch your head."

I checked my watch. "I'll go after it later, then."

"You're so busy at the dispensary."

I rolled my eyes, mock tired. "Too busy. The Doctor worked his interviewers all holiday long, so we've accumulated questionnaires in piles high as anthills."

"I'm glad I don't have that job," she cheerfully declared. "I'm too busy with Chance."

It was a stab at reconciliation; I relaxed. In the chair across from her I was sweating as if melting, but the neutral sound of her son's name struck me like a breeze.

"Where is Chance? Why didn't you bring him, too?"

"He's with Mama Zola. He's gotten fat," she complained, acutely proud.

"That means he's healthy, no?"

The stray insect roared through the doorway then as if missing a muffler; swooped. Ducking, Mpovi and I set up a racket, hilariously yelling, scaring the creature off so that, circling, ricocheting, it slammed out of the room. Still laughing, Mpovi mimicked how I'd covered my head, I mimed her brusque yelps, and we were sharing something then, something magical, sublime. I was laughing at her exactly as she laughed at me; it was an African exchange and it was human, too. I felt as if I'd managed an African trick—that of tapping into a moment, of letting the past and future go. That moment it was Mpovi and I laughing at ourselves, and nothing else could possibly matter just then. It was sorcery; it worked.

Gleefully, she swayed, manicured hands holding her head. *"C'est vraiment possédé!"*

Possessed or not, however, the bug left us in peace, and we quieted down. "Miss," she picked up where we'd left off. "I wanted to ask you about Chance. About those pictures you took?"

Airily, I lifted my arms. "I sent the negatives to a U.S. lab. It'll take a while to receive the prints. Hopefully they'll be waiting in Kimpiri the next time I go."

"When?"

"When I get paid. April. Or, if I'm lucky, someone will visit and bring my mail. My supervisor's supposed to come."

"When?"

"Whenever he gets bored in Kimpiri, I guess."

"Miss doesn't get bored in Kimpiri," Mpovi ventured playfully.

"Ehi, yes, I do. I can't stay there more than a few days. I miss it here."

"You do? You miss Mampungu?"

"I do. I missed it while I was gone."

"What did you miss?"

"I missed the singing." I had, indeed, missed the choir songs drifting across the mission at twilight.

"Ehi, but then you should have stayed!" she smiled wistfully. "I was sorry you could not hear the church songs at Christmas. Beautiful, beautiful singing all day."

"They haven't practiced since I've been back."

"Nobody sings now. But before Easter, they'll sing again. You can start again with the mamas' choir," she teased.

"I can't sing."

Simultaneously, we noticed voices outside. "The *salongo* team is here to slash my lawn," I explained as the lazy French banter drew near.

"Your lawn is long," she disapproved.

"In America I never had to worry about snakes. People there only cut lawns for looks."

"No snakes!"

"Well, there are snakes, but most are benign. We don't think much about them there."

"It's a good place, with no snakes. You won't go back soon?"

"My contract is for two years."

"Chance will be a little man by then. Miss," she looked away. "You went many places last month."

"I like to travel. That's why I'm here." The boys' chatter had already given way to the machetes' slow swish. Rising, I moved a curtain, blinked. When my eyes had adjusted to the light, I focused through the screen on the row of shiny black backs, the graceful twist of each loose stroke. I recognized students; out of their uniforms, they looked happy and strong.

"I went first to the beach," I continued, squinting at the emerald glare. "Then to Kilu for a night, then to Lufwidi camp. Then I went to Kimpiri, and now I'm home."

"You had a good time?"

"Yes." Dropping the curtain, I turned, slid into my seat. Somewhere, the imprisoned insect thrummed.

"But why didn't you stay with Bwadi at the beach?"

"He left. He ran away at night. He'd been planning all along to cross to Angola. I just wanted to go to the beach."

"You see," she scooted her shoulders forward. "He likes you."

"No, Mpovi. He does not like me."

"Yes, I'm sure. I'm sure he'll come back."

"I'm sure not. He took me along to pay his fares. That's all."

"But he was nice, wasn't he?"

Her insistence pissed me off. Resentfully, I felt my throat clog, my sinuses burn; the spicy astringence of the freshly cut grass could not be blamed. "He's a racist," I blurted, and then turned my face to hide my eyes squeezed shut. This was definitely how it was supposed to look; this was how it was. "He hates me," I clenched my fists. "He hates all Americans. White people have ruined Africa, he says; Americans are only here to get rich. He's going to fight in Angola. He's probably going to die."

I stopped. Mpovi didn't speak; the room swelled with the soft smack of steel against weeds, the rustle, the whir of sliced air, again, again, again. The strokes were not timed together, each boy hacked alone, nevertheless there was a choreography at work. How did they manage not to cut each other, not to step and swing too close?

I'd begun to censor news of Angola from my student texts, to tune out BBC's foggy analyses of negotiations and maneuvers, its official death tolls. In class I'd been steering clear of President Mankanzu's support for Savimbi's rebels, of his arrangement with the CIA. I'd been trying to be smart. But, more than that, I understood now, I'd been trying to not think of Bwadi dead.

The cut grass was pungent as smoke. In the dry season my nostrils had burned when all the fields were on fire. The brittle moonscape of Mampungu in September had indeed grown lush, too fetid, too sweet. I felt sick.

Mpovi touched my arm. "He's just hard," was her response. "All African men are hard. They have to be stronger than us women, they don't know. It's their way." She chose not to comment on Bwadi's war, on whether or not I had trespassed in her country as a white. "Remember how you took his picture that day? I remember how he looked at you. He liked you then, I know."

"He liked my camera," I lowered my voice. "He fooled us both, Mpovi. He snuck in and stole it while I was out of town." I'd meant to tell no one of Bwadi's heist, not out of loyalty or fear, but because I knew the story would sound absurd. She might as well believe I'd hidden the camera all along myself.

"Pas possible," she did, indeed, scoff.

"He's the one who stole my camera," I insisted in a whisper, determined now to prove her wrong. I pictured the *Préfet* irate.

"How do you know?"

"Because he gave it back. I'll show you." Abandoning her, I strode into a spare bedroom, flushing the panicked insect away from the chest of drawers. The Pentax felt sullen in my hands, and as I returned to Mpovi the sight of her craning optimistically caused something in my soul to erupt: I let the camera fly. Lurching, red nails flashing, she caught it against her chest.

I sagged back into my seat; she watched, shocked. "I'm sorry," I sighed. A few seconds passed. "Go ahead, take a look."

Resettling herself slowly, she unsnapped the case, and then propped the camera on her knees as if anticipating tricks. Charmed, entranced, she seemed to forget my outburst, to forget I was there. It looked like nothing but a camera to me. I didn't care who pushed the shutter anymore, who eyeballed through the viewfinder, closed down the lens.

"But if he stole it," she finally lifted her gaze, "why did he give it back?"

"I guess he was ashamed. He was supposed to be so morally superior, you know."

"*Alors,*" Mpovi stared into the lens. "*C'est vraiment un homme manqué.*" Loser: *homme manqué.* "But he returned your camera after all, so at heart he must be good. And if he didn't like you," she brightened, "why did he give you his moped?"

"It's broken-down." It depressed me to think of love as bought and sold, affection as measured in gifts. Did she see the crusty moped as a good bride-price? "You were wrong to dress me up for that wedding in Lufwidi," I said. "Like a Tambalan *femme.*"

Her sleek head jerked, adamant. "There was hope for you and Bwadi before that wedding. But Diabelle's sister was there. She steals everybody's man."

"Did she steal the *Préfet?*"

She fiddled with the aperture ring, frowned. "She tried, but he was too good. Maybe you are right. Even if he meant well, Bwadi is too weak. Maybe the American is better for you."

I raised my eyebrows at this. Whether or not the *Préfet* had pushed her into dropping by, I sensed now that she'd had an agenda of her own. She'd meant to make me dump Mitch. Clearly unbriefed by her husband, she'd refused to consider Bwadi gone for good, had clung to her dream of me pregnant in a *pagne.* Why? But then why did Westerners want so badly to see African women with careers? Didn't it amount to the same thing?

"Where did you meet him?" she was asking, about Mitch.

"In Kilu. After Bwadi left me at the beach, I stopped in Kilu. It was Christmas Eve. I met him at the post office." Suddenly I wanted to tell her everything; who else was there to tell? With Diabelle I'd reserved that wall of detachment, the student-teacher rift. Sly fertility jokes were OK, the details of our affairs were not: my choice. In the final analysis, Mpovi and I had more in common where men were concerned; I was a romantic, like it or not. Mpovi probably knew I wished I could love Mitch. Certainly she guessed I did not.

"So do you have enough to tell the *Préfet* now?" I bared a cynical grin. Her smooth face froze, but then expanded in a guilty smile. Coincidentally, the armed boys were laughing outside; our frantic bug sounded raucous as well. This time, however, my sense of humor failed; I could not shake the sense of scaffolding around us preparing to collapse.

"You can tell him what I said," I told Mpovi, sincere. "I honestly can't explain anything Bwadi did. He said the moped was a gift."

"And now you have the camera and the moped, both."

"No. It's your camera, now. Take it home and hide it, so no one will steal it again."

She cracked up, scandalized. "People will think I was the thief!"

"You?" I kissed the air with ornate contempt, banishing the thought. "I would give you the camera when I left Tambala anyway. Take it now, instead."

"Why?"

"It makes me sad. Sad about Bwadi."

After she left, camera strapped beneath her *pagne,* I wondered what it meant when prized possessions kept changing hands. Why Bwadi's moped had found its way to my door. Why my camera had attached itself to Bwadi, returned itself to me, floated off like a baby tied to Mpovi's back. Bwadi takes my camera, leaves it with me, I give it to Mpovi as if shunting a curse. Perhaps, not unlike the mad insect, the camera really was possessed, ricocheting slow motion house to house. Perhaps the moped would move on to haunt Diabelle.

What Diabelle really wanted was Mitch. When his red truck slid to an unexpected halt outside the clinic, splattering the Doctor's parked Land Rover with mud, she froze.

"*C'est lui?*" she breathed, watching through the window. "He's your American?"

Removing his sunshades, adjusting his granny glasses as he swung forward through the screen door, he let it slam. Pale and wild as an apparition, he combed his fingers through his dark halo of a mane, and his collarbones gleamed between the undone buttons of his shirt. Diabelle wanted it all.

He focused, however, on me. "Nice sign," he grinned up, back, as if he'd never have found me without the squat black letters against fresh white: *Centre de Planification Familiale*. Someone had redirected him, of course, from my house. "So this is your dispensary, huh?"

Sheepishly, I smiled. I felt as if caught play-acting, my pretend clinic revealed as a shabby, stuffy front. Pinzi receded in his corner, Diabelle arched. Standing slowly, I glanced at the stacks of questionnaires rising like stalagmites from the floor. "I just work here."

Mitch scanned, jolly, territorial, the quintessential technician come to fix things up, and I understood how the Tambalans must see us, me and Mitch and everyone white. Arms folded, glowing whiter than human, he reminded me of Mr. Clean, the tidy pirate in TV commercials who appeared unsummoned to housewives in distress, the muscled and righteous agent of some omniscient force whose domestic standards the poor drudges had failed to achieve. I didn't want any help from Mitch.

I shook his hand anyway Tambalan style and then walked him forward to meet Pinzi, idly installed for the Doctor's sake. After delivering the new questionnaires this morning, the Doctor had left on foot for our hydroelectric ruins, but Pinzi expected him back for beer. Deferentially, he squeaked at Mitch.

"So you're the nurse?" Mitch squinted furrily at Pinzi's proverbial stethoscope. "Seen any of that bronchitis I've got over my way?"

For once I was glad that Mitch did not speak French; I steered him over to Diabelle. Eyes shy, she dangled behind her desk, loose and limber, tall. Taller than I'd thought. Like a flower swelling, inadvertent, toward light. Above, the ceiling sockets gaped. Sidelit instead by the gauzy sunshine filtered through branches and the peeling screen, she waited, unlikely as an orchid, timid and pretty in the humid gloom. Mitch ducked forward, shook her long hand, recoiled. The African geometry of her neatly anchored braids and the gently sloping forehead fired gold seemed to take him by surprise. He cleared his throat. I should have seen everything then, should have seen what was going to happen next, what had already happened a month before, a year before, a whole history before I'd been born.

"She looks familiar," Mitch blinked at me.

"He's the one who gave us a ride," she informed me shakily in French.

This was news to me. "She says you gave her a ride."

"That's it!" he snapped his fingers, relieved. "She sat up front in the cab. Didn't speak any English, though. I didn't know she worked for you."

"He says you don't speak English," I translated for Diabelle, mock hurt.

She refused to practice on Mitch. I felt her discomfort as a pang inside my elbows; I let her off the hook. "She's one of my best students," I told him. "She understands more than you think."

"Right." He rubbed his hands together. "Look, I've got a care package for you in the truck. Is this the fridge you use?"

"Couldn't it wait till Saturday?" Edgy, I wanted him to leave. Whether I was embarrassed of Mampungu or of him, I wasn't sure.

His beard went slack. "Thought you'd be happy to see me. Came spur-of-the-moment, like; I had to drop off a patient in Mwindi and I thought I'd stop on the way home. Made him wait while I packed your box."

Reluctantly, I smiled.

He took charge then, galvanized. "I have a few things in the cooler, too. Hold on." The screen door banged.

I looked at wobbly Diabelle. I'd never seen her so askew, not even after Mpovi had called her too skinny to have kids. Seated, flawless and pitiful, she would not look at me. While I was gone she was what I'd missed the most. I'd missed the twilight choirs and my solo cigarettes beneath the empty stars, the roosters at the rim of my deep sleep and the hollow clang of buckets against outdoor pipes as mamas drew coffee water at dawn. I had not really missed this clinic, this paperwork breeding on the floor. I had missed Diabelle. I had missed how, in class, she leaned forward into my every word, how, coding questionnaires, she'd flow through a gesture I recognized as mine, wrist slanting with a flourish across her dry brow.

I'd told her right away that I'd seen the bridge site. I'd told her about the camp buildings and the riverfront and the cook afraid of crocodiles; I'd described the fireworks as explosions in the sky and she'd listened reverentially, as if in church. I didn't tell her about Mitch. Then last Saturday I took off in his truck and Monday, at the clinic, she'd pinned me down.

"You have an American man now?" she'd asked, hefting a pile of paper from the floor to her desk. Pinzi had disappeared.

"I guess I do."

"Mintela told us he saw you drive away."

"My friend took me to Lufwidi camp for the night."

"And then he brought you back."

"Right."

"There are many men there, Miss," she'd reminded me.

"Yes." Flipping through my stack, I sought an easy questionnaire with which to start, one free of the interviewer's evocative notes, clean with simple answers: yes, no, a date, numbers that added up.

Diabelle persisted. "What does yours look like?"

"Like a monkey," I giggled, ill at ease. "Hair all over his face. You wouldn't like him."

"But there are many men there with long hair and beards." She looked concerned.

"Many." We each focused down, pencils busy. She turned a page. "Isn't Bwadi coming back?"

"I don't know."

"But you have the moped." She sounded impressed. She had stopped her work.

"I don't know." I wrote the code number for "hysterectomy." The Doctor had apparently performed quite a few.

When I met her eyes she looked pleased indeed, happy with admiration. "It's good."

"What's good?"

"It's good to keep Bwadi's moped. It's good to have something from a man. You are like my sister Catherine. She always takes something from the man."

"I don't agree."

She tilted her head, mouth pursed. "But you have succeeded, don't you see?"

I sighed. Aimlessly, I asked, "Is Catherine in Lufwidi still?"

"With the refugees."

"Does she have American friends?"

"No. Those men don't come to Lufwidi. Our boys go to work at the camp. My sister who got married, her husband works there now." I detected pride, envy, something athwart. I wondered about the girls.

"It's yours," I decided.

"*Comment?*"

"The moped. I don't want it. *C'est pour toi.*"

"Me? Ehi, no, Miss, what if he comes back?" She shook her pencil as if threatening a fly. "Why don't you want it?"

"Because it's his."

This threw her for a loop. "But it's a moped. If Bwadi is gone, it's yours. It's a moped, Miss."

"Then I'm free to give it away. Maybe when I leave."

"Will you leave soon?"

I slammed my pencil down. I clutched my head, fed up. I rubbed my eyes, wiped the perspiration from my fingers on my skirt. "Why does everybody think I'm about to leave?" I turned on Diabelle, and she looked betrayed, jaw dropping, nostrils and mouth swelling open as wounds.

Could I really make her cry? Surprised, I leaned over, taking hold of her warm arm. "Diabelle, I'm sorry!" I watched her, flustered; I was touched. "It's just that when people act as if I'm about to quit, I get angry, because they seem to be telling me I should. You're the last person I want to tell me that."

Mucus clung to her upper lip; wetly, she sniffed. There was no Kleenex in Africa. Crying children wiped their faces on their shirts. Swinging from her waist, she reached for the hem of her *pagne*.

"What's really the matter, Diabelle?"

"*Ça va.*"

"Because one day I'll leave?"

"*Oui.*"

"Nothing else?"

"*Non.*"

"Nothing?"

"*Non,* Miss."

It was easy to believe her that day. It was easy to believe the image of myself she made me see. Endowed with white luck, I was sacred as an idol, precious as a god carved from tusk. It was easy to believe she could cry about me. But the minute Mitch showed up, the minute she spotted him at the wheel of his vehicle and froze, I knew it was more than me. I knew that even a precocious *femme fatale* who considered Bwadi's moped a good catch could fall in love.

"*Voilá,*" Mitch barked gregariously, backing into the clinic now with his box. After dumping it onto the conference table, he cracked his fingers, defensively smug.

"You don't have to bring me stuff."

"It's for everybody. *Tous,*" he declared, his gaze including Pinzi, Diabelle. I bit my lip. Half hidden behind her desk, illuminated as if beneath a forest canopy, her round gaze was locked on Mitch, and her okapi eyes brought to mind the figure I'd seen through his chain-link fence.

"No," I blurted.

Mitch flinched, tennis shoes shrill as he spun to face me on the concrete floor. "What is it with you today? I thought sharing was the AfricEd thing."

"I've got work to do, Mitch." Lamely, I indicated the questionnaires bivouacked around my desk. "It's a bad time."

"Real slave driver, huh?"

We squared off, at egregious odds.

"I'm outta here," he conceded suddenly, hands lifted in defeat.

"No, no. Go ahead, play sugar daddy if you want."

"Sugar daddy? I don't get it. You didn't mind living it up in Kilu. You don't mind the royal treatment at camp. I had no idea a care package would be out of line."

He was right, I knew; I wasn't being fair. Yet something about him standing there put me on the offense. Was it territoriality? It was disgust at myself, perhaps, for having accepted his favors thus far.

"Can we talk about this later?" I snapped. "I'm supposed to be at work."

"Christ."

"I'm supposed to be a role model for this girl, not a concubine."

"Didn't seem to mind the Kilu prostitutes," he muttered, diving defiantly at his box as if to sweep it all away, but he hadn't finished yet. "I thought you fit right in, go-go dancing; looked thick as thieves with those whores." He grabbed something from the top. "Come on over, guys," he waved his arm theatrically, in the manner of one whose words often don't work. Pinzi's chair scraped; Diabelle drifted close, apart. Her glance evaded mine.

Reconnoitering, Mitch approached her cautiously with a cellophane packet of cheese. "For you."

She took it in both hands, dipping to curtsy, touching her arm at the elbow in the village gesture of respect. I cringed.

Mitch abandoned her then as if stung. I supposed she could have that effect on a man.

"And you, my friend," he fished for something else. The bag of Fritos crackled in Pinzi's grasp.

"And," Mitch said at me, brusque, "yogurt for you."

I made no move; he set the sweating carton on the table, swiped more into his arms. "These here perishables are just off ice, they better get into the fridge."

"Perishables?" I asked, as if that were the worst possible crime.

He persevered. Loaded up with my yogurt, a six-pack of Coke, sandwich ham from Denmark, he marched toward the refrigerator, firm.

Pinzi was quick to his post. Courteously, he pulled open the *frigo* door as if he expected Mitch to climb inside.

Mitch laughed. "This all yours, Nickie?"

Coming up behind him, I saw the shelves flush with Empereur bottles on their sides. No serum to be seen.

"Quite a project you've got planned. Guess we'll hold off on the tour; you better get to work."

Chuckling sarcastically, he stuffed the groceries where he could, and then ducked past to pose in the entryway's screened glare. Backlit, supercilious, shirt stained where the perspiring perishables had bled, he shrugged me off. *"Bon travail.* There's salsa in the box."

Pinzi was left holding a bottle aloft in Mitch's wake; he replaced it slowly, as if hurt. Diabelle finally looked at me. I don't know what she expected me to do. What I did was to crumple at my desk, clutching onto my head as if for dear life. It could become a habit, this forensic anguish; I pictured my anarchic students in stitches at the sight. Diabelle didn't laugh. I didn't know what was wrong. I knew I didn't want Mitch.

Silence reigned among us three as Mitch's engine roared awake. His tires skidded in mud; his gears meshed. He drove like an angry male.

Massaging my temples, eyes still closed, I heard the Doctor squishing up the path. He entered; I mustered a weary hello. The door clicked discreetly shut.

"Bonsoir, bonsoir," he stalled, egalitarian, wondering with whom to shake hands first. He advanced on me, tattered briefcase in tow. "You've had a visitor?"

I assented; his hand was bony, light. "I'm sorry you missed him. He didn't stay long."

"An engineer?"

"His name is Mitch Voight; he's the Eckhart medic at Lufwidi camp."

"Ehi, yes, the one I've heard about. A good man, yes. You gave him a tour?" His elderly gaze swivelled to Pinzi, keeper of the key.

Pinzi uttered a faint no.

"He left too quickly," I explained.

The Doctor's meticulous shoulders appeared to deflate. The rolled up cuffs of his white European shirt were red with dust, his leather shoes crusty with mud. I'd always admired him as spiffy and intellectual, yet suddenly he seemed less like Mampungu's oracle of progress to me. "What's the story with these hysterectomies?" I heard Mitch's voice ask. "Abortions are taboo, so he's mass-sterilized instead? Family planning, huh?"

Having greeted Pinzi and Diabelle, the Doctor was gravitating toward the box. "But what is this?"

"He brought a few gifts."

"Ah, bon." He hovered, setting down his floppy briefcase, peering through his wire rims as if to diagnose. A possessive hand shot out, probed. It extracted a tube of shampoo. "This is to disinfect?"

I told him what it was.

"No medical supplies at all?"

"He didn't expect to find me here. He thought I'd be at my house."

"So it was not an official visit. No wonder he did not wait so we could meet. These provisions all belong to you."

"No, he instructed us to share. Pinzi got a bag of chips already; Diabelle got cheese." Looking uninformed, Diabelle sat recessed, her cheese out of sight.

"Bien." The shampoo went into the Doctor's breast pocket.

"Shall we begin?"

Lifting the box to an empty place beside my desk, I could not help but peek. Reaching for the jar of salsa, the tortilla chips, I spied Marlboros. I curbed my impulse to secret the carton away and arranged a snack instead to complement Pinzi's beer. For once, Diabelle had Coke.

"My excursion has given me quite a thirst," the Doctor amiably began to pour.

"It's a difficult walk," I observed. I'd been escorted to the obsolete dam by Lukau and Shamavu when I'd first arrived and hadn't been back since. We'd hiked an hour down scrubby savannah thickening into woods, holding our arms up to protect our faces from weeds arching across the path until we'd arrived at the little brick house. Invisible water had churned, and I remembered half expecting to find inside a *ngando* in human form. Rather, we'd opened the door upon a dead turbine choked with brush.

"The canal is growing grass," the Doctor extended his beer, proposing a toast. "That water may run there again."

We all sipped.

"The generator has become the home of bats. It's impossible to breathe in the shed."

"You went inside?"

"I confess I did not. I made my observations from the door and windows. One window held a tree."

"A tree?"

"The trunk has pushed out a pane."

"Do you think it can be repaired?"

"Pistache can perhaps provide a *salongo* team to clear away these plants. Without funds, however, I can buy no replacement glass."

"I mean the dam."

"Ah. *Exactement.* My new proposal is in progress now." Ingratiatingly, he cocked his head. "Perhaps your friend could be of help."

Deflecting his angular gaze, I reached for a chip, submerged an edge in sauce. "This is popular in California," I crunched. "Mexican cuisine. Help yourself."

"I will invite him for an official visit," the Doctor persisted. "I will prepare a letter using my government seal." He scanned as if excavating possibilities from the stuffy air above my head. "A road would be of considerable help."

The chips were stale. Chewing, I watched Pinzi venture a small hand. Beer foam laced his upper lip. Diabelle looked stoned.

There had used to be a road. Swaths remained exposed. Lukau, Shamavu, and I had followed a piece to a swimming hole famous among the kids. The water had frothed, loud. I hadn't seen where to swim. We'd picnicked on bananas and peanuts and I'd been bit; we'd watched the speck on my wrist grow to a numb welt. I hadn't seen the bug.

A road would be a cinch. The whole hydroelectric dam would be a cinch for those Goliath engineers. Compared to their mammoth bridge, this river was a trickle, our turbine a toy.

"*Excellent!*" the Doctor erupted, swallowing. "So this is what they eat to build a bridge."

I managed a laugh. "It's never worked for me. Have one, Diabelle."

Grimly, she smiled.

"*Bon.* Our business today will please everyone, I trust." The Doctor's glass was empty; Pinzi poured. "You will see that I have not neglected my duties as *chef.*" His expression, sneakily benevolent, brought to mind Mitch. From his briefcase, the Doctor pulled a white envelope.

Accepting it, Pinzi grimaced, pleased. I believed it was the first time I'd seen him smile.

As Pinzi's envelope vanished into his slacks, the Doctor profferred another to me.

"*C'est quoi?*" I asked.

"Your salary."

"In kulunas?"

The Doctor's cottony eyebrows expanded; he nodded, amused.

"I thought I had explained. I don't accept compensation. I'm paid by AfricEd."

Diabelle had woken up; Pinzi stared, serene. The Doctor gave the envelope a significant shake. "Redistribute the funds, if you wish."

I balked.

"This is not the Tambalan way," he reprimanded me. "Whether

or not you belong to AfricEd, you are in Tambala and there are certain ways we do things here. Think of this as an accounting task, part of your job."

He deposited the fat envelope beside my beer. He then put away his green shampoo, placing it from his shirt pocket into his briefcase, securing the flap.

"What about Diabelle?"

Slowly, he exhaled between his teeth. "Diabelle's father receives her salary."

"What?"

"That is our arrangement. That is how he agreed to my engaging Diabelle. He receives her salary to put against school fees."

Diabelle looked ashamed.

"Did you know?" I asked her.

She stared down at the table as if she hadn't heard.

"Tell me about the bridge," the Doctor refilled my glass. "How large is the camp generator? What exactly does the electricity serve?"

"I don't know," I abandoned Diabelle, confused. "It's loud. The generator's in a building about as big as Mampungu's water tank, maybe half as high."

"And how much power does it produce?"

"I can't say." I fingered my envelope, watching Diabelle sulk. "About twenty Americans live there now. They all have electric cassettes, air conditioning. More are supposed to come. So far they've built a couple big barracks for living quarters, a kitchen, dining hall, clinic, supplies sheds. I don't know what else. I don't know anything about how the engineering will work."

"And the clinic? You've seen that?"

"It's small, but well equipped. Air-conditioned. Clean, bright."

"I would very much like to see." He blinked up at the old light socket as if beseeching God. "Ehi, with electricity we could have a real clinic here!"

I glanced at the medieval exam room's door. As far as I knew, since my official visit with Diabelle, it had remained locked. The refrigerator gurgled, chugged. Pinzi appeared proud, well paid. The Doctor continued to quiz and pour, Diabelle to pout. She hadn't touched her Coke. I wondered if she understood that the Doctor saw my salary as hers.

By the time he rose to shake hands good-bye, I was antsy to win her back. Finally Pinzi escorted the Doctor to his car, and I prepared to pounce. She had recovered her cheese.

"Wait a moment," I said.

Fatalistically, she halted in her tracks, and I tensed, irked. I did not care to be lumped with those whom she obeyed. As if to prove her point, I barked, "Take this stuff away."

Obediently, she set down her orange cheese and stooped, lifting Mitch's box. "To where, Miss?"

I dropped the white envelope on top. "It's yours."

She put the box on her desk beside the cheese.

"Diabelle, why didn't you tell me about this arrangement with your father?"

"I don't like to discuss my father with you."

I missed a beat.

"Miss, you don't understand fathers here. You will think we must fight him, and we must not."

"We must trick him instead."

Mildly, she shrugged.

"Whatever works," I gave up. "I don't want to get you into trouble, Diabelle. Maybe keeping secrets from me does makes sense."

Retrieving the envelope, she extended it to me. "Thank you for sharing these things, Miss, but this one isn't mine."

"It is, now." I stepped back.

She studied it, eyelashes dense. When she looked up, her expression hinted at hope. "You're sure?"

"Absolument."

Yet something troubled her still. "How should I spend it, Miss?"

"Save it. Or spend it. I don't care; it's yours. But if I were you, I'd save it for moving to Kimpiri."

"I'll save it to pay for those pills," she said in a brave rush.

I nodded, straightening my desk, readying to go. "Why not? I see now why you can't trust the Doctor here. After you graduate, we'll go together to Kimpiri and I'll find a clinic for you. We'll tell your father it's a business trip, that he'll get paid."

Decisively, she knotted the envelope at her waist. Dropping her cheese into the box, she hoisted it with great purpose in her arms. "It's good, sharing, isn't it?" she turned to me.

I agreed, commandeering a pile of questionnaires to take home. Catching up with the box, I fished, claiming the red-and-white carton of cigarettes. "I'll take those," I said.

She looked away, at me, away.

"What is it?"

"Nothing," she decided.

"Tell me."

"It's good to share, that's all." She allowed herself to smile. "I used to think Americans don't like to share, but you're different."

"I hope so. Americans like their privacy, it's true. Sharing is an African attribute I'm trying to learn."

Below our evangelical sign, the heat flattened out. Diabelle lingered, despositing the box on the porch. The Doctor was frowning as he pointed out the mud splatters Mitch had made on his car; Pinzi was shaking his shaved head. Bending at her knees, long back straight, Diabelle dipped to lift the box to her head; rising evenly, she adjusted the weight, her narrow shoulders solid and smooth and bronze. With grizzled admiration, the Doctor waved.

A few sticky steps along the road, she glanced at me sideways, neck locked. "Miss."

"Yes."

"Miss," she ventured once again. I could see her trying slantwise to read my face. "You don't like him, do you?"

A bubble of silence shimmered, popped. "I guess not."

She opened her mouth, on the verge of asking more.

"He's yours," I hazarded, utterly sick of Mitch. Then I laughed, hearing what I'd said. Diabelle laughed too, chin tightly tucked against her stoic neck; the blithe box floated full sail ahead.

Teaching had become a struggle since Bwadi had left. Whatever the students had thought of my liaison with him, they openly ridiculed me and Mitch. "Miss will be getting money now," one boy had smirked during a structure drill. "Miss will be getting white child."

Stranded among the hecklers, Diabelle would squirm. Luckily, she was not a member of the class that finally went too far—that caused my sanity, however briefly, to snap. She'd have had to take the students' side, all for one. She'd have had to skewer Mitch. Or maybe not. Certainly she'd have refused my quiz. It was Friday, the morning after his visit to my clinic, the morning he came back. I suppose I should have been flattered by his urgent return; he'd assumably dropped his job so we could reconcile. He caught me, however, in the midst of this student mutiny.

A few boys had just received fat red zeros for cheating on homework, and in a show of solidarity the whole class was boycotting my questions on the board. Rows of folded arms confronted me, of soldierly chins. *"On fait la grève,"* the class president informed me; then, in English, "we are on strike." Tiny, wily as Napoleon, he usually took my part.

"Then zeros for you all."

Unanimous, they glared.

I picked up my grade book, my red pen. "No quiz, no points."

Solid immobility.

I sank into the chair behind the teacher's desk, my angry gaze stuck on the smudged, peeling wall. The room was silent; I felt pinned. I folded my arms. I could call Pistache, and the Doctor's turbine would be free of trees. I looked around, down. Graffiti had eaten the desk. *Biri désormais,* I remembered from the Nkisi train; *nous souffrons.* Often I'd puzzled: who had suffered; why? Before me, hearts like valentines bore initials like scars. I began etching "AFRICA" with my red pen.

"Singe," I heard someone whisper as a distant motor whined.

The growl was unmistakable.

"C'est son singe."

"Like a monkey," I'd giggled to Diabelle; had the whole school heard?

Whispers eddied; for a long time the truck approached. Doodling, I underlined "AFRICA" with a snake, inspired by the itinerant hiss. The vehicle closed in; toddlers lined the mission drive. I could hear them cheering. "Bye bye bye bye! Miss Nicoli, bye bye!"

Then, as if to echo the commotion outside, a hushed chant rose from within my class, sudden and cohesive as a breeze. Something about *le pont,* I understood; something "the bridge." Furiously veining a red wreath of leaves, I heard the whole phrase. *"Fait-moi le pont, fait-moi le pont,"* again, again, *"fait-moi le pont."* "Make me a bridge." The message was sexual, obscene. Breathy grunts kept time.

Grabbing my books and chalk, I fled for home. The red truck blocked my path. Sinister as a lobster, it had taken the schoolyard, claiming a place below the slack Tambalan flag on its pole.

"What do you want now?" I bellowed at its ludicrous grill.

Mitch was descending, dusting himself off. "What the . . .?"

"Can't you leave me alone?" I attacked.

All good will retreated behind his dark shades, his beard.

Mutely fuming, I trembled, struggling for self-control. "Look," I finally articulated. "You can't just come here whenever you want. I'm teaching now!" I yanked back my arm to indicate the students billowing at the windows; some had spilled out doors. He lifted his own wrist slightly as if to block a punch. "Muhammad Ali!" someone called.

Dropping his defense, Mitch gave me one last chance. "I just wanted to explain about yesterday."

"I don't want to know."

"Good." Swinging open his red door, he launched himself inside. "Don't say I didn't try."

I was already walking around him, advancing against the flow of half-clad toddlers gathering to watch. The show was over; possibly I heard applause. I didn't look back at the school. I didn't want to see Diabelle. I didn't want to see if the *Préfet* had emerged to offer Mitch a tour.

Mitch stayed away Saturday and I was glad. Things were meant to end between us in any case, but they might have ended differently, more civilly at least, if I'd had him to myself. Yet one never really has anything to oneself in Africa. Kids are always peering in; voices float. One is expected to share. Isn't this exactly what I'd sought, after all, across the fence from that fairy-tale *paillotte* with the pool? In America my mother had died, my brother had strayed, and my father had tried to forget; I, however, had returned to search soft-focus for that *paillotte* of my past, for that vast black family spanning the night.

9
METAMORPHOSIS

In February the mangos fell. The mission reverberated with voices that were mischievously festive, rich and liquid with anticipation and bliss. Echoes haunt me still: the musical rush of shivering leaves and then the pop as kids aim stones to shoot down the ripest fruit, their Bantu yodels of delight. Rewalking the mission, I risk slipping on discarded rinds or rotten fruit; I suck deep into my lungs its insidious scent.

When less ripe, the skins showed green and I knew not to touch those pieces. I'd learned way back in West Africa when, while climbing a tree in the school yard, an American boy had taught me how to peel back the rind with my teeth. The next day, allergic to the unripe rind, I'd developed a rash like poison oak that blinded me for a week. In Mampungu I knew to maneuver the peel with fork and knife, to resist the stringy mango flesh until I'd cut the toxic rind free. Even so, at times my mouth would tingle, going slightly numb with a minute reaction so that I went more than once to check my reflection in the mirror, to see if my mouth weren't actually swollen, to see how African I had become. Each time I found the change invisible, my lips bleak and thin as ever, my chin just as white.

Everything was suddenly in season. Earlier we'd gone through one food at a time at the *petit marché*, peanuts, then bananas, then an occasional misshapen tomato. Worst had been September during the tail end of the dry season, when I'd arrived equipped with my beans and rice and canned pilchards from Kimpiri, when I'd given my sugar and milk to Mpovi and her kin. Yet I had survived, and now all kinds of produce were turning up simultaneously at Mampungu's *petit marché*: corn and squash and manioc, the leaves of which I cooked like spinach, avoiding the roots. Mama Zola, the Pastor's kind, ducklike wife, brought papayas to my door, and Jetaime presented me with a prize avocado the size of a coconut, velvet yellow inside. As the local harvest generated profits, commerce picked up. One woman traded her produce for flour to bake rolls fresh daily in a makeshift kiln that looked like something Peace Corps had thought up. Religiously, I did my part as consumer to make the project work.

The month grew greener and greener, too green, almost black. Leaves pressed against panes of glass, pushed through broken screens. If it wasn't raining, the sky was too blue, too beautiful, a constant shock. The tall grass along the trails stung my calves, and the insects' steady sound of panic sent goosebumps along my arms. I had learned to use my hand slapping insects as the Africans did, my palm falling like a glove with a resounding smack.

Toward noon at school I'd be wilting, perched against a table edge or downright sitting, fanning myself with a *cahier* while squinting through the crazy heat at the basketball hoop undulating in the hot distance. Left scribbling at their desks, the students would drop their heads one by one to their crossed arms, the last pens feeble and erratic against the lullaby of bugs, the wave upon creaking wave.

Even the class that had ambushed Mitch went limp. The week after my performance in the courtyard they had conceded to my quiz, settling into a stale state of truce as if the incident they'd witnessed was enough. Ultimately it was too hot to fight. The snide asides that did surface I allowed to drift; what the kids sought, after all, was my pink embarrassment, my flamboyant, humid despair; finding me immune, they dozed.

They could not shake their fascination, however; like oglers at a zoo, they'd stare. Sometimes I'd glance from the basketball hoop to spot among the sea of fuzzy heads one or another face gazing, curiously absorbed, innocently sure of the right to look. Cynically, I'd smile, and the face would come to life with a grin.

I stared, too, more prudently, perhaps, but with the same objectivity, amazed at the exaggerated reach of a brown arm writing on the board, angling adeptly from narrow shoulders as the other hand dangled, stretching almost level with a knee. Those long hands! I was forever dazzled by the elongated palms waving above the plateau of dark brows.

At the clinic Diabelle's reserve was a relief. When I told her I'd sent Mitch away for good, she'd swallowed, sitting tall, brown irises like flecks of cellophane suspended in white surprise. When I'd turned away, dismissing any questions before they could form, she'd picked up her pencil, and she hadn't mentioned him again. I assumed she was respecting the barrier I'd meant to erect between our personal lives. I assumed she was growing up. Skirting the issue, we fossilized our routine. Coding, jumping each time a mango fell squatly on the aluminum roof, we spoke of cures and crocodiles and hypothetical boys.

Everything seemed to stick: paper to my wrists, hair to my temples. Sweaty with apathy, I was more than bored with my private Shangri-La. Mitch was banished, Bwadi lost; mired in my endless idyll, I simmered, eyes glazed. I didn't see it as a lull, as a slow-motion lag before the repercussions hit. But Mampungu had never existed in a vacuum; the world was destined to catch up.

The first intrusion on our peaceable kingdom was peaceable himself, entirely unconnected, I'm still convinced, with the trouble that lay ahead. He was an ex-missionary; and although I'd always denounced his type as hypocritical twits, I found him different, his visit a pleasant jolt to my enervated funk. He did not condemn our family planning project; apparently he and the Doctor were old friends. They showed up together mid-February in the rickety old Land Rover—the new one had yet to arrive—and the Doctor escorted him around, announcing each mango rind lurking in their path while the Pastor, eternally amicable, deferred. Red-cheeked, bushy-browed, English-speaking, Carl was an American returned from the States to pay tribute to his old stomping ground. Ambling about like an inspector, he blinked his dark, soupy eyes, his mouth hooking under at the corners, hands clasped behind his back. He was tall, taller than anyone at Mampungu, and he stooped as if hard of hearing; more likely, he'd forgotten some of his Kikongo, which he spoke.

I wasn't there when Carl saw the dispensary, and I couldn't help wondering if the conscientious Doctor hadn't orchestrated a speedy exodus of all the beer from the fridge. Yet Carl didn't begin to fit my stereotype of the Bible-thumping tyrant. Cautious and polite, if somewhat down at the mouth, he addressed the *Préfet* with deference, humming approval at our array of texts, which, of course, dated from Carl's day. He, himself, had been the *Préfet* ten years before, and, appreciating his keen interest, I invited him to observe a class.

"I'm impressed with their speaking skills," he told me later, reclining in one of the low armchairs in my *salon*. With his legs crossed comfortably in their khaki trousers, a white sock bunched at his ankle revealing a doughy strip of calf, his long fingers inter-twined before his concave chest, he seemed to belong to the chair. "I'd forgotten," he observed, "how quick they are with words. It's a different scene completely in the States."

"You mean they're brighter here?" I poured our tea, apologizing for my dearth of sugar and milk. Both were now available as our *petit marché* boomed, but I hadn't bothered to restock.

"Oh, I lived here, too, you know," he waved away my concern, "and there were times . . ." His voice trailed off, he took a sip, then perked up. "I lived in this very house, did they tell you? Built that table there myself." He gestured at the rough-hewn dining table scattered with my teaching things, my little army of lamps. The wood was stained where petrol had leaked.

"But the kids, I was going to say, there's something singular about these Tambalan kids. Fresher, sharper, less inundated with our plethora of useless information, the television, the printed matter plastered all over the u.s. Nobody can touch a thing anymore before reading a label. Our children are shorting out, I'm convinced, with this overstimulation. They don't grasp an iota of what I say." He changed gears, exhaling with content. "Ah, my, but it's invigorating, so elemental here in Africa."

I smiled. "What is it you teach, in the States?"

"Languages. French, and Kikongo, at University of Ohio."

"Kikongo! That's obscure."

"Quirky, perhaps, but we fulfill a requirement for international studies, and there are quite a few kids who hope to get to Africa. Like you." His great eyebrows tightened in a sort of salute. Almost completely dark, they were oddly incongruent with the white hair at his temples.

"My son," he confided, "would like a job out here. He's always wanted to come back; he's finishing up his master's now, in economics." Endearingly unable to conceal his pride, Carl dimpled, and I was reassured to see his mouth curl up as readily as it did down.

"That's like me," I agreed. "I mean, I don't have a master's, but I lived in Africa with my family, and I couldn't stay away." I thought again of Sadie, and it seemed more likely than ever that she, too, had returned.

"Ah." He tilted his head inquisitively. "And how do you find it now? As you'd expected?"

"No," I said vaguely, suddenly confused. "Different. I'd lived insulated in American communities, and had romanticized the African lifestyle, I think. Living here, I've found out it's not all dancing around drums."

"No, it's all gone to pot. Mampungu's a ruin."

"You mean the electricity."

"Everything." Replacing his cup and saucer on the coffee table, his hand trembled, from emotion or fatigue, I couldn't tell. "This used to be a top-notch mission, with the generator on line, all the buildings maintained, the roads nice and smooth. Now look at it: screens peeling, windows broken, the whitewash streaked with rust. A simple paint job would do wonders, but no one wants to bother. The generator, I don't know; I'm not sure I want to see."

The Doctor and Pastor were due to arrive any minute at my door to take Carl on a hike to the dam.

"The mango trees have thrived," I offered him one from a bowl.

"Oh, they've always done well," he waved it away. "I've had today's allotment already, I'm afraid, and I know from experience what happens when you eat too many at once. It becomes a mania, these mangos, I suppose because the season is so short. But then nothing lasts long here."

"I've been thinking the opposite lately, that nothing seems to change."

"You're referring to the sanctity of tradition here, of course, and you're right. It's the innovations, the new, the trappings of industrial society superimposed onto the agrarian, it's these things that bite the dust. The generator. The mission, the whole, pitiful place."

"Mangos aren't industrial."

"No, but they are superimposed. Mampungu's founders planted this crop when they built the mission, 1906. Not indigenous at all."

"Don't you think, though, that the mission's better off in Tambalan hands? They'll flounder at first, but shouldn't they make their own mistakes and learn from them? Ultimately, this is their country."

"Yes, yes, there's all that," he agreed, surprisingly. Clearly, he was an educated man with his own bone to pick in Africa, just as I had mine, both of which were buried alongside, independent of, the purposes of Church and State. "Still, it's a crying shame. After what went into putting this place together, to see the deterioration is a shame. The tennis court," he quizzed me, "I bet you don't even know where it was."

"The tennis court?"

"Right over there," he pointed, through a wall. "I levelled the court myself with our road equipment, and I showed them how to keep it up when I left. Now there's nothing but a dusty clearing studded with a couple of no-good stakes."

"And the hoops," I reminded him. He was describing the court where the students played basketball.

"Oh, yes, we put those up, too. So they still play basketball, at least?"

I nodded, distracted by the thought of Bwadi in tennis whites, calling serves. Curious, I asked, "Why was it that you left?"

"My wife was ill," he shrugged. "Passed away finally last year."

Not wanting to pry, I waited for him to elaborate, thinking of my own mom. He only stared into his empty cup. I poured him more tea.

"How long is left on your contract, then?" he inquired, to change the subject, I guessed.

"A year and a half."

"It'll fly. Just fly. I was here six, and I could have stayed six more. Leaving was terribly difficult. Believe it or not, though, coming back has been almost worse."

He seemed startled by his observation, and looked away. I busied myself with the tea. Lately I'd convinced myself that without caffeine I would slow to a full stop, lured like Dorothy in the poppy fields to a lush nap. I wondered if leaving Africa would be hard; would I promise myself, this time, to return? Perhaps ten years from now the walls would be whitewashed, the electricity restored.

Dispirited and stumped, toeing the rubble of his crumbled empire, Carl made me sad. Instead of feeling that his disappointment served him right for playing chief in someone else's country, I felt sad.

Leaving with his escorts, Carl lingered a moment on the porch, shaking his head at Bwadi's moped. One weed woven through the spokes had grown higher than the handlebars. "You're not using this?" he asked.

"It's broken-down."

"Anyone tried to fix it?"

"I don't know."

Perplexed, he looked at me, his eyebrows two tangled knots. The Doctor was looking, too. Evenly, he explained, "It belongs to a teacher who's been away."

"Must have been gone some time."

I counted back. "Two months."

The Pastor was smiling; the Doctor concurred. What did he know about it? He'd never mentioned Bwadi to me. And what about Carl, for that matter; had he come equipped with rumors of a local subversive skipping town? Planted dolefully before the moped, he sagged. He didn't look like any spy to me. Yet he had brought my mail from AfricEd; I had to assume he'd report back—to Gus, at least, if not directly to the CIA. No: that was ridiculous;

I took a slow, equatorial breath. His history here was verifiable: a library of *National Geographic*s and *Getting Things from God,* a hydroelectric dam. He was no Ian Fleming agent with a cross—as if anyone outside Mampungu would really want to bother with us here. No: I'd been in the bush too long.

Dropping a dirty tennis cap onto his balding head, he offered a clammy handshake; heading with the Doctor and Pastor into the yellow afternoon, he left me to my life. He made me miss my dad.

The next day, the Doctor ferried Carl off for three weeks in a village, but not much later I heard from Pinzi that, struck with stomach troubles, Carl had been rushed sick to Kimpiri in a red Eckhart truck.

For a while I kept thinking about God and about how stupid and useless we mortals could be. I kept picturing Carl's neocolonial station superimposed on dingy, contemporary Mampungu, his tennis courts and tennis whites, and one night, during the wide silence that precedes dawn, between the scratchy resonance of a rooster's calls, I thought I heard, again and again, a tennis ball pocking against rackets, crossing back and forth above the net to be slammed into reverse, a ghostly, predictable echo not unlike a slow drumbeat across a lagoon.

The *Force Intérieure de Tambala,* or FIT, was not a myth. Practically on Carl's heels, a contingent of the president's personal security branch galumphed into town in two army lorries like rhinos on the loose. Whispers travelled the classroom, alarm bloomed. *"Ce sont des militaires!"* a boy up front informed me as the trucks lurched past. *"Autorités,"* others hissed; *"gendarmes."*

"Why would they come here?" I asked in French.

Unanimous, the students clammed up, limbs retracted where they sat as if the slightest move would capsize a desk. In back, Diabelle froze.

I understood. This was not hostility or impishness; this was not about me. Returning to our text, I read from the top, cultivating honey in my voice, miming calm. At least I'd given up my lessons on current events; this story was my adapted synopsis of *2001.*

"One day some prehistoric apes find an enormous black door without a knob," I read. "It is standing in the ground. It wasn't there before. After finding the door, the apes become smart. They evolve.

"Millenia later, in 2001, some men find another enormous door on the moon." The students were watching me, eerily angelic, like little dark ghosts. "Astronauts travel through the solar system to learn more about this door. Their spaceship has a very intelligent computer like a brain. The computer's name is HAL. HAL can talk. HAL can play chess. At first the astronauts and HAL are friends. But then HAL goes insane."

A knock interrupted my narrative; Pistache called me outside.

"*C'est* FIT," he declared, pronouncing it "feet."

"And what does that mean?"

He blinked, twice. "We don't know yet. They've parked at the dispensary. We must proceed as normal until otherwise advised." He marched on toward the next room.

Inside, I continued to read. "HAL tries to kill all the astronauts. One man survives. He disconnects the computer and HAL dies. Lastly, the man flies alone through the mysterious door." I wondered if an eavesdropping soldier would construe this as allegorical, treason. If a soldier would understand.

"What is this story about?" I checked for comprehension in my class.

The students stared. I'd intended a discussion on technology, on the implications of machines that can think. On extraterrestrial possibilities, on the futuristic door. Normally these kids were an imaginative lot, but the scenarios now brewing had nothing to do with HAL. The boys risked conscription at gunpoint, if the accounts I'd heard were true. For the first time, I actually pictured *militaires* thumbing my *cahiers*, the *plans de travail* which the *Préfet* inspected once a month, which documented what I'd taught: Nkrumah, Angola, dialogues, drills. Thank God I'd destroyed the essay on the green *fou fou* strike.

Rows of kinky coiffures—some cropped into afros, some knitted into tresses, carved into parts—congealed as, one by one, the boys and girls looked down toward their copies of the text. I understood. If they were too distracted to discuss *2001*, they could at least pretend preoccupation at their desks. I concluded that they should write. On anything, I said. On apes or doors or spaceships with brains. On where the last astronaut went.

At the end of the hour I received a lot of artistic doodles, helpless shrugs. I told Diabelle to skip the clinic that afternoon; her nod was circumspect. My next classes were the same: restrained expectation, dodged cues. Nobody was permitted into the courtyard at recess; kids huddled restlessly in classroom corners hatching hypotheses, hushing when I came near. I understood. At the last bell, they all slunk together toward the refectory, an undulating filament of uniforms, quietly navy and white.

I retreated home. No laundry hung outside; the floors were scuffed and dull. It had been Jetaime's day to clean. No avocados on the counter, no sign of him at all. It seemed medieval, the whole village aquiver as if overrun by Huns. Jagged with outrage, I puttered and fussed, stuck on the image of my mother under house arrest in Conakry, dust cloth snapping in irate surrender; was this how she'd felt? Certainly she'd resented the flinty inconvenience, the elaborate folly of official thugs—certainly she'd panicked that she might actually fail to protect us from harm.

Facing down a stack of questionnaires, I jumped when something boomed: a knock. Rather than allowing air to circulate through the screen, I'd left the front door shut.

Pistache was waiting, pigeon-toed. Inadvertently shifty, his gaze evoked crossed eyes.

"All state employees must report to the dispensary for fingerprints," he said.

"Why?"

Unable to focus on me, he turned to the destitute moped, muttered something bureaucratically baroque.

"Like a census, you mean?"

"Each state employee is to be identified," he erupted then, clicking into gear, addressing me for the first time ever in his disciplinary voice.

"*Ça va.*" I shrugged.

Once again, he strode off; I did as told, heading straight for the clinic after locking up my house with the *Préfet*'s spare key, homing as usual toward my sacred roost as if to cultivate my paperwork, to nurture Diabelle. As if Tambala had no police.

And I found it under siege. The line of suspects that stretched from the building onto the plush lawn included everyone: cohorts like Lukau and Shamavu, strangers from the church. Sober eyes avoided mine. Nobody touched.

I took my place at the end. The two trucks, parked slipshod, dominated the mango's shade; a bevy of soldiers slumped and drooped. Swimming in camouflaged fatigues, they looked sleepy and petite, combat boots loose, M-16s dangling from their shoulders like broken yokes. They looked like kids.

The Doctor's old Land Rover occupied its spot as well, oddly aristocratic beside the Goliath trucks. From where I stood, I could see into one of them through gaps in the canvas draped across the top. Bulky shapes and boxes lurked. Were they transporting ammunition to an arms cache nearby? Peering, I strained for clues of American manufacture: an eagle on a cardboard flap, a word stencilled in English: DANGER; BEWARE.

One soldier nudged another; they all stared, wide-mouthed, sly. They looked more apt to break into song than to shoot. I quit studying the truck. One by one, people emerged below the Doctor's ambitious sign: *Centre de Planification Familiale, Location de Luzawa, Département de Santé Public, République de Tambala*, the words all curling around a map of the country shaped like an elephant's ear. Each time someone exited, the next in line went in. Nobody lingered; discreetly, they fled. The sun blared. We inched ahead. Tiring of their vigil, the soldiers smacked their rifles against the mango branches and charged the falling fruit, toeing, kicking, soccer-happy, laying claim. They peeled the mangos with their teeth; chins dripped juice onto their camouflaged shirts. Coddled in their fatigues, they looked like military preppies to me, a different breed entirely from the ragtag toughs at roadblocks. Could these infant forces really make Mampungu cave? I wanted to clap the end of recess with my hands, to order them all back to school, but then I flashed on Conakry, on the Guinean ambassador whose execution proved how blind to trouble we Americans had been.

Citizen Limbewa, the science teacher, slid into line. His pink flared slacks, circa '67, made me want to smile; I put out my hand instead.

"Bonjour," he mumbled politely. He did not smile; I decided not

to smile. Yet he watched me, alert. Then he asked, "What is this about a black hole in your class?"

It was evidently not a joke. He was a sort of African Poindexter, his grasshopper head tapering like a stylized lozenge, eyes ballooning behind thick Clark Kent frames. As an absentminded professor, he, at least, could ignore the lilliputian *militaires*.

"My students came from your class," he continued, "asking about the door to the black hole. They showed me your text, but alas, my English is not so good."

"Really? Who?"

"Kinkela, Bakitula, all of them." Mildly accusatory, he said, "You've been teaching science, it seems."

"Not about black holes," I marvelled. "I don't know where they got that."

He drew himself up tall. "From my lessons in astronomy, of course."

"Ehi! I wish they'd told me. Actually that's quite a sophisticated interpretation of the text. I gave them a science fiction story, about a film I'd seen. A mammoth rectangular slab of alien black substance keeps appearing, once on earth, once on the moon, once in outer space. I called it a door to help them visualize."

"They told me a man disappears into it."

I nodded.

"It's a black hole," he sniffed, dismissive. "A collapsed star."

"That settles that."

He was as immune to my irony as to Mampungu's ominous guests. I moved forward to just below the sign. It was almost my turn. The *militaires* had settled around the jam-packed truck, loitering in clumps.

Craving the relatively cool clinic gloom, I squinted through the screen door. Miasmic, President Mankanzu floated in his leopard cap above some murky activity at Diabelle's desk. It was a poster, of course, hung for the occasion; each of my classrooms sported the same portrait above the blackboard, but we'd never had one here. Ten demerits, I cringed, and then scolded myself; already I'd allowed this Big Brother voodoo to hit me with guilt.

The silent woman in front of me disappeared, sucked into the office dusk, then reappeared, stepping past me, out. Eagerly, I advanced. Crossing the threshold, however, I went briefly numb with dismay. The darkness was certainly welcome shelter from the brazen equator outside, but this was not the clinic I knew. The president loomed like a guardian angel from hell; a sleek, beefy man in khaki officiated from Diabelle's desk with nepotistic aplomb. The air was nearly palpable, thick with presence, breath, beer. Suddenly the *gendarmes'* sleepy frivolity made sense. The room evoked a college frat in summer, with the added ingredient of something like horses—an odor of leather mingled with sweat.

Mr. FIT was waiting. My eyes were slow to adjust, what with the curtains we'd installed as decoration pulled shut, but then I recognized the Doctor and the *Préfet* recessed on either side of the bulbous fridge. The chairs eternally empty of patients accommodated yet more soldier boys, some cherubically asleep. The mission's wimpiness suddenly made sense. Boys chasing mangos or dozing in uniform were merely picturesque; with Mr. FIT in charge, however, they boded ill indeed. And in Africa there was always someone in charge; this was what Americans found so hard to grasp. Above each village hovered a *chef,* above each family a *père,* above each citizen some zombie gangster like Mankanzu in his pelts.

I didn't see Pinzi. Questionnaires blistered across the floor. I was not introduced to Mr. FIT. Another man in khaki stood aside at slack attention, hands behind his back.

"Name."

I said it, spelled it; Mr. FIT wrote.

"Occupation."

"English teacher at the secondary school. I'm with AfricEd."

The *Préfet* looked dimly tidy, tense. The Doctor looked unperturbed. If he'd evacuated the *Préfet's* beer from the fridge for Protestant Carl, they'd apparently restocked. Possibly the Doctor appreciated the ability of Empereur to mollify police, considered it prudent to keep a case put by. Possibly he was in cahoots. How else could he come up with salaries while the rest of Mampungu went unpaid? With family planning grants, bids for electricity? He was progressive at a cost, perhaps, ends justifying his means. I took solace anyway in the fact that, as collaborator, he might have pull. He'd do his best to protect us, I was sure, if only in his own interests; the scandal of trouble at his site would jeopardize international funds.

I did not see the Pastor or Pistache. Voices percolated from the exam room along with that faint hint of ammonia and mold. The khaki assistant stepped forward, inviting me to press my thumb into an ink pad; I obliged. He then attempted to manipulate my print onto the form; I let my hand flop in his scratchy grip. Mr. FIT lifted the paper, squinted, annoyed at the result—as if he could even begin to distinguish swirls and whorls in this light. The obsequious assistant then produced from his khaki pocket a Bic pen and scribbled directly onto the pad, resupplying ink. Why not simply scribble directly onto my thumb, I wanted to ask. He took me in hand again; I produced a gloppy smudge. They seemed appeased.

Attempting respect, I lingered, anticipating further questions, a request to check my new passport, my national ID. Neglected, I turned to go.

Mr. FIT commanded, *"Là-bas."*

"Where?"

Wordlessly, the assistant scooted forward to open the exam room door. The Doctor looked engrossed in a questionnaire at his feet. This had always been taboo territory; I'd only ever entered once. Could it have fallen under enemy control?

It had. The odor of ammonia and mold swelled. The latch clicked behind me, and I stood facing yet another clique of *militaires*. Seven or eight sat draped across the bed frames; more encircled a steel table that made me think of the vet's. The frames were all that remained of the beds—the mattresses and sheets were gone. The boxes were all gone. The glass cases gaped, empty. No jugs of pills and cures, no rusting scalpels, no rubber gloves. All looted clean and piled into that lorry, that morning, done. Piled into the very truck where I'd envisioned ammunition from home.

The soldiers scrambled to produce a battered stool. Gratefully, I sat, watching a boy prepare me a beer; adroitly, he plucked a bottle from the vet's table to swish that superstitious splash in the bottom of a glass, to spill it out the window for the ancestors *comme au village*. The windows were all open in here, flung wide as if someone had been desperate for ventilation; it dawned on me that the urinary smell I'd associated with ammonia was more likely from bats.

I toasted the soldiers and sipped. They must proliferate like spores, I thought; soon they'll be cluttering up classrooms, roaming through my house. Each wielded a glass; none had guns. Among themselves they chattered and hiccuped; they looked too young to drink. They spoke in army dialect, the tongue of the president's tribe. A mango bonged onto the roof and I jumped as if shot; they went uproariously wild. Minutes passed, an hour; I wished for cigarettes. The muffled sounds of fingerprinting dragged on. I was American, I told myself. I was white. I was stupid and guilty and possibly insane. What if I'd never actually entered this room with Diabelle, never seen it dingy and equipped, never watched her arching like a child before candy as she quizzed about the pills? Perhaps I'd never cringed at the sight of surgical tools—the very ones probably sequestered, at this point, in the camouflaged pockets of fatigues.

Probably I should call Mitch. Should sneak over to the two-way radio kept in the church and tell the world, "Mayday." In an hour or two these bozos would be back on their merry road and I could publicize their crimes. Report them to Amnesty International for holding me hostage in a pillaged clinic, for appropriating beer. Tipping back my glass, I took the last flat sip.

Yet nobody had actually told me I wasn't free to go. As far as I knew I was a distinguished guest at this bash, expected to sit enjoying my refreshment just as I would at a wedding *au village*. The soldiers were crouching, feet flat, tossing one-kuluna bits in a game that looked like jacks. Mitch would probably laugh. Besides, I'd have no idea how to isolate his frequency—how to even turn the transmitter on. In Conakry the authorities claimed to have detained us under house arrest for our own protection; perhaps it had been true. Or perhaps this was how denial worked. Inflicting a mental pinch, I reminded myself of Patty Hearst's survivalist lust for her guard. Perhaps I should have been hating Africa all along.

Yes: I had to assume that at this very moment cadets installed in my *salon* were rifling through my English *cahiers* for subversive vocabulary, for offensive texts. That all the paltry belongings I'd intended for friends—my backpack, my radio, my first aid kit— now belonged to the state. That I was going to be sent home.

That first, however, I'd be interrogated about Bwadi by Mr. FIT. But then Bwadi had insisted that they never asked questions here, that, abruptly, they carted you off. So far Bwadi had been right. Certainly they were after him, after me as a link: I was, after all, the sole detainee. The fingerprinting was but a tactic, I was sure, indicative of accusation, guilt, a ploy to start us all cataloging in our minds whatever infractions we might have managed to commit. Because if they really hoped to match my fingerprints with anything of Bwadi's, that blob of ink wouldn't get them far.

Blue smears adorned the glass in my lap. Luckily I'd ditched my camera with Mpovi, out of FIT range. Or maybe not. Could they possibly invade the *Préfet*'s house? He never had adequately explained his suspicions about Bwadi's flight. But I was glad I didn't know. I didn't want to know; I was paranoid, intimidated by my own thumbprint. And this was exactly what the authorities wanted, what every other Mampungu civilian was likely up to as well—ruminating over what had been said when, to whom, where. Over what had been touched.

The interior door swung open; precariously, the tipsy troops stood. Mr. FIT waddled forward smilingly, for all the world an ally. I stood, too. Pouncing, he shook my hand as if I'd won a prize. And then he let me go. "Thank you for your cooperation," he growled happily. Not a word about Bwadi, Angola, me. I thanked him for the beer and left.

I saw no one in the office. The *militaires* outside looked hung over, spent. Lightly, I tripped past as if my feet were airborne, gifted with wings. Swift and apprehensive, I floated home. The road was free of pedestrians, of goats, of late afternoon noise. No gleeful kids kicked their soccer ball made of rags wound up; no women clanged cooking pots against pipes. All was quiet *chez moi*.

But Bwadi's moped was gone. The tall weed lay crippled on the porch in the midst of crumbled debris, the crusty mud shaken loose. I hadn't heard a motor. Of course not—the tires were flat, the engine broken-down.

At first I felt relief—that this milky blue ghost had finally gone away. It hadn't been mine to keep. And then I found the front door as I'd left it, locked; the floor equivalently scuffed. And I felt addled, thrown. No soldiers greeted me from my *salon;* none sat browsing through *National Geographic*s, boots propped up, unlaced. My teaching materials waited, neatly stacked, unsmudged. All my bundles of cash lay intact beside my photo album in the drawer. My mattress remained where I'd left it, the bunched sheet contouring where

I'd left. Nothing was amiss. And yet the place appeared rearranged. Peopled, tricked. As if, turning, I might catch a blur of short soldiers leering in the passage, a murky contingent bivouacked behind a desk. Intangibly, they'd moved in; I never did get them out.

Later the lorries barrelled off into the sunset. From my kitchen window, I watched through the raspy veil of my own smoke; edgily, I puffed. I was not under house arrest. I had been neither interrogated nor carted off. Presumably the authorities had chosen to load up on drugs rather than boys. Presumably by now our students had scattered to the far corners of the bush. Presumably I should quit.

That night, the *Préfet* responded to this concept with surprise. "But why?"

The virile glow of an Aladdin lamp brightened his front room; the ornamental faces in Mpovi's photographs gleamed. "Never mind. I thought maybe the trouble was about me. I don't want to cause any trouble here."

"No, no, no." Dismayed, he shook his head too long. Still dressed as school principal, short-sleeved jacket buttoned up, he seemed stuck. "Nothing was about you," he finally said.

"What was it about?"

"Nothing. They come around sometimes. They monitor. It's always like this."

"They always rob the dispensary?"

"Two years ago they stole from the clinic at Mwindi." With infuriating patience, he sighed.

"Why did they detain me?"

"I don't know. They don't know. You never know."

Mpovi was motioning behind the *Préfet*'s back, almost out of reach of the lamplight. She was holding something aloft, a small dark bundle: my camera in its case. She wanted me to see.

"They took Bwadi's moped," I said to the *Préfet*.

"Yes."

"Was that why I was detained?"

"I don't know."

"And what about the students? *Ça va?*"

"They've all run away to hide."

As soon as the kids returned, he said, school would resume. I told him that when it did I'd teach. After managing a wink at Mpovi, I left him to his relentless photographs, to his secrets and his private guilts, my storm lamplight skimming before me across the lawn.

By the time the Doctor showed up later, I'd begun to seethe. "It's unacceptable!" I ushered him inside. "How can they just drive off with clinic property?"

"It is terrible," he agreed, upright in my living room, unfazed. "We are lucky, however, that we had not yet stocked the birth control. At least they did not find that. And things may yet work out for the best. Now I can apply for emergency supplies from *Médecins Sans Frontières*. This situation may actually provide us with the opportunity to update our equipment, to modernize."

On foot, I gaped. I forgot to offer him a seat. My hot skin crawled. Had he engineered this heist himself? Brainstormed a sort of inside job? I tried, quickly, to rethink: Mr. FIT had come not for Bwadi, not for me, not even to kidnap my graduating class, but for the Doctor's moldy inventory, at his request. Was this the only way to requisition supplies? The Doctor was sly indeed, a benevolent rat. Gambling, he'd put us all at risk—caused the whole village to hunker down before those impish *militaires,* to roll over, belly up.

"Are they coming back?" I demanded.

He raised a careful, whitened eyebrow. "I don't think so."

"Why did they detain me?"

"I imagine they wanted something. The motorbike was enough."

"What were they really doing here?"

Dangling in my poor lamplight, he hesitated; his shadow swayed. "Taking fingerprints."

I blew up. "That's ridiculous! They couldn't tell a fingerprint from a squashed cockroach. I want to know what's going on."

"Miss Nicole," he sternly said, "it's best not to ask."

I shut up then. I recalled Bwadi shrugging when I'd prodded about the cost of his petrol. *"On se débrouille,"* he'd said: you manage, you do what you can. Whatever you have to. *On se débrouille:* back off; don't ask. An answer that Tambalans tended to respect. I shut up then, and I decided to radio neither AfricEd nor Mitch.

That night the Doctor insisted that the family planning project must proceed. And I told him, yes, I'd reorganize the collapsed stacks of questionnaires; I'd carry on. But then I kept waiting for

Diabelle. Jetaime returned the next morning bearing a pineapple, and for the next few days the AWOL students dribbled back. For the next few days I strolled, sweating in the shade of the bounteous *petit marché,* chatting with people in the road. And nobody said a thing. Disoriented, I was circling, vividly blind—just as when, months ago, I'd lost my way from choir practice and listed in my blind circle at night. This time, nobody laughed. Nobody said a word. When I shared a beer with Mpovi, her lack of politics felt like a front.

By the next week the only absent student was Diabelle. We went on with *2001.* At home, nothing felt like mine. Methodically, I went through my portfolio of photographs and saw each image violated, caressed by baby *militaires,* by sticky fingers pressed directly onto the emulsion of my life.

Diabelle did not come back.

She'd been to the clinic for chloraquine. Pinzi told me she'd come and gone; I hadn't seen her at school. But I hadn't seen a lot of kids—while enough had returned for me to teach, at that point Diabelle was merely one among many away.

She'd had no idea, he said, that the clinic had been robbed, that there was nothing to dispense. Her pulse had been normal, her forehead cool to the touch—the malarial cycle presumably spent while she was hiding from the *militaires.* He hadn't asked where she'd stayed. He sent her to the dormitory to rest.

According to the girls, she'd never showed up. And then the next week she was the only student still gone. The *Préfet,* imperiously reassuring, told me she was in Lufwidi, getting well. That she'd be back to school soon. I suspected bluster, facade. Since I'd glimpsed him as a wilting civil servant, his unction inspired less confidence, although I liked him more. Meanwhile, the Doctor was in Kimpiri, soliciting new scalpels and syringes, writing up reports. Mama Zola convinced me she was ignorant, uninformed by her family in Lufwidi about Diabelle. Days passed, a whole week, two. I should have tracked her down.

We were now in March. Rain was expected on the seventeenth. I went daily to the dispensary, loyal to family planning, to Diabelle.

Having tidied up the ravaged questionnaires, I continued to code. The door to the exam room where I'd awaited deportation remained closed. I kept expecting her to slink across the office, her golden fluidity oblivious to the inklings of stale beer. I was hurt, of course, that she'd consulted Pinzi rather than me, that she'd left no message on my desk.

In retrospect, the students seem to me incongruously cheerful then. Smug with self-preservation, they celebrated their impromptu break. They celebrated me. No more grungy innuendoes about my love life, no more industrial action against my grades. Or perhaps I focus only on the moments when they smiled, on the rare, fixed frames I prefer to recall.

Because I want to forget what happened next. To block out the images that rise, again and again, as if to the surface of a deep lake at night. The glinting skin that seems to span a canvas of water like glass, the expressions silverized by a moon. Again and again, I fall in.

We were into March, the mangos were on the wane, it was afternoon. I was coding alone, waiting for Diabelle. Wispily, an engine strained in the distance, too soprano for the lumbering FIT. Too red. I was in the road, hands on hips, by the time it roared into view, honking, scattering pedestrians. Arcing around me, it nearly buckled to a stop.

The man behind the wheel was skinny and clean-cut, a denuded Mitch, his beard shaved away, his hair shorn. He didn't smile, or bother to get down. "A student of yours is sick and asking for you in Lufwidi," he called, "can you come right away?"

I swallowed. "Diabelle?"

His nod blurred.

Instructing a *petit* to explain my exit to the *Préfet,* I reclaimed my old spot in the cab. Mitch was taciturn, harried; he seemed a step away from gray. Nearly two months had passed since I'd chased him off.

"She's OD'd," he informed me as we lurched down the road. "I'm sure of that. I'm not sure on what. She keeps asking for you."

I fixed on the dusty dashboard, stunned. She could not possibly have tried to kill herself—suicide was an anathema to any Bantu mind. *Why don't your people want to live?* the Doctor had once quizzed.

"I thought she had malaria," I turned to Mitch.

"I wish." We bumped along. "Look, I don't know how to tell you this. She's overdosed on something to induce abortion."

"She's pregnant? How do you know?"

"I'm a doctor."

He wasn't, really, not a full-fledged MD. Something clicked. "Chloraquine."

"Say what?"

"She came here looking for chloraquine. They use it for abortions sometimes."

"Could have been." His exposed chin gleamed, damp with our eternal, white sweat. "Makes sense."

"We didn't have any, though. We were looted."

"I know."

"You heard?"

"You should see the roadblock outside Kilu now. A regular pharmacy. She could easily have bought your chloraquine there."

He offered me a cigarette; I simply could not smoke. Strands from my schoolmarm bun were blowing loose; I took the pins out. Matted hair slapped my cheeks, and I recalled how, long, long ago, I'd sat beside Tembo on my way to Lufwidi for a wedding, hair knitted *à la Tambalaine.*

"I would have come by," Mitch finally said, "if I'd really thought you needed help. I heard everything was OK."

"It's not."

He looked at me, his interest antiseptic, scrubbed. Unsmilingly, he drove.

I said, "She came to me for birth control."

"It's my fault," he wanted to make clear.

"She went to you, too?"

"No, I mean—" he snapped his mouth shut on air, chewed. "It was probably my kid."

And I was sinking then, my world awash in unfamiliar hues, the savannah swerving from green to red as if light filters had been screwed before my eyes. I faced the open window, clenched shut my fists.

"It just happened," his voice snaked on. "After I left you at Paul's in Nkisi. Remember? On my way back to camp I gave a bunch of kids a ride. They were just hanging out in the road. Later that same night the guard tracked me down; he'd found a girl outside who asked for me by name. He said she was from Mampungu, so I thought it probably had to do with you, and I went to see. And there she was, one of the kids from the truck. We could barely communicate—she refused to let the guard interpret—but there was no doubt what was on her mind.

"She kept sneaking from the village all that week. Then she went back to school, I guess, and I went to Madagascar, and I assumed that was that. I didn't see her until she showed up again in December. You were at the beach. Then I saw you in the post office Christmas Eve."

"So that's why you hadn't come by."

"You don't have to believe me, but I wouldn't have seen her again after Christmas. I mean, I didn't, until I came to your clinic that day. I honestly had no idea she worked for you. We couldn't communicate. But then she came back to camp a couple weeks ago, and what she wanted then was clear. 'No baby,' she kept saying, 'I don't want baby.' I tried to tell her I can't do an abortion myself, that I'd try to figure something out. She must have given up."

He'd been so hygienic in bed with me, so expert at protected sex. "How pregnant?" I suddenly asked.

"Ten weeks?"

"Weren't you using anything?"

"'Course. I'm a doctor, for Christ's sake."

"You keep saying that."

"Nothing works one hundred percent."

"Are you sure it was yours?"

He gnawed on more air. "No."

Animosity simmered. I was busy calculating Diabelle's deceit. It appeared that when I'd chosen her to train, she'd already been with Mitch. When I'd christened her "Virginia" and we'd giggled about men. Of course, she'd assumed mine would be Bwadi, not someone white. I'd never mentioned Mitch. Never told her he'd given me a lift to Paul's. I'd thought secrets were best. Long before he came to the clinic that day for me, she'd been with Mitch. Now I understood her acute chagrin, his awkward ire as he handed out our gifts. If his calculations were correct, she was already pregnant then, although she'd likely not yet guessed. If this were not a lie. Why should I think he'd lie? I was the one who'd fostered distance, ignorance, even with him. I'd never asked about his children, the status of his wife. Whatever he'd hidden could be partly blamed on me.

But not what he'd done. Salty with anger, my eyes burned. Behind my back he'd grown into a prototype, the quintessential male, the evil, predatory being who ravages and then abandons women at will. Diabelle was the victim, innocent; I'd take her back under my tarnished wing in a minute if she would just be OK.

"This morning,"—Mitch would not shut up—"Mvutudi, her brother-in-law, appeared at my clinic hysterical, begging for me to come. When I heard it was about Diabelle, I dropped everything. It was too late."

"What do you mean, 'too late?'" Foliage strained past, too vivid, cruel.

"They always wait till the last minute to call *bwana* doctor; they've got to give the healers first crack. They were smart enough to induce emesis, but it wasn't enough. She should have had her stomach pumped right after ingestion, which must have been yesterday. Now the stuff's in her bloodstream; cyanosis has already hit."

"You just left her there to die?"

"I told you, it's too late." He scowled ahead. "She kept asking for 'Miss Nicoli.' Coming after you was the only thing left to do."

I couldn't imagine why she would call for me when, seeking chloraquine from Pinzi, she hadn't bothered to leave me a note. Mitch had come because he was scared, I decided; because he needed a compatriot in Lufwidi, someone white with whom he could compare notes.

We were inching up the incline, close. An eerie choral whistle, something like sirens, lapped the edges of our first-gear whine. The back of my neck crawled. "What's that?"

Drumless, the voices wavered and dipped, weaving a song against the dry blue sky.

"They're crying for her death."

I panicked. "I thought she was still alive."

"They've been doing this for hours. Longo said that from their viewpoint, she was already in a preliminary stage of death when we arrived this morning. You die in stages here, you don't wait for the heart to stop."

"Then why did they ask for your help?"

"My question exactly." He shrugged thinly. "Sometimes the patients do get better. I guess they're hoping for a miracle."

As we crested the plateau, the rising top of the old wood cross appeared to be holding up the sky. I hadn't been back in Lufwidi village since the wedding in November, yet I felt as if I'd been here yesterday. I might have been beginning all over, arriving this time in Mitch's truck instead of Tembo's *camionnette*. I might once again nearly faint from the heat, make friends unwittingly with a prostitute. I might shell peanuts, sitting side by side with Diabelle's aunts.

I might have hooked up with Mitch from the start. Instead of turning my self-righteous back in the Yank Tank, I might have befriended him the night I sat drinking with Paul. I might have arrived at Mampungu equipped with a boyfriend off-limits to Diabelle. She might have never climbed his fence.

"A miracle," I mused aloud, craning my neck as we approached the giant cross. The ethereal voices surged, echoing each other, fading out.

"He said the women do this send-off thing so the patient doesn't die alone." Mitch's voice gained confidence; he leaned forward, scanning, looking left and right. Primed for emergency, he was in his element, and I understood that it was in crises that he thrived.

Knots of people suspended in their yards squinted after us, blinking in the dust, their fists immobile at their thighs, at their cheeks, clasped atop their heads. Then I saw the wailing women, flanking the very house I'd sat outside while sipping my warm Coke. Twirling in isolated circles, trampling the edges of their drooping *pagnes*, slapping at their heads, bawling, singing, ten or so women had worked themselves to an attenuated pitch that approximated more accurately than anything I'd ever heard what it must sound like to die.

Following Mitch through the door, I balked at the aggressive stench, wishing I could turn and run, unwilling to connect the odor with Diabelle. Undeniably human, the stuff of bowels and stomach and blood, metallic, pungent, and bitter, the smell struck the back of my throat; I put a hand to my mouth. Hesitating while my pupils adjusted to the dark, I detected the low moans of mur-mured prayer coming from a group of figures slumped along the wall. I had lost Mitch, but I made out, farther inside, a circle of people on foot.

Breathing through my mouth, I realized that a path was clearing before me, that I was, indeed, expected at Diabelle's bedside. But why weren't these villagers angry; how could they not hate me and my white world? Perhaps they did not know as much as Mitch or I. Or perhaps they knew all about Diabelle's affair, but truly were holding out for a miracle, for another little Portuguese cannon that could shoot God into the sky.

I wondered which poor woman was Diabelle's mother; several pressed my arm as I passed; several wailed outside. That day at the wedding, I had not bothered to fix her in my mind; I remembered only someone birdlike, pinched.

Advancing to the crowded bedside, I stepped to the front. Across a barrier of candles placed on the floor, Diabelle lay on her back in bed, a *pagne* separating her flesh from the scratchy woven hemp. That night in November, I'd used the same sort of bed; it had not been soft. Her head and chest were elevated, propped against a flour sack. I should have brought my sheets, I thought. In the flickering light of the candles, her skin looked ceramic, glossy and rigid, the contours of her cheekbones and eye sockets exaggerated, her mouth parched and shrunken, her coloring a dark extension of the shadows in the room; she might have been an old woman too thin for wrinkles.

Breathing with effort, she wheezed as she inhaled, stalling each time she emptied her lungs, threatening to stop. I gauged the rising and falling of her chest, and her labored breathing seemed to swell, to drown out the wispy song encircling the house and the prayers coming from the corner, as if Diabelle were causing the mud walls to expand and contract. In, out. As if there were no other sound on earth.

This is Diabelle, I told myself, I must think of her as Diabelle, I must be ready with a smile when she wakes up. I must be ready to cry. Nothing I could think of to do made sense. I watched and watched until her closed eyelids twitched and her face hardened and then Mitch dove forward—I had forgotten he was there—and pressed a cloth against her mouth. All at once she reared up from the spine, her chest bowing out, and when a garbled noise came from her mouth I looked away. The wailing outside hit a narrow note and I bit my knuckles, fighting the urge to run, swerving against somebody's shoulder, and for a moment I allowed the scent of perspiration to block out the putrid atmosphere. Then I found my way back to her bed.

She never did open her eyes. Why had she asked for me? What could she have to say? Nothing, I guessed; not a single thing. She had simply called for me out of desperation. After consulting her traditional healers and then Mitch, she had called for the American Miss who had appeared out of nowhere in the bush, who had endowed her with a magical passkey to the West, who she thought must save her life.

Each time she convulsed I looked away. Eventually I was in a chair, the same stiff-backed sort in which I'd waited with such boredom for the wedding to begin. The rhythm of her breathing and the lack of air cast a spell.

When people started stepping forward, one by one, to whisper in her ear, to press her wrist or touch her chin, I shrank against the unyielding planks of my chair. A few taps and nudges, however, sent me toward the bed: it was my turn: go. She was breathing still. Taking her papery hand, I cradled it, palm up. Her fingers curled inward, her thumb tinted purple inside the tip as if her dark pigment had bled. The hand was warm enough, but it was not Diabelle's, not the one that waved so elegantly in my class, not the one that fiddled nervously at braids. Staring at the predictable beige of her upturned palm, where the thumb's spreading bruise had not yet reached, I saw that, at heart, her hand was much the color of mine.

I returned to my place, patient as a crocodile, patient as a rock. I could have waited forever; it happened too fast. The next time I touched her flesh, it was cool as stone.

The sky was white and numb. They laid her out beneath an acacia in milky bloom. The leaves rustled above; there must have been a breeze. Some of the women wore *pagnes* over their heads and shoulders; they must have been cold. Everyone was singing; I caught a few words: *mwindi, ngolo, kiadi, masa.* Light, strength, sadness, water. The water of the afterworld. She was swimming now, in a pool, in the sea. She lay wrapped in white, wrapped like a mummy with only her eyes, nose, and mouth exposed as if she could breathe.

The students were in uniform, the dust on their faces streaked with tears. Lufwidi was a blur. School had been suspended for a day and Tembo, the chauffeur, was shuttling people back and forth to the wake. The teachers faltered at the Doctor's new Land Rover parked beneath the rotting cross. He'd just driven the car off the dock in Kilu, he told me, had driven it straight to the funeral. "There is, however, one mistake. The steering wheel is on the right."

I looked at him, confused. "She was afraid of her father's curse."

The Doctor bowed his head. "It's a terrible thing."

"As bad as suicide."

"As bad," he agreed. "And yet it was not suicide."

"I know." It had been a curse. It was greed and ego and a father's toxic love. I could see him across the plaza keening on all fours. Frightened chickens clucked and flapped. I could see that he'd loved his daughter, that he was rabid, damaged with grief. I could see that she must have loved him, too.

My own father had never forbidden me a thing, but what if he had condemned some choice I'd made, wouldn't I, too, have been miserable, figuratively cursed? My father hadn't trusted his own judgment after my mother's death. Pacing the basement of the mortuary where the coffins were displayed, our progress had been mechanical, distracted, until finally I had pointed at the one lined in powder blue. At home, we had stood gaping at her closet until finally I had suggested the gray wool dress she'd worn last to church.

I pictured Diabelle's mother gently sifting through her things: that classy black *pagne*, English *cahiers*. The Doctor's head was still bowed, ministerial. "And all that salary she'd saved?" I asked him point-blank.

He indicated Diabelle's father thrashing on his back in the dirt. Nobody went near him. Nobody tried to help. "Whatever is left is his."

"Is he all right?" I had to ask.

The Doctor swallowed, twice. "He will mourn like this until she goes into the ground. The mother mourns in the dark."

I couldn't feel a thing. I strayed. At the river Mitch came up behind me; I took a cigarette: truce. He'd wanted to explain, he said, that day he'd charged into the school yard and I'd headed him off. To explain and to promise not to see Diabelle again. I nodded at the river, slate gray. The eccentric *bac* floated motionless; the water slid by. No kids splashed. I told Mitch how my crude students had put me on the spot, how I didn't want his luxuries, how his relative wealth compromised my credibility as a white who accepted, adopted, even, Africa on its own terms.

"But do you?" he asked, sincere.

I picked up a stone, measuring its cool, smooth weight. "Accept, yes," I answered seriously; "adopt, I don't know." I inhaled smoke; exhaled. "See, I don't want to be the white who comes in pushing everyone around, living high on the hog at the expense of the Tambalans. When I was growing up in Africa, my nice standard of living, the servants, the pool, everything was a function of cheap labor. Why should we live like that in their country, when they can't, and we couldn't, either, back in the States?"

"But then what is it you have to offer, if you just want to live like them?"

"Why do I have to offer anything?" I tossed the stone; it plunked weakly beyond the water's edge. "I'm only human. I'm not Santa Claus, and I'm not God."

Reaching toward me, Mitch dropped his arm. There was nothing else to say. The singing rose and fell. We smoked, apart. Diabelle stared. Upriver, Diabelle stood and stared. I remembered she was dead. She inched closer, stopped. Her face was cut and puffy, her mouth dark, unsmiling, sealed. "Look," I told Mitch.

"Diabelle's sister," he commented, raising a hand; she waved. "I patched her up a few days ago."

I turned, surprised. Clean-shaven, intrinsic, he was the village doctor now. Of course, he was right; he had something to give. "What happened?"

"*Militaires.* Came questioning about some friend. Something political, I think."

I took a step, trapped. It should have been me. Why hadn't they questioned me? *We're American,* I heard Mitch again at the road-block; *they wouldn't dare.* And I was lurching toward Catherine then; I broke into a run, ditching Mitch. She stood her ground.

"*Kiadi!*" I was sobbing as I reached for Catherine's hands. She was tentative, her sore face dry as a mask. "*Kiadi. Je regrette.*" I saw she thought I meant Diabelle. I realized I did. She pulled me against her and we swayed, rocking, rocking, although it was only I who cried.

There was no such reconciliation with Bwadi; there still is none today. I've only got him up against a tree, against yellow brick, his dark pupils almost soft. I've got photographs of me crowned with tresses like snakes. Photos of baby Chance. I've got pink sunglasses scratched at the bottom of a drawer, ivory crocodiles. The one from Christmas with Mitch found the one like it from West Africa; empty of innards, they claim a place on my desk and I've forgotten, by now, which crocodile is which.

I went to Kimpiri for the devaluation and then I was gone. Up to two thousand old kulunas could be exchanged for new at the bank. Everything else was trash. There were no lines; people bunched. *Militaires* paced. I had all my salary from January; the *Préfet* told me to go. I packed my straw bag with the stacks like bricks, the one-kuluna bills bound by the hundred in frayed twine. I didn't say good-bye. I took travel documents and toiletries and Mitch's croco-dile. It had remained where I'd dropped it at Christmas inside my bag. Diabelle was dead. Outside the banks, submissive crowds sighed. Civil servants, market mamas set up camp. A parade of black Mercedes ushered rich officials to a separate door. Days passed, intermittent volunteers. I saw Paul, too. He'd joined a local sect following a prophet, an African Christ, he said. We did not dance. Nothing was open; nobody was taking the old bills. The banks ran out of cash. The mint in Germany was printing more but all the airports were closed. Nobody complained. St. Ignatio's, where the black market Catholics had sold such pretty money to Mitch, posted guards. People were burning money in the streets. *Militaires* laughed. The post office agreed to accept my defunct cash and I placed a call to my dad. "I'm coming home," I said, realizing it was true. Jolly, as if I'd called from the corner store, he said, "Good."

I gave my cash to a cook where we volunteers were housed. I told Gus at AfricEd I quit. He knew all about the *militaires* at Mampungu; he suggested a new post. I didn't tell him about Diabelle. My prints were back from the lab; I could not look. Not even on the plane. When the airport opened they put me on the plane. Through my cartoon glasses, I watched Africa recede, green and indistinct. I thought I saw Bwadi at war. He'd taken something from me, an indistinct something; I was empty, a husk. Long ago people thought that airplanes stole you for the afterworld, that once you reached the sky you were irrevocably dead. That those who did return were actually doubles playing tricks.

Mpovi had seen it coming. It's what she'd hated so much about me and Diabelle. She'd known Diabelle would be seduced by my freedom from strings—my freedom to travel, to teach, to buy myself blue jeans and cameras and birth control pills. She knew that Diabelle was brainy and beautiful and bored with village life—but that to escape it she'd need more than me.

Diabelle had never wanted to be a real working girl, to go it on her own; what she'd wanted was a man, a modern man, a white guy to protect her in Kimpiri's urban jungle, to set her up with hairdos and nightclubs and electricity. To encourage her to learn and to grow, to buy her a business. To buy her father's blessing and make her a wife. And to father her kids. What she'd wanted was a rich white guy who could take her on junkets abroad. She'd never wanted to leave Tambala for good.

This is what Mpovi had seen: that as a single working girl I had nothing to offer Diabelle. My ambitions at the time did not involve men—yes, maybe I needed them for romance or sex, but not to survive. And this was too advanced for Diabelle. Diabelle saw that I was free; Mpovi saw that I was free and alone. That any African woman in my shoes could only be sad.

Perhaps Diabelle triggered in Mpovi some image of her own dissent, long since quashed. With the *Préfet* and her baby, she'd seen the light. She'd even tried to convert me. Before having experienced the bliss of living for one's family, why should anyone know what they want? She'd never been seduced by me; all she'd wanted were my things. Not my world; my things. Sugar, a high-tech bra, photographs—things to fuel the pride she took in her placid beauty and her skills as a *femme*. I don't believe Mpovi held this all against me; in her simple, black-and-white way, she was philosophical. She'd felt angry instead at Diabelle. As if, as an alien, I was helpless, not responsible for what I was. Mpovi's idea of a solution was to make me black.

Diabelle put me on a pedestal; Mpovi saw the whole picture—she saw it like an image in a mirror that could break into shards. That day she'd dressed me up for the wedding, when she'd left me at the truck with Diabelle, she'd seen how Diabelle's future as a happy *femme* would splinter if she tried to be like me. The girl would have to cross her father; what's more, no African man would want her like me. I can't say that Mpovi foresaw Diabelle's death; more likely, she saw Diabelle alive without a family, tense with regret. Meanwhile, the prototype, what Diabelle was supposed to be, shattered like a mirror, the fragments reflecting a mess of glimpses—someone you might have known, schizophrenic angles needling the dust.

Bwadi understood me best. I was Mpovi's protégée, Diabelle's idol, but I was Bwadi's charlatan, a fraud. I'd wanted so badly to not exploit. I'd thought I was better than missionaries and their white God, better than the multinational crews colluding with Mankanzu to milk the copper and the oil. Better than the dumb diplomats. I'd wanted to go back and play fair. To see ivory and crocodiles for what they were. And yet I'd brought along in my photo album my portrait of that trinket, the ivory crocodile carved hollow inside. It's an emblem, I see now, of our expatriate idyll, of ivory as dinner table art, of crocodiles as cute. Part of this trinket's charm, of course, is how it caricatures crisis and blood. Africa to us then was a cartoon, kitsch—nothing that could ever touch us in our air-conditioned dining rooms with our houseboys in twill. By the time Mitch gave me the duplicate, I'd grown amorphously aware of what it was I'd wanted to leave behind in the States: this American impulse to exploit, to exoticize what lurks beyond the fence. We pretended there was nothing to fear—no riots, no executions, no crocodiles at all. Growing up like this, you imagine only dancing around drums.

Bwadi knew what I was. And loved me still. I do believe that. Despite our differences, he loved me honestly for what I wanted to be, wanted not to do. And yet as I write this I see I haven't changed a bit. That he is my noble savage still.

Bwadi was no angel, but I'll only ever see him as wronged. I don't feel he betrayed me; he stole my camera for a cause. He used me for a cause. Just for a moment, just for a chore. To provide some photographs, to escort a man on the run. Perhaps in this one respect I did something for Africa on Africa's own terms.

When Ali stole my mother's pocketbook in Conakry, I felt betrayed. Now I want to excuse even him. What were we doing in his country at that time—a time when his president kept asking Americans to leave? Perhaps in his world he'd had every right.

Diabelle's betrayal was ingenuous—a mistake. She didn't know I'd been seeing Mitch. And if she had? Would I fabricate a reason for her, too?

Diabelle could have died of an abortion without knowing me. According to the Doctor, this was a common tragedy. Diabelle hadn't needed me to introduce her to Mitch. She didn't need a white man to conceive a child. Yet it shouldn't have happened with me there. And I wax paternalist again, American to the core. As if I were responsible for the world, as if I had the power to divert disaster. It's an arrogant idea. Because of it I will always blame myself. I had returned to Africa feeling guilty for my white advantage; I left feeling guiltier still. And have not gone back.

And what about this place where women dance topless in bars? Where the deranged take potshots at presidents, where the depressed take their own lives? Those questions of the Doctor's haunt me still. I can only intellectualize; I don't know. Perhaps we are too crowded here; we go like lemmings off the cliff. Perhaps we really don't have enough sun. If suicide happens more to the north, as they say, perhaps this is mother nature's way of evening out the score, of controlling populations where people find it so difficult to die. They say we hardly give birth anymore in the North. Down near the equator, there are lots of babies, lots of deaths, no suicides.

It's easy to theorize. Perhaps it's because we are so afraid to touch each other that men watch women dancing naked in bars. Perhaps it's our spiritual emptiness that makes us want to die. Our reliance on ourselves: we teach our children to be strong, to take care of themselves, to grow up and move away. We don't expect help: not from parents, children, friends. We put our old in institutions, ditch our kids in day care. And toil away. We eat each other up. Now and then one of us snaps. Perhaps we simply have too many choices—too many things to want, too many to do wrong.

Diabelle's choice was between two things only—the village or the city—and still she died. She died, really, of too much family, too much dependence. She died of her love for her father, her need for his support. She could not bear for him to know she'd disobeyed. And what sort of family is that? I can't say families are better in Africa than here.

I was at Mampungu for less than a year. I've been back ten. Yet Mpovi, Diabelle, Bwadi, and Mitch refuse to fade; they temper who I am. I am American, now. I often regret my country's character and policies, but I can, at least, speak out. I can vote; I have legal rights. I can inform myself and try to understand. I can see a doctor for birth control. I can work; I can buy a car and a television and, if I'm lucky, a house. I can take for granted electricity and gas lines, plumbing and telephones. I am less likely than I was in Africa to cause inadvertent harm to my friends.

After I returned, I got a job, went back to school, back to the darkroom. I see my father often now, my brother now and then. I fell in love. My family is American; I see no reason to go back.

My husband and I talk of having children, and I can't help thinking of the only other man who ever brought it up. Bwadi, that last night at the beach, saying, "It would be all right." I still can't fathom what he meant. That it would have been all right for me to slink back to the States—as he knew I would—carrying his child? That it would have been all right for me to raise it alone? He'd never asked about my background. I had only a father and a brother I hardly knew; I'd been brought up to not need help. He flattered me. He thought I could nurture a child in this country where we eat each other up. I try to picture this mulatto offspring, but I can't see where in the world it would fit. Not in the States, not Africa. The dialectic between me and Bwadi will not resolve.

So I see no reason to go back. I can tell you what has happened in Tambala, even so. The cross at Lufwidi teeters; *camions* cross the bridge. Paint is peeling; it's been ten years. Twenty since missionary Carl ran the school. No whitewash hides the rust stains on the walls, no new screens replace the old. No electricity brightens the windows at Mampungu, except, perhaps, during storms.

People suffer still from malaria and parasites; everyone is prey to AIDS. The epidemic that hadn't quite surfaced in my time there has now laid siege.

The money is like dust. Nobody has a job. The president in his leopard cap is mythically rich from the nationalized mines. His policy of ethnic cleansing subdues rival tribes. The army pillages and loots. Opposition festers; anarchy impends.

The Americans have left.

The Cubans have left Angola, where Bwadi's fighting malingers and erupts. Now we call the conflict tribal rather than a cold war front.

In Conakry the blue-and-white tiles lining the pool slid down the drain and washed up around the lagoon. They were collected and then lost, like shells. Now they're buried deep within the ocean floor, or beneath the weighty strata of landfill. Or maybe they continue to glitter in the sand, flipping end over end when the tide comes up. I wonder if they drift.

I'm in love with Africa still. It's a chronic, impossible devotion, like an eight year old's longing for someone else's father, or maybe for her own; it's an exquisite loss. It's like a perfect photograph printed big enough to claim a wall, mounted behind glass, black and white, an uninhabitable moment in someone else's life. My handprints on the glass are as close as I can get.

Lately I've been photographing shapes, experimenting with soft contours wrapped around mean angles, black and white. Although I haven't done portraits for a long while, I keep looking for the faces underneath, the ones shrouded by curtains, drowned in pools of light. For Mpovi, Bwadi, Diabelle.

This is the image that haunts me most. It's not a photograph. It's the African face framed by the window of a subway train, the bold features carved of patience, the panic of recognition in the eyes. Was it me or Sadie that he saw? I keep turning as I pass, looking back, over my shoulder, hopelessly aware that in another instant the glass imprisoning his moving lips will begin to shift backward, backward, will be sucked into the tunnel with the train.